MW01146953

Love, Letters and Lies

Renata McMann
&
Summer Hanford

Cover by Summer Hanford

Copyright 2018 by Renata McMann & Summer Hanford
All rights reserved

Acknowledgment

With special thanks to our editors, Joanne Girard and Betty Campbell Madden.

By Renata McMann and Summer Hanford

The Second Mrs. Darcy

Georgiana's Folly (The Wickham Coin Book I)

Elizabeth's Plight (The Wickham Coin Book II)

The above two books have been published in a single volume as:

Georgiana's Folly & Elizabeth's Plight: Wickham Coin Series, Volumes I & II

The Scandalous Stepmother

Poor Mr. Darcy

A Death at Rosings

Entanglements of Honor

From Ashes to Heiresses

The above two stories have been published in a single print volume as:

Entanglements of Honor with From Ashes to Heiresses

The Fire at Netherfield Park

Courting Elizabeth

Her Final Wish

Believing in Darcy

Foiled Elopement

The Widow Elizabeth

The Forgiving Season

Hypothetically Married

The Long Road to Longbourn

Caroline and the Footman

Mr. Collins' Deception

Mary Younge

Lady Catherine Regrets

The above four stories (and two additional stories) are collected in:

Pride and Prejudice Villains Revisited – Redeemed – Reimagined A Collection of Six Short Stories

Other Pride and Prejudice variations by Renata McMann
Heiress to Longbourn
Pemberley Weddings
The Inconsistency of Caroline Bingley
Three Daughters Married
Anne de Bourgh Manages
The above five works are collected in the book:
Five Pride and Prejudice Variations

Also by Renata McMann
Journey Towards a Preordained Time

Books by Renata McMann writing as Teresa McCullough

Enhancer Novels: Stand-alone novels in the same universe
Enhancers Campaign
The First Enhancer
The Pirates of Fainting Goat Island
The Enhancer with Meg Baxter

Bengt/Tian stories:
The Secret of Sanctua A Bengt/Tian novel
Kidnapped by Fae: a Bengt/Tian Short Story

Other stories:
The Slave of Duty with Meg Baxter
Lost Past

Thrice Born Series by Summer Hanford

Thrice Born Novels:
Gift of the Aluien
Hawks of Sorga
Throne of Wheylia
The Plains of Tybrunn
Shores of K'Orge

Under the Shadow of the Marquess Series:
The Archaeologist's Daughter
The Duke's Widow

Ladies Always Shoot First Half Hour Reads Series:
Captured by a Duke
To Save a Lord
One Shot for a Gentleman
Anything for a Lord

A Lord's Kiss Half Hour Reads Series:
Last Chance for a Lord
To Know a Lord's Kiss
A Lord's Dream
Deceived by a Lord

Installments in Scarsdale Publishing's Marriage Maker Series:
One Good Gentleman
My Lady of Danger
Rake Ruiner
Dreaming of a Gentleman

Chapter One

Elizabeth peeked over the top of the book to find her sister, Jane, finally asleep. With a quiet sigh, Elizabeth marked her place and closed Wordsworth's volume. She enjoyed poetry, but not so much as Jane did. An hour spent reading aloud Wordsworth's work constituted a larger dose than Elizabeth cared for, especially when Jane asked to hear a poem a second time. With a few of the poems, that was two more times than Elizabeth liked.

She looked about the elegant cream and powder-blue bedchamber, taking in the silk clad walls with their subtle floral pattern, the plush ivory carpet dotted by clusters of blue roses, and the flickering candles set in silver candelabras. Heavy curtains were pulled tight against any night air that might endeavor to seep between shuttered panes and infiltrate Jane's still weakened frame, though her fever had broken that morning.

Elizabeth rose quietly. She set Wordsworth's volume on a side table where a pitcher of water and a glass waited. She poured a glass of water and placed it on the smaller table beside the bed, within easy reach for Jane, who slumbered peacefully, braids framing her pale visage against the pillow. Slippered feet all but silent on the thick carpet, Elizabeth moved to stir up the fire before flittering about the room, extinguishing candles. Her route ended at the door where she took up the final candle and slipped out.

She looked up and down the hall with its evenly spaced sconces. Dinner long past, Elizabeth imagined the five other people in residence at Netherfield Park with her and Jane still lingered in the parlor. Little desirous of sleep, Elizabeth also had no wish to converse with her housemates. She turned and headed toward the opposite wing of the home where what passed for a library waited. Perhaps she could find something more entertaining to read, or at least a different book of poetry to divert Jane on the morrow.

As she quietly traversed the corridors, Elizabeth reflected that her behavior lacked graciousness. As a guest of Mr. Bingley's, the gentleman renting Netherfield Park, she ought to seek her host, his relations and his friend, and provide what amusement her company could offer. She owed as much to Mr. Bingley, and to Jane.

Him, because of his kindness and generosity in letting Jane remain when she fell ill while visiting his sisters, and for taking in Elizabeth to tend her. Jane, because Elizabeth felt her sister to be at least half in love with Mr. Bingley, though it was difficult to tell. Jane kept her feelings to herself. In love or not, Jane would wish Elizabeth to make a favorable impression on him.

Elizabeth peeked around a corner, though she'd yet to find another person in the drafty hall to which the library was relegated. Empty corridor stretched away before her, a single flickering candle offering a swaying pool of light outside the library door. Apparently, at least one of the servants had noticed Elizabeth's use of the room and decided to light the way for her.

Elizabeth looked back over her shoulder in the direction she'd come. Outside, she could hear wind whipping past, but inside remained silent. Not that she expected otherwise. The parlor they frequented after dinner was a floor down and in a different wing of the grand manor. Were Elizabeth a better person, more dutiful and mindful of her mother's ambitions, she would be in that parlor.

Candle held high, Elizabeth faced forward once more and marched toward the little library. Jane's fever had broken. That meant that soon Jane would be well enough to travel, and they would be able to go home, to Longbourn. Maybe even tomorrow, if their father could spare the carriage, something that seemed unlikely when their mother had already made Jane ride over under threat of rain in the hope she would be unable to return until the next day. Elizabeth clenched her teeth as she strode down the hall, still angry their mother would risk Jane's health and comfort just to see her catch Mr. Bingley.

Worse, for success would only leave Mrs. Bennet vindicated in her plotting, the way Mr. Bingley asked after Jane, the expression on his face when he did, gave every indication that their mother's plan had worked. Not that Elizabeth held any ill will for him. In fact, she liked Mr. Bingley, but spending time with his sisters and that Mr. Darcy was worse than reading the same Wordsworth poem a thousand times over. In the rain. Standing on one foot. In a puddle.

She turned into the library. Surprisingly, the fireplace and several candles were lit, all near the door. Whatever servant had been so thoughtful deserved better than Mr. Bingley's unwed sister, Miss Bingley, as a mistress of the house. Miss Bingley didn't seem very devoted to her role as her brother's hostess. She would far rather curry favor with Mr. Darcy than manage Netherfield Park. Then again, Mr. Bingley seemed a kind master, assuming he took any note of the staff at all.

Elizabeth went around one of the oversized, decorative pillars to the far side of the room, where her favorite highbacked armchair and a modest collection of books on the natural world waited. Between the pillars, fireplace and many windows, there was hardly space for shelving. The room offered a sparse collection, kept only for show.

Reaching the shelves she sought, Elizabeth held up her candle to survey the titles, but her mind was too full of thoughts of Miss Bingley to concentrate on the books. Miss Bingley and her sister, the third sibling, Mrs. Hurst, were horrible. Although they were Mr. Bingley's sisters, their personalities were very different from his. He was friendly and accepting, while they were neither. Mrs. Hurst's husband, so far, defied assessment. He seemed so determined to remain in the background as to have completely suppressed any show of personality.

At least Miss Bingley and Mrs. Hurst were kind to Jane, thus far. That was more than could be said for Mr. Bingley's other guest, Mr. Darcy, who wasn't kind to anyone. Insufferable... that was the only word Elizabeth could use to describe the proud, withdrawn Mr. Darcy. Through his behavior, he made no secret of his belief in his superiority over Elizabeth, her family and, indeed, all of Meryton. Likely, all of Hertfordshire. On top of that, he'd deliberately insulted Elizabeth before they'd even been introduced, saying, quite obviously within her hearing, that she wasn't handsome enough to dance with. Mr. Darcy was a boor.

Yet, for Jane's sake, Elizabeth had suffered him for some days now, her only solace that she enjoyed sparring with him. It amused her to attempt to show him the wrongness of his outlook. Although she did not believe she'd changed his mind on anything, for the imposing Mr. Darcy wouldn't condescend to be wrong on any count, she felt she'd made valid points, which he must consider. Sometimes, his expression even ventured into consternation.

A smile turned up her lips at each recollection of stumping Mr. Darcy. The real wonder was that he didn't avoid speaking with her altogether. Of course, he would never back down from someone who, in his eyes, was so much lower than he. To avoid her would be tantamount to defeat.

Her smile even wider at the thought of Mr. Darcy ever admitting defeat at her hands, Elizabeth focused her gaze on the spines before her and yanked free John Coakley Lettsom's *The Naturalist's and Traveler's Companion*. She took book and candle to her favorite armchair, its back pressed against one of the decorative pillars, which were wide enough for both a chair and small table to hold her candle. Setting down the latter, she curled up in the chair and flipped open the weighty, dry volume, the perfect antidote to Wordsworth.

Without, the wind continued to howl, but inside the library, ensconced in the large armchair, Elizabeth felt snug enough. She paged past the preface and started reading. The first section, which spoke of how to properly catch and preserve insects, conjured a new vision of Miss Bingley and another smile.

Elizabeth had nearly dozed off by the time she reached Lettsom's recommendation for where to find flies but came more fully awake at reading a rather gruesome description of how best to catch and pin butterflies. Precisely where to stab a pin into the beautiful creatures constituted more of a foil to poetry than she required. She was about to close the book and seek another when footsteps sounded in the hall. In moments, someone entered the room.

The conscientious servant come to see if the room still required light? No, the firm footsteps in the hall most likely meant one of her companions sought a late night read. As the tread was too heavy to be feminine and Mr. Bingley didn't strike Elizabeth as the reading sort, she could only assume the intruder on her solitude was Mr. Hurst at best and, at worst, Mr. Darcy.

Whoever it was, for the moment, fortunately, they browsed the shelves near the door. Should she announce herself or remain hidden and hope to go unnoticed? If the gentleman made his way between the pillars to the far side of the room, she would certainly be seen. Better to alert him to her presence now. She eased forward in the chair and opened her mouth to speak.

New footsteps sounded, the light patter of slippers heard only once they tapped on the wood planks just inside the library door. Mrs. Hurst come to join her husband in selecting a book to read in bed? Elizabeth closed her mouth over her greeting and eased back again. Perhaps, if they came around the pillar, she should feign sleep?

"Good evening, Miss Bingley," Mr. Darcy's voice said.

Elizabeth cringed. Worse than the Hursts. Two of her least favorite people.

"Good evening, Mr. Darcy," Miss Bingley replied in a honey-coated voice.

Elizabeth stifled a gasp. Heaven above, she did not want to bear witness to a tryst. But surely, despite his many faults, Mr. Darcy wouldn't—

"I do not mean to intrude," Mr. Darcy said. "I will make my selection and depart, so you may make yours."

"I'm not here for a book," Miss Bingley said. "I must speak with you."

"Then you should do so in the morning, not alone with me, late at night." Cordiality bled from Mr. Darcy's voice.

"You won't wish anyone, even a maid, to hear what I must say."

Grimacing, Elizabeth realized she'd long since missed her chance to inform them of her presence. She curled more tightly into the chair. She could only pray they didn't come to the back of the room.

"I find it difficult to believe you and I have anything to discuss privately, Miss Bingley," Mr. Darcy said. "If you will excuse me?"

A shuffle of footsteps and swishing skirts ensued.

"Please step out of my way," Mr. Darcy said, voice touched with anger now.

"Not until you hear me out," Miss Bingley declared.

"Say what you feel you must."

One of them, likely Miss Bingley, drew in a long breath and let it out again. "I don't know how to say this, but you have shown an unbecoming interest in Miss Elizabeth."

Elizabeth grimaced, muffling a groan which threatened to turn into a laugh. Interest in her, indeed. Only Miss Bingley would conjure such an idea, born of how badly she coveted Mr. Darcy. Or, rather, Mr. Darcy's connections and wealth.

"I? In Miss Elizabeth? Preposterous."

Elizabeth pursed her lips. Despite how his sentiment mirrored her own, Mr. Darcy's tone held scorn enough to sting.

"You watch her," Miss Bingley accused.

"Not particularly."

"Oh, really?" Miss Bingley countered. "When I stood up and walked about the room, you ignored me. When I invited her to join me, you put down your book and paid attention." She sounded aggrieved. "Your gaze is always on her."

"I do not think so."

Even Miss Bingley, Elizabeth thought, must hear the frost in Mr. Darcy's voice.

"Oh, yes, it is." Miss Bingley sucked in another breath. "You even commented to me once that she has fine eyes."

Elizabeth widened those eyes in shock.

"She does. May I not make an innocent observation?"

"You may, but you didn't," Miss Bingley snapped. "Your observation would be innocent if you didn't pay particular attention to her."

"I do not."

"Don't you? Miss Bennet is very pretty, but you haven't said so. When we spoke about how pretty she is, all you said was that she smiles too much. More importantly, you don't watch Miss Bennet constantly."

Heat rose in Elizabeth's cheeks. She considered standing and coming around the pillar. Her appearance would be nearly comical now. To her, at least.

"What do my comments about one sister have to do with the other sister?" Mr. Darcy asked, words clipped. "Miss Bingley, this is a highly inappropriate conversation. Let me make one thing clear. You are my friend's sister and I will treat you with respect, but I have no interest in this kind of exchange. My opinions of other women are mine. Your observations are distasteful. If you do not depart this library immediately, I shall."

Light footsteps sounded. The door slammed. The lock clicked.

Before Elizabeth could fully register that Miss Bingley had locked them in, her slippered steps sounded again, still in the library. They pattered across the other side of the room at an alarming rate.

"What are you doing?" Mr. Darcy exclaimed as another click sounded. Frigid air swirled in. "What did you throw out? Was that the key?"

Elizabeth stood, alarmed by the consternation in Mr. Darcy's voice. The howling November wind whipped through the library. All around the room, curtains stirred and swayed. Flames, candle and fireplace alike, danced, emphasizing light and shadow. Firm, masculine footfalls crossed to the door. The knob rattled.

"Why did you lock us in?" Mr. Darcy demanded.

"I am tired of waiting for the proposal that will never come," Miss Bingley cried. "I am completely suitable to be your wife, yet you ignore me."

"I beg your—"

"Well, now we are locked in a room together," Miss Bingley continued, speaking over Mr. Darcy. "No one but you ever comes to this wing. If you shout, no one will hear you over the sound of the wind. Even if they do, we are locked in here together. Come morning, you will have to marry me." Miss Bingley's voice rang with triumph. "You cannot spend the night alone with me without consequences."

Elizabeth had heard enough. She squared her shoulders. "But he is not alone," she said, stepping around the pillar to take in two startled faces.

Chapter Two

"I imagine it will be an uncomfortable night, but with us here to chaperone one another, there is no compromising anyone," Elizabeth continued. She quirked her lips into a slight smile. "However, considering how unreasonably you're behaving, I insist on getting the sofa."

Mr. Darcy continued to stare at Elizabeth in astonishment, but Miss Bingley's features contorted into anger. She whirled to face Mr. Darcy.

"You had a rendezvous with her," Miss Bingley spat out. "You let me talk about her, knowing she was here."

"I did not." Mr. Darcy shook his head, gaze still on Elizabeth.

"I do not believe he knew I was here." Elizabeth couldn't keep a certain wryness from her tone. "He couldn't see me from that side of the room any more than you could."

Miss Bingley angled her venomous glare at Elizabeth.

Mr. Darcy turned back to the door. "This is ridiculous," he muttered. He again tried the doorknob, a scowl marring his handsome face. The expression deepening, he patted about the top of the doorframe. "There is usually a second key."

"Maybe in that desk?" Elizabeth said, pointing to the narrow, drawer-filled piece where it stood to the right of the fireplace.

Miss Bingley maintained her vitriol-filled glare at Elizabeth while Mr. Darcy rummaged through the small desk. He didn't find a key but eventually came up with a penknife. Elizabeth returned Lettsom's volume to its place. She turned back to watch Mr. Darcy use the penknife first to attempt the lock and then to try to pry up the hinges. Ignoring the hatred radiating from Miss Bingley, Elizabeth crossed the room, brushing past the other woman to reach the open window. She knew they were two stories up, but the distance appeared even greater than expected as she gazed down at the lawn, lost in a sea of darkness below.

Miss Bingley huffed and returned to the other side of the room, where Mr. Darcy still pried at the hinges. A muttered sound, suspiciously like an oath, issued from Mr. Darcy's place at the door. The penknife clattered to the desktop. A moment later, he appeared beside Elizabeth to look out the window.

"We are too high up to climb down," he said.

Elizabeth glanced left and right, at the long curtains. "Maybe not."

Behind them, the lock clicked. Elizabeth spun to see Miss Bingley swing open the door and dart through. Elizabeth raced toward her, Mr. Darcy outdistancing her in one stride. The door slammed closed in Miss Bingley's wake. The locked clicked at the same time as Mr. Darcy's hand engulfed the doorknob. He twisted. The handle didn't budge.

"Miss Bingley, open the door," Mr. Darcy barked.

A slightly hysterical laugh sounded. "So, you won't marry me. Fine." In addition to the manic note, Miss Bingley's voice held a trace of tears. "Instead, you'll be forced to marry someone highly inappropriate. She may have fine eyes, but you won't like the rest of her, particularly her family." Another laugh, that same strange mix of glee and despair, sounded. It faded as Miss Bingley moved off down the hall.

"Miss Bingley," Mr. Darcy called. He pounded both fists against the door. "Come back here."

Panic surged in Elizabeth. Though tinged with madness, Miss Bingley's words were also true. If Elizabeth and Mr. Darcy remained locked in the library together and were found in the morning, they would be forced to wed. Elizabeth grabbed the doorknob and twisted, then yanked. Her efforts to move the solid wood panel didn't even rattle the hinges.

Mr. Darcy stepped back from the door. Elizabeth tamped down her panic. She forced her hand to unclench the doorknob. Movements slow, she swiveled to face Mr. Darcy. Handsome, haughty, insufferable Mr. Darcy.

He folded his arms across his chest. "I'm afraid we are stuck here."

Elizabeth forced down a fresh surge of panic. "There must be a way out."

"I do not think so." He glanced at the desk, many of the drawers still hanging open. "Miss Bingley had the second key all along."

"Or threw something else out the window," Elizabeth said, feeling slight hope. "She planned this."

He nodded. "Except for the part where you stepped in. Thank you."

"Don't thank me yet." Elizabeth went to the desk to search the drawers again. If Miss Bingley had thrown something else out the

18

window, there could still be a spare key. "If we're found here together..." She didn't complete the thought, which must be as repugnant to him as to her for, although Miss Bingley's assessment of her stung, Elizabeth could see some validity in it, especially from Mr. Darcy's perspective.

After a moment, Mr. Darcy joined her in searching. He checked about the fireplace while she looked inside vases. He patted along the top of the doorframe a second time. Elizabeth peeled back the edge of the carpet. Only dust met her searching gaze.

"I could try to kick down the door," Mr. Darcy offered as Elizabeth stood and dusted her palms together.

A glance at the mantle clock showed the hour to be even later than Elizabeth had realized. She shook her head. "We're on the far side of the house from the bedrooms but the wind is dying down. I've no idea if you can kick down that door, but Mr. Bingley's footmen patrol the household at night. The racket you would make in the attempt could very well draw attention. We'd be discovered and forced to marry." She shuddered at the thought.

"If you do not care for my idea, I am open to suggestions," Mr. Darcy said stiffly.

Elizabeth bit back a rejoinder. Of course, the great Mr. Darcy wouldn't enjoy having his idea dismissed. Well, Elizabeth would not spend her life wed to a man who measured his value as only slightly less than that of the Archbishop of Canterbury. She had to get out of the room without being seen.

A fresh gust of night air blew in. Candlelight, curtains and firelight flickered. Elizabeth narrowed her eyes at the thick, swaying cloth. She crossed and closed the window to preserve the heat.

"We'll make a rope out of the curtains." She looked about, seeking greater height. "Come, help me," she said and dragged a chair over to the first window. Climbing up, she began taking down the curtains.

"It will not be strong enough," Mr. Darcy said but he moved to the window and helped, not requiring a chair to reach.

Once they had both heavy panels in pools on the floor, Elizabeth moved to the next window. Silent, Mr. Darcy again helped, and with another. Soon, they had heaps of fabric about the room.

"This will do, thank you," Elizabeth said after the fourth window.

The library boasted seven windows in total. Although difficult to judge in the dark, she'd seen the exterior of the manor by daylight. They couldn't be all that high up. She didn't need every curtain the room offered.

While Mr. Darcy watched with a frown, Elizabeth retrieved the penknife and started cutting the seam of one of the curtains. As soon as she began, she realized the wide swaths of fabric would still be too thick to tie tightly, so once the seam was out, she took up one side and applied the knife, along with judicious tearing, making no attempt to preserve the expensive material.

"Miss Bingley will not be pleased with the damage to Netherfield's curtains," Mr. Darcy observed, tone sardonic.

"Miss Bingley could have saved her curtains by unlocking the door," Elizabeth replied without looking up from her work.

Mr. Darcy crossed to the fireplace and threw on more wood. Although Elizabeth found the efforts with the heavy fabric invigorating, she was glad of the heat from the fire. He returned to watch her again, his polished shoes visible at the edge of her vision, then went to the back of the library to pace the shelves. To her surprise, he seemed to focus on the same section she had. Then again, among the poetry, gothic novels and worn volumes of Shakespeare, the library's works on the natural world were a welcome deviation.

Once she felt she'd dismantled enough panels, Elizabeth twisted and knotted them into a semblance of a rope. She made it extra-long, so she could tie an end about one of the pillars. She also wanted to make sure her rope would terminate near enough to the ground. If she got to the end and felt the distance was still too great, she didn't imagine she'd have the strength to climb back up and add more length.

Finally satisfied with her work, she knotted one end securely to a column. A glance in the direction of the mantle showed the hour to be quite late, or rather early, her efforts having taken some time. If she didn't get away from Mr. Darcy with no one the wiser, she was well and truly compromised. Lips pressed into a tight line, Elizabeth opened the window nearest the column and tossed out the free end of her so-called rope.

Mr. Darcy's book snapped closed. Elizabeth turned to watch him cross the room. He checked her knot on the end she'd secured to the column, tugging so hard she held her breath until he desisted. He came to the window and looked down, where her makeshift rope disappeared into the dark lawn.

He shook his head. "It's too dangerous." He glanced at her askance.

"We should wait until morning. Someone will come."

"We're not that high up," Elizabeth protested. "If we're found here, together, we'll be forced to marry." Had he lost sight of that all-important repercussion?

Or didn't he plan to do the honorable thing? Miss Bingley had assumed marriage would come on the heels of a night spent sequestered, for her or for Elizabeth, but could Elizabeth, a mere country miss in their eyes, count on the same chivalry? She would suffer greatly from the resulting scandal but to Mr. Darcy, it would mean little.

"I realize we will marry if we remain here until we are discovered," he said quietly, refuting her unvoiced accusation. As he spoke, he pulled in the rope. "I also realize we do not know each other well, but I would far rather wed you than break my neck climbing out a window." He dropped the last bit of rope to the floor and closed the window. "Or see you come to harm."

"That's flattering, and ever so honorable of you, but I am not your wife yet," Elizabeth countered. "The choice is mine. I deem the risk worth the reward." Elizabeth had no intention of wedding a man whose manner was already overbearing.

He folded his arms across his chest and turned so he stood squarely in the window, back to the night. "I will not permit you to take such a risk."

Elizabeth locked gazes with him. His countenance, hard with obstinance and conviction, begged a slap, but she would never best him that way. Deliberately, she issued a sigh and let her shoulders fall, hands loose at her sides. She gave a little shrug.

"This is on you, then," she muttered.

He gave a sharp, satisfied nod.

Mastering a renewed urge to slap the domineering look off his face, Elizabeth broke eye contact and looked about the room. "I suppose I'll read a bit more."

He nodded again, then watched as she crossed to retake both book and chair. She opened the book to the sound of the mantle clock ticking.

"If you intend to read, I shall avail myself of the sofa," Mr. Darcy said. "Wake me when you wish to sleep." He left the window to move about the room, extinguishing all the candles except those she needed to read.

Book open in her lap, Elizabeth listened intently as Mr. Darcy stretched his long frame out on the sofa. She studied the cadence of his

21

breath. Eventually, it settled into a quiet, even rhythm. Movements as slow and silent as she could make them, Elizabeth rose. She set the book on the chair, tiptoed to the window, opened it, and quickly lowered her makeshift rope out.

Chapter Three

Darcy shivered. He reached for his blanket, to tug the thick, soft quilt up around his shoulders, only to find he didn't have one. He blinked his eyes open to recall he lay on the sofa in Netherfield Park's small library. A gust of cold air whipped through the room.

He sat up, swiveling to take in the topmost of Elizabeth's curls before they disappeared from view below the sill. Darcy came to his feet and raced to the window, fears for Elizabeth jumbling through his brain.

Was she mad? A fall was likely to break her leg or worse. Netherfield was not some squat, mean dwelling with ceilings to endanger a man's skull. The sill was high enough to kill someone who fell from it, and she hung from curtains.

He gained the window and thrust his head out into the night. She clutched the curtains, far down her makeshift rope already. As well as he could estimate in the dark, she neared the ground. She gazed downward. He only saw her dark curls.

She skidded, a startled squeak issuing between her lips. Darcy dove forward and grabbed the rope, for what little good that did. Elizabeth's feet hit lawn. She clung to the rope for a moment, ragged breath discernable even from so far above, then released the curtains. Shaking her hands, she looked up, met his gaze, and grimaced.

"Are you well?" he called in as loud a whisper as he dared.

"That last, inelegant bit merely bruised my pride," she whispered back.

Darcy let out a relieved breath.

She looked about her. "I don't think I can find the key. I can hardly see my own feet, and I know where *they* are." Her delicate features angled back upward. "I'll see if I can find a way in, then send a servant for the housekeep. Maybe she has another key."

Darcy shook his head. Even if she often vexed him, he couldn't, in good conscience, leave Elizabeth out there alone in the dark, cold night. Besides, there may not even be another key, if Miss Bingley truly had thrown one out and kept one. "No, I am coming down."

Elizabeth offered a shrug and stepped back from the rope.

Darcy left the window to retest her knot encircling the column. It seemed solid, as did the next, binding two sections of cloth together. He returned to the window, offered a silent prayer that all of Elizabeth's work was of a similar quality, and climbed onto the sill.

She was brave, he realized, feeling the precariousness of leaving the windowsill to put all his weight on the rope. Hanging there in the dark, the ground seemed even farther away than he'd estimated. Arm under arm, he descended, though tension left him once he was halfway down. Even if Elizabeth's makeshift rope gave way, he wouldn't sustain injury from the shorter fall.

Her rope proved as solid as her resolve. Soon, his feet touched lawn. He glanced about, reaffirming the lack of use in searching for the key, and turned to face her. In the dark, Elizabeth was a swath of porcelain skin and a pastel gown, the night swallowing her rich curls. "You should not have taken such a risk." The words came out harsher than he'd intended.

"Would you rather be wed to me?" she countered in a tone rich with scorn.

"Than see you dead or permanently harmed?" Did she think he had so little honor? "You question my standing as a gentleman if you think otherwise."

To his astonishment, and vexation, she held out her arms in a dismissive gesture. "The point is moot. We're down now and the hour only grows later."

Much as he would prefer to argue the point and gain the gratification of an apology, he let the matter drop. "Let us see if we can find an open window. If we do not by the time we round the building, I will enter through the front door and come back to open one for you. I wish it could be otherwise."

She nodded, rubbing bare arms against the chill. "It's a reasonable plan. My reputation would never survive me appearing at the door in the wee hours of the morning."

Holding back the rejoinder that yes, of course his plan was reasonable, Darcy offered, "Would you like my coat? You are cold."

"No, thank you," she replied. "I daresay we won't be out for long. I don't wish to be caught wearing it."

Annoyance slicing through him, Darcy pivoted to stride along the side of the house, searching for windows in the dark. She wouldn't even accept the offer of a coat, which she could return before they parted ways. His pique mounted, growing nearer to anger. He'd been foolish to make the offer. What did she care of coldness? She'd risked her life climbing out that window. A chill was nothing to that. Apparently, avoiding marriage to him was worth any danger or discomfort.

He located a window and drew in a breath. He should be relieved, as he didn't wish to marry an aggravating country miss with a horrible family and no connections. Still, her determination stung. No woman had ever treated him thusly, especially not one with so little to offer a man. By all logic, she should throw herself at him. He tried the window, perhaps with more vigor than required.

Elizabeth reached his side. "Will it open?"

"Would it, I should have it open by now." He moved to the next.

They made their way along the wall in silence, Darcy attempting to open each window. At least Elizabeth didn't insult him by trying them a second time, he reflected as he reached for another. She had some faith in him, even if she found the idea of wedding him abhorrent.

The window slid open. Darcy rocked back slightly, surprised. They'd only tried five.

They were doubly fortunate, for the sill stood only a few feet off the ground. He turned and offered his hand. Elizabeth placed cold, delicate fingers in his. He helped her through the window, though, he reflected, she did not require his help. He did not have time to warm her hand before she gained entrance.

Darcy climbed in after her, then turned and closed the window. He patted around until he located the lock, the darkness inside more complete than the starlit night without, only to find the mechanism not in working order. He shrugged, unable to rectify the broken latch, and turned away.

"I think we're in a parlor," Elizabeth whispered. "There's a chair to your left and to your right, with a small table set between. Don't knock it over. Follow my voice."

Deciding she was correct in leading the way, her slight form much less likely to topple anything, Darcy followed in Elizabeth's wake as they made their slow way across the room. With her whispered instructions guiding him, they found a door without mishap. Elizabeth cracked it open to let in a dim, welcome line of light. Miss Bingley's housekeeping might not extend as fully as it ought to window maintenance, but fortunately did reach the level of leaving no corridor completely dark at night.

They stepped free of the room to find a single candle in the center of a long hall, likely directly below the library. Unerringly, Elizabeth turned toward the more frequented portions of the manor. Darcy continued to follow, somewhat enthralled by her grace and the ephemeral quality of their journey as she drifted down little used corridors in the night. They truly were quite scandalously alone.

Soon enough, they were in sight of familiar ground, the spell her slight form wove unraveling. Darcy blinked several times as they neared this better lit area, a man coming out of a dream. Before they reached that haven of the known, Elizabeth stopped. She turned to face him.

"No one needs to know I was in that room with you," she whispered.

There was enough light to see her features again now, and he read the worry in what truly were lovely eyes. "Miss Bingley already knows," he countered. "I will not lie if she comes forward." What would it be like to have those eyes look at him every day?

A slight frown turned down Elizabeth's lips. "I think her actions were from momentary pique. Locking you in the library because you made her angry is a more charitable explanation for her behavior than locking in both of us together, although I am sure she'd prefer to pretend nothing at all occurred."

"I hope she sees it that way." He wasn't certain how he was going to explain the destruction of the curtains, without betraying Miss Bingley's actions.

"She will. She won't so easily give up on her dream of having you." Elizabeth's mouth quirked, the frown gone. "In view of which, you might consider having your valet sleep in your bed," she said as she turned away, voice light with amusement. With that, she strode quickly to the end of the corridor. She looked left and right, bundled her skirt slightly, and dashed from sight.

Darcy was left alone with that parting vision of well-turned ankles and a sparkle of mirth so palpable as to almost shimmer in the air in her wake. He took a half step after her, then stopped. He shook his head, counted out several long minutes to ensure he wouldn't encounter her should her pace slow, and headed in the direction of his rooms.

He still could not believe how adamantly Elizabeth didn't want him. She'd rejected marriage to him as strongly as possible. The Miss Bingleys of the world did everything they could to get him to marry them. Elizabeth Bennet had that union handed to her, through no conniving on her part, and she'd baulked. She'd risked injury or even death to avoid that fate.

Her actions stirred anger, and confusion. Why be angry when he didn't want her, either? Was he truly that proud, that every woman in England must desire him? Or was his sense of self-worth that fragile? Darcy didn't care for either assessment. He tried to tamp his anger down.

Rather than dwell on his shortcomings, he turned his attention to Elizabeth's parting comment. He could tell she issued the words as a jest, but he considered the idea with care. When he reached his room, he rang for his valet, who appeared immediately.

"Sir?" Hawkins said, coming to attention with near military precision. Well trained, he made no comment about the late hour.

Knowing he could trust Hawkins discretion when required, Darcy said, "What I am about to say goes no further."

"Understood."

How to sum up his rather unusual evening? "Miss Bingley tried to force me to compromise her."

"I see, sir," Hawkins said without inflection.

"By chance, her plan did not work," Darcy continued. Circumspect as Hawkins was, Darcy saw no point in mentioning Elizabeth. "Either Miss Bingley or I will leave tomorrow. We shall never again be under the same roof. It occurs to me that she might guess that and try again, as one last chance. I have a key to my door, but I suspect, as manager of Bingley's household, she does as well."

"Almost certainly, sir," Hawkins agreed.

"I would like to sleep somewhere else." If he could sleep at all after the events of the evening. "Furthermore, if you sleep in my bed, I can at least find out if she really intends to go that far. I am probably overreacting, but do you have a suggestion as to where I might sleep to be safe from her?"

"I could sleep on the floor here," Hawkins suggested. "You could keep your bed and have a witness."

Darcy shook his head. "I do not wish to make you sleep on the floor and, frankly, you snore abysmally."

One side of Hawkins' mouth twitched, as if he might smile, but he didn't. "My snoring has been mentioned by the other servants from time to time, sir."

"I imagine so. The few occasions I have been made to endure the racket have left a very strong impression. That is why I gave you your own room at Pemberley and at Darcy House, as a kindness to all." Though for many years, until his daughter married, and his wife died, Hawkins had lived in a small cottage near Pemberley, an accommodation not afforded most valets but a precedent set by Darcy's father.

"And here I thought it was out of deference to my years of faithful service to both you and your sire."

In his late forties now, Hawkins had become Darcy's valet when Darcy's father died and Darcy's previous valet left him, taking advantage of the money Darcy's father had willed to every servant. Hawkins had accepted a pension but, Darcy later learned, sent that pension to his daughter, wife of a tailor.

"The rooms are out of gratitude for your service as well, of course," Darcy said. "But back to our current trouble."

Hawkins expression grew contemplative. "If I may suggest a course, you could take my bed in the servants' quarters here. The others might appreciate a night free of me, all else aside."

"How would we explain my presence?" Darcy asked.

"You shall merely keep silent. I shall explain before you come in." Hawkins hesitated a moment. "You won't enjoy the accommodations, sir."

Darcy shrugged. He'd seen the servants' quarters at Pemberley and Darcy House many times. Even the group rooms, as he supposed his servants had been given as those of a guest, were perfectly suitable. "I'll manage. Lead the way."

Darcy followed Hawkins through a small servants' door, then a narrow corridor, and up a steep flight of steps. Finally, they reached a hall that ran the length of the attic of that wing. Even in the narrow hall, the slope of the roof's peak was visible. Darcy could only stand upright in the center.

Hawkins held up a hand, then disappeared through one of the small doors, taking the flickering light of the candle he carried with him. Darcy heard voices, made out the words 'letter' and 'bet' on the other side of the thin wood. He tried not to listen, wanting to be as little part of Hawkins' subterfuge as possible. Still, he heard very clearly when someone said in jovial tones, "He can't snore any worse than you, Hawkins."

The door opened and, head ducked slightly against the slope of the room, Hawkins gestured Darcy in. "Welcome to your accommodations for the evening, sir. Watch your head."

Hawkins, and the candlelight, remained until Darcy removed his shoes, which Darcy set under the cot, and settled onto the creaking little bed, which was too short for him. The mattress was almost non-existent and the blanket quite inadequate for a room without a fire, but Darcy didn't issue a complaint.

"Thank you for permitting the intrusion," he said instead. "Sleep well."

"You as well, Mr. Darcy," one of the others returned.

Hawkins gave a parting nod and disappeared with the light. Cold and uncomfortable as he was, his mind trouble with a mild nagging of conscience over Hawkins' lie, it took Darcy some time to fall asleep. Fortunately, none of the servants in the room with him appeared to snore.

Chapter Four

Far too early for Darcy's tired mind and limbs, the servants started moving. Someone cracked open a rickety shutter. It wasn't full light out, but near enough that the room brightened to the point where the occupants could see to strike flint in a tinderbox. One of his men lit a tallow candle and passed it over. Remembering not to slam his head into the low ceiling, Darcy accepted the wavering bit of flame. He set it down to put on his shoes, then made his stooped way from the room, happy to leave the frigid chamber behind.

As he drew near his rooms, a muted rumbling reached his ears, then grew with every step. He entered to find Hawkins sound asleep in the bed, buried under a deep quilt, fire burned low in the grate. Darcy crossed to stir the coals. His gaze fell on a pair of feminine slippers beside the bed. Eyebrows raised in a mixture of surprise and disdain, Darcy threw a log onto the fire.

"What? Who?" Hawkins muttered.

Darcy turned from stirring the blaze to find his valet sitting up in bed, blinking. "Sleep well?" he asked, amused.

"I did, sir, if you don't mind me saying so."

"Not at all." Darcy gestured to the slippers. "I see you had a visitor."

Hawkins swung his feet to the floor. His gaze settled on the incriminating footwear. Surprise flittered across his face. "I didn't think she'd left evidence."

"What happened?"

Hawkins blinked several times, seeming to gather himself. He scratched at the stubble on his cheek and Darcy realized he'd never seen his valet in a state outside perfection. He wondered how early Hawkins rose each morning to be ready to appear the moment Darcy called.

"Well, sir," Hawkins said. "I reckon I was sound asleep when someone lay down next to me, under the blankets, and wrapped an arm around me, but I woke up pretty quick, let me tell you. She said, 'You won't get away from me this time, Mr. Darcy,' and I recognized her

31

voice, so I said, 'Begging your pardon, miss, but Mr. Darcy's not the type to dally with servants, so you'd best be on your way,' so as to give her a chance to leave. She let out a little squawk and darted out of here faster than a rabbit set on by the hounds."

Darcy nodded. Though colorful, Hawkins' description was approximately what he expected. He eyed the expensive, flower embroidered slippers with grim amusement. Miss Bingley had gone too far and been foolish enough to leave evidence of her machinations.

"What shall I do with those?" Hawkins asked with a gesture to the slippers.

"Put them somewhere safe." Recalling that Miss Bingley held the master keys to the household, he added, "Somewhere she cannot unlock. Speaking of which, did you lock this bedroom door last night?"

"I did, sir, so you were correct, she used her key." Hawkins stood and tugged his rumpled clothing into better order. "I have just the place for the slippers, don't you worry."

"I'm not," Darcy said. He had complete faith in Hawkins.

"Well then, let's make you presentable, Mr. Darcy, if you don't mind the assistance of a rather bedraggled valet?"

Darcy shook his head. "I do not mind, but I would consider it a boon if you would go about your usual routine while I catch a bit more sleep. Do not let me doze for too long, though. I wish to speak with Bingley before breakfast. Our discussion should prove quite interesting."

"I should think so, sir." A hint of a smile formed on Hawkins' face. "And if I may, sir, if the young miss wants to save her good name by marrying me, I'm open to it. She won't even have to see me again, after the ceremony."

"She is unlikely to settle any of her dowry on you," Darcy observed as he removed his coat and vest. Darcy didn't usually sleep clothed, but he'd been grateful for even the slight additional warmth of his coat.

Hawkins stepped forward to take the wrinkled garments. "I'm sure I could pry free some small portion of her funds," he said as he examined the coat. "I'd start by asking for a quarter of it, but I think I would accept a thousand pounds. For fifty pounds a year, I could live with my daughter and not be a burden to her. I could even help in her husband's business. I do a bit of sewing for you and I'm pretty good at it. Speaking of which, there's a nasty tear in your coat, sir."

"I must have torn it climbing out the window," Darcy said as he pulled his shirt over his head. "Will you be able to mend it?"

Hawkins nodded, giving no reaction to the news that Darcy had climbed out a window. "When I am through with it, you won't even know the tear was there," he said confidently, before helping Darcy into his nightclothes and leaving the room.

Darcy felt as if he'd hardly closed his eyes when Hawkins, face clean shaven and clothing perfectly starched, woke him. Darcy shook off sleep, pleased to find a coffee service at hand, and readied for the day. By the time he felt prepared to face Bingley, his pocket watch claimed nearly nine. Earlier than Bingley usually descended to the breakfast parlor but not, Darcy felt, too early to seek his friend. Bracing for a scene, Darcy left his room and marched down the hall in the direction of Bingley's door.

Fresh, unlit candles rested in the evenly spaced sconces of the hall, Darcy noted, nerves seeming to stretch the short walk and emphasize every detail. At both ends, curtains stood open to permit daylight to enter, though the windows remained closed against the November chill. Darcy glanced down, taking in the polished gleam of his shoes and the nearly chaotic red and gold pattern of the runner.

He considered Bingley a good friend but wasn't completely sure how the news of Miss Bingley's behavior would be received. Friendship could grow complicated when mixed with family. He reached Bingley's door and knocked.

The door opened to reveal Bingley's valet. "Mr. Darcy."

"Stevens," Darcy acknowledged. "I requite a word with Mr. Bingley."

"I'll ask if Mr. Bingley is receiving visitors yet, sir." Stevens disappeared as the door closed.

Darcy heard Stevens' baritone, then Bingley's lighter voice. He made no effort to eavesdrop. Bingley's surprised, 'Darcy?' came through the wood quite clearly, but nothing else. Darcy reflected that the bedroom doors on this level were much thicker than the ones on the servants' quarters above.

Bingley's door swung wide. Stevens stepped back with a bow. He turned to face the room as Darcy entered. "Mr. Darcy to see you, sir."

Bingley still wore his nightclothes, covered by a thick, densely embroidered robe. He was on the sitting room's lone sofa, facing the door, but stood. "Darcy. Rather early for socializing, isn't it?"

"I wish to speak with you before breakfast," Darcy said, crossing to the small array of sofa and chairs.

"Yes, certainly," Bingley replied, tone confused. He gestured to a chair. "Please, sit. Stevens, send for coffee. Darcy, would you care for coffee?"

Darcy nodded and took the indicated chair while Bingley resumed his place, expression both curious and weary. "I'm afraid," Darcy began, "That you will not care for what I have come to tell you."

Bingley grimaced. "Can it wait until after coffee?"

"If you insist."

"Thank you."

They sat in strained silence while they waited. After what the mantel clock claimed was but a brief time, but Darcy deemed an eternity, a coffee service arrived. Bingley poured a cup then gestured for Darcy to do the same. Across from Darcy, his friend settled back in the sofa, took a long sip, and let out a sigh.

"Now, what is so urgent as to push you beyond the realm of civilized behavior, Darcy?"

"I hardly think requesting your time at nine is uncivilized."

"Coming to a man's room, glowering, before he's had even a taste of coffee is downright barbaric," Bingley said and took another sip.

Darcy cleared his throat. "If you feel that is barbaric, you will need a new word to describe a woman who would lock herself in a room with a man in order to force him into marriage, and then, when he escapes, climb into his bed in the middle of the night."

Bingley's eyebrows shot up. He set down his coffee. "Truly? Who did that? Don't tell me it was Miss Elizabeth? She's a bit unconventional, but I didn't think she was chasing you."

Darcy grimaced, his pride re-stung. "You will soon understand that saying she is not chasing me is an understatement."

"Then who?"

A wave of pity washed through Darcy, cooling some of the anger sparked by the prospect of retelling his evening. Bingley really didn't understand how low his sister could sink. Darcy disliked being the one to disillusion him. "Your sister."

"My sister what?" Bingley's wide, honest face reflected his confusion.

"Last night, Miss Bingley followed me to the library." Darcy aimed to keep emotion from his voice. "She postulated that I am enamored of Miss Elizabeth and proceeded to say some rather unflattering things about that miss. She then locked the library door and threw, or pretended to throw, the key out the window. She said I would have to marry her come morning."

Bingley's jaw hinged open.

"Miss Elizabeth, who had been in the library the entire time, in a chair behind one of those ridiculously overdone pillars, then revealed that your sister and I were not alone."

"Wait," Bingley said, learning forward. "What was Miss Elizabeth doing hiding in the library? You said she doesn't care for you."

Darcy suppressed another grimace. The whole mess was so sordid. "I can only guess, but I imagine she hoped I would select a book and leave and then, once your sister arrived, did not wish us to know she heard our conversation. Once we were all locked in, she must have realized she could not remain hidden. She announced herself as a potential chaperone to spare the need for me to marry your sister."

Bingley shook his head. "You're telling me Caroline locked herself in the library with you to trap you?"

"I am."

"But Miss Elizabeth was there the entire time. Perhaps you misunderstood my sister's motives."

"I would that were true," Darcy said, and proceeded to detail the rest of his night to Bingley.

When they reached the part about Miss Bingley climbing into bed with Hawkins, Bingley went white. Then, as Darcy passed along Miss Bingley's words, his friend turned red. He slumped on the sofa, coffee cooling where it rested on the table.

"I don't believe it," Bingley muttered. "I can't believe it." He raised beseeching eyes to Darcy.

"I have Miss Elizabeth and Hawkins as witnesses," Darcy pointed out. "I also have the slippers that were left behind in my room, and I imagine that if you go to the library, you will find some measure of disarray."

Would Miss Bingley have gone back? She must have, to know to seek him in his room. Had she cleared away the makeshift rope? She wouldn't have been able to replace the curtains.

Bingley pushed a hand through his hair. "This is terrible. Unconscionable."

Darcy agreed, but all he said was, "As you can imagine, I cannot spend another night under the same roof as your sister."

"No," Bingley murmured, expression dazed. "No, most certainly not."

"Therefore, unless you have somewhere to send her immediately, I shall depart today," Darcy continued, forcing a gentler tone than his simmering anger over the debacle warranted.

Bingley's expression sharpened as he focused on Darcy. "Where will you go? You may have to marry Miss Elizabeth. You will want to be in the neighborhood."

"Were you not listening?" Darcy couldn't keep a bitter note from creeping into his voice. "She does not wish to wed me. She worked for hours to fashion a rope, then climbed out a dangerously high window, all to avoid that fate."

"If word gets out about what happened…" Bingley trailed off, eyes going wide. "If her mother finds out, neither you nor Miss Elizabeth will have a choice. You'll have to marry."

Darcy shook his head. "That will not happen. I certainly will not be spreading the tale. Neither you nor Miss Bingley will wish to share the story. And with how adamantly Miss Elizabeth wishes to avoid marriage to me, I highly doubt she will tell a soul."

Chapter Five

Elizabeth, sitting at her sister's bedside, told Jane what happened as soon as she woke up. Jane, still pale and too-thin from her recent illness, listened to the tale with wide, incredulous eyes. At several points, she shook her head, almost as if denying Elizabeth's words, but she didn't interrupt.

"You climbed out the window?" Jane demanded when Elizabeth finally fell silent. "You could have been hurt."

"I did scrape my arm somehow." Elizabeth peeled back the sleeve of her gown, chosen for covering her arms to her wrists, and showed Jane the shallow cuts. "I think I did it while climbing over the windowsill." She held up her hands, still red and sore. "And this is from when I skidded down the last bit of curtain."

Jane's eyes became, if possible, even rounder. "I'm glad there's nothing more serious." Agitated fingers plucked at the heavy quilt that covered her. "I'm also glad you both got out of that room. What if no one came? What if there was a fire?"

"No harm came of it," Elizabeth said soothingly. Perhaps she should have remained silent. She hadn't realized how strongly the news would affect her already weakened sister. "All that happened is that I learned Mr. Darcy is even more vexing than I thought."

"How can you say that?" Jane exclaimed. "He defended you to Miss Bingley and he offered to do right by you."

"He didn't defend me to Miss Bingley," Elizabeth countered. When she'd had time to think over the evening, she'd been a bit put out by the lack. "He said he found her observations distasteful."

"That is a defense."

Elizabeth shook her head. She stood and paced to the window. "No, he simply dislikes gossip." She pulled back the curtains to permit daylight to enter. They were on the same floor as the library. With the sun up, the distance to the lawn appeared even greater than it had in the dark. "And he never once offered to marry me. He informed me that we would marry." His arrogance still rankled.

"That's nearly the sa—"

"On top of which, he permitted me to go through the considerable effort of making a rope, all the while with no intention of allowing me to use it," Elizabeth continued. "You should have seen how... how haughty and proud he was as he ordered me not to go out the window." Elizabeth worked to press down her anger. No one ordered her about that way. "If he hadn't fallen asleep, we'd probably still be locked in there."

"And you would have to marry him."

Jane's voice had an odd dreamy quality that caused Elizabeth to turn. Her sister's unfocused gaze rested on the door and a smile curved her lips. "Jane," Elizabeth was aghast. "You aren't enamored of Mr. Darcy?"

"Me?" Jane's face swiveled toward Elizabeth and her eyes focused. "No. Of course not."

"Then why so dreamy?" Elizabeth pressed, still alarmed. Her sweet gentle sister could not end up with the pretentious, officious Mr. Darcy.

Pink stained Jane's cheeks, adding much needed color to her face. "He's Mr. Bingley's dear friend. Whomever marries Mr. Darcy will be much in Mr. Bingley's company."

Elizabeth rushed to the bed, anger with Mr. Darcy fleeing before happiness for Jane. "So, you do care for Mr. Bingley," she cried, clasping Jane's hand.

Jane's blush deepened but her smile returned as Elizabeth perched on the edge of the bed. "Oh, how could I not, Lizzy? He's so kind, and warm, and dear."

"And handsome," Elizabeth added.

Jane flushed an even brighter red.

Elizabeth chuckled. She squeezed Jane's hand before letting go. "I'm very happy for you. Mr. Bingley is a wonderful choice."

Jane dropped her gaze. "It's not as if it's a set thing, Lizzy."

"But it will be. I've seen the way he looks at you," Elizabeth said. "We all have. In fact, I count it a wonder Miss Bingley hasn't tried to dislodge you from his presence, ill or not." Elizabeth shrugged. "Then again, she's obviously been wrapped up in plans for her own future."

A giggle left Jane. "It is very odd, you know. You climbed out of a window to avoid marrying Mr. Darcy while Miss Bingley went so far as to lock him in a room to try to catch him."

"As far as I am concerned, she may have him," Elizabeth said, her tart tone belying the smile Jane's happiness brought to her lips. Then Elizabeth, too, laughed. "No. On second thought, even Mr. Darcy doesn't deserve Miss Bingley."

Jane tsked. "For shame. She can be very nice."

"Can be?" Elizabeth pulled a face. "You are always nice. Miss Bingley has shown me a side of her character I find unreasonable, to say the least."

"You are right," Jane admitted, but looked sad rather than indignant. "She should never have locked you in the library. She's been very nice to me, and I tend to think well of people who are."

"You think well of people, regardless," Elizabeth said without censure. Jane's open, caring nature was to be cherished, not suppressed. "And I wouldn't change that about you. Not for a moment."

Jane rewarded that avowal with a smile.

"Now," Elizabeth said, standing. "You look and sound much improved. Should you care to dress and have breakfast in the parlor, or shall I bring you food? This morning promises to be rather interesting."

"I should like to dress and eat in the parlor, and not because I hope to see Miss Bingley reprimanded, as you obviously do," Jane said. "But because I'm feeling much more myself today and, in view of Miss Bingley's behavior toward Mr. Darcy and you, I'm worried there will be a scandal, which means we really ought to go home, even if I must walk."

"You will certainly not walk," Elizabeth said firmly. "That would undo all your rest. If need be, I'll go demand the carriage, but you, dear Jane, will neither walk nor ride, but will sit calmly in a snug, warm carriage and be driven home."

Jane made no argument as she rose to dress. Elizabeth maintained an easy, cheerful manner while she assisted her sister, for Jane's sake. Inside, worry gnawed. Elizabeth knew Mr. Darcy wouldn't publicize the events of the night, for marriage to her must strike him as worse than never wedding at all, but she wasn't certain about Miss Bingley. Would Miss Bingley continue to want to force Mr. Darcy into an unwanted marriage, and thus continue in the vein that saw them locked in the library? Would vindictive pettiness cause her to deem the damage to her own reputation worth ruining Mr. Darcy's future, and Elizabeth's, by revealing the scandal and forcing them to wed?

By the time they reached the breakfast parlor, mulling over her concerns still hadn't offered any relief from them. They entered together to find Mr. Darcy alone at the table. He stood at the sight of them.

"Miss Bennet," Mr. Darcy greeted with a nod. "Miss Elizabeth," he added before turning back to Jane. "May I say you appear much improved this morning, Miss Bennet."

"Mr. Darcy." Jane hurried across the room toward where Mr. Darcy stood at the table. "Elizabeth told me—"

"A fascinating story," Elizabeth cut in, reaching Jane's side. She nudged her sister with an elbow, then rolled her eyes toward the waiting footman and maid, but Jane was looking at Mr. Darcy.

"Yes, about that," Mr. Darcy said. He moved to pull out a chair for Jane, waving the footman off. "My carriage is at your disposal this morning, if you should care to depart," he said in a low voice. He pushed in Jane's chair.

Elizabeth didn't know if he intended to assist her, but she sat before he could. "I think that would be for the best," she said, making no effort to be overly quiet. "Jane is feeling much better today and, though we're both very grateful for Mr. Bingley's hospitality, we should like to return home."

Mr. Darcy pivoted toward the footman. "Please have my carriage made ready. Ensure my driver knows the way to Longbourn."

"Yes, sir," the footman said and left.

Mr. Darcy turned next to the waiting maid. "Please fetch pen, paper, sealing wax, a lighted candle and ink. I wish to write a letter."

The maid dropped a curtsy and hurried away. If she thought Mr. Darcy's desire to write a letter at the breakfast table odd, she gave no indication. Instead of sitting, Mr. Darcy crossed to the hall door and looked out, then repeated the process with the servants' door. Finally, he returned to the table and sat.

"If you would forgo breakfast for a moment, I believe we should discuss last evening, while we are alone," he said.

"Elizabeth told me what happened," Jane said.

"So I gathered, and I told Bingley this morning, but unless Miss Elizabeth wishes to marry me, which I ascertain she does not, the information should go no further." Mr. Darcy's tone was dry and touched with reprimand. "Especially not to the ears of servants."

"Oh," Jane said, expression abashed. "Yes, of course."

Elizabeth flushed and clamped her lips over sharp words. Even if she'd been thinking the same thing when Jane nearly mentioned the incident in front of Mr. Bingley's staff, Mr. Darcy had no right to reprimand her sister. If Elizabeth thought it would make any impression on him at all, she'd say as much.

"You should know," Mr. Darcy said, shifting his attention to Elizabeth. "I consider myself honor bound to marry you, given the circumstances."

"That's truly not necessary," Elizabeth protested, meeting his gaze. "I would rather we each find happiness than torment one another for the remainder of our days. After all, you and I both know nothing untoward happened."

He nodded. "I agree. However, I plan to visit your father today and tell him what occurred and of my offer. If the incident is ever made public, I want it clear that I will fulfill my obligation by offering to wed you."

"That's not really necessary," Elizabeth repeated as the maid returned.

"I insist," Mr. Darcy replied.

They fell silent as the maid set out paper and other writing accoutrements beside Mr. Darcy, then disappeared to fetch more items. As she left, the footman came back in and returned to his place. The maid returned almost immediately with a fresh candle. Elizabeth tamped down her anger at the lack of privacy and stood.

"Jane, what would you care for? I'll fetch you a plate," Elizabeth offered.

While Mr. Darcy wrote, Elizabeth fixed a plate for Jane and another for herself. Jane requested tea for them both. When Elizabeth returned to her seat, food in hand, Mr. Darcy slid a page across the table.

"Read this and then I shall seal it," he said.

Piqued afresh by what sounded, to her ear, like an order, Elizabeth nonetheless dropped her gaze to his even, bold script.

To Whom it May Concern,

I, Fitzwilliam George Darcy of Pemberley, in Derbyshire, owe Miss Elizabeth Bennet of Longbourn, in Hertfordshire, a considerable debt. If she presents this note to you, please give her whatever aid she requests and then return the note, if she so wishes. Bear in mind that I shall consider assistance rendered to Miss Elizabeth Bennet as I would assistance rendered directly to me.

Elizabeth looked up from the signed and dated page. "Return the note?"

"To be reused, for I doubt one favor will be thanks enough," Mr. Darcy stated.

"No, I imagine not," Elizabeth murmured, amused. Not that she didn't feel the same. A hundred favors wouldn't be enough to thank someone for not forcing her to wed Mr. Darcy. He, likely, multiplied that number by ten when compiling his gratitude for not being made to marry her.

Mr. Darcy tapped the page. "This may never help you in any way, but it is all I can think to do at this juncture." He left unspoken that anything more would compromise her anew. Even the note, though not, strictly speaking, a letter and composed while Jane looked on, was outside the bounds of propriety.

"It's very kind of you," Jane said.

"And unnecessary," Elizabeth added.

Mr. Darcy folded the page closed and reached for the wax. He angled the wax toward the candle and used his ring in place of a seal. "I do not have a title, and thus no crest," he advised, "but I have used this ring enough times that many people I know will recognize the mark. It was my father's, and his father's before, and so on back." He passed the now sealed note to Elizabeth.

"Thank you," she murmured, unsure what else to say. She tucked the folded page into her skirt, then reached to pour tea.

Another footman entered the room. He headed up the table to where Mr. Darcy sat and bowed. "Sir, Mr. Bingley requests your presence somewhat urgently."

Mr. Darcy nodded, then turned back to Elizabeth and Jane. "My carriage is at your disposal this morning. I am afraid I must ask you employ it as soon as reasonably possible. I shall have need of it the remainder of the day."

"Thank you. We will," Elizabeth said.

Mr. Darcy stood and bowed. Without another glance, he strode from the room, the footman trailing in his wake.

Elizabeth prayed Mr. Bingley's summons didn't mean Miss Bingley was threatening to reveal the events of the night before. As far as Elizabeth was concerned, it would suit her perfectly if Mr. Darcy's proposed visit to Longbourn later that day was the very last she ever saw, or heard, of Fitzwilliam George Darcy of Pemberley and his pompous ways.

Chapter Six

To Darcy's surprise, the footman directed him to Netherfield's library. Darcy found Bingley inside, pacing the inadequate space. When Darcy entered, Bingley whirled to face him, then summarily dismissed the footman to the end of the hall.

"And don't let anyone come down here," Bingley called after the retreating form.

If the servants hadn't thought anything was amiss before, they surely did now, Darcy reflected. "You asked to see me?"

"There's no rope," Bingley blurted.

Darcy glanced about the room. Elizabeth hadn't ended up using all the curtains they'd taken down, but four of the seven windows remained bare, regardless. Likewise, the column bore the marks of their escape. "Yes, but there are quite a few missing curtains." He pointed. "And the plaster is rubbed off that column where Miss Elizabeth secured the rope she fashioned."

Bingley hurried to the column and bent low to investigate. He moved to the window and ran a hand over the sill. Darcy joined him to find marks there as well.

"I spoke to Caroline. She admits to locking in the two of you, but says she came back almost immediately and found you both gone," Bingley declared. He cast Darcy a darting glance. "She swears to me she never went to your room."

Darcy turned from the window to stare at Bingley for a long moment, wondering if Miss Bingley's behavior would ruin a valued friendship. "If by almost immediately you mean hours later, then your sister told you the truth. It took Miss Elizabeth quite some time to fashion that rope." On which she'd worked diligently, as proof of her determination not to marry Darcy.

Bingley glanced back at the array of marks, expression indecisive.

"As for your sister's second transgression, you forget that I have evidence," Darcy added.

"A pair of slippers and your valet's word it was my sister," Bingley scoffed. "Like as not, Hawkins is trying to get Caroline's dowry."

Sorrow weighed in Darcy's breast, but he wouldn't so easily give up Bingley's friendship or permit Miss Bingley to slander Hawkins. "The slippers are rather distinct. Perhaps there is someone who could identify their owner?"

Bingley paced away. He turned back. His shoulders slumped. "Darcy, it can't be true. Caroline has always had silly dreams when it comes to you, but she wouldn't go that far."

"Apparently, she would." Darcy permitted a touch of anger to color his voice. Bingley was coming dangerously close to labeling him a liar. "Shall I call for Hawkins and the slippers? You may examine both."

Expression tormented, Bingley scrutinized the pillar again, then the windowsill. He turned his troubled gaze out into the dreary November morning. With a sudden exclamation, he wrenched open the window and leaned out, pointing downward. "What's that?" Bingley asked, voice light with surprise. He stepped back, gesturing for Darcy to look.

Darcy stuck his head out. A cold breeze tousled his hair. He looked about, downward, where Bingley had pointed. There was nothing. He'd no idea what had caused such excitement. Below lay lawn, and more lawn, and— "The key," Darcy exclaimed, catching sight of the gleaming metal. "So, she did have two copies."

Behind Darcy, Bingley sucked in a breath. "Let's send for Hawkins, these slippers and my sisters."

"Both sisters?" Darcy asked, turning from the window. He'd hoped no one else need learn of last night's escapades.

Bingley's expression firmed. "If I decide I must discipline Caroline, Louisa will need to know why."

Darcy nodded, relenting. As Miss Bingley's and Bingley's sister, Mrs. Hurst would eventually need to be told, if she didn't know already. Miss Elizabeth had obviously informed her sister immediately that morning. "Whatever you think best."

Bingley headed across the library. "Shall I send for Miss Elizabeth?"

Darcy shook his head. Bad enough he should have to recount how fervently the country miss had rejected him. He did not need her to watch him speak the words. "She and Miss Bennet are readying to depart Netherfield Park. Let us not interrupt unless we must."

"Miss Bennet is leaving?" Bingley asked, halting just inside the library door.

"Miss Elizabeth told Miss Bennet what occurred. You can hardly expect her to remain."

A surprisingly hard look settled over Bingley's features. "A good point," he said, and strode into the hall.

Without, Darcy could hear Bingley ordering the footman to fetch both of his sisters, Hawkins, the 'items Hawkins would know to bring,' and to send someone for the key lying in the lawn. Darcy grimaced. Some sort of scandal would be born of all the strange goings on.

Bingley returned, expression still grim, and resumed his pacing. Darcy went to the fire and tossed on a few more logs, noting that they'd nearly emptied the reserve. He also noticed the wood he threw on the fire caught quickly and boasted cobwebs. Apparently, Netherfield's library was seeing much more use than usual.

Darcy turned to watch Bingley, face troubled, pace. In deliberate contrast, Darcy moved to the windows. He selected a bare patch of wall beside one, where curtains once rested, and propped a shoulder against the silk cladding to wait with outward calm while the minutes ticked by.

Hawkins hurried into the library, carrying something wrapped in cloth and a larger package. With a bit of amusement, Darcy recognized one of the curtains, presumably wrapping the remaining rope. With a quick movement, Hawkins lifted the other cloth to reveal the slippers. Bingley didn't halt his pacing but cast Darcy's valet a glare that stopped Hawkins three steps into the room. He turned worried eyes on Darcy.

Straightening, Darcy gestured Hawkins to the far side of the library. "Why don't you take that armchair, Hawkins. The one with its back to the pillar. It is perhaps best for you to remain aloof from this discussion unless needed."

Hawkins moved deeper into the room, expression somewhat dubious until he rounded the pillar and spotted the chair. Darcy realized his valet hadn't even known the chair existed, it was so well obscured. Hawkins, the rope and the slippers, disappeared from view.

Darcy allowed himself to feel mild, grim amusement at concealing Hawkins in the same place Elizabeth had sat to elude detection. Hopefully, Miss Bingley would confess and not need a second unwelcome surprise from that quadrant. Then again, if Miss Bingley developed an aversion to ostentatious pillars and hidden armchairs, that would be her own doing.

A different footman entered. He handed Mr. Bingley a key. Bingley dismissed him and put the key in the lock, where it worked perfectly. He cast Darcy a troubled look, tucked the key into his vest pocket, and returned to pacing.

The patter of footsteps preceded Mrs. Hurst's entrance, Mr. Hurst inevitably on her heels.

"Charles, we were told you urgently wish to see us," Mrs. Hurst said. "We haven't even breakfasted yet. Whatever could be so important? And why have you dragged us to this dreary corner of the manor?" She turned to Darcy with a nod. "Good morning, Mr. Darcy."

"Mrs. Hurst, Mr. Hurst," Darcy acknowledged. He moved to stand before the fireplace once more, gesturing that they should take their choice of the two chairs and sofa arrayed there. "Bingley," Darcy added as Bingley continued to pace.

Bingley changed his trajectory, coming to plop down in one of the armchairs beside the fireplace. Mrs. Hurst perched on one end of the sofa, Mr. Hurst taking the chair opposite Bingley. Darcy continued to stand.

Before anyone could speak, Miss Bingley burst into the room, face flushed. She glanced around, gaze skittering away from meeting anyone's eyes. "Mr. Darcy, Charles, Louisa, Mr. Hurst."

"Caroline," Mrs. Hurst said on the heels of Miss Bingley's greeting. "Did Charles send for you as well?" She looked back and forth between her siblings, obviously noting the angry glare Bingley leveled at Miss Bingley. "Have you any notion why? He hasn't said a word yet. He's just sitting there, glowering."

Miss Bingley swallowed. She shook her head, then dropped her gaze to the carpet.

"Miss Bingley." Darcy gestured to the sofa on which Mrs. Hurst sat. "Please sit."

Without looking at him, she complied, ignoring the question clear on her sister's face.

"Will the Miss Bennets be joining us?" Mr. Hurst asked. "We'll need more chairs."

"The Miss Bennets are preparing to depart Netherfield," Darcy said. "I do not mean to disturb that process unless required."

Miss Bingley's cheeks reddened. She kept her face angled downward, hands clasped tightly in her lap.

"Depart?" Mrs. Hurst echoed. "Whatever for? Is Miss Bennet feeling well enough to travel?"

"Required for what, Darcy?" Mr. Hurst asked, frowning.

Darcy drew in a deep breath and squared his shoulders, keenly aware he stood as an outsider before a family. "Last night, Miss Bingley locked herself in this library with me in an attempt to force me to wed her."

Mrs. Hurst gasped. Miss Bingley turned an even brighter red. Bingley watched his sister through angry, narrowed eyes. Mr. Hurst sat up straighter in his chair, expression surprised.

"Neither of us realized Miss Elizabeth was in the room," Darcy continued. "When Miss Elizabeth revealed her presence, Miss Bingley ran from the room and locked Miss Elizabeth and me in the library, saying that if I would not wed her, she would force me to wed someone totally inappropriate to my circumstance."

"Caroline," Mrs. Hurst cried. "Is this true?"

Miss Bingley raised her face to look at her sister but didn't speak.

"I believe it is," Bingley said.

"Caroline," Mrs. Hurst repeated, voice full of reprimand.

"I'm very sorry." Miss Bingley turned a pleading expression on Darcy. "I came back to let you out, but found you gone."

"You told me you returned almost immediately," Bingley said. "But Darcy tells me Miss Elizabeth spent hours making a rope from the curtains and then they both ended up climbing out the window." He made an angry gesture in that direction.

Mrs. Hurst twisted to take in the windows. She frowned. "There are quite a few curtains missing. How long did you really wait, Caroline?"

"I don't know," Miss Bingley whispered.

"I don't care when she came back." Bingley's voice was colored with never before heard anger. "I care about what other lies Caroline told me when we spoke about the incidents of last night."

"Incidents?" Mr. Hurst repeated, catching Bingley's emphasis on the word. "There's more?"

Mrs. Hurst held up a hand to silence her husband. "Mr. Darcy, are you attempting to tell us that Caroline has forced you to propose to Miss Elizabeth?" she asked, voice so full of worry as to be nearly a shriek.

Darcy did his utmost to fend off the anger and embarrassment her question evoked. "I tendered the offer. She did not appear interested in accepting."

"She won't marry you?" Mrs. Hurst gasped out.

Darcy cleared his throat. "No, she will not. Miss Elizabeth did most of the work in making the rope and climbed out the window first.

Indeed, I thought it was not safe, and would not have let her go, but she waited until I was asleep. She expended considerable effort to make the rope, only having a dull pen knife. I must assume she adamantly does not want to marry me."

Miss Bingley laughed, the sound almost hysterically. Everyone turned to stare at her. She emitted another giggle. "I knew Miss Elizabeth was strange and wild, but I didn't know she was foolish enough to climb out a window to avoid marrying you, Mr. Darcy." Another sound, half giggle half hiccup, escaped her.

Mrs. Hurst watched her sister with worried eyes for a moment, then turned back to Darcy. "Well, as you shan't be forced to wed Miss Elizabeth, no harm's been done."

"You said incidents," Mr. Hurst said in a quiet voice, the comment directed at Bingley.

"I did." Bingley's syllables were clipped. He hadn't left off glaring at Miss Bingley since she entered. "There's more."

"What more can there be?" Mrs. Hurst said. "Caroline behaved abominably and forever ruined her chances with Mr. Darcy, but he won't have to marry Miss Elizabeth and we'll all agree never to speak of their time in the library together, so all ends well."

Darcy angled a hard look at Miss Bingley. "Do you wish to tell them what else happened last night, or shall I?"

"What happened?" she repeated with a good show of innocence, ruined by the red staining her cheeks.

"I admit, I have only secondhand information, so I would rather you narrate," Darcy continued, ignoring her pretense.

"Perhaps we should not discuss it," she said.

"It must be discussed." Darcy raised his voice slightly, calling, "Hawkins."

"No," Miss Bingley whispered as Hawkins appeared from around the pillar and started across the room, slippers in hand.

Chapter Seven

Darcy watched Miss Bingley pull horrified eyes from Hawkins to turn back to him.

"Don't do this," she pleaded.

Darcy firmed his visage.

"That man has been listening to us the entire time?" Mrs. Hurst demanded in outraged tones as Hawkins came to stand beside Darcy. Her brow furrowed, confusion chasing some of the anger from her expression. "Why is he holding the slippers I gave you, Caroline?"

Miss Bingley shook her head, face white now, and clamped her lips tightly closed.

"Caroline?" Mrs. Hurst pressed.

"This is my valet, Hawkins, a longtime, trusted member of my staff," Darcy said. "I think it would be best if we permit him to explain." Ignoring Mrs. Hurst's frown and Miss Bingley's beseeching visage, he gestured to Hawkins to speak.

"Mr. Darcy and I exchanged sleeping quarters last night, as Mr. Darcy worried Miss Bingley might not give up in her attempts to ensnare him." Hawkins spoke in an unemotional voice. He might have been suggesting what Darcy should wear. "I locked the bedroom door, but Miss Bingley came into the room and climbed into bed with me. I told her that Mr. Darcy did not wish maids to do that, hoping to preserve some small portion of her dignity. She left these," he added, tipping up the slippers.

"Are you sure it was my sister?" Bingley asked, words thick with anger.

"Yes. I recognized her voice." Hawkins cast Darcy a quick glance and received a nod in reply. "Besides, she had to have a key to get into the room. Very few persons have access to the master set and I had the spare in the room with me."

Miss Bingley surged to her feet. "A maid stole my slippers," she cried. "And my dressing gown, and the key. Everything. It wasn't me."

"Caroline," Mrs. Hurst bemoaned.

Bingley stood as well, expression suffused with anger. "Stop lying, Caroline. You're only making this worse."

"You would take their word over mine?" she cried, gesturing to Darcy and Hawkins.

"I would take Darcy's word over King George himself," Bingley declared.

Bingley glared at Miss Bingley, who glared back. Mrs. Hurst looked back and forth between them, worry and sorrow etching lines on her face. Miss Bingley brought clenched hands to her mouth. She pressed them there, as if to hold in whatever words would escape. She looked around the room, Darcy following her gaze to find little sympathy, save from her sister.

Miss Bingley burst into tears. "I wanted to marry Mr. Darcy," she sobbed.

Mrs. Hurst stood, leaving only Mr. Hurst seated, his expression baffled, as if he couldn't credit what he heard. Mrs. Hurst moved to her sister and touched her hand. Almost childlike, Miss Bingley flung her arms about her older sister and buried her head against Mrs. Hurst's shoulder.

"I'm sorry," Miss Bingley babbled through her tears. "I wanted to be mistress of Pemberley. I wanted to be Mrs. Fitzwilliam Darcy. I wanted it more than anything. More than anyone has ever wanted anything."

Bingley's face folded into lines of disgust. Darcy, embarrassed for Miss Bingley despite her horrendous behavior, gestured for Hawkins to leave. Hawkins issued a return gesture to call attention to the pile of curtains behind the pillar. Darcy nodded. His valet set the slippers on the little desk that Darcy and Elizabeth had rummaged through and slipped out. Darcy hoped, and didn't doubt, that Hawkins would begin packing their things immediately.

Bingley took Miss Bingley by the shoulder and pulled her away from Mrs. Hurst. "Darcy is leaving here because of you," he said, voice dripping anger and disdain. "I can't say I blame him. I don't think you are fit to be under the same roof with any wealthy single gentleman. You're lucky I don't insist you marry Hawkins."

Miss Bingley gasped. "You wouldn't."

"I should." Bingley crossed his arms over his chest, looking more obstinate than Darcy had ever seen him.

"He's a servant, Charles," Mrs. Hurst said, tone worried.

"Hawkins' grandfather was a gentleman," Darcy murmured. Hawkins' mother had run off with a footman.

Both of Bingley's sisters cast him horrified, angry looks.

Bingley let out an explosive breath, too anger-filled to be a sigh. "What were you thinking, Caroline?"

"I don't know," she cried, wiping at her eyes. "I couldn't wait any longer for Mr. Darcy to propose. I'm perfect for him and he refuses to see it, and then he said she has fine eyes, and I saw the way he looks at her and I knew I would lose him."

Darcy raised his eyebrows. The woman was obsessed with his innocent observation.

"Fine eyes?" Bafflement was added to Bingley's anger. "What are you blathering about, Caroline?"

"Miss Elizabeth. He fancies her," Miss Bingley sobbed. "He wants her, when I've been trying for ages and am so perfect for him."

Darcy shook his head.

"Stop babbling about Miss Elizabeth," Bingley snapped. "Darcy doesn't even care for her. All you've done is prove that not only aren't you perfect for him, you likely aren't fit to be wife to any gentleman." Bingley stared at her for a long moment. "I can't in good conscience have you in my household. I'm hoping the Hursts will take you for a while, but I plan to send you to Aunt Dowding."

"She won't take me." Miss Bingley's voice held a note of triumph. She pulled out a kerchief and dabbed at her face. "You know how tightfisted she is."

"Charles, Caroline, please," Mrs. Hurst said. "Calm yourselves. Let's speak reasonably here."

"Stay out of this, Louisa," Bingley said without looking at his other sister. "For all I know, you put this mad scheme in Caroline's head. You're always encouraging her to go after Darcy. Don't think I haven't noticed." He scowled at Miss Bingley, ignoring Mrs. Hurst's gasp. "Aunt Dowding will take you if you pay her, Caroline."

Miss Bingley angled her chin in the air, some of her usual arrogance returned. "I won't."

"No, but I will, from your money," Bingley said. "I've been letting you handle your own money, but I am your guardian."

"My guardian?" Miss Bingley scoffed. "You're only two years older than I am."

Darcy remained still, a tactic he noticed Mr. Hurst had also adopted. Darcy felt he intruded on a family matter now but leaving would only draw attention. Besides which, he admitted inwardly, he was too curious about what would be decided to depart.

"Our father's will made me your guardian and trustee," Bingley said to Miss Bingley. "I've let you handle your money, but I shouldn't have. You will be given the same allowance you had before our father died. The rest of your money will go for your upkeep and be saved to increase your capital."

"You can't send me away," Miss Bingley cried.

"Now, now," Mrs. Hurst soothed, placing a hand on Miss Bingley's arm. "Aunt Dowding moves in circles with many wealthy men. You will have a good chance to find a suitable husband."

Miss Bingley whirled to stare at her sister. "In trade, Luisa. I want to move in the best circles. You always say I'm destined for the highest echelons." She made a gesture toward Darcy.

Darcy didn't bother to hide his grimace of distaste.

"You are unfit for the best circles, Caroline," Bingley said. "This isn't a debate. You're going to Aunt Dowding."

Desperation clear on her face, she turned back to Bingley. "You need me. You can't run Netherfield Park without me. Oh, you might last a month or two, but it needs a woman."

"She's right," Mrs. Hurst said, tone thoughtful. "The servants can handle things when you aren't in residence, but your housekeeper isn't really up to managing a household this large for any length of time."

"And Louisa can't do it, because she has her own household to manage," Miss Bingley said, triumphant once more. "It's hard to find a good housekeeper. You need someone. You need me."

"I'll find a way to manage." Bingley's tone brooked no argument. "Go to your room and tell your maid to pack. You will be leaving. Oh, and you will be responsible for your maid's wages and upkeep from your own money."

Miss Bingley sputtered a refusal.

"I said go, Caroline," Bingley ordered, mien and voice like ice.

Darcy was surprised at Bingley, and impressed. From the shocked looks on the Hursts' faces, they were also surprised, and Darcy thought he caught a touch of approval in Mr. Hurst's expression. Darcy had never seen Bingley be so firm. He hadn't even realized Bingley was capable of assertive behavior. Yet, the situation warranted action. Miss

Bingley could hardly go unpunished or be allowed to try her tactics on another of Bingley's friends.

Miss Bingley turned to Mrs. Hurst, who shrugged, expression remorseful. Miss Bingley turned back to her brother, fists clenched at her sides. "I hate you," she said, looking first at Bingley and second at Darcy. She whirled and raced from the room.

Mrs. Hurst shook her head. She glanced from Bingley to Darcy. "I'd best go help her pack," she said and hurried after Miss Bingley.

Darcy stood, silent, unsure what to say. Bingley sank into his vacated armchair, looking spent. Mr. Hurst sat forward.

"You're doing the right thing," Hurst said in a quiet voice. "She went too far. She can stay with us for a couple of months, but she really should not mix in polite society." Much as his wife had, he shook his head, then levered to his feet and left.

Bingley looked up at Darcy. "I'm sorry."

"It is not as if you told her to behave that way," Darcy said.

"Not only for her behavior," Bingley said. "For that whole scene. Sorry you had to witness it."

Darcy took a moment to choose his words. "I cannot say I enjoyed what just transpired in any way but be assured that I agree with Mr. Hurst. You are doing the right thing." He wondered how to say more without appearing condescending. "I'm pleased you were able to be so firm. Appropriately firm. And, if I am not overstepping, a touch surprised as well."

Bingley flashed him a humorless smile. "My father was in trade but gave me a gentleman's education. He even encouraged me to spend my holidays with the right people." Bingley shrugged. "But I spent some of my time at home and watched my father being firm. I realize that sometimes sternness is needed. Caroline has been over spending her inheritance. She has an income of a thousand pounds a year and my father died less than a year and a half ago. I recently discovered she is three hundred pounds in debt, although her capital is intact. When I confronted her, she was contrite and apologetic. She said she would be very good and pay her debts soon. That was three days ago."

Darcy realized there was more to Miss Bingley's sudden desperation to snare him than just a silly, baseless worry over his mention of Miss Elizabeth's eyes. "And if I had married her, I could hardly be upset that her supposed twenty-thousand-pound dowry was actually three hundred pounds less."

"Exactly." Bingley looked up at Darcy, expression apologetic still. "You don't have to leave. Caroline and I will."

"Today?" Darcy asked, though he had no intention of remaining.

Bingley shook his head. "No, I suppose not. First, I'll write Aunt Dowding to see if she'll take Caroline. I think she'll be happy to if Caroline's money pays her enough. That may take some negotiating." He frowned, then shrugged. "I'll make it work. Tomorrow, I'll take Caroline to London. She keeps a portion of her possessions at the Hursts' and she'll want them."

Darcy nodded.

"We'll stay in London while I negotiate terms with our aunt," Bingley continued. "Then I'll escort Caroline to Aunt Dowding."

Darcy nodded again, finding no flaw in Bingley's plan. "Are you planning to return to Netherfield Park afterward? Miss Bingley's assessment of your housekeeper's skills may be correct. She may not be up to running Netherfield for a long term without someone to oversee her." Darcy's thoughts went to the window he and Elizabeth had used to climb into the house. Obviously, Miss Bingley wasn't competent, or she would have discovered the problem, but two were at fault. A competent housekeeper would have found the broken latch and had it repaired. One or the other should also have seen to better blankets for the staff.

For the first time that morning, a real smile lightened Bingley's expression. "I definitely plan on returning." Something akin to mischief sparked in his gaze. "And I do have some ideas about who can run Netherfield when I do, but this is hardly the time for that discussion."

Darcy's eyes narrowed. Somehow, he thought Bingley alluded to more than simple housekeeping. He hoped Bingley wasn't planning on running Netherfield Park himself, for that would surely end in disaster. Not that it was any of Darcy's concern. Bingley was a grown man and could see to managing his own estate.

"When you do decide, you will probably also want to decide what to do with the other item Hawkins brought here. I doubt these can be repaired and rehung." Darcy stepped behind the pillar and brought out the rope. He shook it out, to show it could indeed reach the ground. A note flittered out of it.

Darcy stooped to retrieve the page. "Found in the servants' quarters," he read aloud. "It must have been placed there after all the servants were up and about for the day." It was unsigned, but Darcy recognized Hawkins' handwriting.

Experimentally, Bingley tried to untie a knot. He couldn't. "It's too bulky to burn without untying it," he commented. "I suppose I should be pleased Caroline realized that and attempted to hide it instead. She could have burned the house down, along with her other crimes."

Darcy nodded, unsure what to say. In truth, he had no comfort to offer his friend.

Chapter Eight

Elizabeth tried not to hover as Jane descended Netherfield's steps and crossed to the carriage. Really, Jane did seem a great deal better. Elizabeth would have rather kept her abed a day or two more, not had her pack up and travel the first morning she seemed improved, even for so short a distance. But they could hardly remain. Nor should they pass up the offer of Mr. Darcy's carriage.

A footman handed Jane into the large, gleaming conveyance, then turned back for Elizabeth. If the size and the rich wood of exterior hadn't been indication enough, the moment Elizabeth ducked into the spacious carriage, she realized it was the finest in which she'd ever ridden. The seats were plush, the interior upholstery extravagant. The curtains were better than any in Longbourn. She trailed a gloved finger down one, considering taking off her outerwear to touch the soft fabric.

"What a lovely carriage," Jane said, voice touched with awe. "It's very kind of Mr. Darcy to lend us the use of it."

A smile quirked in Elizabeth's lips. "It's the least he can do to thank me for not forcing him into a union." She said the words very quietly, although she knew the footman and driver couldn't hear.

Jane cast her a repressive look, which Elizabeth ignored. Her smile widened as they started down the drive. The carriage rode smoother than any other in which she'd sat, as well. She supposed it wouldn't do Jane much harm to travel in so fine a conveyance. She could see why Miss Bingley coveted the position of Mrs. Darcy.

Not that any number of fine carriages, homes, gowns or what-have-you were worth behaving as Miss Bingley had. Not simply because Mr. Darcy would likely be a condescending, highhanded husband. Perhaps Miss Bingley, unlike Elizabeth, would bear his nature to enjoy his wealth. What, though, of pride? Of honor? Miss Bingley had behaved with neither, showing she had none. Truly, she'd acted inexcusably.

Elizabeth wondered what, if anything, would be done. Miss Bingley was a member of a wealthy family. Usually, the more wealth the fewer repercussions, by Elizabeth's estimation. Miss Bingley's offence was against Mr. Darcy, though, who possessed even greater wealth. He didn't seem the type to let her actions be forgotten or forgiven. Not domineering, stern Mr. Darcy. No, he would want retribution.

Elizabeth shrugged and settled back more fully in the seat. Truly, Miss Bingley's fate wasn't her concern. So long as word of the library incident didn't get out, Elizabeth was satisfied. She didn't know what she would do if it came to living with a lost reputation or with Mr. Darcy. A terrible choice, and one she hoped to never be forced to make.

She turned to Jane for a change of topic, and found her sister rode with eyes unfocused, a dreamy smile on her face. Elizabeth raised her eyebrows. Certainly, that joyous expression didn't result from their destination. Even Jane couldn't be that happy to return to Longbourn.

"Whatever is the root of your cheer, Jane?" Elizabeth asked.

Jane blinked. Her eyes focused on Elizabeth. A slight blush bloomed in her cheeks. "Nothing."

"Jane Emma Bennet," Elizabeth gasped. "You've never lied to me before."

Jane's blush deepened. "And I do not mean to now, Lizzy, save for it's a very private thing. My mind lay on an exchange I had with Mr. Bingley, shortly before we departed."

"You saw Mr. Bingley? When? Where was I?" Elizabeth ran the actions of the morning through her mind.

"In the foyer, right before you saw him," Jane said. "Do you not recall? You went back to recover your bonnet, having left it on your bed, and when you came down, he bid us both a most cordial farewell."

"I remember very well. It wasn't a quarter of an hour ago." Elizabeth shook her head, bemused. "But you must have stood with him only a moment and a not alone, with Netherfield's staff about. What could he possibly have said?"

"Said? Nothing you did not hear."

"Jane, his was a cordial adieu, but hardly worthy of daydreams."

Jane smiled, radiant. "Under the guise of bidding me farewell, while you were coming down the steps, he pressed a small, folded page into my hand."

Elizabeth gasped, joy shooting through her on her sister's behalf. "Well, that is scandalous, is it not? And what is contained on that page?"

"I have no idea. I haven't read it."

"Read it now," Elizabeth urged.

Jane shook her head. "I will not. I shall wait until I am well and perfectly alone, and safe from Mama. We'll be home in little time. I avow that if I don't manage to put Mr. Bingley's note from my mind, Mama will somehow sense I have it and make me show it to her."

As much as Elizabeth longed to know what the letter said, she could see some truth in Jane's fear. She might be able to dissemble before their mother, but Jane never could. Out of love for her sister, Elizabeth swallowed curiosity and embarked on an animated, somewhat one sided, critique of Netherfield's cook.

They rumbled up the drive to Longbourn in good time and must have been spotted from the house because their mother and three sisters spilled into the yard, along with servants to gather their things. The carriage rolled to a halt. It briefly dipped as Mr. Darcy's man leapt down. Mr. Bennet's carriage would have swayed and shook.

"What a beautiful carriage," Mrs. Bennet cried without. "Oh, it must be Mr. Bingley's, it's so lovely. If only my Jane could marry a man with a carriage like this."

"You know it's not Mr. Bingley's," Mary, their middle sister, rejoindered as the carriage door swung open. "You've seen Mr. Bingley's carriage, Mother. This is Mr. Darcy's."

Mr. Darcy's man proffered his hand to Jane, who accepted.

"I can't believe that," Mrs. Bennet said. "Not for a moment. A man as terrible as Mr. Darcy couldn't possibly have so wonderful a carriage."

Jane climbed out.

"Mr. Bingley might have more than one carriage," their youngest sister, Lydia, chimed in.

"Oh, Jane, whatever has happened to you?" Mrs. Bennet cried, as if she didn't know Jane had been ill and hadn't seen her a few short days ago. "You're too pale and too thin. No wonder Mr. Bingley has sent you away."

Mr. Darcy's man reappeared in the doorway to offer his hand to Elizabeth. His expression was a study in neutrality, but Elizabeth felt sure she read amusement and distain in his eyes. She accepted his hand, suppressing a sigh. Miss Bingley was somewhat in the right to criticize Elizabeth's relations. There was no use, she suspected, in asking the man not to repeat her mother's and sisters' silliness. On the other hand, she hardly thought Darcy would encourage his servants to gossip.

"Mr. Bingley did not send me away, Mama," Jane said as Elizabeth climbed out.

"Then why are you here?" Mrs. Bennet demanded in aggrieved tones. "I didn't send for you. How can you capture Mr. Bingley if you're here and not there? I arranged everything so perfectly, went against your father to have you ride, and this is how you repay me? By returning unattached?"

Elizabeth couldn't hide her grimace.

Jane sighed. Even with her forgiving nature, she obviously found their mother's behavior troublesome.

Mr. Darcy's man, expression showing a touch of sympathy now, relinquished Elizabeth's hand. "Will you require anything more, Miss?"

"No, thank you," Elizabeth said.

The man bowed and turned to check that the luggage had been unloaded, then swiftly mounted the carriage.

"But where are they taking the carriage?" Mrs. Bennet cried.

"I wanted to look inside," Kitty, youngest save for Lydia, wailed.

"I did as well," Lydia said. "Lizzy, call them back."

Elizabeth turned to face her family. "That is Mr. Darcy's carriage and he has need of it. He didn't loan it to us so we could pile in our relations as if it's a paid attraction. Furthermore, Jane is not fully well and must be permitted to go inside, either straight to bed or at least into the parlor to sit."

Mrs. Bennet propped balled fists on her hips. "If Jane is so unwell, why are you here? You should have stayed at Netherfield, with Mr. Bingley."

"Mr. Darcy offered the use of his carriage this morning," Elizabeth replied. She took Jane's arm and began to steer her around their mother. "It seemed impractical not to avail ourselves of it."

"But why did he offer it?" Mrs. Bennet demanded, following as they went inside. "He doesn't like you, nor you him. Why would he up and…" A gasp escaped their mother. "There's been a scandal, hasn't there? Oh Lizzy, what did you do?"

"Nothing, Mother." Elizabeth turned Jane in the direction of the parlor, sure their mother would only follow them should they go above stairs.

"Nothing? Oh, it must be something. Mr. Darcy wouldn't hurry you away for nothing," Mrs. Bennet wailed.

"I bet she was too outspoken," Lydia muttered, somewhere behind their mother. "She probably told Mr. Darcy what she thinks of him and hurt his pride."

Elizabeth's lips twitched toward a smile. In a way, she had told Mr. Darcy what she thought of him. In all likelihood, his pride was wounded. Her near-smile dipped into a frown. Yes, his pride must be injured, no matter his relief at not being made to wed her. Yet, he still behaved honorably and cordially, which spoke well of him. Better than she would have expected. She pulled Jane down onto a sofa beside her, to face their mother with a united front.

"Vanity and pride are different things, though the words are often used—" Mary began, with her usual art of trying to sound wise but missing the mark of conversational relevance.

"I didn't say he's vain," Lydia said, cutting Mary off. "As if a man as handsome and wealthy as Mr. Darcy has any need to be vain."

Elizabeth rubbed her forehead, her sisters' skittering, illogical trains of thought instantly starting an ache there. Beside her, Jane sighed again. Mrs. Bennet momentarily filled the center of the parlor with her girth and a great fluttering of movement, then collapsed into a large armchair. Elizabeth's and Jane's other sisters filed in to sit, Mary wearing a scowl.

"Out with it, Elizabeth," Mrs. Bennet demanded. "What did you do to Mr. Darcy?"

"Nothing," Elizabeth repeated firmly. She could justify her statement as being true, if blows to his pride weren't counted.

"It wasn't Lizzy's fault," Jane added.

Elizabeth elbowed her sister.

It was too late. Mrs. Bennet's eyes lit with malicious glee. She threw her arms up, fabric fluttering. "I knew it. I knew you would ruin us all, Elizabeth Isabella Bennet. How could you be so selfish? How could you ruin Jane's happiness this way? And Lydia's? I'm sure that once Jane and Mr. Bingley wed, Lydia would have dazzled each and every one of Mr. Bingley's acquaintances. She would have had her pick. Oh, my poor Lydia."

"I shouldn't have dazzled Mr. Darcy," Lydia said. She turned to Elizabeth. "What did you do, Lizzy?"

"Absolutely nothing," Elizabeth repeated, trying to be as firm in this statement as her previous one, since she wasn't being entirely honest.

Sadly, her relations would not be content with that answer. Elizabeth spent the majority of the next two hours fending off their persistent questions and ridiculous speculations. Her sole accomplishment was to see Jane escorted, by Mary, to the room Elizabeth and her older sister shared, where Mary remained to read to

61

her.

Elizabeth regretted ever begrudging Jane even a moment of Wordsworth. How she would prefer to read poetry to her sister, rather than remain in the parlor. Instead, her torment continued, the hypotheses spouted by her mother, Kitty and Lydia growing more outlandish every minute, until the knocker interrupted them.

Elizabeth craned her neck to look out the front window. Mr. Darcy's elegant carriage stood without. Her mother and youngest two sisters fell silent, snatching up embroidery and books. These, they contemplated with the utmost intensity as Mr. Darcy could be heard striding down the hall. He did not enter the parlor, however, or even glance inside, but went straight to Mr. Bennet's library.

Lydia sniffed. "He didn't even say hello."

Mrs. Bennet twisted in her chair, attention so entirely directed toward the library, she didn't appear to hear. "I should go ask the kitchen staff to put the kettle on, in case Mr. Darcy wants tea."

"I'll go, Mother." Elizabeth sprang from her seat. She darted out of the room to the sound of her mother's protests.

She did not go to the kitchen, doubtful that Mr. Darcy would require tea and positive the staff would have put the kettle on the moment a visitor arrived, as always. Instead, Elizabeth took up a position down the hall from her father's library. Not near enough to hear, for she didn't wish to commit the transgression she knew her mother longed to. Simply near enough to ensure no one could put an ear to the door.

Not a quarter of an hour later, Mr. Darcy emerged. His expression showed some surprise to see her there. He dipped his head in acknowledgment.

"Ah, Lizzy, just who I wish to see," Mr. Bennet said, emerging in Mr. Darcy's wake. "Mr. Darcy, you will excuse me if I don't walk you out?"

"Certainly." Mr. Darcy looked back to nod to Elizabeth's father. "Mr. Bennet. Miss Elizabeth."

"Mr. Darcy," Elizabeth replied, dipping her head in turn.

She remained where she stood until he passed by her in the narrow hall, scents of fresh coffee and shaving soap lingering in his wake, then turned to her father. Mr. Bennet held out an arm to gesture her into the library.

"I only hope Mr. Darcy's presence keeps your mother occupied long enough for us to speak," Mr. Bennet murmured as they entered. "It was smart of you to guard the hall against her eavesdropping." He ushered Elizabeth to the chair opposite his, then went around his desk to sit. "I take it from your diligence that you do not wish to wed him."

"No, I do not," Elizabeth agreed.

"He's very wealthy and seems honorable."

"I don't like him," Elizabeth countered.

Her father regarded her for a long moment. Finally, he nodded. "I would like to hear your description of what happened."

As briefly and quietly as she could, although her mother would have no reason to suspect Elizabeth spoke to her father, she recounted the library incident and breakfast the following morning.

Mr. Bennet nodded along, as if agreeing with already known facts. When she finished speaking, he rose, tiptoed to the door, and cracked it open. He turned back with a relieved expression and crossed to retake his chair. "And did Miss Bingley make a second attempt? Mr. Darcy didn't mention your warning in his recounting."

Elizabeth shrugged. "I don't know. I gave the warning mostly in jest. I didn't think to ask at breakfast." She frowned slightly. "It could be construed as odd that only Mr. Darcy occupied the breakfast parlor, but Miss Bingley and the Hursts sleep quite late. I should think, though, that if Mr. Bingley got word Jane was up, he would have come, had something not occupied him."

Mr. Bennet nodded. "Well, I suppose that isn't really any of our concern."

"No, I suppose not. I daresay, sadly for Jane, we shan't see any of them again." After the words left her mouth, Elizabeth's thoughts went to Mr. Bingley's letter, hidden somewhere about Jane. She'd pushed the page from her mind so thoroughly, she'd all but forgotten. Maybe, then, they would see Mr. Bingley again, depending on what the letter said.

"As you don't wish for the union, I can agree with that hope," Mr. Bennet said. "However, you should know that Mr. Darcy is concerned that what happened may get out. If it does, or if you simply change your mind about marrying him, he's given me several ways of getting in touch with him."

"For how long?" Elizabeth said, surprised at Mr. Darcy's continued and exceedingly honorable care for her reputation, especially in view of their mutual dislike and his lack of culpability.

"He didn't stipulate a time limit," Mr. Bennet said, a layer of amusement in his tone.

"But, what if I change my mind in a year, or two? What if he's about to wed and I hear of it, and write him?" Not that she would.

Her father shrugged. "He either did not think of or is not concerned about those eventualities. As he seems an intelligent man, I'd guess the latter."

Elizabeth sat back in her chair, thoughtful. Barring his general highhandedness, Mr. Darcy's behavior throughout their shared incident did not match with the proud, entitled image of him she'd built up in her mind. She began to wonder, despite spending several days much in his company, if she really knew Mr. Darcy at all.

Chapter Nine

With a frown, Miss Anne de Bourgh folded the letter from her young cousin, Georgiana Darcy. She stood from her armchair and crossed her room to a large desk. With a quick glance about, though she stood alone in her own chamber, Anne pulled a key from her bodice. Before applying it to the raised front of her desk, she checked the lock for signs of tampering, as always. Aware how her locked away correspondences galled her mother, Lady Catherine de Bourgh, Anne remained ever vigilant.

Finding the lock undisturbed, this time, Anne applied the key and lowered the lacquered panel of wood that, when closed, secured the many rows of drawers and, when open, became her writing surface. Her gaze scanned over labels for friends and relations, lingering on her cousin Fitzwilliam Darcy's drawer for a moment. She needn't page through his letters, all kept since they were old enough to write, to know he'd never, not once in all those years, mentioned a young lady.

Likewise, as she placed his sister Georgiana's letter in her drawer, Anne knew she didn't need to reread any of those. Her gaze flicked to their other cousins' drawers. Of them, Colonel Richard Fitzwilliam knew Darcy well enough that he might have heard mention of a young lady, but Richard wouldn't have written Anne about that. No, only Georgiana would, or possibly Darcy, but that was less likely. Regardless of who might, Anne was quite certain neither ever had written about an eligible lady catching Darcy's attention.

Instead of making notes on Georgiana's letter and composing a draft in reply, as she normally would, Anne tapped the folded page against the desktop. Georgiana hadn't meant to gossip, and certainly not to alarm Anne. Miss Georgiana Darcy did little outside of attend her lessons, especially of late. Her inclusion of her brother's mention of a young woman certainly stemmed from a void of anything other than her brother's correspondence about which to write.

Georgiana couldn't know the significance the information held for

Anne. In his twenty-seven years, Darcy had never noticed any particular woman well enough to write about her, especially not her beauty and wit. And he'd definitely never been inspired to speak well of a young woman to his treasured, coddled little sister. That he recommended this Miss Elizabeth Bennet to Georgiana and said he hoped they should meet one day was the doom knell of Anne's happiness.

Anne slapped the letter down on the desktop, thin lips pursed. This was going to cause her trouble. She'd known her present, precarious truce with her mother couldn't last. She'd hoped for a few more years, though. A few more years of Darcy single, her mother's hope alive that he would marry Anne, before Lady Catherine turned her sights on someone else. Someone who might be amiable to wedding Anne and who, when combined with her mother, might attempt to force the union into existence.

The sound of a knock had Anne closing the desk front, letter inside. She turned the key in the lock. She would reply to Georgiana later, including no indication of the consternation her cousin's letter caused, of course. Anne was not vindictive. She'd give her young cousin no reason to dislike this woman of whom Darcy was enamored.

The knock sounded again. "Miss de Bourgh," Mrs. Jenkinson, Anne's so-called companion and one of her mother's spies, called. "Mr. Collins has arrived. Your mother sent me to ask you to join us for tea."

"I'll be along in a moment," Anne called back. Just like her mother to send a gentlewoman, even if under her employ, on a maid's task. Lady Catherine had almost certainly issued the order in the presence of Mr. Collins, a local clergyman and Lady Catherine's toady, in some sort of devious, subtle show of authority. One likely lost on the sycophant Collins, but not on Mrs. Jenkinson.

Anne tucked the key to her desk away, then went to the mirror to adopt a lack of expression. She slumped her shoulders slightly and dulled her gaze. Then, steps slow, she headed from the room.

Anne had to work to keep her footfalls a light, unassuming patter, so as not to hint to Lady Catherine that anything had changed. She supposed her upcoming confrontation with her mother was inevitable. Lady Catherine wished her to wed. Anne preferred not to do so. At least, not in the way her mother wished.

Marriage led to marital relations, and those to childbirth. As she passed a tall, gilt-framed mirror, Anne glanced askance at her diminutive, too-thin form. She feared childbirth. Feared it more than she wanted love, and far more than she feared her mother's wrath.

Her father had two sisters, both lovely, ethereal women built similarly to Anne. Both had died trying to bring children into the world. One, least remembered, died during her first attempt, though the child lived. Everyone said that was a blessing. Anne supposed it was, but not for her aunt.

The other, better recalled and sorely missed, died during the birth of her fifth child. Anne's new little cousin died, too. No one called that a blessing. Anne still recalled standing with her four cousins, tears streaming down her cheeks, the littlest clinging to her, for they'd been visiting, Lady Catherine insisting she could help with the difficult pregnancy.

Three of Anne's cousins on the de Bourgh side had been female. They'd all died in childbirth, two leaving behind living children, one not. All their husbands had remarried, as had one of Anne's uncles. Her relations were now relegated to mere footnotes on those men's family trees.

She knew not all women died in childbirth, but all slender, petite de Bourgh women seemed to. Perhaps someone as formidable as her mother, with hips that had hardly needed hoops during that ridiculous trend in fashion and shoulders to do any gentleman proud, could bear up under the strain. Anne, however, doubted she could. Further, she had no intention of wagering her life to find out.

She'd even made it clear to Darcy once, some time ago, that they could wed, as their mothers wished, yet not consummate the union. They got on well enough, after all, and, unlike her other cousins, he'd shown no inclination toward a wife and children. His reply had been an oblique mention, the next time they spoke, of his hope to someday have a family and pass down the Darcy name. Despite that polite refusal to her nearly-asked question, he'd very kindly, on her behalf, refrained from refuting her mother's wish for them to wed. Once Darcy took a wife, though, even Lady Catherine would be forced to give up on the idea of him and Anne.

Anne drew near the parlor, her mother's voice snaking outward. She stopped and availed herself of yet another mirror, Lady Catherine being fond of them, to regain an uninterested, unagitated expression. She must put thoughts of wedlock, children and Darcy from her mind. If Lady Catherine sniffed out the topic, she would latch onto it and shake it like a terrier with a rat. Shoulders drooped, Anne shuffled into the room.

"Anne, there you are," Lady Catherine boomed. "Where have you been? You have made us all wait. You are to serve the tea. You must keep in practice for when you are Darcy's wife."

Mr. Collins and Mrs. Jenkinson both stood as Anne entered. Her mother, as usual, did not. Anne moved to take her place, so everyone could sit.

"I, of course, have not minded," Mr. Collins said, addressing Anne's mother. "Waiting for tea gave me more time to avail myself of your wisdom, Lady Catherine."

"You should mind," Lady Catherine replied. "It is the height of poor manners to keep guests waiting. You will need to do better once you are Darcy's wife, Anne."

Anne reached for the teapot, expression bland. Apparently, she would be forced to endure talk of marriage even if she didn't give away her fears over Darcy's upcoming defection. Well, if that was the case, at least she could speak of someone else's nuptials. "Speaking of wives, Mother, weren't you telling Mrs. Jenkinson and me, only last night, that it's high time Mr. Collins secured one?"

Anne ignored the slightly panicked look Mr. Collins cast her and prepared her mother's tea. She handed the cup to Lady Catherine and secured another, all while Mr. Collins sputtered. Anne set to fixing his tea, which he preferred with a sickening amount of sweetener.

Lady Catherine sipped her tea. She always checked Anne's preparation immediately in order to know if she could carry on conversing or needed to complain. She turned more fully to Mr. Collins, apparently satisfied with her beverage. "That is so, Mr. Collins. You lack a wife. It is not proper. It is not correct for a man of your standing. I will not have it."

"Yes, why haven't you married yet, Mr. Collins?" Anne asked with feigned concern, passing him his tea.

"Yes, well, of course, I wish to. All men wish to," Mr. Collins stammered.

"Well, then, find a wife," Lady Catherine said. "I recommend the married state to any young man. It shall improve you and be only proper for a clergyman."

Anne poured a third cup, for Mrs. Jenkinson.

"My position, yes, that's exactly the thing," Mr. Collins said. "You see, that's the hold up. Normally, I should bow to your ladyship's wishes immediately, aware of your great wisdom, but in this case, I realize certain facts are missing."

Anne suppressed a smile. She noted a like glimmer of amusement in Mrs. Jenkinson's eyes as she passed her tea. Anne hadn't realized Mr. Collins would baulk at the topic. The exercise promised amusement, as he usually capitulated to Lady Catherine like a coward facing a loaded pistol. It seemed Anne had stumbled on an even greater diversion from talk of her and Darcy than she'd anticipated.

"Facts?" Lady Catherine repeated. "There are facts of which I am not aware? How is this?"

"Ah, that is, you are, of course, your ladyship." Mr. Collins, cup and saucer in one hand, tugged at his collar. "Prospective brides may not be, however."

"Remind me why this is," Lady Catherine ordered.

"I did mention to your ladyship that I have an estate coming to me at some time in the future, and you bid me write, which I did, and offer to go in person to visit, and tender my apologies."

Anne suppressed the desire to ask how else one might visit but in person.

"Yes." Lady Catherine tapped a nail on the side of her teacup. "What was it I disapproved of, regarding the estate? I recall disapproving, and recommending you make some amends."

Finally, Anne poured a cup of tea for herself.

"Ah, the entail, your ladyship," Mr. Collins said, then took a quick gulp of tea. "The estate is entailed away from my five cousins, all being female."

"Ah yes, that was the trouble." Lady Catherine nodded. She leveled a hard look on Mr. Collins. "What does the estate have to do with your state of matrimony?"

"I, ah, feel I might secure a better quality of bride once I lay claim to it, my lady."

Anne sipped her tea, watching her mother digest that. She took in the tightening of Lady Catherine's lips, the way the lines at the corners of her eyes deepened. Anne considered serving the cakes that accompanied the tea to break the tension, but she didn't want her mother's attention turned back on her.

"Your difficulty is easily solved," Lady Catherine declared. "As is the immorality of the entail."

"Immorality, my lady?" Mr. Collins ventured.

"Yes. Entailing property away from female relations is immoral."

Anne dabbed at her lips with her napkin to hide a smile. Trust her mother to inform a clergyman of what was and was not moral.

"It is?" Mr. Collins asked, sounding a bit weak.

"Certainly," Lady Catherine declared. "But you have in your power the very means to alleviate your condition and set that matter right. Where is this estate again?"

"It is Longbourn, in Hertfordshire," Mr. Collins offered. "My visit draws near. Your ladyship kindly gave me permission to make the journey, as you'll recall."

"And of your cousins? I seem to recollect none of the five are wed. What are their ages?"

"I believe between fifteen and twenty-two."

"That is ideal, then, giving you all five from which to choose the most suitable."

"M—most suitable?" Mr. Collins stammered.

Anne fancied he could see his fate before him, but no way to avoid it. He always conceded to her mother and must know that her continued patronage, which he seemed to very much enjoy on most occasions, if not that day, depended on his capitulation. He might be destined to inherit an estate someday, but he didn't have it yet and thus depended somewhat on Anne's mother's continued generosity to make his life bearable while he waited for his relation to pass away.

"Wedding one of your cousins alleviates your unfortunate condition of being unmarried, removes your reason for waiting until you can attract a better sort of woman by ensuring your wife is worthy of your estate, and would go some way toward rectifying the wrong created by this entail." Lady Catherine's expression was insufferably smug.

"Ah—that is, um," Mr. Collins stammered. "Do you know, I'm not positive I agree with cousins wedding."

Anne hid a wince on Mr. Collins' behalf.

Lady Catherine's eyes narrowed dangerously. "Nonsense. Anne is to wed her cousin, Mr. Darcy. The nobility do so often. It is only proper, to keep wealth and property where they belong. Do you deny that wealth and property should be kept where they belong?"

"Ah—no. No, certainly not. Ah—"

"It is settled, then," Lady Catherine said, cutting him off. "While on your visit, you shall select the most suitable of your cousins for your wife. In fact, I shall loan you one of my smaller carriages to make the journey, so pleased am I with this plan." She narrowed her gaze. "Only remember, I do not expect you to return unattached, Mr. Collins."

"No, of course not, my lady," Mr. Collins said, managing to allow very little resignation and misery into his tone.

A strained silence fell.

"You may thank me for my advice and the loan of a carriage," Lady Catherine finally said.

Mr. Collins blinked. He swallowed, Adam's apple bobbing. "Thank you, as always, for your treasured and valuable advice, my lady, and for the loan of your carriage, in which I am honored to be permitted to travel."

"As you should be," Lady Catherine replied, expression satisfied. She turned to Anne. "Anne, why are you not serving the cakes? With the way you daydream instead of performing your duties, it is fortunate you are promised to Darcy. I cannot imagine any other man would take you."

"Yes, Mother," Anne murmured. She reached for a plate and began assembling cakes, aware her respite from her mother's attention was over.

As Lady Catherine rattled on about Anne and Darcy, Anne served the cakes, then another round of tea. Her mother's voice an unintelligible buzz in her ears, Anne reflected that there must be someone out there for her. Someone who would wed her and then leave her alone. Perhaps a widower, who'd already had children, already learned the price childbirth could take. She didn't even care if he was wealthy. In fact, if he saved her life by keeping his hands off her, she didn't even care if he held the status of gentleman. Any kind, intelligent man, of any rank, would do.

The only trouble was, Anne never met anyone, entrenched at Rosings with her mother. Lady Catherine ensured that. It was a circular problem. She couldn't get away from her mother until she wed, and she couldn't find a man to wed while with her mother.

Anne popped cake into her mouth, narrowing her gaze. She wouldn't live like this always. She would have her own home. Stuck at Rosings or not, Anne would find someone to wed, somehow.

Chapter Ten

After several days of breakfasts punctuated by her mother's sniping, Elizabeth was dismayed to hear Mrs. Bennet once again trundle toward the parlor earlier than usual. Normally, her mother could be avoided by rising while the day was young, but Mrs. Bennet had achieved such a state of agitation over Elizabeth's imagined expulsion from Netherfield and Mr. Bingley's subsequent departure from Hertfordshire without proposing to Jane, as to render her unable to sleep.

In moments of hearing Mrs. Bennet's tread, she burst into the room in a flutter of agitation that caused Elizabeth to suppress a sigh. Kitty and Lydia trailed in behind her, looking sleepy. From Mr. Bennet's, Jane's and Mary's faces, Elizabeth guessed they felt similarly to her regarding Mrs. Bennet's new morning hours.

"How is this?" Mrs. Bennet cried. "Elizabeth, move to the end of the table. You are disgraced. All of your sisters shall sit above you, not only Jane. Mary, take her spot."

Mary glanced at Elizabeth, expression conflicted.

"Sit down, Mrs. Bennet," their father said. "Elizabeth is not a disgrace and the meal merely breakfast. No one is moving."

"Well, I shall not eat at the same table with her, no matter where she sits," Mrs. Bennet declared.

Kitty and Lydia stepped around their mother, moving toward the sideboard. Lydia rolled her eyes at Elizabeth. Even Elizabeth's silliest sister was tired of Mrs. Bennet's morning tirades.

"You will sit, Mrs. Bennet," Mr. Bennet ordered. "You will set aside your grievances, for I have a matter of some small importance to discuss with you."

"Matter? About Elizabeth?" Mrs. Bennet asked, taking her usual chair.

"Not about Elizabeth." Mr. Bennet took a sip of coffee, a glare leveled on his wife. "It is my hope, Mrs. Bennet, that you have ordered a good dinner today. I have reason to expect an addition to our family party."

"An addition?" Mrs. Bennet turned to look at Jane. "It is Mr. Bingley?"

"Mr. Bingley left Hertfordshire, Mama," Mary protested. "They all left. Miss Bingley, the Hursts, everyone."

"Even that terrible Mr. Darcy, so you must be happy, Lizzy," Lydia chimed in as she and Kitty reached the table, full plates in hand.

Elizabeth shrugged, perfectly indifferent to Mr. Darcy's whereabouts. She did note, though, a slight coloring in Jane's cheeks. Elizabeth still hadn't managed to tease the content of Mr. Bingley's note from her sister, but deemed his words encouraging, for Jane didn't seem sorrowful.

"That doesn't mean Mr. Bingley can't come back," Mrs. Bennet said. "And where should he come once he does, but right to Jane's side?"

"It is not Mr. Bingley," Mr. Bennet stated. "It's a gentleman I've never set eyes on in my life. My late brother's son, Mr. Collins."

"Mr. Collins?" Mrs. Bennet gasped. "Oh, do not speak that odious name in this house. The vile, horrible man. What can he mean by coming here?"

Mr. Bennet took another sip of coffee. "Vile and horrible he may be, but, as he wrote last month, he wishes to come view Longbourn and to offer some sort of apology for his eventual possession of the estate."

"Apology?" Mrs. Bennet's voice dripped vitriol. "He could well apologize by not tearing our home away from us."

"Last month?" Elizabeth cut in, before her mother's typical rant about the entail that awarded Mr. Collins their home upon Mr. Bennet's death enveloped them. "Papa, you've known he was coming for so long, yet didn't tell us?"

Mr. Bennet offered a slight smile, eyes gleaming. Elizabeth supposed she shouldn't begrudge him his delight in secrets. After all, he kept one for her which she certainly wouldn't wish passed along.

"You're a terrible creature as well, Mr. Bennet," Mrs. Bennet cried. "Imagine, not warning me until today. Oh, but there's so much to be done. You're no better than Mr. Collins."

"Not telling us about a letter isn't the same as casting us out," Mary said. She turned to their father. "What sort of man is Mr. Collins?"

"From his letter, I deem him a silly sort of man," Mr. Bennet said. "Pompous and servile all as one, and overly devoted to his patroness, Lady Catherine de Bourgh."

Elizabeth stifled a sigh. Another pompous gentleman. Apparently, the world was rife with them.

"Elizabeth, Jane, you shall have to ready the guest room," Mrs. Bennet said. "Go now. Air the sheets before he arrives. Air the room. Check under the bed and in the corners of the wardrobe." Mrs. Bennet's hands fluttered about in a shooing gesture. "I shall never live down Mrs. Gardiner finding a litter of mice in the desk. Oh heavens, check the desk."

Elizabeth looked at her mostly finished breakfast, then at Jane, who'd hardly eaten. "I'll go start," Elizabeth said.

"As well you should," Mrs. Bennet agreed. "Any extra chores should go to you, not Jane. Jane isn't a disappointment to me."

Elizabeth ignored her mother, nodded to her father, and stood from the table.

"I'll have to go over the menu. I'm sure what I have planned isn't enough," Mrs. Bennet continued as Elizabeth left the room. "Oh, if only I'd known. I would have sent for a goose. Two geese, and a pheasant. And trout. Oh, we shan't have any trout at such late notice. Mr. Bennet, do you see what you've done? You shall embarrass me in front of your…"

Much of the tension left Elizabeth's shoulders as her mother's voice fell far enough behind to become unintelligible. Elizabeth went first to the room she shared with Jane and retrieved the book of Greek myths she was reading, then to the guest room. Their housekeeper perfectly competent, the room seemed, as she'd expected, to be in good order.

Even so, Elizabeth threw curtains and window open wide. A chill wind swept through the room, made tolerable by a bright swath of sunlight. Elizabeth took up the coverlet and shook it out the window, scattering a thin layer of dust. The sheets, stored clean on the bed, she deemed perfectly acceptable. She returned the coverlet to its place and then dutifully inspected the room for vermin. Finding none, Elizabeth closed the window against the November chill and sat in the chair beside it, since the window allowed in good light by which to read. She propped her feet on a footstool.

After more time passed than Elizabeth expected, Jane entered, sewing in hand. "Mother is in a state over Mr. Collins' impending arrival." Jane gestured to Elizabeth's feet. "May I have the footstool? I should like to keep out of her way as well."

"Yes, but you may also have the chair," Elizabeth said. "I'll read on the bed. I'm sure our cousin won't mind."

Jane smiled. "Our cousin won't know," she said as she took the chair Elizabeth vacated.

"That is why he's sure not to mind." Elizabeth settled wrong way round on the bed, the light better that way, her feet irreverently beside Mr. Collins' pillow. She pretended to read while Jane got settled into her sewing. After a time, Elizabeth ventured, "You're being terribly vexing about this note you received."

Jane didn't look at Elizabeth or slow her stiches. A fresh smile turned up Jane's lips. "The content is between me and Mr. Bingley."

"It's highly improper of him to give you a note," Elizabeth said, not for the first time.

"Hmm," Jane agreed.

"And to think I endured Miss Bingley and Mr. Darcy to tend you while you were ill," Elizabeth prodded.

Jane finally looked up, smile beatific. "His note specifically asks that I keep his confidence."

Elizabeth let out a lugubrious sigh.

"I can, perhaps, tell you how he signed it," Jane offered.

"Yes, do." Elizabeth didn't hide her excitement. "I shall content myself with that, on my honor."

Jane's expression took on a slightly foolish cast. "Forever yours, B."

Elizabeth gasped, jumping from the bed. She hurried to embrace her sister. "Oh, but Jane, that's wonderful."

"But nothing is settled, you understand," Jane cautioned as Elizabeth released her. "Nothing can be until he returns."

"Did he say why he went? Where to? For how long?"

Jane shook her head, tight lipped. "You gave your word to be content, Lizzy."

Elizabeth couldn't tell if that meant Mr. Bingley hadn't said or meant Jane wouldn't divulge more, but she had given her word, so she returned to the bed and took back up her book. Still, she couldn't help the occasional glance at Jane, who appeared as serene and untroubled as a woman possibly could. Cheerful and well occupied, Elizabeth and Jane passed a very pleasant hour before their consciences got the better of them and they returned downstairs to further assist their mother.

Later, when the hour of Mr. Collins' arrival approached, Mrs. Bennet shooed Elizabeth and Jane upstairs, saying, "If Mr. Collins sees Jane, he might become enamored with her, which simply wouldn't do."

Frowning, she added, "Elizabeth, you are not allowed to meet guests first, considering how you behaved. You'll give a bad impression."

They retreated to the room they shared and ignored the sounds of Mr. Collins arriving. Before too long, though, their three younger sisters bustled into their room.

"He's wretched. Not nearly as handsome as an officer." Lydia plunked down on the edge of the bed. "You will never guess why that Mr. Collins is here."

"Why is he here?" Elizabeth asked as Kitty and Mary found places to sit.

"I thought he came to apologize for the entail," Jane said.

Lydia nodded. "We were barely introduced to him, and he closeted himself in the library with Mama and Papa, and he did apologize, which Mama didn't take well."

Elizabeth grimaced. That was to be expected. The true surprise was that she and Jane hadn't been able to hear their mother yelling all the way from the library.

"You could hear her from the parlor," Mary said with a grimace of her own, thoughts paralleling Elizabeth's.

"But that's not the good part," Lydia continued, voice low. She looked about to make sure she had all their attention "Mr. Collins told Mama and Papa that he's going to make things right by wedding one of us."

Jane gasped, expression horrified.

"Don't worry," Lydia said. "Not you, Jane. Mama told him you're about to become engaged."

Jane colored but nodded, her smile returning.

"She also told him he can't marry Lizzy because you," Lydia said, turning to Elizabeth, "behaved so badly at Netherfield Park that Mr. Darcy had you escorted home and then came to speak with Papa about how you acted."

Four sets of eyes turned toward Elizabeth, Jane's sympathetic and the other three curious. Elizabeth maintained a placid expression. Knowing how well her youngest two sisters kept secrets, she had no intention of ever telling them the truth. Mary would keep a secret, but subject Elizabeth to some sort of boring, only tenuously related sermon, as payment.

After a short silence, Lydia shrugged. "And Mr. Collins said he should never wed someone who has offended Mr. Darcy, because Mr.

Darcy is the nephew of his patroness, Lady Catherine de Bourgh." Lydia scrunched up her nose. "He sure does talk about her a lot."

"And Papa didn't defend Elizabeth?" Jane asked, surprise in her voice.

Lydia tipped her head to the side. "No, which is odd, isn't it? Papa never lets anyone criticize Lizzy, because she's his favorite, but he didn't correct Mr. Collins." She turned to Elizabeth again. "You must have done something truly awful. I hope it was fun, at least."

Elizabeth fought against a smile but didn't open the conversation to questions by offering a defense. She also forwent pointing out that their father criticized her the most of all his daughters. Of course, that was because Jane never did anything wrong and Mr. Bennet had given up on his youngest three children.

"I'm sure if Elizabeth would show she's properly repentant, both Mama and Papa will forgive her," Mary said.

Elizabeth knew her mother would never forgive her for not marrying a rich man and her father did not feel there was anything to forgive.

Lydia eyed Mary. "Do you suppose he'll start with the oldest, then, of us three, and see who he prefers?"

"He won't prefer me," Mary said with a glum certainty that tugged at Elizabeth's heart.

"Well, if he doesn't want to marry Mary, I won't take him," Kitty said. "I'm not desperate."

"Mama is," Elizabeth said. "Especially since Mr. Bingley left." It took all Elizabeth's will not to exchange a quick smile with Jane, who smiled enough on her own to arouse suspicion. Not that any of their younger sisters were in the habit of noting other peoples' feelings.

Lydia flounced, setting the bed bouncing. "Mama may be desperate, but I plan to have lots of fun before I get married." Her expression grew thoughtful. "Although, I would love to get married first."

A sudden thought occurred to Elizabeth. She turned a suspicious look on her tall little sister. "It's not like Mama to tell you all of this, Lydia. How do you know it?"

"I eavesdropped," Lydia said with a complete lack of contrition.

Jane gasped.

Mary made a tsking sound.

Elizabeth shook her head. "Lydia, really."

Lydia shrugged. "The servants do it all the time."

"It is not proper for us to model our behavior on the servants," Mary said. "We should be models of good behavior for them."

"If we were to behave like the servants, we would work hard and not need so many servants," Elizabeth said, amused by Mary's typically sanctimonious reprimand. "If they were to behave like we do, nothing would be done."

"That is true," Mary said thoughtfully. Her expression firmed. "We should all try to do our best behavior in our own sphere."

The rapid beat of their mother's slippers in the hall alerted them all in time to turn toward the open door.

"There you all are," Mrs. Bennet said, bursting into the room. "I've wonderful news. Simply marvelous. Mr. Collins wants to marry one of you." She preened, looking about, only to become crestfallen at their lack of reaction. "Yes, well, I persuaded him that Jane is likely to be engaged soon, she being, of course, his first choice." Mrs. Bennet swiveled to face Elizabeth. "He then asked about you, Elizabeth, but I informed him you've behaved badly. Do you know, his patroness is Mr. Darcy's aunt? So, you would never do. I'm sure of that, even if Mr. Bennet won't tell me what happened and said I should not ask you about it, or even bring it up with you." Mrs. Bennet's eyes narrowed into a glare. "It's unfair and improper for a mother not to know how her child has behaved. Mr. Bennet won't even let me punish you for what you've done."

"I believe Papa knows best," Elizabeth said, relieved to have confirmation of Lydia's report that she would not be the subject of Mr. Collins courtship. Though Elizabeth hadn't met him yet, she trusted her father's assessment that he was a pompous, silly man.

"You always agree with your father," Mrs. Bennet groused, as if that agreement were a crime. She shook her head. "It doesn't matter," she declared, and turned from Elizabeth. "Mr. Collins is not happy with the idea of you, Mary, because he saw that you aren't pretty."

Mary flushed.

Mrs. Bennet turned to her youngest two. "I persuaded him that you would be unsuitable because of your ill health, Kitty. A clergyman requires a strong wife."

Kitty frowned but didn't speak.

Mrs. Bennet turned a happy expression on Lydia. "So, you see, my pet, I've secured Longbourn for you. You shall be mistress here when I'm gone. Lydia, you are the lucky one who will get to marry Mr. Collins."

Lydia gaped at their mother. "No," she wailed, her shriek surely audible to the far corners of the house.

Chapter Eleven

Elizabeth went down to dinner with a feeling of dread hanging over her. Her mother's and Lydia's battle of wills, following Mrs. Bennet's pronouncement of Lydia's fate, had lasted nearly an hour... with Elizabeth, Jane, Mary and Kitty trapped in the room, their mother's broad frame barring the doorway.

Lydia had argued. She'd begged, pleaded and cried. Finally, Mrs. Bennet got tired of standing and left.

Lydia appeared just in time for dinner. Mary and Elizabeth followed Mrs. Bennet with Mr. Collins, then Mr. Bennet escorting Jane, into the dining room. Mary whispered she'd heard Mrs. Bennet tell Lydia that if she wasn't on time for dinner, she would not eat again until breakfast. Inside the dining room, they found place cards, written out in their mother's hand. Mr. Collins was visibly nervous, his florid countenance evidencing great eagerness and hope. So much so, as to evoke a pang of pity in Elizabeth.

Elizabeth tried to see what he must, uncolored by association with her sister. Lydia had stalked into the room tall and well proportioned. Her curls gleamed. She possessed creamy white skin, smooth and glowing by candlelight. Certainly, a catch for the stoop-shouldered, weak-jawed, puffy-cheeked Mr. Collins. Yes, in appearance, Lydia was everything amiable and desirable.

But Elizabeth knew better. If Lydia's mulish expression and deliberate near tardiness were any indication, soon Mr. Collins would as well.

The unusual presence of place cards put Lydia next to Mr. Collins, who moved to pull out her chair, but Lydia grabbed the back before he could and yanked. The heavy piece skidded backward. Mr. Collins jumped out of the way. Lydia plunked down in the chair and scooted it forward, legs squealing on the floorboards. Elizabeth winced at the sound. Her sister certainly was starting with strong defiance.

Nor did Lydia's behavior improve as the evening commenced. She blatantly ignored Mr. Collins. She reached across the table to take up dishes, and continuously conversed with Kitty, who was across from her.

Elizabeth didn't know if she was more appalled or amused, but Mr. Collins' feelings were clear. By the time dinner ended, he could hardly look at Lydia. Instead, he dedicated his conversation, what little was possible over the din, to Mary, who sat opposite him. For Elizabeth, the only good thing about their evening was the early end to it.

The following morning, they received an invitation to join their Aunt and Uncle Phillips for cards that evening. Mr. Phillips, an attorney, kept their household in the nearby town of Meryton. Mrs. Phillips, their mother's sister and a competent hostess, enjoyed the buzz of a room full of young people. For her part, Elizabeth looked forward to a reason not to speak overmuch with Mr. Collins or her youngest sister.

Lydia was silently sullen all day but showed high spirits as they departed Longbourn. Elizabeth knew this stemmed from Mrs. Phillips promise to invite officers from the militia stationed in Meryton. For Lydia, the prospect of a room full of red coats overshadowed any dismay at Mr. Collins being invited to accompany them.

Not that Mr. Collins showed any interest in Lydia as the six of them set out, on foot, toward Meryton. Instead, he chose to walk with Mary, the two discussing scripture. That suited Elizabeth, who preferred to strike out ahead with Jane, who was fully recovered from her fever. Elizabeth knew the arrangement pleased Kitty and Lydia as well, as they liked to walk together behind, lingering and giggling.

When they reached the Phillips', Elizabeth and Jane entered a room already full of young ladies and officers, finding the atmosphere quite stuffy after their invigorating walk. Smile wide, Aunt Phillips hurried across the room in their direction. Conversation and laughter rang through the oversized parlor, the room perfect for Mrs. Phillips' soirees.

"Jane, Elizabeth, lovely as ever," Mrs. Phillips cried as she neared.

"Aunt Phillips," Jane said, voice warm. "Thank you for inviting us."

"And who is this with Mary?" Mrs. Phillips asked, seeing Mary and their cousin coming down the hall. "Rumor is you have a guest at Longbourn."

Elizabeth smiled. "For once, rumor does not lie." She turned and gestured to Mr. Collins, who even then reached them. "This is our cousin, Mr. Collins. We hope he is a happy addition to your gathering this evening. Mr. Collins, our aunt and your hostess, Mrs. Phillips."

"Mr. Collins, how delightful to have you with us," Mrs. Phillips greeted.

Mr. Collins bowed. "Mrs. Phillips, I am honored to make your acquaintance and to be invited into your home." He glanced about as he straightened. "And a lovely home it is. Why, I was just saying to Cousin Mary, Lady Catherine would approve of so fine a—"

"La, Colonel Forster," Lydia called loudly, brushing past Mr. Collins, deliberately knocking her shoulder into him. "I'd so hoped to find you here tonight, sir."

She strode through the room toward the commander of the local regiment, waving and calling to various acquaintances, Kitty in her wake. Mr. Collins stared after, jaw left hinged open. Mrs. Phillips watched with raised eyebrows, Mary with a scowl.

Mrs. Phillips turned to Elizabeth, expression questioning.

Elizabeth chuckled. "Come, Aunt, greet Mary and direct her and our cousin to a table for cards, and I shall tell you about the day we've been having, and yesterday as well."

Mrs. Phillips, expression bemused, complied. Soon, Mary and Mr. Collins were seated at a table with two people and a freshly shuffled deck. Elizabeth steered their aunt away and, Jane beside her, began the tale of Lydia's even-less-decorous-than-usual behavior. As they spoke, Mr. Collins could be heard droning on behind them, expounding upon Lady Catherine de Bourgh's opinion of whist.

On the other side of the room, Lydia's laughter rang out where she all but clung to Colonel Forster. Elizabeth resolved to ignore Lydia's behavior, which was never decorous, but now bordered on crude. Hopefully, her sister would soon realize that Mr. Collins no longer had any intentions toward her and return to her usual, somewhat more acceptable, antics.

"Lydia and your mother at odds?" Mrs. Phillips said once Elizabeth finished her tale. "I never thought I'd see the day."

"We can only hope it won't last long," Jane said with all evidence of sincerity.

Mrs. Phillips turned to Jane. Her eyes brightened as if her mind was struck with an idea. "Jane, dear, have you any notion why your Mr. Bingley departed so precipitously? We're all dying to know."

"I, ah…" Jane cast Elizabeth a pleading look.

"No one told us why they had to go, but Mr. Darcy did, kindly, loan us his lovely carriage in which to ride home," Elizabeth replied.

"Pardon me," a voice said to Elizabeth's right. "I do not mean to intrude, Mrs. Phillips, but did I hear mention of a Mr. Darcy? A Mr. Fitzwilliam Darcy of Pemberley, in Derbyshire?"

"Why, Mr. Wickham," Mrs. Phillips said with warmth.

Elizabeth turned to find a singularly handsome young man in an officer's coat. Light of hair and eye and possessed of an easy affability, he offered a bow to each of them. When he straightened, it was to Elizabeth he turned. She flattered herself to think him attracted, an unusual happenstance when she stood beside Jane.

"I do not believe I'm acquainted with these lovely guests of yours, Mrs. Phillips," Mr. Wickham said.

"Only because you are new to town, sir," Mrs. Phillips replied. "Mr. Wickham, may I present my nieces, the prettiest young women in all of Hertfordshire, the Miss Bennets. Jane, Elizabeth, this is Mr. Wickham, lately arrived from London."

"Mr. Wickham," Elizabeth murmured and dipped a curtsy, mimicked by Jane. "You overheard rightly. We spoke of the same Mr. Darcy with whom you seem acquainted."

An almost imperceptible tension tightened the skin about Mr. Wickham's eyes and shifted the set of his shoulders. "And is Mr. Darcy about this evening?"

"I'm afraid not," Mrs. Phillips replied. "He was staying with Mr. Bingley over at Netherfield Park, but the whole lot of them, Bingleys, Hursts and Mr. Darcy, up and left all of a sudden."

Mr. Wickham's tension fled. "Do you know if he means to return soon?"

"I doubt it," Elizabeth replied. Return? After all the humiliation he'd received there? It wasn't likely.

"Do you know Mr. Darcy?" Jane asked.

"Very well. I knew the whole family."

"We've only met Mr. Darcy," Jane said, "but I understand he has a sister."

"He does," Mr. Wickham said, smirking.

"What can you tell us about Miss Darcy?" Mrs. Phillips asked, obviously encouraged by Mr. Wickham's demeanor.

"She thinks very highly of herself and her select circle and barely tolerates others," he said. "Much like her brother."

No wonder Mr. Bingley's sisters thought so well of her, Elizabeth reflected. They shared values.

"Speaking of Mr. Darcy," Mrs. Phillips said. "I have some gossip."

Mr. Wickham's eyes lit from within, increasing his good looks. "Oh? Do tell, Mrs. Phillips."

"It isn't unhappy, is it?" Jane asked, looking worried. "Only, I don't like to give heed to unpleasant gossip."

"And wise you are, dear," Mrs. Phillips said. "However, this is of the happy sort. It seems that Mr. Darcy arranged for every servant at Netherfield Park to get a fine, heavy blanket. They even have their names embroidered on them."

"Why would he do that?" Mr. Wickham asked.

Mr. Wickham sounded as confused as Elizabeth felt and Jane looked. A kind gesture, but Elizabeth wondered about his motivation. She recalled her joking suggestion Mr. Darcy should be leery to sleep in his own bed. Had he, in fact, taken her words to heart? Would the proud Mr. Darcy truly have slept in the servants' quarters?

Mrs. Phillips leaned nearer, as if she didn't intend to share her news with every person in the room, which she surely would. Mrs. Phillips tended to enjoy telling a story repeatedly to a small group, as if imparting something precious, to telling it once to everyone. "They say he lost a bet with someone and had to spend a night in the servant quarters. He said the blankets were inadequate and decided to correct that. He said the new blankets are the servants' personal property, to take with them if they leave."

"What a charitable gesture," Jane said.

"An odd one, as well," Elizabeth murmured. Could her aunt's rumored explanation be true, or had a lie been planted to cover Mr. Darcy's true reason for sleeping somewhere other than in his own bed? From what little she knew of him, she didn't feel Mr. Darcy would be party to subterfuge.

Mr. Wickham frowned. "I didn't think Mr. Darcy was a betting man."

Elizabeth felt the same and added that to the oddity of Mrs. Phillips' gossip. "How well do you know him?" Elizabeth asked, wondering if Mr. Wickham had insight into a man who was honorable enough to offer to do right by her, good enough to buy blankets for servants, yet almost too condescending and officious to bear.

Mr. Wickham turned his charming smile on her once more. "We were boys together. I am the son of Mr. Darcy's father's steward. Old Mr. Darcy was very good to me and gave me a gentleman's education."

"That was kind of him," Jane said.

"Indeed." Mr. Wickham's smile grew. "Perhaps the blankets were Darcy's attempt to emulate his father, who was very generous." Mr. Wickham shook his head, affecting a sad look. "But since his father's death, Darcy and I have gone our separate ways. I am not a member of the landed gentry and Darcy is contemptuous of people not in his class. But, considering how well I was treated by old Mr. Darcy, I shouldn't speak ill of any Darcy."

Elizabeth agreed with Mr. Wickham's self-deprecating advice, even as she couldn't help also agreeing with his assessment of Mr. Darcy. "Then it is doubly odd that he gave blankets to servants." Even as the words left her mouth, she frowned. Mr. Bingley was leasing Netherfield Park and so, presumably, didn't own an estate. That meant he was not a member of the landed gentry. Yet, Mr. Darcy treated him with respect and affection. He'd even spoken believably to Miss Bingley of treating her with respect.

"Maybe that was part of the bet," Mr. Wickham said. "The blankets might have been his payment."

"That must be it," Mrs. Phillips said.

Elizabeth could all but see her aunt setting Mr. Wickham's postulation as fact, to be added to the tale for the next rendering. If Mr. Darcy had not behaved honorably with her, Elizabeth might have believed Mr. Wickham's guess as well. Besides which, although she knew little of men betting, it seemed odd to have two consequences of losing. The little she knew suggested that a bet either required a payment to the other party or having the loser perform some humiliating action, but not both. Not that she would unravel Mr. Darcy's actions now. She gave her head a small shake and returned her attention to the conversation, for Mr. Wickham chatted on.

If Mr. Darcy was an enigma to Elizabeth, so was Mr. Wickham. He was attractive and charming, yet willing to malign the man he claimed he owed an inherited loyalty toward. After enduring a few more almost random seeming complaints about Mr. Darcy, Elizabeth decided it was time to change the subject. "You must be a very brave man, to join the militia in these times," she ventured.

Mr. Wickham stood straighter, chest puffed out. "I'd like to believe so. What I do, I do for love of king and country."

"Very commendable of you," Mrs. Phillips said. "If you young people will excuse me?" Without awaiting an answer, she hurried to join another group of guests, probably to repeat the story of the blankets, with Mr. Wickham's words added.

"Yes, it's very honorable of you to join the militia, Mr. Wickham," Jane said, renewing Elizabeth's change in conversation, interrupted by Mrs. Phillip's departure.

"I should hope so." Mr. Wickham offered Jane a smile. "Half the reason I did so was to charm beautiful ladies into a dance with me."

Elizabeth laughed, surprised by his brashness. Perhaps this Mr. Wickham wasn't the most reasonable of men, but he was well-favored and amusing. Certainly, he would make a pleasant addition to their society and liven their evenings.

Chapter Twelve

Lydia arrived at dinner the following evening shortly before they entered the dining room, wearing her most subdued gown and a meek expression. Mrs. Bennet leveled a glare on her youngest, eyes hard as she took in Lydia's every move. From the way her little sister winced when she sat, Elizabeth guessed their mother had done more than simply speak to Lydia about her behavior toward Mr. Collins.

For his part, Mr. Collins didn't so much as look at Lydia. Instead, he offered Mary, seated across from him again, a smile. Elizabeth couldn't blame her cousin. Self-absorbed though he was, even he must have noticed Lydia's display with Colonel Forster the evening before. For all her outward beauty, Mr. Collins couldn't help but realize Lydia would make him a terrible wife.

"Lydia," Mrs. Bennet said into the awkward silence of the table. "Didn't you spend the afternoon reading Genesis? I specifically recall you saying you wished to discuss a verse with Mr. Collins."

Lydia cast their mother a panicked look. Elizabeth felt a bubble of amusement. If Mrs. Bennet wished Lydia to speak on the Bible, she ought to have coached her on a passage first.

"I've been led to believe Miss Mary is the expert on scripture among your daughters, Mrs. Bennet," Mr. Collins said. "Which is most laudable of her. My patroness, Lady Catherine de Bourgh, says all young women should spend at least an hour a day reading the Bible."

Elizabeth used her napkin to cover a smile. Once she had her facial expression under control, she observed, "This must be directly after she spends an hour on Italian, yet before her hour at the pianoforte, the one spent drawing, and those devoted to sewing and embroidery."

"Don't forget riding," Lydia added brightly.

"Or dancing," Kitty put in.

Mr. Bennet's lips twitched. He reached for a plate of potatoes. "Indeed."

Mr. Collins frowned. "I'm not certain of the order. To my shame, I thought not to ask. I'm sure Lady Catherine would be happy to advise you on the proper scheduling of your accomplishments, Cousin Elizabeth. I shall include the inquiry in my daily letter to her."

Elizabeth covered her mouth with her napkin again. Daily letter! Would even someone as wealthy as Lady Catherine want to pay to read Mr. Collins' daily letters?

"You speak very highly of Lady Catherine de Bourgh," Mary said to Mr. Collins. "Can you tell me more about her?"

Mr. Collins' entire demeanor livened. "She is the most magnificent lady. She is wise, condescending and helpful to all of those around her."

"Can she really be all those things?" Mary asked with what seemed like genuine interest.

Prompted by Mary's occasional questions, Mr. Collins eagerly went to considerable lengths to illuminate that yes, Lady Catherine de Bourgh was all he claimed and more. As dinner wore on, the Bennet family received a physical description of Lady Catherine, her clothing, her house, her furniture, her hats, her jewelry, what one might be served for dinner or tea, and a brief mention of her daughter. Mary looked rapt. Everyone else looked bored.

After dinner, Mary asked him about the Hunsford Parsonage, to general and poorly concealed dismay. With her encouragement, they heard about every room, most of the furniture, and what livestock Mr. Collins kept. They also received Lady Catherine's opinions and advice about every space, object or breed mentioned. Elizabeth's mind was stuffed with unwanted knowledge of distant Kent as she placed her head to her pillow later that evening.

The next morning, Mary returned to seeking Mr. Collins' opinion on various religious writings. Elizabeth cut her breakfast short, inviting Jane to walk with her. Kitty and Lydia set out for Meryton, their goal to urge their aunt into another gathering. Elizabeth hoped they succeeded. An evening bantering with the handsome, gregarious Mr. Wickham would be highly preferable to one captured at a dinner table with Mr. Collins answering Mary's questions.

Besides, Elizabeth should like to learn more about Mr. Darcy. It interested her to hear the thoughts of someone who'd known him for so long. The dichotomy of the man confused her. On one hand, he'd refused to dance at his first assembly in Hertfordshire and insulted her within her hearing. On the other, he'd slept in the servants' quarters and then bought them blankets. More than that, in suggesting they wed, he'd been willing to forgo happiness for the sake of honor and reputation.

Despite twisting and turning the enigma of Mr. Darcy in her mind the entire day, Elizabeth failed to unravel him. Kitty and Lydia, however, succeeded in their goal to persuade their aunt to host another gathering. Sadly, Mr. Wickham wasn't in attendance. Colonel Forster was, though, and once again received the bulk of Lydia's attention. Fortunately, that regard took a less manic form, which seemed to please him.

The following morning at breakfast, before Elizabeth could think of an excuse to leave, Mr. Collins stood from the table. "Mr. Bennet, I am sorry to interrupt your coffee, sir, but I can contain myself no longer. I must speak with you in private, regarding Miss Mary."

Lydia gasped. Mrs. Bennet clapped her hands together, face aglow. Mary turned pink.

"Well, if you must, I suppose you must," Mr. Bennet said. He set down his cup and paper and stood, then gestured for Mr. Collins to precede him to the library.

"How wonderful, Mary," Jane said in a soft voice as the two men disappeared down the hall.

"Oh, my sweet, beautiful girl," Mrs. Bennet gushed. She wiped an imagined tear from her eye. "I've always said you would do well."

Mary turned to their mother, surprise clear on her face.

"I wanted to be married first," Lydia groused. "Imagine, I should be above you all, then. Even you, Lizzy."

Elizabeth raised an eyebrow at that but turned to Mary. "I believe you shall be truly happy."

Mary smiled a shy, becoming smile that made her nearly pretty.

"Oh, but how will you stand this Lady Catherine?" Kitty asked.

Mary turned blinking eyes on Kitty. "Stand her? Lady Catherine sounds a paragon of advice."

Elizabeth cast Kitty a stifling look and said, "She does, at that." Then, acutely aware that Mary, as the middle child, was often shorted in so many things, Elizabeth jumped up and went around the table to hug her. "Best wishes, Mary," she said.

Jane hugged Mary next, followed by Kitty. Lydia's well-wishes lacked some of the sincerity of the others, but she managed the right words. Then Mrs. Bennet stood. Real tears made tracks down her face. Cheeks gleaming, she enveloped Mary in her arms.

"Oh, my baby," Mrs. Bennet wailed. "My sweet Mary. Leaving me. How shall I live? How shall I cope without you?"

The look Mary directed over their mother's shoulder held such a keen mixture of panic and confusion as to nearly pull a laugh from Elizabeth. She gestured to Jane. Together, they freed Mary from their mother and got Mrs. Bennet back in her breakfast chair so they could all continue eating. Talk turned to a lively discussion of Mary's upcoming nuptials, with only Lydia seeming to mind.

Lydia disappeared immediately following breakfast, presumably to her room to sulk. Mary, cheeks stained pink once more, headed out for a walk with Mr. Collins, who wore an insufferably pleased look. Smile benign, Mrs. Bennet insisted Kitty follow at a distance as chaperone, then held her back until Mary and Mr. Collins were mere specs down the lane.

Relieved of the duty to listen to their cousin, Elizabeth turned to Jane. "Shall we employ ourselves in mending, or did you wish an hour each of Italian and drawing first?"

Jane shook her head, smiling. "And who would instruct us?"

"Hm, there is that." Elizabeth shrugged. "Mending it is. Let's see if we can pry Lydia from her room to help. Somehow, she always gets out of chores."

They went to their room to fetch their work, then to Lydia's door. A knock received no reply. Elizabeth rolled her eyes at Jane.

"Lydia, do come out," Jane called.

Only the creak of the house, a reply more to the autumn wind than Jane, answered. Jane raised her hand to knock again.

"Oh, let her sulk," Elizabeth said. "She enjoys the activity too much to deny it to her."

"I suppose that's true," Jane said.

They joined their mother in the parlor and the morning progressed enjoyably and productively. Elizabeth was nearly finished with everything she'd brought down by the time Mary, Mr. Collins and Kitty returned. They settled into the parlor as well, with talk of the partridges they'd seen, and the deer, which soon reverted to a discussion of Mary's wedding day.

The front door opening met with general startlement, for no one had knocked. Steps sounded in the foyer. They all turned to the doorway as Lydia bustled in, hand clasped firmly about Colonel Forster's, whom she dragged along behind her.

"Where is Papa?" Lydia demanded, expression triumphant. "Colonel Forster would like to speak with him." She angled a smile over her shoulder at the tall gentleman. "Wouldn't you, Thomas?"

Colonel Forster came forward into the room, doffed his hat and bowed. Elizabeth set aside her mending to stand, everyone else scrambling to their feet. She dropped a curtsy.

"Mrs. Bennet, Miss Bennet, Miss Elizabeth, Miss Mary, Miss Kitty," Colonel Forster greeted. He nodded to their cousin. "Mr. Collins."

"Lydia, what is the meaning of this?" Mrs. Bennet cried.

"Thomas and I are to be married." Lydia tipped up her chin, smug. "As soon as possible."

"Oh, my sweet, beautiful girl," Mrs. Bennet cried and rushed across the room to fling her arms about Lydia.

They all moved to offer their best wishes. If Mary's well wishes were a bit subdued, Elizabeth couldn't blame her. As they all clustered about Lydia, except Mr. Collins who frowned to one side, Colonel Forster came to stand beside Elizabeth. He cleared his throat and she turned to regard him.

"Miss Elizabeth, could you direct me to your father?" he asked, grip on his hat brim tight enough to dimple the thick material.

"Certainly, sir." Elizabeth slipped past the gaggle in the doorway to lead the way.

"Lovely girl, your sister," Colonel Forster said as the hubbub behind them faded.

"I'm happy you think so," Elizabeth replied and quickened her pace. "Here we are," she said when they reached her father's library door. She knocked, then raised her voice slightly to call, "Papa, Colonel Forster is here to see you, about Lydia."

A moment later the door opened on Mr. Bennet, bushy eyebrows raised. He looked first to Elizabeth, who offered a smile and a shrug, then to the colonel, who bowed.

"To see me about Lydia, is it?" Mr. Bennet asked.

"Yes, sir," Colonel Forster said.

"So be it. Come in, sir."

Elizabeth waited until the door closed, then headed back to the parlor. She couldn't help the amused smile on her face. Hopefully, the expression would be taken as happiness for her sister, not mockery.

"...thought you said you wanted to have lots of fun before you married," Mary was saying as Elizabeth approached, tone a touch petulant.

Elizabeth entered to see Lydia shrug. "I wanted to, but Thomas

93

assures me that I will enjoy being a Colonel's wife." She turned to Kitty, expression bright. "And Kitty, he says you can come with us, when the militia leave for Brighton this summer. Isn't that fabulous? We'll find you a red coat, too."

Elizabeth's smile vanished at the thought of her two most silly sisters together in Brighton with a sea of red coats.

Kitty, however, clapped her hands in glee. "Oh, that will be wonderful, Lydia, thank you."

Mary frowned. "Yes, well, I shall invite people as well, shan't I, Mr. Collins?" she asked, turning to her intended for a moment before whirling back to face her sisters. "And I shall have a proper home, a parsonage, not barracks, and the benefit of Lady Catherine's excellent company to bestow."

"Yes, well," Mr. Collins said. "I cannot deny that anyone would benefit from Lady Catherine's excellent advice. Anyone, indeed."

"Thomas is a colonel," Lydia said with a disdainful sniff. "We won't live in the barracks. And he has nine hundred a year over his pay."

"Only nine hundred?" Mrs. Bennet cried. "Oh, but Lydia, you'll starve."

"She will not starve, Mama," Elizabeth said. "She will be very comfortable."

"I shall have as many gowns and ribbons as I like," Lydia declared. "And sweets and carriage rides."

Mary glared at Lydia for a long moment, then stepped back to stand beside Mr. Collins. "Well, we shall have plenty of room for guests, and tea and dinner at Rosings with Lady Catherine de Bourgh herself." She elbowed Mr. Collins. "Won't we, Mr. Collins? Have guests?"

"Yes, well, yes, certainly," Mr. Collins said. "Perhaps Cousin Jane might come."

"Absolutely not," Mrs. Bennet said. "Jane must remain here. Mr. Bingley is sure to return any day to ask for her hand. She can't be off in Kent. He might forget all about her."

Because Jane looked so relieved, Elizabeth forwent pointing out her mother's illogic, for how could not seeing Jane in Hertfordshire make him any less likely to forget her than not seeing Jane in Kent?

"Well, then, Elizabeth can come," Mary said.

"Cousin Elizabeth?" Mr. Collins frowned. "I won't bring scandal to Lady Catherine's doorstep."

Elizabeth imagined her relief to be at least as keen as Jane's. She could hardly think of a worse fate than enduring Mr. Collins for days on end with no respite.

Mary offered Mr. Collins an earnest look. "But don't you see, Elizabeth would benefit most from association with Lady Catherine. Who better to instruct her on how to mend and maintain her reputation?"

Elizabeth suppressed the urge to kick her sister in the shin.

"Elizabeth shouldn't be permitted any trips," Mrs. Bennet said. "Mr. Collins is wise. Elizabeth is to be punished for her shameful behavior at Netherfield Park."

Jane opened her mouth to protest, but Elizabeth silenced her with a glare. Mary appeared mulish, the expression adopted with the ease of use. Elizabeth could only hope her middle sister didn't have as much influence over her husband to be as her youngest obviously did. The last thing Elizabeth wished for was a trip to Kent.

Chapter Thirteen

After the newly united Mr. and Mrs. Collins left for Kent and Lydia, now Mrs. Forster, moved out of Longbourn, Elizabeth had the leisure to observe Jane more. Jane pined for Mr. Bingley, though she tried not to let her feelings show. Each night, just before bed, she would take Mr. Bingley's cherished note, which she still hadn't given Elizabeth permission to read, from their hiding place beneath one of the floorboards, where it rested beside Mr. Darcy's more mundane penning. Sometimes, Jane would read the note. Others, she would simply hold the page for a moment, smile, and put it back.

Finally, after over six weeks with no sign of Mr. Bingley, Elizabeth couldn't help but speak. "You're sure you understood his note aright?" she asked as they climbed into the bed they shared.

"It's very plain," Jane said, tugging the comforter up around her shoulders.

"He's been away some time," Elizabeth ventured. She leaned over and blew out the candle.

Jane's sigh filled the darkness. "Yes, he has. I would write to Miss Bingley to inquire, as she always treated me with kindness, but in view of how she treated you and Mr. Darcy, I can't bring myself to do that."

"No, don't write her," Elizabeth agreed. "I still worry she did worse than we know."

Jane shifted. "How do you mean?"

"Well, I suspect Mr. Darcy didn't sleep in the servants' quarters because of a bet. You heard Mr. Wickham, who knows him well. Mr. Darcy is not a betting man." Even without Mr. Wickham's words, Mr. Darcy didn't strike Elizabeth as a gambler... but not as one willing to be part of a lie, either. Would circumstances make anyone a liar? She did not consider herself to be a liar, yet she'd lied when she told her mother and sisters she'd done nothing at Netherfield Park. "I believe Mr. Darcy slept with the servants because of my warning, which I meant as a jest."

"Warning?"

Elizabeth nodded, though the room was dark, realizing she'd left out that unimportant seeming detail in her recounting to Jane. "Before I left him that night, I suggested he not sleep in his own bed, lest Miss Bingley try one final time to trap him."

Jane shifted again, and Elizabeth realized she shook her head. "Just because you warned Mr. Darcy of that, and even if that is why he slept with the staff, that doesn't mean she actually went to his room. Besides," Jane's tone brightened, "if he didn't sleep in his room, how would anyone know if she went there?"

"I suppose that's true," Elizabeth agreed, letting the matter drop more because she didn't wish to debase Jane of her illusions than because she felt her postulation lacked merit. "You could write Mrs. Hurst."

"No," Jane said the word slowly, as if testing her answer. "Her loyalty must be to her sister. Also, she never gave me her address. I always felt she didn't quite care for me, the way she looked at me."

"I think that's simply her normal expression," Elizabeth said. "Likely a reflection of her inner state."

"Elizabeth, that's not very kind to say."

"True, but to lie is never kind."

"Equally true, but the kindness could come in the form of not speaking at all," Jane countered.

Elizabeth smiled. "She isn't here to hear me."

"You're being contrary," Jane declared, her words trailing off into a yawn. "And keeping me awake. You'll make me regret not taking Mary's room."

"You'd never be happier in that closet-sized room than here with me, your favorite sister," Elizabeth countered, but said no more.

Soon, Jane's breathing relayed her state of sleep, but Elizabeth's mind kept working. She wished Jane would permit her to see the letter. Without reading Mr. Bingley's words, Elizabeth had no means to assess the validity of Jane's continued hope. With her tendency to see all in a golden light, Jane could easily have taken an overly cordial adieu as a promise.

Her mind working at the problem far into the night, Elizabeth slept late the following day. She woke to find Jane already gone from their room. Rubbing sand from her eyes, Elizabeth sat up, taking in the excess of light behind the curtains. She yawned. Her gaze fell on the floorboard under which they hid things from their mother, then drifted to the closed door.

Elizabeth slipped from beneath the covers. She tiptoed across the room to the loose board. It would be wrong to read Jane's correspondence, but Elizabeth was beginning to feel she must, for Jane's sake. If Mr. Bingley wasn't coming back, Jane must be prepared. Elizabeth knelt and reached for the loose board.

She stayed her hand, rocking back on her heels. She must keep her word. She might be a liar, but she was still honorable. She objected to her mother's and Lydia's eavesdropping but was considering doing something worse. Jane was not stupid. Reading the letter would not only violate Elizabeth's word but would insult Jane's intelligence and ability to manage her own life.

A shriek rent the quiet morning. Elizabeth sprang to her feet, heart pounding. Another shriek sounded, and she realized the screeches emanated from her mother. Elizabeth grabbed her robe and ran from the room, tugging the garment on over her nightclothes.

Elizabeth sprinted through the manor and careened into the front parlor, robe clutched closed, to find Mrs. Bennet sprawled on a sofa. Jane bent over her, expression solicitous, alongside the also bent form of— "Mr. Bingley," Elizabeth gasped.

"Miss Elizabeth," Mr. Bingley said, straightening with a smile. His eyes widened, and he quickly turned his back. "Uh, Miss Elizabeth, I beg your pardon but you're in a state of undress."

That brought both Jane's and Mrs. Bennet's heads up.

Elizabeth looked down at her nightdress and robe, both of which covered more than most of her gowns. She tied the belt on the robe. "I do apologize. I heard Mama scream and I ran to see whatever was the matter."

Jane's face split into a wide smile. "Nothing is the matter. Mr. Bingley asked me to marry him."

"My sweet Jane," Mrs. Bennet said. "Lydia's and Mary's husbands are nothing compared to Mr. Bingley. What jewels and carriages you will have. What a lovely home. Homes, even, for you must have more than one, and…"

Shaking her head, Elizabeth stop listening. She murmured, "If you'll excuse me," and retreated toward the staircase to go to her room to dress properly.

"Lizzy, I'll be right up," Jane's voice called above their mother's rambling. "I must show Mr. Bingley the way to the library. Papa's in there."

"Of course," Elizabeth called back. "Again, I apologize for my appearance."

Elizabeth hurried back to the room she and Jane shared… or at least would share for a short time more. A stab of sorrow cut through her happiness for Jane, but she shrugged it aside. They couldn't, after all, remain as they were forever. Jane, at least, was bound to wed. Elizabeth counted it a great fortune that happy state would be entered into with someone as kind as Mr. Bingley.

A short time later, but longer than it ought to take to walk Mr. Bingley to the library, Jane entered. She went immediately to the mirror to check her hair, cheeks flaming and smile wide.

Elizabeth, who'd been attempting to do up the buttons on the back of her gown, hid a grin. "I didn't realize Mr. Bingley had returned."

"Nor did I," Jane said, tucking up a curl. "No one did. That is, he hadn't. He arrived late last night but didn't want to wake us. He came here when he woke up. You and Kitty were still in bed. Mama claimed she had something to do in the kitchen." Jane's cheeks, which had begun to regain their normal creamy tone, reddened again. "Once we were alone, he told me what called him away and then he proposed." In a calmer tone she added, "Let me do up those buttons."

Elizabeth obediently turned, one arm holding up hair she hadn't yet pinned. "You never doubted him for a moment."

"No, though I was growing quite miserable over his absence."

"You're very steadfast, Jane. I'd begun to doubt," Elizabeth admitted.

"You wouldn't have if you'd read his letter," Jane said as she fastened.

"Which you would not allow." Elizabeth permitted a touch of annoyance. She should like to have been less worried for Jane, even if Jane hadn't worried for herself.

"It opened with, 'My dearest Jane,'" Jane said, tone filled with delight. "He then went on to apologize if he'd misconstrued and ought not address me as such. That was followed by his wish I not share the information in the letter with anyone. He said, 'I love you with all my being and wish for nothing more than to make you my wife, but you may not care for me when you find out why I've gone, so I shall not ask you to decide until I may return and explain. If you still care for me once you know my family's scandal, it will be my honor if you'll marry me.'" Jane let out a dreamy sigh. "And you know how he signed." She fastened the top button.

Elizabeth turned to face her sister, somewhat stunned. "Why, you spoke truly, then, didn't you? He could hardly be plainer than that, saying he loved you and wanted to marry you. No wonder you've been so sure, despite his absence."

"I told you that you needn't worry," Jane admonished.

"So, you did." Elizabeth smiled, happy to be proven wrong. "But what is this scandal? Is it truly awful? Weren't you worried?"

Jane took Elizabeth's hand and led her over to the bed to sit on the edge. "I wasn't worried one wit. Mr. Bingley could never be capable of doing anything that would alter my love for him."

Thinking of Mr. Bingley's nature, Elizabeth supposed that might well be true. "What then?"

"You already know half of it," Jane said. "It's Miss Bingley. Not only did she lock herself in the library with Mr. Darcy, and then you in with him, forcing you to climb out a window, but you guessed aright, Lizzy." Jane lowered her voice to a whisper, although surely, they were the only two people in that part of the house. "She did sneak into Mr. Darcy's room, and climbed right into his bed with him, only it wasn't him. He'd switched beds with his valet."

Elizabeth gasped. "I didn't think she would go so far." She blinked several times. "It seems Mr. Darcy hasn't changed much from his childhood. Mr. Wickham was correct in his suspicion that Mr. Darcy isn't one to gamble." In more ways than one.

"Mr. Bingley left to escort Miss Bingley to London," Jane continued. "She stayed there until Mr. Bingley could negotiate her living with their aunt. Then he had to bring her there, because he didn't trust her to go with only a maid." Jane shrugged. "All of that took time. He didn't want me to answer his proposal until he'd settled Miss Bingley and I knew the whole of her reprehensible behavior."

"That's understandable, though I'm sorry you had to wait so long."

Jane's smile returned tenfold. "Mr. Bingley was worth waiting for."

Elizabeth hugged her sister again, truly happy for Jane. It occurred to her, though, to wonder if she would ever wed. Somewhere out there, was there a man Elizabeth would find worth waiting for? Was he, even now, waiting for her?

Jane and Mr. Bingley were wed as soon as possible after the banns were read. The ceremony was attended by only a pinch-faced Mrs. Hurst and a bland Mr. Hurst on Mr. Bingley's side, and the Phillips, Forsters and Bennets, minus Mary, on Jane's side. Jane moved into Netherfield Park that very afternoon. Elizabeth, though overjoyed for her sister, couldn't help but be a bit sad that evening, as she readied for bed alone in her empty-seeming room.

With three daughters married, and all married well, Elizabeth thought her mother would be less worried about the remaining two, but there was no cessation of activities. Mrs. Bennet continued to entertain as fervently as ever. On top of that, she alternated visiting Lydia and Jane almost every day she could get the horses. Lydia was very welcoming, but Jane confessed to Elizabeth that she and Mr. Bingley found the visits somewhat overwhelming. For her part, Elizabeth had taken to walking to Netherfield, especially when their mother visited Lydia or the horses were needed for the farm, so she could have time with Jane without Mrs. Bennet's constant haranguing.

"It's not that I don't want to see Mama," Jane said to Elizabeth one afternoon as they made their way down elegantly appointed corridors from Netherfield's foyer to Jane's favorite parlor. "But she comes so often, Lizzy. Mr. Bingley and I dread what will happen when Lydia leaves. We're afraid that all the time she now spends with Lydia, she will then want to spend here."

"Should I drop a hint to Papa that the horses need to be unavailable more often?" Elizabeth asked as they entered the parlor, a splendid yellow and white affair with songbirds painted on the ceiling.

"I have a solution," said Mr. Bingley, looking up from a writing desk set between two windows along the far wall. Elizabeth had long since assured him he needn't stand for her when she entered a room, something Mrs. Bennet still insisted upon. Mr. Bingley tapped a script-covered page before him. "Darcy wrote. He's invited us to London. Maybe some time in town will help?"

Much of the anxiety fled from Jane's face.

Elizabeth shook her head. "But what about when the weather turns warm again? You'll want to return here. Lydia will be gone, and nothing will stop Mama from visiting."

"We will worry about that when the time comes," Mr. Bingley said, shrugging. "If nothing else, I'll give up my lease next autumn and find another country residence."

Elizabeth couldn't quite stifle a dismayed gasp.

Jane put a hand on her arm. "Yes, we've talked about it, and if we do go, you'll come stay, we hope, for so long as you like." She turned back to Mr. Bingley and smiled. "Some time in London sounds delightful."

"I'll write and let him know." Mr. Bingley pivoted in his chair and pulled free a fresh sheet.

Jane gestured to a pair of sofas in the center of the room. "Now," she said as she and Elizabeth sat, "How is Mary? I'm afraid I'm letting her down in my correspondence."

"That is to be expected," Elizabeth replied. "You're newly married and learning to run this household." She made a sweeping gesture. "And dealing with Mama."

"Still, I feel awful for her, there alone in Kent."

Elizabeth excused Jane again but, as she embarked on a description of Mary's doings, she realized she was their middle sister's most frequent correspondent. Jane truly was busy. Neither of her parents wrote letters often. Lydia and Kitty acted as if they'd forgotten they had another sister. Well, Elizabeth thought as she described the state of the Collins' chickens to Jane, at least Mary had her. Watching the way Jane's attention kept drifting away from their conversation, her dreamy eyes on her new husband, Elizabeth reflected that, in turn, she was fortunate that she, at least, had Mary.

Chapter Fourteen

Darcy sat in his office at Darcy House, his London residence, left index finger tapping a slow rhythm on his desktop. He'd a letter to reply to, but no desire to have the missive out when Georgiana answered his summons. Both the reason behind his request to speak with his sister and the letter vexed him. Darcy did not care for being vexed.

The letter, in a very neat hand, had arrived that day from a Mr. Phillips, or Hertfordshire. Darcy had met the man only briefly. An uncle to the Bennet sisters, Mr. Phillips was nothing more than a country attorney with a mildly silly wife and a small rural practice.

Initially, on noting the sender, Darcy had suspected the letter had to do with Elizabeth and his promise to wed her should the tale of their time in the library come out. Her delicate features and flashing eyes had come readily to mind, as they were rarely far from his thoughts, and the idea of returning to Hertfordshire to take her as his bride hadn't been as unpleasant as he would have guessed. He was still bemused, and mildly piqued, by this country miss who'd fled out of a window instead of becoming Mrs. Fitzwilliam Darcy. The incident had left him disgruntled, which undoubtedly explained why he found her so often on his mind. That and, of course, the fact that her sister, Jane Bingley, resided with him for the time being.

But the letter did not hold any reference to Miss Elizabeth Bennet and Darcy's promise to wed her should circumstances call for it. Nor did Mr. Phillips mention his niece, Mrs. Bingley, which would have been Darcy's second guess as to a reason the gentleman would write. No, much to his surprise, Mr. Phillips' letter was about George Wickham.

Darcy's mouth pulled down in a scowl. Wickham. Darcy's onetime friend who'd gone from playmate to lazy, avaricious backstabber. First, Wickham had asked Darcy to buy out the living Darcy's father had left him. They should have remained cordial after that, as Darcy didn't fancy Wickham would make a very good clergyman, anyhow. They were both pleased with the arrangement.

But Wickham had gambled away that money, so far as Darcy could tell. At the least, he hadn't used the funds to pay his debts to the merchants around their childhood home of Pemberley. No, Darcy had paid those, knowing the craftsmen and women of Derbyshire had only extended Wickham so much credit because they associated him with the Darcy name.

Even that, Darcy might have excused. His father had helped raise Wickham to be frivolous, after all. Darcy felt his family somewhat responsible.

Wickham's greatest crime, however, and the reason Darcy had Mr. Phillips' letter locked tight in a drawer as he awaited Georgiana, was the incident in Ramsgate. Darcy's eyes narrowed in anger at the recollection. In Ramsgate, Wickham had attempted to elope with Georgiana, a girl of fifteen, so that he could claim her dowry. That, Darcy would never, could never, forgive.

Nor could he ever exact retribution. To seek any would draw attention where Darcy did not wish attention turned. No one must ever learn that Georgiana had nearly eloped with Wickham. Her reputation would be ruined and her prospect of a good marriage along with it. Not to mention, Darcy's inadequacy as a guardian would be exposed.

His gaze flicked to the mantel clock. Where was his sister? He'd sent for her nearly a quarter of an hour ago. What was it that afternoon, drawing?

His fingers twitched with the desire to compose his reply to Mr. Phillips, who'd written of a new transgression on Wickham's part. It seemed, as Darcy wasn't in Hertfordshire to refute him, that Wickham had told every merchant that they were still as close as brothers and that Darcy regularly paid his debts. The merchants of Hertfordshire, having briefly dealt with Darcy that past autumn, knew him to be reliable. Most of the merchants were not fooled and only offered no more credit than to anyone in the militia, but a few believed him and let Wickham rack up large debts.

Somehow, with an astuteness that did him credit, Mr. Phillips gathered enough information to recognize that Wickham's total debts were substantial. He'd taken it upon himself to warn Darcy. Also, to Mr. Phillips' credit, he'd phrased his letter so adroitly as not to call Wickham out or imply Darcy owed the merchants of Hertfordshire a farthing, guarding against insult should Wickham be telling the truth, and against pressing Darcy when he, legally, bore no obligation.

Mr. Phillips had also provided several options, including that he discreetly show a letter, provided by Darcy, warning the merchants to forgo any additional credit. Darcy would take Mr. Phillips up on that offer. Though Mr. Phillips letter in no way demanded Darcy cover Wickham's debts, yet again, Darcy had considered doing so. Not for George Wickham, but rather for the hard-working men and women of Hertfordshire.

With some reluctance, however, he'd concluded he should not pay the debts. Instead, he ordered an agent of his to arrange the repair of some of the roads in and near Meryton. That should compensate everyone without actually helping Wickham.

A light knock sounded. Darcy's eyes snapped up from the drawer front hiding the letter bearing Wickham's name. If Darcy had his way, Georgiana would never hear that name again.

"Come in," Darcy called, recognizing that tentative tap as his sister.

The door inched open and Georgiana's tall form slipped in. She came halfway across the room and halted, as if afraid to come any nearer. Darcy tamped down anger. He'd never raised his voice to his sister, or even reprimanded her. At most, he'd shaken his head and admitted disappointment in her behavior. Still, she acted as if he were an ogre of a guardian.

She hadn't been that way before... Ramsgate. Georgiana used to be lively. Cheerful. Even outspoken, at least with him.

That was before Darcy failed her as a guardian. Before George Wickham failed them both as a friend. Before his sister became burdened with a secret that would ruin her. Darcy scowled.

"You sent for me, Fitz?" she all but whispered.

"Some time ago," he said, then winced as she dropped her gaze to the floor. He cleared his throat. "Which is neither here nor there. Please, sit." He gestured to the chair before his desk.

She glided forward and perched on the edge of the chair, as if a loud noise would startle her into flight. She darted a glance up, then returned her gaze to her hands, clasped in her lap.

Darcy waited, but Georgiana didn't speak. Unable to stop the comparison, he contrasted her to Elizabeth. Would the quick-witted country miss inspire his sister to greater bravery? Mrs. Bingley was exceedingly kind to his shy sister, to little effect. He could tell Georgiana no longer feared speaking before Mrs. Bingley, yet she still rarely did so. Did his sister fear that any conversation, no matter how mild, might lead to a misstep? An inadvertent revealing of her secret?

"We are having guests to dinner," Darcy began, bringing his thoughts back to the trouble at hand. "Mrs. Bingley's aunt and uncle."

"Oh," Georgiana said into the silence. To Darcy's surprise, she looked up. "You think I will embarrass you by not speaking to them."

Darcy's eyebrows lifted in surprise. She was near the mark but had his reason for calling her in twisted the wrong way around. "Quite the contrary." He'd been contemplating a delicate phrasing. "I wished to warn you that Mrs. Bingley's aunt and uncle are in trade."

Mrs. Bingley, sweet as she was, didn't know that when she put the question to him, she was cornering Darcy into inviting her relations against his will, realizing one of his greatest fears in inviting the Bingleys to reside in Darcy House. True, the Gardiners were not Mrs. Bennet or the younger sisters, but they were likely close. If Darcy was fortunate, Mr. Gardiner would be levelheaded, like Mr. Phillips, but as Mr. Gardiner was brother to Mrs. Bennet and Mrs. Phillips, he was likely silly, and a silly man would have a silly wife.

"Mr. Bingley has family in trade," Georgiana ventured, each syllable tentative.

"Yes, but he was raised as a gentleman." Darcy shook his head. "Mr. Gardiner was not raised as a gentleman and is in trade. I worry the Gardiners may be too crass for you."

His sister's eyes widened. "But Mrs. Bingley is everything genteel. Surely, they are like her."

"There is always that possibility," he allowed, though he didn't think that likely. "I am going to instruct Mrs. Annesley to remove you if the company seems too vulgar. You are to stay near her and leave if she presents a reason to do so."

Georgiana gave a halting nod. "So, I do not need to speak with them?"

"Indeed, I would prefer if you do not."

She sagged back in the chair in obvious relief. "Thank you."

Darcy could think of no reply to that other than a nod. "I shall see you in the parlor before dinner, then, with our guests."

"Yes." Georgiana popped up out of the chair and scuttled away.

Darcy frowned after her. He rang for a servant and sent for Mrs. Annesley.

At least, Darcy reflected as he awaited Georgiana's companion, he wasn't required to entertain the Hursts. Mr. Hurst, he didn't mind, but

Mrs. Hurst often grated on him, just as Miss Bingley had. Mrs. Hurst, however, was angry over Bingley's treatment of Miss Bingley and refusing to see him. Darcy found Bingley's actions perfectly reasonable, even laudable, and saw no reason to promote a reconciliation between siblings.

A knock returned Darcy's thoughts to the present. He bid Mrs. Annesley to enter.

After imparting his instructions and learning that Georgiana had been painting, and then had to remove her smock and properly stow her implements before she could answer his earlier summons, Darcy wrote back to Mr. Phillips. It took all his will, and an inability to come up with a suitably casual phrasing, not to ask after Elizabeth. He tried to exercise similar restraint on her hold over his thoughts but failed. After slogging through several more correspondences, he went to dress for dinner.

Once ready, Darcy entered his parlor to find Mrs. Bingley and Mrs. Annesley listening to Bingley expound on fox hunting. Darcy selected a seat off to the side, near his silent sister, and made no effort to join in their conversation. Georgiana gazed straight ahead, expression abstract, as if she didn't even listen. Already put out, though nothing had yet gone wrong with their evening, Darcy selected a point on the mantlepiece across from him on which to fix his gaze and settled into his worries.

At precisely the time they'd been invited, the Gardiners were announced. Darcy stood as they entered. Mr. Gardiner, average height and slightly thick of build, met Darcy's gaze with candid, intelligent eyes before executing a precise bow. Mrs. Gardiner, slender and at least as graceful as Mrs. Bingley, curtsied beside her husband. Her warm, bright eyes turned almost immediately to Mrs. Bingley, who rushed forward with a smile.

Throughout the hubbub of greetings and obligatory pleasantries, Darcy could find no flaw in the Gardiners, in accent or manner. Nor in dress, for they were clad fashionably, though not flamboyantly. To his eye, their coin had been spent on quality fabric and craftsmanship, not ostentation. Precisely how Darcy managed his wardrobe, in contrast to Bingley who enjoyed a bit of flash and urged Mrs. Bingley in that direction as well.

Once seats were retaken, Darcy found himself between Mr. Gardiner and Mrs. Bingley. Mrs. Gardiner sat beyond Mrs. Bingley, to the right of where Georgiana shared a sofa with Mrs. Annesley. Darcy would have preferred to stay nearer his sister, to monitor her conversation, but he could hardly begrudge Mrs. Bingley a place beside her aunt.

"So, Mr. Darcy," Mr. Gardiner said. "I hear your country seat is in Derbyshire?"

"It is," Darcy replied.

"Fabulous countryside," Bingley added.

"Decidedly," Mr. Gardiner agreed. "We visit often. Mrs. Gardiner is from the region. Some of the loveliest land in all of England, I warrant."

"And fabulous hunting," Bingley said, returning to his earlier topic.

Darcy cast about for a means by which not to hear, for a second time in one evening, Bingley's thoughts on fox hunting.

"Indeed?" Mr. Gardiner said. "I warrant so. I'm more interested in brooks and streams, myself. Give me a grassy bank over a gallop any day."

"We have an ideal setting for fishing at Pemberley," Darcy said, happier to talk of trout. Luring in a fish to dine upon always struck him as more sporting than setting hounds on a fox. Aside from which, he enjoyed the quiet of fishing.

"He does, if you really care for that sort of thing," Bingley said on a chuckle. "Hours standing still, naught but birdsong to keep you company."

Mr. Gardiner gave a cheerful nod. "Mark my words, Mr. Bingley. Someday, you'll have a house full of little ones and no peace to be found, and birdsong will be a respite."

From fishing, Mr. Gardiner moved their conversation through a series of topics, broadly ranging through farming to proposed canals, to the affairs of Parliament. With seemingly no effort, he spoke intelligently and reasonably on any subject raised, never baulking from his opinion, but not overly forceful when faced with disagreement. Rather, he seemed more interested in rooting out and examining the basis of any discord than in pushing his view on the matter.

Darcy became so engaged, in fact, that it wasn't until near the hour they were slated to retire to the dining room that he noticed Georgiana was speaking. Nearly losing the threads of his own conversation, he realized his sister had been talking for some time.

"...was a wonderful dance instructor," Georgiana was saying. "He retired, though, and I don't care for his son, who replaced him."

"That's very good to know," Mrs. Gardiner said. "I'd heard mixed opinions and couldn't imagine why. I'm afraid I'm terribly behind in selecting instructors for my eldest. She'll be ten this summer. If you do not mind, I should enjoy hearing your thoughts on Italian instructors as well. Your insights into dance and the arts were very helpful."

"Has she had no languages at all?" Georgiana asked.

"She has, but not in the dedicated way I should like," Mrs. Gardiner said. "Drawing is her best skill. You should see the lovely sketches she does of all of us."

"I would enjoy to," Georgiana replied.

"We could come for tea," Mrs. Bingley said.

"Could we?"

Darcy had rarely, if ever, heard such hope in his sister's voice. He supposed, as Mr. Gardener and Bingley drew his attention back to a discussion on the land tax, that he should be alarmed. The Gardiners seemed eminently pleasant, however, and Mrs. Annesley obviously wasn't perturbed. She had her instructions, after all.

Both conversations broke off soon thereafter as dinner was announced. They moved to the dining room, Darcy taking the opportunity to study his sister. She walked on the arm of Mr. Gardiner without any nervousness. From what he could hear, Mr. Gardiner's questions were general and delivered in kind tones.

As they all sat to dinner, Darcy realized that was where Mrs. Bingley fell short with his sister. Mr. Gardiner, as well. Mrs. Gardiner spoke to Georgiana as if she were not cripplingly shy. Not bumbling and out of place, or too young to be minded, or too old to act as she did. Simply as an equal and with great interest and attention to his sister's replies. That was how Elizabeth spoke to him and, he now realized, to similar effect.

Bemused, Darcy took his place at one end of the table, Georgiana at the other. As they all sat, his sister looked about. She seemed to shrink into her chair, obviously recalling her role as hostess now that they'd reached the dinner table. Darcy stifled a mixture of regret and annoyance.

"Before we dine, I should like to make an announcement," Bingley said, and Darcy realized his house guest still stood, and held a raised glass. "Jane and I are enjoying our time in London so fully, due in large part to those gathered here this evening, that we shall begin the hunt for a London residence of our own."

"Oh, that's wonderful news," Mrs. Gardiner said.

"Felicitations," Darcy added.

"Not that we do not very much enjoy Darcy House," Mrs. Bingley put in, with a smile for Darcy and then Georgiana.

"To our new home," Bingley said. He raised his glass and took a sip, a gesture they all mimicked, and finally sat.

"Where will you begin the search?" Mr. Gardiner asked as the first course was brought out.

While Bingley replied, Darcy noted, and tried not to be seen noting, that Mrs. Annesley offered whispered encouragement to Georgiana as the soup terrine was placed before her. With that encouragement and a kind word from Mrs. Gardiner, Georgiana served the soup without incident. When the last bowl was filled, Darcy relaxed marginally.

That set the tone for the remainder of the evening. Dinner was punctuated by interesting, intelligent easy conversation. Darcy couldn't recall a time he'd seen Georgiana converse so freely, even from before Ramsgate. Being candid, he noted that he spoke more than usual as well. All in all, as when they'd first entered his parlor, Darcy could find no fault with the Gardiners. With that discovery, something in his mind, and heart, rested easier.

Chapter Fifteen

Winter passed uneventful and quiet, save for Mrs. Bennet's continued harping. Come spring, it came as no surprise at all when Elizabeth, sitting in the parlor at Longbourn, opened a letter from Mary and read her sister's invitation to visit. Though at the time of the Collins' departure the previous autumn Elizabeth had heard all she ever wished to about Lady Catherine, Rosings and Miss Anne de Bourgh, by now she quite welcomed the diversion.

Jane and Mr. Bingley had extended their stay in London, enjoying the activities there enough to seek a residence. Kitty spent all her time in Meryton with Lydia. Mr. Bennet, as always, hid in his library. In short, Elizabeth had been left alone with her mother for much of the winter and knew, with certainty, that if she didn't get away soon, she would go mad.

She lowered the letter and endeavored for an easy tone. "Mary's asked me to visit."

Mrs. Bennet, seated on the other side of the parlor, didn't look up from her needlework. "How good of Mary to take you in, even for a short time, when you must be an embarrassment to her."

"Embarrassment?" Elizabeth couldn't help asking.

"Yes," Mrs. Bennet said, adding a beleaguered sigh. "What with a horrible scandal in your background and, well, how old you are. I mean, you're nearly an old maid."

"Yes, well, despite my horrible scandal and equally horrendous age, Mary has tendered the offer and I should like to go."

"Of course, you must go," Mrs. Bennet said. "You can't find a husband here. You must try your luck in Kent. If you'd as much sense as Kitty you would be at Lydia's side every day, to secure an invitation to Brighton. Kitty has a good chance of meeting an officer there." Mrs. Bennet finally looked up. She tipped her head to the side, jowls creasing, expression thoughtful. "Someone in the regulars might be better than someone in the militia."

113

Elizabeth couldn't quite suppress a sigh, tired of the same topics. She folded Mary's letter and stood. "I'll ask Papa if I may go," she said as she left the room.

Perhaps she should seek a husband. She'd had some hope, when she first met the amiable Mr. Wickham, but he only showed interest in better dowered women. Besides which, rumor had it he used Mr. Darcy's credit so freely that Mr. Darcy had informed the merchants of Meryton that he had never extended such a credit. Though Mr. Wickham was appealing to the eye and easy to converse and dance with, Elizabeth suspected he lacked the substance to be a good husband.

Not, she mused as she turned down the hall to her father's library, that she expected to find a gentleman in Kent. Mary's letters spoke of Lady Catherine and two farmers' wives with whom she'd formed friendships, but no single gentlemen were mentioned. Elizabeth reached her father's door and knocked.

"Enter," he called.

She stuck her head into the room to find her father at his desk, an open book before him. "Papa, Mary's invited me to visit. May I?"

"Despite the fact that I shall miss the only reasonable conversation available to me, you may," he said. "I suppose you'll wish to leave promptly?"

"I certainly shouldn't mind."

He gave a nod and closed his book. "Begin packing, then, if you like. I can't imagine the journey will be too difficult to arrange. Plan for the day after tomorrow."

"Thank you, Papa," Elizabeth said and withdrew her head from the library.

She went to her room, though she didn't truly need to begin packing immediately. She opened the wardrobe, so sparsely filled with Jane's things absent, to the same feeling of nostalgia that assailed her every day. Just as the wardrobe, the room seemed overly large and overly empty. Elizabeth had tried spreading her things out in the drawers and across the small dressing table, but that only seemed to emphasize the truth. Jane would never return. Elizabeth was alone.

Shaking her head as if that might shake off her dejection, Elizabeth removed each dress and checked it over for suitability. By all reports, she would be called on, at times, to dine at Rosings with Lady Catherine and Miss de Bourgh. Elizabeth wished to look her best for those occasions. She truly didn't want to embarrass Mary.

After deciding which gowns to take, she crossed to return those few she would leave to their place. Beneath her tread, the loose floorboard creaked. Elizabeth smiled down at it, their hiding place, recalling Jane kneeling there on the floor each evening, painted lovelier than ever by candlelight and joy, rereading Mr. Bingley's words before stowing his note away.

That note was gone now, along with everything of Jane's that she treasured. Elizabeth frowned. Mr. Darcy's strange letter still lay beneath the board, however.

She knelt to retrieve it. One thing Elizabeth could say for her mother was that Mrs. Bennet didn't rifle through her daughters' rooms. Still, the board creaked, and Elizabeth would be away for some time. She didn't even want to imagine what Mrs. Bennet would do should she stumble upon the note. Better to burn it, really.

Then again, if ever Elizabeth might need Mr. Darcy's assistance, wouldn't it be while she traveled? Not that the journey from Hertfordshire to Kent should offer any obstacles. Still… Elizabeth shrugged and tucked the note away in her luggage.

A few days and a short journey later, Elizabeth arrived in Kent to find the Hunsford Parsonage precisely as Mr. Collins had described. The quaint dwelling and outbuildings were well maintained, and generously sized for a parsonage. The glebe looked to contain enough land to provide all that the household needed to eat, likely with enough left over to sell. When the Collins showed her about, Elizabeth praised everything she saw, not so much because it deserved praise, although much of it did, but because she saw that Mary required the praise. Or, rather, Mary needed Elizabeth to praise everything to please Mr. Collins.

At dinner, served in a charming if stark room dedicated to the purpose, Elizabeth decided she would give a more general favorable comment. She'd quickly learned, during his time in Hertfordshire the previous autumn, that a flattered Mr. Collins was an easier to deal with Mr. Collins. "I am happy to see you so well settled," she said to Mary.

"Thank you," Mary said, looking at her husband. "It took me quite a while to learn to manage a household. I wish I had spent more time learning what goes on in the kitchen than learning how to play the pianoforte."

"Lady Catherine has been very helpful," Mr. Collins added.

"She has," Mary said. "But I needed more help than she could give me directly. She put me in touch with some local women who helped me learn what I needed to know. I didn't realize how complicated running a household is."

"You didn't get much assistance from Mrs. Williams," Mr. Collins said with a frown.

Mary's gaze darted to Elizabeth. "We already spoke on this matter," she said to Mr. Collins, tone beseeching.

Mr. Collins' frown deepened. "Yes, and determined you should find more ways Mrs. Williams can help. Lady Catherine recommended Mrs. Williams. She will learn that you didn't properly use the resource she gave you. She learns everything."

"I met Mrs. Lewis through Mrs. Williams," Mary said tentatively. "She was most helpful."

"But Lady Catherine didn't recommend Mrs. Lewis," Mr. Collins said. He shoved a forkful of mutton into his mouth.

"Mrs. Williams is too busy to help me," Mary said, twisting her napkin in her hands. "She made that rather clear."

"Perhaps Lady Catherine knew that Mrs. Williams would introduce Mary to the right person," Elizabeth offered, hoping to alleviate Mary's distress. "If Lady Catherine is as wise as you said, that might be what she planned."

The tension in Mr. Collins' expression eased. He swallowed his lamb. "You may be correct, Cousin Elizabeth. Lady Catherine is very wise."

Mary offered Elizabeth a grateful smile. "She is," Mary said, tone full of forced cheer. "She even advised us on what to plant in the garden."

Taking that cue, Elizabeth cheerfully helped the conversation move on to vegetables and how best to grow, harvest and employ them. Mary's moment of distress disturbed Elizabeth, though. When, later that evening, Mr. Collins left them alone in the parlor while he retired to work on a sermon, the exchange still weighed on Elizabeth.

"Must Lady Catherine truly be so thoroughly obeyed?" she asked Mary.

Mary grimaced. "It seems she must. She's very domineering and thinks she knows best in all things."

"Thinks?" Elizabeth repeated, hearing the emphasis Mary put on the word.

Mary went to the door and stuck her head out to look up and down the hall. She returned, taking the other side of the sofa on which

Elizabeth sat. "Lady Catherine had visited Mrs. Williams, and saw she has a beautifully run household," Mary said in a low voice. "Mrs. Williams' household is beautifully run, but it's run by Mr. Williams' widowed sister, who not only runs the household, but contributes enough money so that they have more servants."

"In other words, Lady Catherine doesn't know everything," Elizabeth said.

Mary's features contorted into a mixture of annoyance and resignation. "She tries to. I had to answer all sorts of prying questions. I would like to be able to tell her to mind her own business, but Mr. Collins…" Mary's voice faded into nothingness.

"Thinks it is her business," Elizabeth supplied.

Mary sighed. "I was annoyed before I married that no one paid attention to me."

Elizabeth felt a stab of guilt. She was one of the people who hadn't paid attention to Mary. That her sister's voice and expression were both devoid of recrimination only made Elizabeth feel worse.

"Now, Mr. Collins insists on reading all my mail, both what I receive and what I send," Mary continued, giving no indication she realized Elizabeth's discomfiture. "He practically interrogates me every evening. He wants to know everything I do each day. It's not that I have any secrets, but I would like to be able to have them."

"And our parents hardly care what the other one is doing," Elizabeth observed. The difference must make Mr. Collins' interest even more disconcerting.

"I'm not unhappy," Mary said quickly. "I was prepared for the possibility of Mr. Collins not caring. I'd much rather he cares, even if his attention is a bit overwhelming."

Elizabeth would rather describe Mr. Collins' behavior as stifling and obsessive, but never would. Mary was wed now and must make the best of her marriage. Harsh words would offer no help. "But you are happy?"

"Yes, happy enough." Mary plucked at a stray thread on the sofa. "It would be nice to be permitted more of a say in some aspects of our life, though. Mr. Collins always thinks Lady Catherine knows best. If she doesn't have an opinion on something, he thinks he knows best. He doesn't, at least not all the time. I know I had a lot to learn when I first moved here, but I am learning. I feel like I am being treated like a child."

"Maybe time will help?" Elizabeth tendered, hoping she was right.

"Maybe," Mary said but her tone lacked hope. She shrugged and stood. "Regardless, we should go to sleep. Mr. Collins allotted only one extra candle a week for your visit. If we aren't careful, we'll be in the dark by Sunday. You take that one to light your way, but do please blow it out as soon as you're able. I'll put these out and then I'm off to the kitchen to make sure the staff have their instructions for Mr. Collins' late meal."

Elizabeth could think of nothing positive to say about any of that, so she nodded, stood, and took up the suggested candle. Why Mr. Collins required more to eat when they'd so recently dined, she didn't know, but she also realized she didn't care. Dutifully, she headed toward her room.

When she rounded the corner in the upper hall, she saw light disappear into one of the rooms. She frowned, sure Mary couldn't have passed her unseen. Had Mr. Collins been roaming the hall? Like as not, he'd been on his way to order them to extinguish the parlor candles.

Elizabeth found her door slightly ajar. Her frown deepened. She'd closed the door firmly earlier.

Hadn't she?

She went in, candle held high. Nothing appeared amiss. Everything seemed in the exact order in which she'd left it when she went down to dinner. Still, something felt odd.

Elizabeth shook her head, set the candle down, and began preparing for bed. She was being fanciful. What reason would anyone have to go in her room? She had little money and no possessions of any real value. If anyone had been in, it was probably a maid, to check the water in the ewer or some such thing. Elizabeth's disquiet likely stemmed from her first night in new surroundings.

If she did suffer from disquiet, the feeling didn't hinder her rest. She woke early the following morning and didn't linger in her room. If she wouldn't be allowed occupation in the evenings, she deemed it wise to take advantage of the morning light. She dressed quickly and went to see who else was awake.

Mary must have been of the same mind, for Elizabeth found her sister already up and nearly finished with breakfast. This she took in the kitchen, with many fewer options than Mrs. Bennet served, saving work all round. As she dished up a plate and availed herself of a stool, Elizabeth decided she heartily approved of Mary's frugality.

While she ate, Elizabeth took in the two bustling staff members, once kneading bread and the other stirring a large pot of wash. "Does Mr. Collins eat in the kitchen as well?" she asked Mary, unable to picture

118

the officious clergyman in the cozy kitchen.

"Oh, no," Mary said. "I'll take him up something soon. He eats in his study, once he wakes. He prefers to work for a time before luncheon."

"Once he wakes?" Elizabeth parroted. "How can he sleep so late when we were abed so early?" She didn't necessarily laud her cousin but hadn't thought him slovenly.

"He stayed up quite late, working on his sermon for Sunday." Mary stood and began gathering her dishes. "Did you not hear me say I would make arrangements for his late-night respite?"

"He stayed up late?" Elizabeth said with mild indignation. "When I hadn't a candle by which to read?"

Mary took her dishes to a basin of sudsy water and set them carefully inside. "He was working, Lizzy. His work is very important."

"Sunday is days away. He has plenty of daylight by which to work between now and then."

Mary turned to face Elizabeth, shaking her head. "He must finish by tomorrow morning, so Lady Catherine has time to read the sermon and suggest improvements."

Elizabeth stared at her sister.

Mary's expression begged her not to speak. Her gaze darted toward the diligent staff.

Finally, with a shrug, Elizabeth applied herself to finishing her breakfast.

"I haven't seen that carriage before," Mary said.

Elizabeth looked up to find her sister crossing the kitchen.

Mary stopped at a small side window that looked up the lane. "They're turning up the drive," she exclaimed. "That looks like a rented carriage." Mary left the window to hurry from the room.

Elizabeth stood and swiftly gathered her dishes. These, she set beside the basin, uncertain if they ought to follow Mary's into the suds, and hurried from the kitchen to follow her sister.

She found Mary standing in the open parsonage door and joined her to watch luggage being handed down from the carriage. Elizabeth agreed the conveyance appeared rented, nondescript and dingy as it was. Once the luggage was down, one of the two men without climbed back up into the driver's seat. The other opened the carriage door and extended his hand.

A woman descended, tall and rather attractive. She turned back and lifted out a child. The little girl, whom the woman placed on the ground, was old enough to walk on her own but clung to her mother.

Footsteps sounded at the far end of the hall, somewhere behind Elizabeth. She recognized her cousin's heavy tread but didn't bother to look.

"Will that be all, missus?" the man who'd helped the woman out of the carriage asked.

"Yes, thank you," she replied in cultured tones as Mr. Collins' footsteps drew near.

The coachman nodded and climbed up beside the driver. The woman turned, spotted them, and squared her shoulders. She pried the little girl's hands from her skirt and captured one. A tentative smile on her face, the woman started toward them.

Mr. Collins came up behind them. "Mrs. Collins, Cousin Elizabeth. I've been waiting for my breakfast. Whatever are you doing at the doo—"

He broke off. Elizabeth glanced over her shoulder to take in the shock on his face.

"Mrs. Fortescue," he exclaimed.

"Susan," she corrected, not halting as she and her little girl walked up the path to the door. "How often must I tell you, William, to address me as Susan?"

Chapter Sixteen

Elizabeth glanced at Mary. Her sister gaped at the newcomers.

"It is not appropriate for me to address you as anything other than Mrs. Fortescue," Mr. Collins replied in his most censorious tone.

"Don't be absurd. I'm your sister."

Sister? Elizabeth relaxed, then nearly laughed aloud. What had she thought, that Mr. Collins... She shook her head. Askance, she saw Mary hinge her jaw closed and adopt a smile.

"Half-sister," Mr. Collins corrected. "Why are you here?"

"We're moving in," Mrs. Fortescue said. "For a week at least. More if you'll have us."

Mr. Collins pushed between Elizabeth and Mary and trotted down the parsonage steps to meet his half-sister at the base. "Why aren't you with your father?"

Elizabeth exchanged a quick look with Mary, who shrugged, expression confused.

"Our father is dead," Mrs. Fortescue said, emphasizing the 'our.' "If you are referring to my deceased husband's father, he wanted an unpaid housekeeper." She frowned "No, worse, he wanted me to pay him twenty-five pounds a month to be an unpaid housekeeper. I decided to leave."

"Twenty-five pounds," Mary exclaimed.

Mr. Collins cast her a stifling look over his shoulder, then turned back to his half-sister. "If your husband is dead, why aren't you in mourning?" He folded his arms across his chest.

Elizabeth couldn't see her cousin's face, but she could envision his scowl.

"It's been more than a year." Mrs. Fortescue frowned. "Which you would know if you ever opened my letters."

"I don't accept letters from Father's side of the family," Mr. Collins declared.

Yet, he would accept Longbourn, Elizabeth thought, but managed to forgo pointing that out.

"You are such a prig, William," Mrs. Fortescue snapped. "Furthermore, what went on between our father and my mother has nothing to do with me, or with you."

"You are the product of Father's illicit—"

"It was not illic—"

"He was still married to my mother," Mr. Collins roared.

"He divorced her in Scotland, quite legally," Mrs. Fortescue rejoindered.

The little girl pulled free of Mrs. Fortescue's hand and buried herself in her mother's skirt. Mr. Collins and his half-sister glared at each other. Mary looked to Elizabeth, face twisted in concern.

"I need a place to stay, William," Mrs. Fortescue said, tone almost reasonable once more.

Mr. Collins drew himself up. "There is no room under my roof for a basta—"

"May I ask, Mrs. Fortescue," Elizabeth cut in, stepping out onto the stoop. "What made you finally decide to leave? I'm Elizabeth Bennet, by the by," she added, improperly introducing herself. "Mr. Collins' cousin. On his father's side."

Mrs. Fortescue raised an eyebrow at that. She gave Mr. Collins a tart look before turning back to Elizabeth. "I'd spent the entire day doing the wash and mending," she said. "Beatrice came into the kitchen, seeking me. I hadn't seen her since luncheon." She stroked the little girl's curls. "She tried to climb into my lap and accidentally touched a pot I'd only recently taken off the fire." A flash of misery crossed Mrs. Fortescue's face. "My late husband's father came barging in to find out what the crying was about." Her scowl returned. "He accused me of being lazy because he found me holding Beatrice, trying to get her to open her hand so I could see the burn. He said I coddle her too much and that it's good for her to cry, and she'd touched the pot deliberately to take my attention from my work." Mrs. Fortescue drew in a slightly shaky breath and glanced at Mr. Collins and Mary, as if realizing she spoke with too much passion. "It wasn't the first time he's ordered me to neglect my daughter, but it was the last."

Elizabeth looked at Mr. Collins, who glowered at his half-sister. Elizabeth was afraid he would turn Mrs. Fortescue and her child away. It was obvious Mrs. Fortescue wouldn't be there if she had anywhere else she could go.

"I'm here visiting my sister, Mrs. Collins," Elizabeth said, gesturing to Mary. "If I can stay here for several weeks, certainly you can stay for at least that length of time without causing a strain on the household, particularly if you do occasional mending." She added that to mollify Mr. Collins, although she tried to make it sound like a joke. With a quick breath, she moved on into flattery. "You wouldn't believe how large the parsonage is. Your brother was very fortunate to obtain this living." To make sure her comment didn't come across as implying luck on his part, instead of merit, she added, "He has earned a wonderful place to live and raise a family. He is quite the patriarch."

Mr. Collins straightened his shoulders, standing taller, but his dark expression didn't waver.

Elizabeth cast a beseeching look at Mary.

"Generosity," Mary blurted. Everyone turned to look at her. "That is, generosity is the soul of virtue. You're always saying so, Mr. Collins. And… and where else to bestow generosity than a mother and child? You know how Lady Catherine speaks of our responsibility to care for the fairer sex and especially for children."

Mr. Collins' disapproving expression wavered. Elizabeth hid a grin. She should have thought to evoke Lady Catherine.

"Lady Catherine?" Mrs. Fortescue asked tentatively.

"Mr. Collins wise and noble patroness," Elizabeth clarified.

Mrs. Fortescue turned raised eyebrows toward her half-brother.

"Lady Catherine does espouse generosity, especially toward children," Mr. Collins admitted. "You may stay, at least until I've sought her council. Lady Catherine will know what ought to be done with you."

"Thank you," Mrs. Fortescue said. "You're a kind, generous brother."

"Half-brother," Mr. Collins muttered as he turned away. "Mrs. Collins, please arrange room for Mrs. Fortescue and her child, and notify the cook."

"Yes, Mr. Collins," Mary said, expression neutral.

Mr. Collins tromped up the parsonage steps. "And send my breakfast," he added as he disappeared inside.

Mary turned to Mrs. Fortescue. "It's our pleasure to have you visit, Mrs. Fortescue, Beatrice."

Beatrice peeked from behind her mother's skirt.

Mary smiled, then turned to Elizabeth. "Lizzy, could you show Mrs. Fortescue and Beatrice into the parlor? I'll go give the staff their instructions and then we can all go see the rooms I have in mind."

"Yes, certainly," Elizabeth said. She turned to Mrs. Fortescue as Mary hurried away. "This way," she said and led the way inside and to the parlor.

Elizabeth let Mrs. Fortescue and Beatrice settle onto a sofa. The room was rather cold, but Elizabeth didn't want to stir Mr. Collins ire along with the fire. Instead, she crossed to open the curtains, letting in morning light. Without, looking down the side of the parsonage, she could just see two of the Collins' staff hoisting Mrs. Fortescue's luggage. She left the window to sit in one of the chairs near the sofa and offered a smile.

"I didn't mean to cause such a stir," Mrs. Fortescue said, one arm about her daughter, who watched Elizabeth with wide eyes. "Thank you for intervening."

"Think nothing of it," Elizabeth said, meaning her words.

"I knew I took a risk coming here."

"You've nowhere else to go?" Elizabeth said, voicing her earlier guess.

"In a way." Mrs. Fortescue shrugged. "I own the house I grew up in. It belonged to the aunt who raised me. It has tenants now, but their lease will be up in three months. I will move in then."

"If you'd only three months to go, and had already endured your late husband's father for over a year, why leave now?" Elizabeth asked.

"My husband's father lives in a small, isolated village," Mrs. Fortescue said. "Ever since I left deep mourning, I've been looking for a means to leave. I'd resolved that, if I couldn't find a better way by the time the tenants' lease ends, I would simply take Beatrice and whatever I could carry and begin walking. I have possessions, but little coin, you see."

"Couldn't you sell some of what you own?" Elizabeth suggested.

Mrs. Fortescue nodded. "I did manage to sell some items, before Mr. Fortescue put a halt to that. He forbade me to have anyone approach the house and denied me all use of his horse or carriage. Then, at church last Sunday, one of the neighbors told me that her mother was coming for a long visit and would come in a hired carriage."

"Which would go back empty?" Elizabeth guessed.

Mrs. Fortescue nodded. "I thought, well, they'd rather take us and our luggage for whatever I could offer than drive all the way back for nothing. I planned to go into a larger town, wherever they would take us, then sell more of my possessions for fare here. Then I found out that they were headed this way, and therefore willing to take us all the way to Kent." She let out a long sigh, shoulders dipping. "I'd begun to fear we would be forced to go on foot," she admitted. "I'd already given up on the bulk of my possessions, but the way it worked out, I was able to take most of what we own."

"Like my dolls," Beatrice said in a small voice.

Mrs. Fortescue looked down at her and smiled. "Yes, like your dolls."

"And what are your dolls' names?" Elizabeth asked.

This led to more questions, mostly pertaining to the three dolls owned by the young Miss Beatrice Fortescue. Elizabeth enjoyed drawing out the child, who turned out to be somewhat frightened and tired but not actually shy. As Beatrice relaxed, so did her mother. Elizabeth could see that Mrs. Fortescue loved her daughter very much.

When Mary returned, they went up to look at the rooms. While none of the few remaining empty bedrooms had connecting doors, there were two side by side. Though one of these was quite small, Mrs. Fortescue avowed them to be perfect. Mary accepted her praise happily and ordered a crib brought down from the attic for Beatrice, who turned out to be not quite three.

That evening at dinner, Elizabeth listened, amused, as Mrs. Fortescue complimented Mr. Collins on everything from his choice of wife to his home, to the food. None of her praise was untrue, but taken altogether, Elizabeth guessed Mrs. Fortescue as being intelligent enough to realize that Mr. Collins needed flattery. By the end of the meal, he was quite certain Lady Catherine would approve of his generosity in permitting his half-sister and her child to stay.

Mr. Collins headed to Rosings the following morning, both to deliver the draft of his sermon and seek Lady Catherine's blessing on his half-sister's visit. Though Elizabeth tried to believe the day would proceed amicably, she couldn't help but worry that Lady Catherine would order Mr. Collins to turn out Mrs. Fortescue. Judging by the tense expressions of both the lady in question and Mary, they nursed the same concern.

All three of them made liberal use of Beatrice as a delightful distraction, playing dolls with her and arranging her hair, but all activity stilled when Mr. Collins returned. Four pairs of eyes turned to regard him.

"Lady Catherine advises that I'm correct to permit you to remain, Mrs. Fortescue," Mr. Collins announced.

Elizabeth wasn't alone in her relieved sigh.

"In her wisdom, Lady Catherine pointed out that it is not Beatrice's fault if her mother was born to a questionable union," Mr. Collins continued. "Beatrice is a gentleman's daughter and needs our guidance if ever she's to be an asset to society. Lady Catherine advised me that it is our Christian duty to assist her."

Elizabeth saw Mrs. Fortescue's lip twitch, but she managed not to smile. "Then Beatrice, and I, thank your Lady Catherine."

"You shall thank her in person," Mr. Collins said. "She has invited us to tea. She is particularly interested to meet you, Cousin Elizabeth," he added, an odd note, something akin to anger, in his voice.

"And I her," Elizabeth replied, wondering at Mr. Collins' glare.

Mr. Collins continued to glower. "We shall see about that," he said and stomped from the room.

Elizabeth turned a questioning look on Mary.

"I've no idea," Mary said with a shrug.

"Maybe he doesn't wish to share Lady Catherine's attention with you?" Mrs. Fortescue suggested.

"Maybe," Elizabeth agreed, and turned the conversation to an easier topic.

She couldn't keep Mr. Collins' odd malice from her thoughts, though, as they all dutifully walked to Rosings that afternoon. Mr. Collins hardly looked at Elizabeth and spoke as if she didn't exist. She wouldn't have minded at all if his behavior weren't so strange.

Rosings turned out to be a stately, if overly stern and ornate, structure. The building loomed tall as they drew near, statuary high above on each soaring faux turret. The grounds, as well, were sculpted, each plant reined into a perfect order that left little hint of natural beauty.

Even the stiffness of the approach and exterior didn't prepare Elizabeth for the over-gilded ostentation of the interior. Every surface overflowed with adornment. The overall effect, as they were shown down hall after hall and then into a large parlor, was dizzying.

If Rosings seemed formidable, so did the mistress of the house. Lady Catherine, though seated, appeared a good head taller than Elizabeth, with broad shoulders, a vast bosom and ponderous jowls. Her chair was a little higher than normal. A charitable interpretation of that would be that it was made to make it easier for her to rise and was more suited to her height, but Lady Catherine's demeanor did not invite charity.

She did not stand to greet them, instead receiving them as a queen would, one hand resting on an amethyst-topped cane. The Collins went first, Mr. Collins bowing as Mary curtsied. Mary's curtsy was lower than the usual social curtsey and graceful enough so that she must have practiced something more suited to royalty than someone of Lady Catherine's rank.

"Mr. Collins, Mrs. Collins." Lady Catherine dipped her chin slightly.

"Lady Catherine, thank you for inviting us into your home," Mr. Collins said.

"Thank you, Lady Catherine," Mary echoed.

For this, they received a second nod. Lady Catherine made a sweeping gesture left.

Mary and her husband turned slightly. They genuflected again. Elizabeth realized there were two more occupants in the room. Both slender women, though one much older than the other, they occupied a sofa set slightly back from Lady Catherine's oversized armchair.

"Miss de Bourgh," Mr. Collins greeted. "Mrs. Jenkinson."

Elizabeth studied Lady Catherine's daughter, finding Miss de Bourgh not ill-favored, if too thin and pale. She had lovely, wide blue eyes, overlarge in her face, which gave her an innocent, youthful appearance. Elizabeth nearly started when those eyes turned a piercing gaze her way.

Mr. Collins cleared his throat. Elizabeth looked back to see Mary had stepped aside, taking one of two empty chairs on the other side of Lady Catherine from her daughter. Mr. Collins was gesturing Mrs. Fortescue and Beatrice forward. The little girl clung to her mother again, almost engulfed by her skirt.

"Lady Catherine, may I present my half-sister, Mrs. Fortescue, and her child Beatrice, whom we are generously permitting to remain with us in their time of need, as you so graciously recommended," Mr. Collins said.

Even hampered by Beatrice, Mrs. Fortescue accomplished a curtsy so full of elegance as to inspire envy. "Lady Catherine, thank you for your understanding and generous spirit."

"Yes, you should thank me," Lady Catherine said. "Not many would be so tolerant. You are fortunate Mr. Collins is intelligent enough to look to me for guidance."

"Indeed, I am," Mrs. Fortescue said.

Elizabeth heard not a trace of amusement in Mrs. Fortescue's voice, but felt she already knew the widow well enough to read the emotion in her heart.

"You may sit with my daughter and her companion," Lady Catherine said, gesturing to Miss de Bourgh. "Anne adores children. Soon, she will marry and start a brood of her own."

Elizabeth hid a frown. Miss de Bourgh did not look up to brooding anything. Her frame seemed as suited to childbearing as Lady Catherine's to foot races.

"Thank you," Mrs. Fortescue murmured. Prying Beatrice from her leg, she took the little girl's hand and moved to sit with Miss de Bourgh and her companion.

"And this, Lady Catherine, is my cousin, Elizabeth Bennet," Mr. Collins said, voice filled with censure.

Ignoring his tone, Elizabeth came forward to curtsy. She knew she didn't accomplish the act with quite as much grace as Mrs. Fortescue but liked to think her performance at least equaled Mary's.

"Miss Bennet," Lady Catherine snapped.

"Thank you for inviting me to tea, Lady Catherine," Elizabeth said at her most polite.

"I understand, Miss Bennet, that you've met my nephew, Mr. Darcy." Lady Catherine's tone made the statement an accusation.

Elizabeth blinked, taken aback. Was there some reason she ought not to have met Mr. Darcy? "Mr. Darcy of Pemberley?" she supplied. "Yes. He was visiting a neighbor, a Mr. Bingley, for one or two months."

"So Mr. Collins informs me." Lady Catherine's eyes were raptor-like as she studied Elizabeth. "Did you spend much time with Darcy?"

Able to think of no reason for the woman's hostility, Elizabeth couldn't find one to prevaricate, either. "We were frequently at the same gatherings. I spoke with him on occasion. We were never on particularly good terms."

Lady Catherine leaned forward. "Is that all you did? Speak to him? You didn't see more of him?"

"We did both reside in Netherfield Park at once, for several days. My sister fell ill while visiting Mr. Bingley's sister and I went there to look after her until she regained enough health to travel."

Lady Catherine lifted her cane, then slammed the tip to the floor. "So, you saw him at more than gatherings, as you put it." Her eyes narrowed. "Are you in the habit of lying, Miss Bennet?"

"I beg your pardon?" Elizabeth replied with a hint of anger.

"I insist upon knowing all," Lady Catherine declared.

Elizabeth frowned. She didn't care if Lady Catherine was queen of the Orient, her behavior lacked all civility. If she thought, for one moment, that Elizabeth would answer so impertinently asked a question, she—Elizabeth's train of thought shattered as she caught the beseeching expression on Mary's face. Elizabeth let out her anger in a long, low sigh.

Instead of voicing her anger, she said, "Mr. Darcy and I may have spent time in the same household and spoken at various parties in our neighborhood, but except for the generous hospitality of his friend Mr. Bingley, I would not move in Mr. Darcy's sphere. How can you expect me to have any more than a casual acquaintance with him?"

Lady Catherine continued to gaze at Elizabeth as if she were something found on the bottom of a shoe, disbelief clear in her eyes. She snapped her cane down on the floorboards again. Elizabeth didn't so much as flinch.

"Lizzy was only at Netherfield for a few days," Mary said in a rush. "I'm sure she was so busy tending Jane, she hadn't time for anything at all else. Right, Lizzy?"

Elizabeth looked at her sister again. Mary's face was white, save for red splotches on her cheeks. A glance the other way showed Mr. Collins still standing nearby, as if he couldn't sit until Lady Catherine's interrogation finished. He, in turn, appeared livid.

Lady Catherine must know, Elizabeth realized. She knew about the library, or at least some part of the story. She couldn't know about Miss Bingley's visit to Mr. Darcy's room, or Elizabeth wouldn't be the focus of her ire. Somehow, some sort of rumor had gotten out, and reached Darcy's aunt, who must think Elizabeth had tried to trap her nephew. How else to explain her questions and hostility?

Well, Elizabeth would admit nothing. She squared her shoulders, smoothed her expression, and met Lady Catherine's gaze. If awkward silence was how Lady Catherine wished everyone to spend their afternoon, Elizabeth would meet her halfway.

"Mama, I'm hungry," Beatrice said in a small voice.

"Shh, dear," Mrs. Fortescue admonished, her tone kind.

"You should know, Miss Elizabeth Bennet, that Darcy is betrothed to my Anne," Lady Catherine declared. "They will wed."

Elizabeth shrugged, realizing Lady Catherine must think her a threat to that union. "And I'm sure they will be very happy." She glanced at Miss de Bourgh. "You are fortunate. I believe he is an honorable man."

Miss de Bourgh answered with a grimace.

Lady Catherine's ponderous jowls pulled down. Deep lines creased her face. "Well, sit down, girl," she finally snapped at Elizabeth. "You too, Mr. Collins. Mrs. Jenkinson, send for tea."

Mrs. Jenkinson obediently rose. Elizabeth looked around and selected a chair across the room from Lady Catherine, somewhat removed from the others. Mr. Collins took the seat between Mary and his patroness.

Tea proved a slightly awkward affair, peppered by Lady Catherine's jabs and leading questions. Elizabeth managed to maintain her temper well enough to become amused by the situation. It occurred to her that she could confess, in private, so Lady Catherine would understand just how adamantly she did not wish to steal Mr. Darcy from Miss de Bourgh, but even their short acquaintance led Elizabeth to feel her hostess would never believe her.

How like Mr. Darcy, Elizabeth mused, to impede her enjoyment of tea even from afar. First, he insulted her at the assembly. Then, he insisted on daily arguing with her during her stay at Netherfield Park. After that, he inflicted a letter on her which could only cause a scandal if found. Now, he somehow managed to make tea at Rosings—

Elizabeth stifled a gasp. She turned to scrutinize her cousin, who glared at her nearly as consistently as Lady Catherine.

Mr. Darcy's letter.

Elizabeth narrowed her eyes at Mr. Collins. He flushed and looked down. Anger shot through Elizabeth, dispelling any equilibrium she'd found.

Mr. Collins wouldn't have gone through her things. It was one thing, and a distasteful one at that, to go through his wife's possessions. Quite another to go through Elizabeth's. He wouldn't have dared.

Would he?

Her suspicion aroused, tea couldn't end soon enough for Elizabeth. Once they were free of Rosings, she strode out ahead of the others, sure of the way. Upon reaching the parsonage, she raced up the steps and into her room.

Anger making her movements sharp, Elizabeth opened her trunk and yanked out her writing things. She'd left Mr. Darcy's letter tucked into a bundle of others, ones she'd brought with her to reread and reply to.

She didn't find the letter. She went through the pile again, and a third time.

Elizabeth turned a glare in the direction of the parlor, where she imagined her cousin to be. Mr. Darcy's letter was gone.

Chapter Seventeen

Worry gnawed at Anne for the entirety of tea. Her mother's dislike of Miss Bennet, her constant questions, they bespoke of some knowledge, but what? In view of the direction her mother's questions took, her knowledge centered around Darcy.

How had Lady Catherine managed to discover Darcy's interest in Miss Bennet? Georgiana wrote Lady Catherine only twice a year, at the Yuletide and to thank her for birthday gifts. Surely, Georgiana wouldn't have included, in her Christmas letter, mention of Darcy's autumnal words about Miss Elizabeth Bennet.

Which left only one option. For all Anne's care, all her precautions, Lady Catherine was still reading her letters. She must be. Her mother claimed an adult woman had the right to keep her letters private, but her mother often seemed to feel that rules applied exclusively to other people, not de Bourghs. Only in Georgiana's letter to Anne could Lady Catherine have read Darcy's all-too-telling description of Miss Bennet. Seated beside Mrs. Jenkinson, Anne turned a hard look on her mother, who watched their guests file out of the parlor from the vantage of her silly, ostentatious, deliberately throne-like seat.

Anne was nearly beside herself with anger but knew better than to let the emotion show. Her mother loved to quarrel and could never be swayed. Lady Catherine would only deny her snooping. Or, worse, declare it her right. Anne didn't know if she would be able to curb her tongue should her mother take that tack.

"Finally, that woman is gone," Lady Catherine said as Mr. Collins and his guests disappeared down the hall. She swiveled to look at Anne. "You will invite her for a drive tomorrow."

"I beg your pardon?" Anne said, taken aback.

"Miss Bennet. You will take one of the small carriages and invite her on a drive."

"You wish me to visit with a woman you clearly dislike." Anne narrowed her gaze. "Why?"

"I want your impression of her, unfettered by my presence," Lady Catherine said. "Obviously, she was on her best behavior this afternoon, for what that was worth."

"You wish my opinion of someone?" Now Anne knew her mother had an unsavory agenda. Lady Catherine didn't value anyone's opinions but her own.

"Certainly. You are my daughter and will manage Rosings someday." The imperious way Lady Catherine looked down her nose bespoke of how poorly she felt Anne would fare. "You must learn to judge people. Now is the time."

Anne didn't believe that explanation for a moment, but she'd learned patience when dealing with her mother. Lady Catherine must be handled as one would a mountainside. Chip away, let nature erode. Eventually, even rock would crumble to dust.

After breakfast the following morning, Anne dutifully ordered a carriage readied. She set out, joined by Mrs. Jenkinson within and the coachman and two footmen without. Anne didn't expend any effort at speech as they journeyed to the parsonage. She preferred to contemplate what her mother's agenda might be. Besides which, Mrs. Jenkinson would report to Lady Catherine any and all things said, as would anyone else employed at Rosings.

When they reached the parsonage, Anne said, "Wait here. I won't be a moment," and alighted without waiting for the footman, even though Mrs. Jenkinson would report such uncivilized behavior.

She strode up to the door and knocked.

Almost immediately, the door swung open to reveal a maid. "May I help you, Miss?"

"Is Miss Bennet at home?" Anne said. "I've come to invite her for a drive."

"Did I hear the door?" Mr. Collins' voice called from somewhere within.

Anne grimaced to hear his footfalls drawing near. Soon, his tall form loomed behind the maid. Surprise skittered across his face.

"Miss de Bourgh, it's an honor to have you at our door."

"Only think, then, how grand it will be to invite me in," Anne said, able to curtail a tart tone if not her acerbic words.

"Yes. Yes of course. Certainly." He backed away. "Open the door," he hissed at the maid. "You're barring Miss de Bourgh's way and embarrassing me."

The young woman, eyes wide, pulled the door more fully open. She, too, backed away, adroitly ducking around Mr. Collins when she reached him.

"Please tell Miss Bennet I'm here to see her," Anne said to the girl as she stepped into the small foyer.

The maid nodded and darted away.

"You've come to see my cousin?" Mr. Collins' asked, frowning. "Does Lady Catherine know?"

"It is by my mother's recommendation that I am here." Anne kept her expression bland though, as a grown woman in her late twenties, his suggestion that she couldn't decide whom to visit on her own rankled.

"Oh, well, then, would you care for tea?" Mr. Collins said. "I'm sure Mrs. Collins and my cousin are in the kitchen. I can send for them."

Anne shook her head. "No, I should like to go for a drive with Miss Bennet. Mrs. Jenkinson is waiting in the carriage. That is, if this isn't an inopportune moment."

"Inopportune?" Mr. Collins' expression showed alarm. "No, certainly not. How could it be? There's nothing my cousin could be doing that could possibly be as important as a drive with you, Miss de Bourgh."

Ridiculous as she found that statement, Anne refrained from offering a reply. She refused to give her mother's sycophant any more fodder for conversation. They fell into a silence that Mr. Collins, to judge by his fidgeting, felt to be quite awkward. Anne considered the hush amusing. To add to the discomfiture of their silent tableau, cool, damp spring air gusted about them, for the maid had left the door wide open and Anne didn't stir her limbs to close it. Dressed for the out of doors, Anne didn't mind the cold.

Miss Bennet appeared at the end of the corridor leading from the foyer. "Miss de Bourgh," she called as she drew near. "What a pleasant surprise."

Looking past Mr. Collins, who loomed between them, Anne studied Miss Elizabeth Bennet, this woman who, of all women, Darcy had actually noticed. Not much larger than Anne, she managed to convey a lively, unpretentious attitude of vigor and health. Dark eyes, cloaked in long lashes and turned up ever so slightly at the corners, shone with intelligence, honesty and a wry humor. Aside from that, while certainly blessed with moderate outward beauty and a fine figure, nothing about Miss Bennet set her apart from dozens of other English misses.

Her eyes, though, were what Darcy had specifically noted. Her eyes and her wit, which all but shone from those luminous orbs. Of those, Anne admitted, she'd witnessed no parallel. Apparently, for all he'd met many more women than Anne, neither had Darcy.

"Miss Bennet," Anne greeted. "It's a lovely day. I thought you might wish to take a drive?" She gestured in the direction of the waiting carriage.

"She would," Mr. Collins declared. "Of a certainty."

Anne cocked an eyebrow. Behind the officious clergyman, Miss Bennet's expression betrayed amusement. She caught Anne's eye and nodded.

"Lovely," Anne said. "I'll wait without." She pivoted and headed through the doorway and back down the front steps.

"Oh, but you must come in," Mr. Collins called after her, tone worried. "It's cold, and I'll send for tea. I'm sure Lady Catherine wouldn't appro—"

His words were lost as Anne climbed back into the carriage and closed the door. She gave Mrs. Jenkinson a quick, reassuring smile to denote her success in securing Miss Bennet's agreement. Anne settled into her seat and pulled a rug over her legs. It was, in truth, a bit cool.

A short time later, a knock sounded at the carriage door, which then swung open. Miss Bennet looked back and forth between the seats, then climbed up to sit in the backward-facing one, beside Mrs. Jenkinson.

"Mrs. Jenkinson," she greeted, then turned to Anne. "What a lovely carriage,"

"Only the finest for Mother," Anne said, realizing even as the words left her mouth that wasn't the correct rejoinder.

Far from appearing censorious at Anne's lack of properly vacant social niceties, Miss Bennet chuckled. Not a giddy, silly laugh, as Anne had heard from many a young miss. A rich, intriguing chuckle. Had Darcy listened to that warm, beguiling sound and fallen in love?

"There's no point, I suppose, not to have the best, if one can," Miss Bennet temporized. "If it is within taste and reason."

Anne studied the interior of the carriage as they started to move. Plush seats. Thick, embroidered drapes. A deep green and rich oak palette. This was her favorite of her mother's carriages and the only one not gilded inside and out. She doubted the others would meet with Miss Bennet's idea of taste or reason.

"Would you care to share my rug?" Mrs. Jenkinson asked Miss

Bennet.

"Indeed, thank you," Miss Bennet replied. "It is a touch cold, is it not?"

Two sets of eyes turned to Anne. She realized they were giving her the chance to speak, something her mother rarely did. She also realized she ought to take advantage of the rare opportunity to practice her rusty conversation skills. "Yes. Unseasonable so," she ventured.

"But I'm sure we won't notice with such beautiful scenery," Miss Bennet supplied. "At least, the little I've seen of it has been quite lovely. I do enjoy walking but haven't had the time to see much more than I did on the ride here and the walk to and from Rosings yesterday."

"There are some very fine manors hereabouts," Anne said. "None so imposing as Rosings, but others at least as appealing. I shall point them out as we pass, though we'll see little from the roadway."

"Well, seeing a little is better than not seeing anything," Miss Bennet said.

They went on in this manner, speaking of many things and yet nothing, really. Anne sensed that Miss Bennet, as much as she, didn't wish to blunder into any topic which might pose a strain to their burgeoning relationship. They rode together for an hour, cutting a wide country loop around the parsonage before returning Miss Bennet to Mr. Collins' doorstep. Despite the conversation never going beyond impersonal politeness, Anne hadn't enjoyed herself so much since her mother had secluded her at Rosings.

For seclusion it was, she thought grimly as the carriage headed back to Rosings. None of their neighbors liked Lady Catherine, and thus called as rarely as possible. This amounted to one or two brief visits a few times a year, but only from those who were snobbish to the point where they valued the connection enough. Mr. Collins was hardly reasonable company and his wife might mean well, but Anne saw no common ground with her.

And why? All to ensure Anne would wed Darcy, a man who only declined making his lack of interest plain as a favor to her. Anne sighed. She could enlighten Lady Catherine to the impossibility of her and Darcy wedding, fight for a social life. Unfortunately, success, if that unlikely achievement occurred, would only mean a barrage of suitors, all hand-selected and pressed on her by her mother.

Her mind wrestling with how to handle the repercussions of Darcy's inevitable marriage, Anne fell into a glum silence by the time they reached Rosings. The cheerfulness and equilibrium she'd found with Miss Bennet disappeared. After devesting her outerwear, she strode into her mother's favorite parlor in a grim mood.

"Did you have a nice drive?" Lady Catherine asked the moment Anne stepped into the room, eyes glinting.

"Yes," Anne all but snapped. She settled into her usual sofa, to Lady Catherine's right and slightly behind her.

Mrs. Jenkinson, shadow-like, followed and took her place at Anne's side.

Lady Catherine swiveled to face them. "Do you think Miss Bennet likes you?"

Anne wished she could guess her mother's goal, though she was certain she disapproved. "How should I know? She was polite and pleasant."

Lady Catherine nodded. She drummed her fingers on one of the lions' heads that capped the arms of her chair. "I want you to make friends with her. Make her like you." Lady Catherine nodded. "Yes, you are to become her intimate friend."

Anne cast Mrs. Jenkinson a quick look, finding her so called companion's expression deliberately blank. So, whatever Lady Catherine's plan was, Mrs. Jenkinson knew of it. Anne ground her teeth, tired of being spied upon.

"It is difficult to become good friends with someone with so many people eavesdropping," she said, deciding she may as well get some advantage from her mother's scheming.

Lady Catherine shrugged. "You may leave Mrs. Jenkinson home tomorrow, when you invite Miss Bennet for another ride," she said, offering no surprise at or refutation of Anne's implied accusation. "But you will take a maid. I do not like you to be alone in a carriage, even if it is just the distance from Rosings to the parsonage."

"A maid?" Anne frowned. "Only if I may leave her at the parsonage while we ride."

"A maid is nothing," Lady Catherine scoffed. "Only a servant."

"To you a maid is nothing, or to me," Anne said, the second part of her statement a lie. Not only were maids people, they were people who reported everything to her mother. "But to Miss Bennet? Perhaps not."

Lady Catherine appeared to consider that. "True. She is quite low, after all." She shrugged again, the broadness of her shoulders exaggerating the slight gesture. "Fine, when you ride, you may leave the maid at the parsonage. You can also walk on the grounds of Rosings with propriety. Invite Miss Bennet for a walk."

Anne adopted a resigned expression, as if she'd no will to protest. "Fine, Mother. I will do as you wish."

"Certainly, you will," Lady Catherine declared. "And each evening, you will inform me of every topic the two of you discussed. Most importantly, you will find out Miss Bennet's relationship with Darcy."

Anne locked gazes with her mother but didn't speak. So, Lady Catherine wished Anne to spy for her, as everyone else at Rosings did. Anne would never comply.

She suppressed a grim smile and dropped her gaze to her lap. Her mother always took a lack of reply as capitulation. Anne would spend time with Miss Bennet, precisely as her mother wished, but she wouldn't spy. She would use Lady Catherine's suspicions and high handedness to her own gain. Anne would make a friend.

Lady Catherine studied Anne a moment longer, then swiveled back to face the parlor door. "Now, my head aches from this talk of Miss Bennet. Mrs. Jenkinson, play for me."

Dutifully, Mrs. Jenkinson rose and moved to the pianoforte.

Anne angled her body to face the instrument and schooled her features into polite boredom, but her mind ranged far and wide. She would make friends with Miss Bennet, who very well might aid her in finding a way free of her mother and into a relationship of her choosing, with a man who would respect her desire to be let alone. It didn't matter that her mother plotted, for Anne would prevail. As Mrs. Jenkinson played, Anne's fingers drummed out a discordant rhythm on the arm of the sofa.

Chapter Eighteen

Elizabeth was baffled by Miss de Bourgh's repeated invitations, which Mr. Collins insisted she accept. Elizabeth didn't mind. Miss de Bourgh was pleasant enough company. Indeed, she was a better conversationalist than anyone else Elizabeth had met in Kent, except for Mrs. Fortescue. Spending an hour or two a day with Miss de Bourgh was no burden.

They walked outside most days that it didn't rain. When it did, they took carriage rides or walked the halls of Rosings. While they spoke on a wide range of subjects while alone, Elizabeth quickly noted that Miss de Bourgh never initiated any topic when her mother or Mrs. Jenkinson were present. In their presence, Miss de Bourgh replied to direct questions and limited her conversation with Elizabeth to asking whether she was warm enough, or too warm, or comments on the weather.

This trend became so blatant as to require explanation. Miss de Bourgh was an entirely different, and vastly more interesting, person when alone with Elizabeth, and Elizabeth longed to know why. She resolved to ask. When next they walked together, she tried to think of a way to issue the question with delicacy. Finally, she decided there wasn't a subtle way to ask and their friendship had grown enough to support the occasional lack of tact.

"I've noticed you speak less when your mother is present, and on a narrower variety of topics," Elizabeth ventured as they strolled past a row of geometric topiaries.

The corner of Miss de Bourgh's mouth quirked upward. "True, and I'm never allowed to have any friends of my own here, so my mother is always present."

"Yet, you are walking with me," Elizabeth pointed out, for Miss de Bourgh's words, which were noticeably not a true explanation of Elizabeth's observations, seemed to contradict her actions.

Miss de Bourgh stopped and turned to face Elizabeth, expression serious. "Yes, and I feel guilty about why. My mother said I should get

141

to know you and get you to like me, so I may spy on you for her." She placed a hand on Elizabeth's arm. "Rest assured, I do not."

Elizabeth stared at her, digesting that odd declaration. "I do like you," she finally offered. "And I very much thank you for not spying on me, but if your mother dislikes me so vehemently, why does she want you to spend any time with me, even as an informant?" She longed to ask if Miss de Bourgh knew anything about Mr. Darcy's stolen note but didn't want to press their friendship to the lengths of accusing her mother of theft.

Miss de Bourgh looked left and right, though they were alone. She dropped her arm and stepped closer, eyes still darting about nervously. "My mother wants me to marry. Specifically, she wants me to marry Mr. Darcy."

Elizabeth knew that much. "Wants you to? I thought the union was set."

Miss de Bourgh shook her head. "Only in Mother's mind. Not in mine, or Darcy's."

Elizabeth digested that. "That is why she quizzed me on my relationship with him, because she deems me a threat to her plans?" Which she could be, if Miss de Bourgh and Mr. Darcy weren't truly betrothed, but not if they were. That was, if Elizabeth had any designs on Mr. Darcy and if he didn't find her wholly unsuitable. "Does she question every woman of Mr. Darcy's acquaintance in the manner she did me?"

"Not so intently, no," Miss de Bourgh said.

Her eyes darted downward as she spoke. Elizabeth followed that gaze to find Miss de Bourgh's hands tightly clenched. Obviously, Miss de Bourgh knew something more. Something she wasn't telling Elizabeth. Most likely, she did know that Mr. Collins had rifled through Elizabeth's things and taken that note to her mother.

Still unwilling to exceed the bonds of politeness with that accusation, Elizabeth instead ventured, "Why don't you want to marry Mr. Darcy? He seems a bit… stiff," she settled for, not wishing to insult. "But honorable. Certainly, he's well-built and handsome." Those complements she could give without perjury.

Miss de Bourgh shook her head. "It isn't that I don't want to marry Darcy. I don't want to marry any man. Not unless I can find some miraculous gentleman who would wed me in name only. If I can't find a man willing to agree to that, I shall never wed at all."

Elizabeth blinked, taken aback. "But why? A single woman, a spinster, has little place in society."

Miss de Bourgh gave her a long, considering look. "My father had two sisters. They both died in childbirth. They were like me, small. Three of my de Bourgh cousins were women, all of whom died in childbirth."

"Not all women die in childbirth," Elizabeth protested, the words leaving her mouth almost automatically.

"I'm not going to take that chance. Marriage simply isn't worth the risk."

Elizabeth stared at her. "Not to marry... You'll be alone your whole life." She frowned on the heels of her words, uncertain they were true. She'd always thought a woman's only significant choice in life was that of a husband. Admittedly, it was only the right of refusal, but it was there. She'd never considered that a woman had two important choices. Not only whether to accept a specific suitor, but whether to accept any man at all.

Elizabeth had, in a way, exercised her right to refuse a suitor on Mr. Darcy, and likely bruised his not inconsiderable pride in the process. Perhaps if she had not acted, he would have found a way out of the library and spared his pride, but she was already compromised, and it was partly his fault, that culpability robbing her of care for his feelings. If he'd been faster, he might have stopped Miss Bingley from locking the door the second time.

No. That was unfair. Miss Bingley's action could hardly have been anticipated.

Regardless of fault, if Elizabeth had simply accepted his decree that climbing out of the window was unsafe, she would probably be Mrs. Darcy by now, and miserable. Now, her decision seemed laudable on an afore unknown front. She could only imagine the trouble Mr. Darcy wedding would make for Miss de Bourgh.

"Does Mr. Darcy wish to wed you?" Elizabeth asked. Had Miss de Bourgh weighed on his mind that evening in the library? Or would he easily have broken his understanding with her, what little of one existed beyond Lady Catherine's decree?

Miss de Bourgh smiled slightly. "I was concerned that Darcy might marry me, so I confided in him about my fears and said I would only marry if he agreed that the union would be unconsummated." She let out a small sigh. "I wouldn't have minded living out my days with Darcy. He's a very kind man."

Elizabeth did her best to hide her surprise at that statement. Kind? More like arrogant.

"He didn't propose, mind you," Miss de Bourgh continued. "Nor do I believe he planned to propose. The next day, he somewhat awkwardly spoke on how he hopes to have a wife he loves and, more so, that they would be blessed with many children."

"That must have been an interesting conversation," Elizabeth mused, for Mr. Darcy did not strike her as possessing great conversational subtilty.

"I'm glad we had it. Darcy visits several times a year. Knowing his expectations makes those occasions more enjoyable, which, in turn, makes it easier to bear the isolation my mother insists on."

"Isolation?" Elizabeth looked about the vast, impeccably maintained grounds. In truth, they did have a strange, almost unsettling, empty feel. Where children should have played and laughed, ladies picnicked, and men boasted, only silence reigned. As if in answer to Elizabeth's dark thoughts, she noticed a swath of gray clouds on the horizon.

"Yes. It's a form of punishment on me, really." Miss de Bourgh grimaced. "And not difficult for her to achieve. Almost no one visits my mother."

"Why does she want to isolate you?" Elizabeth asked. "To force you to wed Mr. Darcy? I take it she doesn't know the two of you are in agreement not to marry." If Miss de Bourgh only socialized more, perhaps she would find a man who would accept her terms. Or, the romantic bit of Elizabeth's heart added, a man to actually fall in love with.

"She does not know," Miss de Bourgh said. "As a kindness to me, Darcy hasn't informed my mother that we will never wed."

"So, she endures a lack of society to ensure you marry Mr. Darcy," Elizabeth summed up. "Yet you and Mr. Darcy have agreed never to marry. It seems to me, Lady Catherine is mostly tormenting herself."

Miss de Bourgh offered another of her humorless smiles. "Undoubtedly, she is. At Rosings, I am limited, since it is improper for me to call repeatedly on people who won't return my calls, but that means she is also limited." She grimaced. "I think she accepted Mr. Collins for the living because she knew he would visit her, although how she can get any pleasure out of his visits I don't know."

Elizabeth brought a hand to her mouth, stifling a laugh.

Miss de Bourgh's eyes flew wide. "I'm sorry. He's your cousin and since he married your sister, he's your brother. I didn't mean to insult him."

Elizabeth dropped her hand to let her smile show. "You are not saying anything I haven't thought. Between the two of us, I've only known him for about six months and he is not my favorite conversationalist."

Miss de Bourgh's consternation melted into a relieved look.

Elizabeth gestured at the rapidly darkening sky. "We should head back," she said, turning toward the distant shelter of Rosings.

Miss de Bourgh nodded. They fell easily into step, though Elizabeth had to shorten her stride. She looked at Miss de Bourgh askance.

"Well, now I understand why you speak so little around your mother," Elizabeth said.

Miss de Bourgh shrugged. "It's a bit childish, I know, but nothing else is working. I want her to realize that keeping me isolated keeps her isolated. I still have my correspondence and my books. I have tentative friendships with a few of the wives of our tenants, even if I only see them when dispensing charity. Mrs. Jenkinson talks to me more in private, although she isn't a great conversationalist. And I talk to some of the servants. I'm not as isolated as my mother would like me to be."

"How long has this been going on?" Elizabeth asked. The wind picked up around them, swirling their hems.

"Almost a year. We used to spend the winter in London and I had many friends there, all of them married. One of my friends died in childbirth." She looked even more melancholy at that thought. "My other friends still write me. My mother thinks that if I'm isolated from them, I'll give in." Miss de Bourgh sighed. "At least she still permits my cousins to visit, so I have Darcy and Richard."

The wind gusted, bringing an almost wintery chill to the spring day and a few drops of rain. They increased their pace, Rosings growing ever larger before them. Gravel crunched beneath their rapid strides.

"Richard?" Elizabeth asked.

"Colonel Richard Fitzwilliam. He's the younger son of the Earl of Matlock, my mother's brother. He'll be visiting here soon… with Darcy. Richard has little money and is quite charming. I considered marrying him, thinking my mother would accept him as a substitute for Darcy." Miss de Bourgh shrugged. "He would be a reasonable choice, since he must marry for money, but he also wants to have children. Legitimate children."

"That is a common desire," Elizabeth said.

"I know, but I fear what others desire." Miss de Bourgh stole a quick glance at Elizabeth. "Did you ever think that, maybe if the women who are too small don't have children, there won't be any more small women? Like pigs."

"Pigs?" Elizabeth repeated, unsure if she should be scandalized or amused.

"My uncle, the earl, breeds pigs. He wants pigs that grow large quickly. He only breeds the big ones."

"Are you really comparing yourself to a small pig?" Elizabeth asked, incredulous even as amusement won out.

Miss de Bourgh cast her a quick grin as they hurried through the garden. "You're right. I don't mean to compare myself to a pig. I mean a sow. A small sow."

Elizabeth couldn't help but laugh. A large droplet splatted on her cheek, then the rain came down in earnest. Still chuckling, she grabbed Miss de Bourgh's hand and tugged her into a run. Hand in hand, both laughing and gasping for breath, they pelted for Rosings.

They were soaked and out of breath by the time they reached the shelter of the house. Miss de Bourgh tugged now, using their clasped hands to pull Elizabeth into a narrow, hidden servants' stairwell. Releasing Elizabeth to grasp her skirt, Miss de Bourgh headed up. Though the steep staircase was nearly dark, illuminated only by light filtering in through cracks, Elizabeth followed.

They came out in a wide, opulent hall. Unfaltering, Miss de Bourgh turned right and led the way past several widely-spaced and ornately carved doors. Elizabeth bundled her skirt close, keenly aware she dripped rainwater all over the plush red and gold carpet. Fortunately, if the gravel without had allowed any mud on their shoes, it seemed to have come off in the stairwell.

Miss de Bourgh opened the final door in the hall and looked over her shoulder. "My room," she said. "I'll lend you a gown, so we can both change."

Elizabeth followed Miss de Bourgh inside. A room far more understated than the others in the home met her interested eyes. A subtle combination of sage and cream, with the occasional silver accent, Miss de Bourgh's sitting room enveloped them in beauty and tranquility. Elizabeth couldn't help but be impressed. Pleased as well, for she'd begun to admire Miss de Bourgh and consider her a friend, and would have felt some slight disappointment to find her rooms as overdone as the rest of Rosings.

"Come, we can see what I have that might fit you while your gown dries," Miss de Bourgh said, crossing the sitting room to another door. "I'll ring for a maid, and tea."

Elizabeth trailed her hostess into the sleeping chamber. The soothing colors of the sitting room were repeated, joined by a dusky rose. A comfortable looking, somewhat small, canopied bed dominated one side of the room. An oversized, closed desk the other.

"You must write a great deal," Elizabeth said, for the desk stood nearly as large as the bed and appeared at least as prominent in the cozy room, occupying the prime position between two windows and adjacent to the fireplace.

"I do," Miss de Bourgh agreed. "Even before Mother's more recent restrictions. In my youth, I went through a sickly phase. I learned the value of careful correspondence then and have never lost the skill."

A maid came and helped them with their wet hair and gowns. About the time they were once again presentable, a slight commotion in the sitting room announced the arrival of tea. They returned to the outer room to find a tea service set out and two maids departing. Yet another appeared, proffering a silver tray.

"Sorry, Miss," the girl said as she handed over the correspondence. "It's only two letters today."

Elizabeth raised her eyebrows. Only two? Did Miss de Bourgh usually receive three or more letters every day? Were that the case, she wrote a great deal indeed.

Miss de Bourgh set aside the letters, chatting amiably over tea. As they finished the pot and talk dwindled, Elizabeth's dress hadn't yet returned from being dried by the large kitchen fires. Miss de Bourgh's gaze drifted more and more often to the envelopes.

"Go ahead and read them," Elizabeth said. "I can entertain myself with a book while you do, if you've any on hand?"

She was handed the same book of poetry she'd read to Jane. Elizabeth suppressed any outward show of displeasure and dutifully reread a few of the poems. At least she knew where in the volume the most tolerable were to be found.

Miss de Bough looked up from her letters soon enough. "If you'll excuse me, I shall file them."

"File them?" Elizabeth repeated.

Miss de Bourgh smiled slightly. "I'll show you."

They returned to the sleeping chamber and the desk there. Removing a key from her bodice, Miss de Bourgh opened the closed front to reveal rows of small drawers with alphabetic labels on them. She didn't put the letters into the drawers, instead placing them in a smaller, open file, likewise alphabetically delineated. Several others already waited there.

"The ones I haven't replied to yet," Miss de Bourgh said.

"Are all those drawers full of letters?" Elizabeth asked, amazed.

Miss de Bourgh pulled one open, then another, and another, each brimming. "They aren't all letters. I also keep copies of everything I send. Well, not really copies, but my first draft. But these are only my current correspondence. I store the other in the attic." She closed the drawers, hand trailing lingeringly down the fronts. "I live for these letters. Here, let me show you."

Miss de Bourgh took up one of the letters she'd received that day. She opened a different one of the drawers and showed Elizabeth several letters back. She handed that day's letter and the others to Elizabeth. "Read them. They aren't of a personal nature."

Elizabeth felt a bit awkward but complied. Miss de Bourgh's correspondent wrote on many topics, including the various people she visited or entertained, but there was also a running discussion of what was going on in parliament. Miss de Bourgh's replies were written to be drafts, with spaces between the lines for editing. They were heavily edited, and the editing greatly improved the flow of the words as well as the content. Miss de Bourgh's replies showed she read newspapers and understood the issues. Elizabeth did not consider herself to be uninformed, but she quickly ascertained that she paid less attention to the news than Miss de Bourgh did.

After quickly reading the letters, Elizabeth handed them back. "I would be pleased and honored if you would correspond with me after I leave," she said with all sincerity.

"I would enjoy that as well."

A loud knock sounded on the sitting room door.

"My mother," Miss de Bourgh said in a low voice as she slipped the letters back into place and closed the desk. There was a swish as the hall door opened. Movements quick, Miss de Bourgh locked her desk and slipped the key back into her bodice. She and Elizabeth turned to face the bedroom door as Lady Catherine barged in.

Her eyes narrowed when her gaze fell on Elizabeth. "You are still here? Why are you wearing Anne's dress?"

"Her dress is wet," Miss de Bourgh responded.

"Humph. Well, it looks hideous on you. You'll split the seams," Lady Catherine declared. She turned to face Miss de Bourgh. "I would have preferred to speak with you alone, but I must leave immediately."

Elizabeth dropped a curtsy, only too happy to take that cue to leave Lady Catherine's presence.

"Stay here," Lady Catherine snapped in an angry voice as Elizabeth took a step in the direction of the sitting room. "I will not have you leave, only to listen at the door. I will discover the truth." She then turned to look at her daughter. "Because you are too slow, I find I have business to attend to. I will be gone for two weeks. Mrs. Jenkinson is sufficient chaperone. She will know whom to get in touch with in case of emergency."

"May Miss de Bourgh entertain?" Elizabeth asked, her thoughts moving quickly ahead.

Lady Catherine turned her glare back on Elizabeth, studying her for a long moment before looking to Miss de Bourgh. "Certainly. Entertain whomever you wish, Anne. It's time you learn how to be a hostess. You will need such skills when you marry Darcy." Her wide, thin lips pulled into an almost feral smile. "You may even continue to entertain Miss Bennet, if she's still willing to speak with you."

Elizabeth raised her eyebrows, confused.

Lady Catherine met her gaze squarely. "Anne befriended you at my request, for the express purpose of discovering what lies between you and Darcy. She has been spying on you for me." With that, Lady Catherine turned and swept out of the room.

Miss de Bourgh cast Elizabeth a stricken look. "I didn't—that is, as I said, it's not like—" she stammered.

Elizabeth made a sweeping gesture. "Even in the breadth of our short acquaintance, I've come to know you well enough to believe you when you said you were not spying on me."

Miss de Bourgh went limp with relief. "I truly wasn't. When she asked what we spoke about, I told her I could not remember anything you said that would interest her. I only refrained from refusing to spy so that I could enjoy your company. Oh, and I did say that I didn't think you objected to Mr. Collins insisting you accept my invitations."

"That's true. I've enjoyed spending time with you." Elizabeth was not perturbed in the least. She recognized a pattern to how Miss de Bourgh dealt with her domineering matriarch. In many ways, it wasn't dissimilar to Elizabeth rising early to avoid breakfast with her mother, back at Longbourn, or any number of small decisions and daily actions she took to minimize exposure to Mrs. Bennet. "I understand."

"Thank you," Miss de Bourgh said. After a brief silence, where she seemed to gather herself, she opened her mouth to speak once more. "Why did you ask if I might entertain?"

"So that there would be no confusion over the issue if you do, which you ought, as you have this opportunity."

Miss de Bourgh appeared thoughtful. "We could invite the Collins over and then the two farmers wives I mentioned," she offered. "Or, maybe not. They might be uncomfortable at a dinner."

Elizabeth smiled. "I'm not going to discourage you from inviting them over, but you are not taking full advantage of your situation. Are you on calling terms with any pleasant neighbors?" If Miss de Bourgh was so desperate for friendship as to pretend to spy on her, Elizabeth had grander plans for her two weeks of freedom.

"Yes. Somewhat," Miss de Bourgh said, looking curious.

"Well then, drag Mrs. Jenkinson along and make some calls," Elizabeth suggested. "Is your cook up to serving a nice dinner tomorrow? There is still time to give invitations today."

Understanding dawned in Miss de Bourgh's eyes, followed by a slow smile. Elizabeth answered by broadening her own. With a sharp nod, Miss de Bourgh spun, reached for a bell pull, and rang for a maid.

Chapter Nineteen

Darcy, seated across from his cousin, Colonel Richard Fitzwilliam, gazed at nothing as his carriage moved ever closer to Rosings. They'd departed London days ahead of schedule, because disastrous spring rains and a damaged wheel had made them quite late the year before. Punctuality, however, wasn't Darcy's only consideration.

He couldn't remain in London a moment longer. Though the Bingleys had moved into their new London residence, he still saw them frequently. They entertained and went out. Darcy encountered them everywhere and was obliged to visit them often and reciprocate with invitations of his own.

Their company was torture. Rather, Jane Bingley's company was. Not through any fault of her own. Bingley's choice of bride proved to be just as warm, pleasant, lovely and intelligent as she'd seemed at first meeting. More than that, under Bingley's tutelage, she'd become more exuberant and talkative, better able to keep conversation moving freely.

No, the only problem with Mrs. Bingley, and, for that matter, the Gardiners, whom Darcy also saw regularly, was the constant reminder of Elizabeth. What had seemed a mild preoccupation, a slight tendency to dwell on the one woman to ever reject him, had turned into an obsession.

His mind was ever occupied with visions of her. Her flashing eyes. The slight smile she adopted when something sparked her sardonic wit. The candid way she regarded him, without a trace of the sycophantic or subservient. Her lithe form as she strode about. Tresses that shimmered by candlelight.

At first, Darcy had tried distraction, diving into managing his affairs, but to no avail. Next, he'd attempted distance from the Bingleys, by introducing Bingley to a socially sought-after couple, the Hyatts. Darcy's friendship with the earl, Lord Walter Hyatt, dated back to his time at Cambridge. The friendship began with Lord Walter's older brother, Matthew, who'd somewhat replaced George Wickham in Darcy's life, but Matthew, ever reckless, had joined the army and died in Spain.

With Matthew's death, Walter became heir, and later earl. Darcy was Walter's confidant when he was considering marrying Lady Clara, who was the daughter of an earl. The two married and were eminently happy, and very social. Darcy felt them the perfect match for the Bingleys.

A slight smile played across Darcy's face. His motives were not all selfish, however. Quite a few of Bingley's friends were no longer so enthusiastic as they once were. This seemed to stem less from a rejection of Mrs. Bingley's lower status than from the truth about their friendships. It seemed many of Bingley's friends had simply been out to marry him off to their relations. It pleased Darcy to introduce Bingley to an earl, for many of the same people had often sought that kind of introduction, and watch those false friends, those sycophants, clamor once more for Bingley's attention.

Although he'd succeeded in flushing out the false friends of Bingley, Darcy had hardly seen less of the Bingleys. Their group had simply widened to include the Hyatts and some of their friends. Mrs. Bingley and Mrs. Gardiner were still nearly always about, their presence reminding Darcy, in different ways, of Elizabeth.

Now, Elizabeth, the siren who called to him from afar, was in Kent. His cousin Anne had written as much, Mrs. Bingley offering unwitting and unneeded confirmation of Anne's words. The journey would not only rid Darcy of the torment offered by Mrs. Bingley and the Gardiners but put an end to all future discomfort.

For a moment in Elizabeth's presence would alleviate his condition. Of that, he was certain. The power Miss Elizabeth Bennet held over him was imagined. Conjured by his own mind. He'd simply permitted his thoughts to dwell over-long and too-fully on the incomprehensibility of a single woman who didn't wish to wed him. One who would climb out a window to avoid that fate.

Once with her again, he would surely find her not as lovely as recalled. Her mind less sharp than he imagined. Her manners less elegant.

Though, in honesty, he couldn't much fault her relations any longer. Three sisters respectably married, one to his dear friend. Two uncles that, while in trade, proved intelligent, interesting and poised. A father who must not be so neglecting as Darcy had first assumed, for his daughters seemed to be doing well in the world. In truth, if one recalled just how young the youngest two sisters were when first Darcy met them, and therefore allowed for improvement, only Elizabeth's mother and one aunt seemed silly, and the aunt only marginally so.

Really, there was nothing objectionable about Elizabeth's upbringing or standing. Nothing about her family that should prevent a man from wedding her. A man such as Darcy.

He gave his head a sharp shake. No. Not wedding her. She specifically did not wish to wed him, and his trip to Kent would show him that he did not wish to marry her, either.

"What seems to be the trouble, Darcy?" Richard asked. "You look as if someone kicked your horse."

Unwilling to lie outright, but with no intention of sharing his thoughts, Darcy instead said, "We are nearly to Aunt Catherine's. We are days early."

"Well, last spring we were days late." Richard shrugged. "She can't have it both ways."

"She can," Darcy disagreed somewhat sourly. "Either way, she can carp about poor planning."

"I wouldn't let it trouble you," Richard said. "She'll find some fault, no matter what. At least this way you have fair warning what the complaint will be."

"At least I sent Hawkins ahead," Darcy said, having sent his valet off after luncheon, when he realized they would experience no delays. "So we will not catch her unprepared."

"A wise choice. Aunt Catherine hates to be surprised," Richard observed.

Darcy nodded. He turned to the window and twitched the curtain back to find they trundled down a familiar lane. His gaze shifted in the direction of the parsonage, not visible from that point on the road. He closed the curtain, unable to think of any reason they might stop there.

Soon, they turned up the drive to Rosings, but stopped short of where Darcy expected. Sure they hadn't made the turn at the top of the drive, he reopened the curtains to peer out. Three carriages lined up before Rosings' grand entrance, absent and idle servants bespeaking of how long they'd waited or felt they had left to wait.

Darcy pulled the curtains fully back. He turned to Richard and nodded in the direction of the carriages. "Do you think something is wrong?"

Richard leaned forward to peer out. "No one seems agitated."

They alighted, strode down the line of carriages, and jogged up the grand steps, side by side. Before they reached the top, Lady Catherine's longtime, stoop-shouldered butler, Wilks, emerged. He bowed to them both.

"Mr. Darcy. Colonel Fitzwilliam," Wilks said, voice creaking. "Lady Catherine is still away. Miss de Bourgh asked me to advise you that she is entertaining in the formal garden. She says that if you wish to join her and her guests there, you may. Otherwise, I am happy to escort you to your rooms. She ordered your usual suites readied."

Darcy exchanged a bemused look with Richard.

"Still away?" Richard repeated, with emphasis on the first word. "Where did she go?"

"I cannot say, sir," Wilks replied.

"When will she return?" Darcy asked.

"I do not know, sir."

So, Darcy mused, Wilks knew where their aunt had gone, but was under orders not to divulge the information. Also, he didn't know when she might return.

"We did expect her back before your arrival, sirs," Wilks offered. He peered up at them through rheumy eyes. "But you are, if I may point out, quite early."

Richard's chuckle cut off Darcy's frown. "Aye, we are, Wilks. We do apologize."

"No apology is required, sir." Wilks said. "May I enquire as to your preference? The garden or your rooms?"

Richard shrugged. "I'm certainly not tired. By all means, let us meet Anne's guests. We know the way."

Without another word, they turned and trotted back down the steps, heading for a gravel path. Glancing back at the array of carriages, all respectable, Darcy's initial surprise and confusion only grew. Lady Catherine away? Anne... entertaining? He shook his head and lengthened his stride. This, he had to see.

The path wound around Rosings, into a grove of fruit trees resplendent with blossoms, and out again. It then turned and headed through several lines of sculpted shrubs before angling toward the formal garden, itself hemmed in by a wall of green. As they drew in sight of that final visual delineation, they heard laughter.

"Is that Anne laughing?" Darcy asked, nearly halting in surprise. Anne hadn't laughed since they were children. At least, not in his hearing.

"I think so," Richard replied, sounding equally incredulous.

As they neared the arched opening to the formal garden, a small child came running out. Darcy exchanged a startled look with Richard. He turned back to find a woman on the path, hurrying after the child, whom she scooped up. As one, Darcy and Richard halted.

"Beatrice, must you run away?" the woman, dressed too well to be a nursemaid, said. She settled the little girl on her hip and started to head back to the formal garden, then spotted them.

Squirming child and all, the woman turned to face them fully and dropped a deep, elegant curtsy. A smile made her already handsome face all the lovelier. "You must be Miss de Bourgh's cousins," she said. "She expected you later and said we would need to leave early, because she really should spend time with you."

"We wouldn't want to chase you away," Richard said.

Hearing barely concealed delight in Richard's tone, Darcy cast his cousin a quick look. Richard didn't appear to notice, attention riveted to the woman. Under that look, her eyes warmed to match her smile. Darcy assumed, and hoped, that a woman who had a husband wouldn't look at Richard that way, but the child appeared young and the woman didn't wear mourning.

"We promised we would leave when you arrived," the woman said, smiling at Richard as she adjusted the still squirming child.

Richard started forward. "Well, I for one enjoy meeting new people. I wouldn't have you depart on my account."

"We'll have to leave that up to Miss de Bourgh," the woman said as Richard reached her.

He gestured for her to walk with him into the hedged-in formal garden. "Yes, we will, but I wish it on record that I shall be pleased to follow this lovely child on her wandering, if you keep me company. I've been sitting too long in a carriage and would enjoy walking a bit."

"Her name is Beatrice," the woman said as they disappeared into the garden.

Darcy, unsure if he was amused, insulted or scandalized by Richard's ready abandonment, followed.

He entered the formal garden to the sight of men, women and children everywhere. Richard stood halfway across the lawn already, before Anne, who seemed to be introducing him to the woman with the child. She put Beatrice down, and the child immediately set off. Richard proffered his arm and he and his new acquaintance followed.

Darcy started in Anne's direction. Spotting him, she turned slightly and said something in the direction of a clump of females. The lot of them turned to face Darcy. He nearly tripped as he recognized Miss Elizabeth Bennet.

Darcy gathered himself and resumed a steady stride, aware of amusement in Anne's gaze. Elizabeth moved to Anne's side. The other women returned to their conversation, but kept peering his way, as did a group of men, alerted by their behavior. Unsure how Richard had avoided such scrutiny, Darcy marched forward.

He reached Anne and bowed, first to her, then to Elizabeth. "Anne, Miss Bennet."

"Darcy, Mother won't be pleased you've arrived early." To Darcy's surprise, Anne exchanged a look with Elizabeth, who's eyes danced merrily. "But I'm happy you've come," Anne continued. "Let me introduce you around. You already know Miss Bennet and Mrs. Collins."

Darcy nodded, although he hadn't noticed Mrs. Collins stood with the group of women until Anne pointed her out. He was introduced to several other men and women, all local, some of the names vaguely familiar from years spent visiting Rosings. Anne also told him that the woman with whom Richard had gone off to chase Beatrice was Mrs. Fortescue, a widow and half-sister to Mr. Collins. Darcy glanced about for them at that point, but they were nowhere to be seen.

"Mr. Darcy," Elizabeth said, stepping forward. "Would you care to walk as well?"

This forwardness from the woman who'd climbed out a window to avoid wedding him? Had she changed her mind? The sight of her, intelligent looking and lovely as ever despite his predictions, sparked an odd excitement at the thought. Keenly aware of the array of piercing gazes, he endeavored to conceal eagerness and surprise, and nodded. He offered his arm.

They set out at a firm pace, Elizabeth appearing to have no trouble matching his stride. Darcy was pleased. Usually, he had to mince his steps when he walked with a woman. He took them in a wide loop, never leaving sight of the others, but as far from them as the greenery-crafted walls of the garden permitted.

"I'm sorry to importune you in that way," Elizabeth said once they were out of hearing. "I must appear to be an outrageous flirt, but there is something of which you need to be aware. I brought the letter you gave me to Kent. It was locked in my trunk in my writing box, among other letters, but my key was in a drawer. Your letter disappeared."

"I can write you another, if you wish," Darcy said, somewhat confused by the intensity of worry in her voice. Did she desperately require the assistance his letter might bring? Was she in straits? Would marriage to him free her of them?

She shook her head. "That's not necessary. My concern is that the letter was taken."

Darcy shrugged. "It is not really useful to anyone else."

Elizabeth halted. She turned to face him, expression annoyed. "That isn't the problem." She drew in a breath. "I think Mr. Collins took it and gave it to Lady Catherine."

Understanding hit Darcy. He cast a quick look about, as if his aunt, possessed of a fit of rage, might spring from anywhere. "Where is she?"

"I don't know," Elizabeth said. She glanced about as well, then plastered a smile on her face. "People are looking. Don't appear so grim."

"My apologies," he murmured. He couldn't muster a smile, but he eased away his glower. "You have no idea where my aunt is or why? It is not like her to leave, especially without Anne and so near a visit from us."

Elizabeth shook her head, silken curls brushing her shoulders. "I was with Miss de Bourgh when Lady Catherine barged in and said she had to leave for two weeks. That was a dozen days ago."

"That might have nothing to do with the letter."

Another head shake. "When she met me, she seemed already to dislike me. She questioned me quite arduously about my dealings with you in Hertfordshire." Worry shadowed Elizabeth's eyes. "I've no idea how she might have interpreted your letter, but I have the impression unfavorably."

Darcy couldn't refute that, but what, really, could Lady Catherine do? She would hardly tell anyone that he'd written Elizabeth such a letter. The scandal would cause him to have to propose. Of a certainty, Darcy knew his aunt would wish to avoid that. "We should know more when she returns."

Smile strained, Elizabeth nodded. "True. And we should rejoin the others. We don't want to start any rumors."

They resumed walking. When they were again within earshot of the gaggle of females, Darcy said, "I am sorry, but I believe Mr. Bingley probably will give up his lease to Netherfield Park. He and Mrs. Bingley are enjoying London overmuch and I believe they plan to summer by

157

the sea."

"Jane said as much in her letters, but I was hoping you might have a different insight," Elizabeth said, with no indication his ruse startled her or caught her off guard in the slightest. "I shall miss them sorely in Hertfordshire this summer. But I've occupied enough of your time," she added. Taking her hand from his arm, she dipped a curtsy.

Darcy bowed as she walked away. He was then approached by a man he'd met briefly in church when staying at Rosings before. The man's wife was talking to Anne. Elizabeth rejoined the group in which Mrs. Collins stood. For the first time, Darcy realized that Mr. Collins was there. Fortunately, there were enough people around that they seemed to be keeping the unpalatable clergyman occupied.

After about half an hour, all the guests left, but the next day was full of company, and the day thereafter. Richard spent a great deal of time with Mrs. Fortescue. At first, Darcy was surprised. He'd never imagined Richard would court someone with a child. But Richard appeared to be delighted to spend time with Beatrice, and her lovely mother. Anyone with eyes could read their mutual interest. What Darcy couldn't read, or rather wished he were unable to read, was Elizabeth's lack of interest in him.

Chapter Twenty

Although she had a room full of guests in happy occupation in another wing of the manor, Anne stood alone in Rosings' vast, archaic library. She held a letter from her mother, the instrument by which she'd been wrenched from her visitors and sent fleeing for a moment of solitary contemplation in a room which had come to mean much to her in recent days. Unmistakable on the letter in Anne's hand, Lady Catherine's firm, rather blocky script stated that she was on her way home. Unfortunately, Anne's mother hadn't seen fit to date the missive.

Anne let out a long sigh. Over the past several glorious weeks, nearly a month, each time she'd received a letter from her mother, she'd hoped it would be another reporting further delay. Until the one she held, each page had answered that wish.

Anne's hand closed over the thick paper, crumpling it just as she had the previous six. Calling them letters did a disservice to the term. They were notes, hardly worth paying for, except each one had told Anne that she would have a few more days to enjoy the company of her neighbors. Along with the lack of dates, not a single one of Lady Catherine's correspondences had hinted at a return address.

Anne was aware that Mrs. Jenkinson knew where Lady Catherine had gone. Perhaps even why. Everything was so convivial, though, everyone behaving well and getting on so splendidly, that Anne didn't want to disrupt the general buoyancy by forcing a confession. Especially when, in truth, she cared little what her mother was up to. With Darcy there, Lady Catherine couldn't have gone to drag him to the altar. Nothing else could be dire enough to matter.

Now, the worst had come to pass. Soon, Lady Catherine would return to Rosings, and Anne's plans hadn't yet come to fruition. Not that her mother could end them, but she could, and would, hinder them.

Elizabeth would leave soon, and Darcy had apparently yet to realize he loved her, because he hadn't proposed, no matter how much Anne threw them together. Worse than Darcy's obliviousness to his own infatuation, Anne wasn't certain Elizabeth loved him back. Each time he said something pompous, as he was frightfully apt to do, Anne could feel Elizabeth judging him and knew that by Miss Bennet's estimation, Darcy came up short. There were times when Anne wished she could stomp on his foot to get him to be quiet.

At first, she'd thought to discourage the union, for she hadn't found anyone to take Darcy's place, to keep Lady Catherine from devoting all her will to Anne wedding. A slow, secret smile touched Anne's lips. More recently, though, she'd found the answer to her needs. Her focus had changed to securing a place for Elizabeth in her life, as she'd become one of Anne's dearest friends. Her role as Mrs. Collins' sister would have Elizabeth visit perhaps once every five years. As Darcy's bride, Anne would see her often. Anne… and her intended.

"I know that smile," a man's voice said. "It means you're thinking of me."

Anne brought her attention to the library doorway to find Darcy's valet, Hawkins, framed there. Her smile grew. "I was, and how you've come into my life to fulfil my dreams."

Hawkins offered a deep bow. "I live to serve, my lady."

Anne chuckled, an expression of amusement she endeavored to copy from Elizabeth. "Yes, you do, but not once we're wed." She headed toward him, the smile leaving her face as she proffered the crumpled page. "We'll have to go more carefully now. My mother is on her way. All of the servants here are her spies."

Hawkins nodded. "I am aware, Miss." He hesitated, as he always did when unsure where his role of servant left off and his role as her betrothed began. "Shall I warn Mr. Darcy of your mother's impending arrival?"

Anne shook her head, pressing the page into his hand. "I will. In fact, I'll tell him, Richard and Elizabeth right now. I should be getting back to my guests. They've likely begun to wonder at my absence."

Hawkins nodded, never one to waste words. In accord, they turned and set off down the hall. Anne knew Hawkins would drop back, all but disappear, if they heard anyone approach.

"Did you happen to survey the parlor?" she asked.

"Colonel Fitzwilliam is still in deep conversation with Mrs. Fortescue," Hawkins confirmed.

At least one of Anne's plans seemed to be progressing well. She liked Mrs. Fortescue, who had a home and some savings, and would enjoy her as a cousin. Furthermore, Richard's attachment would keep Lady Catherine from settling on him for Anne the moment Darcy made it clear he wouldn't marry her. Assuming he ever acknowledged his feelings enough to pursue Elizabeth. "And Elizabeth? And Darcy?"

Hawkins' gaze briefly met Anne's, askance. "When last I looked, Mr. Darcy sat alone. Miss Bennet, though not appearing interested, conversed with Mr. Collins."

Again, Anne felt Hawkins' hesitation. She had little difficulty guessing the impetus. "Don't tell me," she cautioned.

"No, I cannot," he agreed, but his whole mien, his anguished tone, bespoke of how much he wished to.

There was something between Darcy and Elizabeth, beyond Darcy's unrequited fascination. Anne had guessed as much. Something in how he always watched her, and she avoided looking at him. Knowing them both as she did, Anne couldn't conceive of anything too untoward. Whatever this thing, she was aware that it countered her attempts to bring them together. She also knew that Hawkins was privy to it but didn't wish to break his oath of service to Darcy by speaking.

Anne respected that. She had extracted oaths of her own from Hawkins. How could she ask him to keep those, yet break the ones given Darcy? It was not, after all, as if their secret engagement sprang from a place of deep passion. Rather, it was the product of practicality and honesty. Passion might move a man to break vows. Honesty never would.

They walked together in easy silence. Since she'd found Hawkins in the library in the middle of the night, coat folded over the back of a sofa and a book of Shakespeare's sonnets in hand, Anne had felt unwavering kinship. She'd known of Hawkins, or at least his existence, all her life. Looking past his status as her uncle's and now Darcy's valet, caught up in her newfound verboseness, Anne had sat and discussed those poems, the very ones she'd come to the library to claim that night, at length.

While they spoke, she'd realized that Hawkins was the consummate gentleman. Unwaveringly loyal. Unfailingly honest. Polite to the core. In short, Hawkins was perfect.

He'd been shocked by her proposal, though little emotion had shown. Anne recalled holding her breath, heart pounding, waiting for his answer. Finally, flashing a never before seen smile, he'd informed her that honor and society dictated he could never refuse a lady.

They couldn't marry immediately, although Anne would like to. Mr.

Collins would refuse to read the banns and neither she nor Hawkins had the knowledge or influence to obtain a special license, but they could, and did, make plans… and promises.

Anne glanced at him now, aware he would soon leave her side. They neared the end of the hall. Left lay the parlor and her guests. When they reached the corner, Hawkins held back. Shoulders back, head high and gaze forward, Anne went left. In a few moments, she knew, Hawkins would go right.

She entered the parlor, full of local guests, to find things with her cousins and Elizabeth remained as Hawkins reported. Darcy still sat alone, so fixated on Elizabeth that he didn't appear to notice Anne's return. Likewise, Richard was too engaged bouncing Beatrice on one knee while he talked with Mrs. Fortescue to look Anne's way. Elizabeth, where she stood, literally cornered by Mr. Collins, not only spotted Anne but turned pleading eyes on her.

Anne waved her over, wending her way deeper into the room. She watched, amused, as Elizabeth tendered her apology to Mr. Collins and stepped around him. He turned, and his gaze found Anne. He bowed slightly, then made to follow Elizabeth. His wife adroitly stepped in his way.

Elizabeth reached Anne's side with a smile. "I was beginning to wonder after you."

"My apologies. I received a letter which disturbed me enough to require a few moment's solitude."

"Is all well?" Genuine concern shone in Elizabeth's eyes.

"Yes, everything is perfectly well. It's only, my mother is—"

"What is the meaning of this?" Lady Catherine's voice boomed across the parlor. "Who gave you all permission to enter my home?"

Anne grimaced, then cleared her expression into blandness as she turned to face her mother. "You said I could entertain, Mother," she said in a mild voice.

Lady Catherine, Rosings' butler hovering behind her, glared about the room from where she nearly filled the width of the doorway. "So I did, and so Mrs. Jenkinson reported you were." Her eyes narrowed as she glowered at Mrs. Jenkinson, who went red. "However, I was not informed, and never dreamed, that you would keep sullying our home with that harlot."

She swiveled back to face Anne as she spoke. One ponderous arm rose, pointing. For a moment, Anne thought her mother's anger, disgust and disparaging label were aimed at her. Then, she realized Lady Catherine pointed at Elizabeth.

"I will not have that hussy in my home," Lady Catherine bellowed.

Gasps sounded. Anne realized one of them had issued from her. She gaped at her mother, who lowered her arm but continued to glare.

"That is enough," Darcy snapped, appearing between Elizabeth and Anne's mother. "Aunt Catherine, I do not know what you have heard, but guard your tongue. This will not go as you wish."

"This will indeed go as I wish," Lady Catherine angled her many chins ceilingward to look down her nose at Darcy. "This hussy's hold over you shall end, and you will marry Anne."

"Lady Catherine," Elizabeth's voice, though not loud, was firm as she stepped to Darcy's side. "I believe Mr. Darcy is correct. Please consider containing your emotions. I'd be happy to discuss whatever is troubling you in private."

Anne heard an undercurrent of desperation in Elizabeth's words. Shocked, she eyed her friend askance. Lady Catherine couldn't actually have found something... untoward in Elizabeth's past? That made no sense. Why would Darcy obsess over her and she ignore him if she had aught to hide?

"No, this will be done publicly," Lady Catherine said.

"Mother," Anne began, stepping up to Darcy's other side.

"Everyone here should know the sort of woman they have been fraternizing with," Lady Catherine continued over Anne. "Miss Bennet is unfit for this house. She schemed to force a proposal from Darcy by locking him in a library with her. He climbed out a window to avoid being found there with her, so she settled for blackmailing him into writing a letter granting her carte blanche in seeking favors from his associates, threatening to reveal their few moments of solitude to all." Lady Catherine sucked in a huge breath. "Well, now we know that you were alone together, and we know who perpetrated it, and we know Darcy is not to blame, nor honor bound to anything, and you, Miss Elizabeth Bennet, are a harlot."

"Lady Catherine," Darcy snapped, voice ice-hard with anger.

Lady Catherine jabbed her finger at Elizabeth again. "You will leave this house immediately, never to return. You will go to the parsonage and pack, to leave Kent now. My carriage will take you home, with proper escorts. It will be better comfort than you deserve, but I do not want anyone to say that you were sent away in a way that endangered you." Her arm came around as she tapped her chest. "I will publicize your behavior to ensure you are never permitted in polite company again."

Elizabeth stalked up to Lady Catherine, looking incredibly small before her girth. "I will leave," she said in that same quiet, assured voice. "And please believe that I do not wish to ever return. Not while you reside here. But remember this, my lady, I attempted to avoid this fate. You have brought it upon me."

With that, Elizabeth pushed past Lady Catherine, who, expression slack with surprise, pivoted to let her pass. She swung back as Darcy left Anne's side, obviously intent on following Elizabeth.

Lady Catherine leveled a hard look on Darcy. "If you follow her, you will never be allowed in Rosings again. I will not let you marry Anne."

Anne couldn't see much of Darcy's face, but his shoulders were thrown back and his stance firm as he looked down at her mother. "I can only guess where you heard such lies," he said, voice thick with iciness. "But we shall address that, and how to make up for what you have done, later. For now, rest assured, I will not be marrying Anne. I will be marrying Miss Bennet. This time, I will not permit her to refuse me."

"Refuse you?" Lady Catherine repeated, brow knitting. "She tried to trap you."

Darcy shook his head. "A different person locked me in the library in an attempt to force me into wedlock. Miss Bennet saved me from that fate. In anger, that other person locked Miss Bennet in the library with me. I immediately made it plain that I would marry her, as honor dictated. She, in turn, climbed out a second story window to avoid accepting my offer."

Even from where she stood, Anne imagined that, in the silence that met that declaration, she could hear Darcy grind his teeth.

"So, you see, Aunt," Darcy's voice dripped ire, "Miss Bennet wished nothing more than for the situation to be kept secret. She has absolutely no desire to wed me. Now, she will be forced to do so."

"A different woman tried to force your hand and then locked you in with Miss Bennet?" Lady Catherine asked, expression stunned. "Who?"

"I think you know who," Darcy snapped. "Now, step aside."

"No, Miss Bingley would not lock you and Miss Bennet in

together," Lady Catherine said. "She wanted to marry you. She wouldn't lie. Not to me."

Miss Bingley's name was clearly audible in the whispers that sped around the room.

Darcy shook his head. "I think you will find Miss Bingley would and did lie to you," he said in a tone of disgust.

"No," Lady Catherine screeched. "She did not. You are the one lying. Why, I don't know. My revelation has set you free of Miss Bennet's blackmail. You do not have to pretend any longer, Darcy. You are free to marry Anne."

Darcy reached out, as if he might lift Anne's mother and move her aside.

"I say, Darcy," Richard called.

Darcy turned a glare on their cousin.

Around the room, people shifted. Someone whispered, the words unintelligible. Anne suddenly, acutely, felt the weight of humanity in the room. With the abundance and mixture of the gathering, there would be no way to keep the scene her mother had created from being repeated all over Kent. Quite possibly all over London. Anne grimaced on Elizabeth's behalf.

"Yes?" Darcy growled.

"Do you mean us to believe that Miss Bennet climbed out a window to avoid marrying you, rather than you climbing out one to avoid marrying her?" Richard asked.

Anne glanced back to see his look intreated. He was, she realized, endeavoring to help. His question should enable Darcy to point out a simple, logical flaw in her mother's story. Darcy would never abandon a woman, even one who'd trapped him. His honor wouldn't permit it, as Miss Bingley, the one who'd really attempted to trap him, must have known.

"Not only did she climb out a window, she used a dull pen knife to spend hours fashioning curtains into a rope in order to do so," Darcy said grudgingly. "As for me, I only climbed out after her, to see she got back inside safely. I would never run from the honorable course." He glanced back at Lady Catherine. "And I am insulted you would so easily believe that I did."

Following his gaze, Anne saw the uncertainty on her mother's face. More whispers pushed back the silence. Fabric rustled.

Richard's chuckle broke through the mounting tension. Anne

turned to look at him again, where he sat beside Mrs. Fortescue, a wide-eyed Beatrice in her arms.

"You find this amusing?" Darcy asked.

"After all the women who have chased you, it must be difficult for you to realize you're going to end up marrying one who emphatically demonstrated she doesn't want to marry you," Richard said, though his expression was apologetic.

Anne couldn't let that stand. She wished Darcy and Elizabeth to wed but wanted them to find happiness. "Or emphatically demonstrated that she doesn't want to be forced to marry him," she put in quickly. "Which is not quite the same thing."

Surprise flittered across Darcy's face, as if he hadn't considered that possibility.

"It is neither of those things," Lady Catherine said, voice raised. "You all witnessed Miss Bennet's lack of denial." She raised hands beseechingly to Darcy. "It is all out in the open now. Why do you insist on protecting this woman's reputation?"

"Because she has done nothing reprehensible," Darcy stated. "And while we are revealing all, Aunt Catherine, why not tell us what set you looking into my and Miss Bennet's past association?"

A shock went through Anne. Her letters. She leaned forward. Would her mother confess, before all, to breaking into Anne's desk and reading her correspondence?

Lady Catherine's cheeks became two red cherries, a development Anne had never witnessed before. "Mr. Collins gave me the letter you wrote saying you owe Miss Bennet a favor and suggesting anyone should aid her if she so required."

Another gasp rippled through the room.

Even as Anne felt a wave of relief that her obsessive letter keeping wasn't to blame, she was aware, peripherally, of people moving away from Mr. and Mrs. Collins. Anne whirled to face Mr. Collins. "How did you get the letter?" She narrowed her gaze. "It doesn't seem like Miss Bennet to show it to you." Mrs. Collins cringed, evoking Anne's sympathy, but she kept Mr. Collins pinned with a glare.

"She is my relation," Mr. Collins said with an officious sniff. "She is under my roof. It is my duty to take care of her. To do so, I must know as much information about her as possible. We haven't known each other well or long, so I had to find out about her."

"For heaven's sake, man, she wouldn't have left that letter out.

Where did you have to look to find it, among her under garments?" Richard asked incredulously. "And then, once you found that letter, you showed it to someone else? You violated her privacy and gave that information to a third party."

"There was nothing with her under garments," Mr. Collins said. "The note was with her letters. It was my duty to give it to my patroness, which supersedes my duty to family."

The murmuring in the room swelled to a low babble. Mrs. Collins turned her face, stained red, toward the floor, though Anne doubted she had anything to do with Mr. Collins' snooping. At least, no more so than having invited her sister to visit.

"Darcy," Lady Catherine roared over the din. The room fell quiet once more. "Your duty to family is more important than your duty toward this woman. Pay her off. Regardless of the truth, she will be happy to back out of this marriage for a few thousand pounds. That type of woman can always be bought," Lady Catherine said with confidence.

"Miss Bennet already demonstrated she cannot be bought. I admire that in her," Darcy said. He cocked his head slightly to the side, as if he sighted something in the hall beyond Lady Catherine. "Hawkins?" Darcy asked, tone confused.

"I believe I am required, sir," Hawkins said, slipping around Lady Catherine and into the room. He gave Anne the barest of winks, the gesture so quick even she wasn't sure she'd witnessed it.

"I do not know who sent for you," Lady Catherine said, "but perhaps you can shed light on this. Darcy is mistaken in what he thinks happened at Netherfield Park concerning Miss Bennet."

"I have no direct knowledge of an incident with Miss Bennet," Hawkins said.

"Hah," Lady Catherine barked. "If he does not know, nothing happened. Servants always know."

Darcy shook his head. "Hawkins, please inform Lady Catherine of everything you are directly aware of that happened on the evening before we left Netherfield Park and the next day."

Hawkins nodded, a glimmer of amusement buried deep in his eyes. "Mr. Darcy rang for me quite late. He said Miss Bingley had tried to get him to compromise her but had not succeeded. As we could hardly depart in the middle of the night, he conveyed his concern that she would try to sneak into his bedroom that night, being aware that we would certainly leave the following day and likely in possession of the room's key. We changed places. I slept in his bed and he slept in the servant quarters."

"I knew it couldn't be a bet," Richard crowed. "I heard that rumor, Darcy. I should have realized something was amiss."

Anne saw Darcy wince at that but hadn't any notion what a bet had to do with Hawkins' recounting.

Hawkins looked to Darcy, who gave a miniscule nod.

"Some time later, Miss Bingley entered and climbed into bed with me," Hawkins stated.

New gasps filled the room. Voices raised in everything from shock to disbelief.

Hawkins waited, expression bland, for a semblance of silence. "I chased her away, but she left her slippers," he continued. "The next morning, Mr. Darcy asked me to confirm what happened. Miss Bingley admitted locking Miss Bennet and Mr. Darcy in the library and to climbing into bed with me, thinking I was Mr. Darcy."

"How dare you sully Miss Bingley's name this way?" Lady Catherine roared at Hawkins. "Darcy, I demand you dismiss this man immediately."

Anne tensed, but Hawkins appeared serene. His gaze slid briefly to hers, full of sardonic amusement, before returning to some point high up on the wall opposite him.

"Dismiss Hawkins?" Darcy said to Anne's mother. "I am not the one who brought Miss Bingley's name into this. You did."

"Not that you're honor bound to protect Miss Bingley," Richard said. "Perhaps for Bingley's sake, but the lies she told Aunt Catherine, the trouble she's stirred up for Miss Bennet, those negate any obligation to her."

Lady Catherine opened her mouth for another bellow, but Anne had had enough. She strode forward, the movement catching her mother's, Darcy's and Hawkins' attention. All three turned to look at her, Lady Catherine's mouth snapping closed.

"You like helping people, Mother," Anne said in a hard, overly saccharine voice as she reached Lady Catherine. "And oh, how you've helped. You have created an unhappy situation for my dear friend Miss Bennet and tormented Darcy. In fact, I do believe you've besmirched his honor. You are fortunate you aren't a man, or he would be forced to challenge you."

Her mother stared down at her, expression shocked.

"And for my part, I agree with Miss Bennet," Anne continued. "They did not have to marry. Now they do. You are responsible for the marriage." Anne smiled sweetly. "You helped, as you always do, and I hope you are happy with your interference. I know I am. Miss Bennet will be a delightful addition to my cousins."

"Miss Bingley said that Miss Bennet locked the door," Lady Catherine protested, but her voice was weak now. "I paid her to break her silence. I had to go to London and back to acquire enough funds, her price was so high."

"I don't think you got your money's worth," Richard said somewhere behind Anne. "And I doubt you'll be able to get it back."

Lady Catherine looked past Anne. Her wide-eyed gaze traversed the room. Her face turned red with white, molten splotches. "Get out," she said, voice cracking. She cleared her throat. "Leave, all of you," she said, louder. "Out," she repeated on a screech. She stepped into the parlor and pointed to the hall.

Anne looked at Darcy, only force of will preventing her from seeking Hawkins' gaze. Darcy shrugged. Anne nodded, and led the way out. Everyone else in the room, even the servants and Mrs. Jenkinson, followed.

Chapter Twenty-One

Darcy followed Anne as she marched to the foyer. There he, Richard and Hawkins broke from the crowd. Servants materialized, laden with outerwear. Anne moved to the door, a sort of reverse receiving line forming as she bid each party a brisk farewell. Mr. Collins, broad face livid, dragged Mrs. Collins and Mrs. Fortescue, Beatrice in her arms, around the line of people and out the door.

"Hawkins, please pack," Darcy said.

"Ask my man to do likewise, Hawkins," Richard added. "I'll go order the carriages made ready." With a nod, he jogged away.

"Will that be all, sir?" Hawkins asked Darcy.

"I will come up and get my coat and hat," Darcy said. "Once the carriages are loaded and ready, meet me at the parsonage. Miss Bennet must be nearly there by now. I will ride over to speak to her."

"Yes, sir," Hawkins said. Eyes bright, he added, "Good luck, sir."

Darcy grimaced. "I am afraid I will need it."

"Hawkins," Anne called as Darcy and his valet made to head for his rooms. "Please ask my maid to pack as well." Her attention shifted to Darcy. "I assume there is room for me in your carriage?"

Darcy suppressed his surprise and nodded. "Of course." He felt no compunction about agreeing. Anne was his cousin and well past her majority. If she wished to depart Rosings, then she certainly could. Besides which, Lady Catherine had ordered them all to leave.

It didn't take Darcy long to reach the parsonage. He hoped he'd beaten the Collins there, even though he had to wait until his horse was saddled and they'd taken the direct route, across the lawn. Darcy brought all his deep-seated decorum to bear as he stood at the parsonage door and knocked, then waited. What he truly wished to do was throw open the door and race inside. It felt like an eternity since Elizabeth had strode from Lady Catherine's parlor.

What must Elizabeth be thinking? She would have walked the whole way from Rosings to the parsonage alone. Did she wonder why he hadn't followed? Did she worry about the scene unfolding behind her? Worst, did she fear he hadn't upheld her honor? The door opened to Elizabeth, pale but composed.

"The maids are out?" Darcy asked, then wished he could take back such an irrelevant, almost judgmental query.

"One," she said. "The other is packing my belongings. I told her I would answer. I suspected it would be you. I also told her to have my trunks taken outside the moment they're packed." She stepped away from the door. "The parlor?"

Darcy nodded, feeling suddenly awkward. She led the way down the hall and past the foot of the staircase, then slipped into the small room. Darcy hovered in the doorway. Elizabeth turned back, expression enquiring.

"Should we call for a maid?" Darcy asked.

A sad smile touched Elizabeth's lips. "I don't think it will matter."

She made no move to sit, so he crossed the room to stand before her. He took in her lovely eyes, her silken curls. Delicate features that, even tense with worry, were aristocratically fine.

She interested him. Intrigued him more than any other woman he'd met, but did he love her? Certainly, she filled his thoughts, day and night. The pain of harming her in any way, even besmirching her reputation, stabbed through him like a physical blade. If he considered the idea of any other man possessing her, his vision dimmed with rage.

But was that love? They rarely spoke. Not since the library. Mostly because, even though Elizabeth was often at Rosings, she'd avoided him studiously. He wasn't so obtuse as not to have noticed. Could a man go through life loving a woman who did not love him?

Perhaps he should try to buy her off, as his aunt suggested. He would be generous, of course. Ten thousand pounds. No. Twenty thousand, which would involve selling some profitable holdings, but he wanted Elizabeth to be as wealthy as Miss Bingley.

No one who mattered would blame him for not marrying Elizabeth. She was nothing. A nobody.

She tipped her head to the side, looking up at him. "Mr. Darcy?"

Her tone held question, but not worry. She'd no inkling of his unworthy thoughts. Complete faith in his intention to do right by her, to keep his word, suffused her expression. And he was a gentleman. He had standards of behavior.

Besides, when she tipped her head and looked up at him that way, she was beguiling. He said, "We were not able to keep the incident secret. We must marry."

Lips pressed into a flat line, which he considered to be rather a shame, she nodded. "I concede."

Darcy winced. Concede. The word could mean she agreed. In the context of his statement, it did mean she agreed. He couldn't help but feel it also meant she'd surrendered. Given up on fighting the inevitable.

Any other woman, Miss Bingley included, would consider marrying Darcy a triumph. For Elizabeth to marry him, it was capitulation. He doubted she chose the word carefully, but somewhere in her mind, it was a defeat for her to marry him.

"Miss, your trunks are ready," a voice said behind Darcy. "We had them taken out."

"Thank you," Elizabeth said, looking past Darcy. She mustered a smile.

A smile for a maid, but all Darcy got was, 'I concede.' He frowned, listening to the girl's footsteps patter away down the hall. "My carriage will arrive soon. Richard and Anne will depart with me. May I assume you wish to as well, or would you prefer to take Lady Catherine's proffered carriage?" Assuming his aunt recalled the offer and had the presence of mind to send the conveyance.

"Miss de Bourgh will accompany us?" Elizabeth smiled again, the expression suffused with more warmth this time. "I would be more than pleased to ride with the three of you. I don't wish anything to do with Lady Catherine ever a—"

A loud bang sounded, the parsonage door being flung inward. "Why is Mr. Darcy's horse here? Are those Cousin Elizabeth's trunks in the yard?" Mr. Collins voice demanded. "Well?"

"We walked over with you," Mrs. Collins said tentatively in an obvious effort to remind him that she had no more knowledge than he did.

"How we would know anything about that horse that you don't is beyond my ability to fathom," Mrs. Fortescue said, voice at least as strident as her half-brother's. "As for the trunks, if anyone should recognize Miss Bennet's luggage, it should be you."

Darcy cast Elizabeth a quick look, finding her gaze narrowed in anger. Footsteps in the foyer brought Mrs. Fortescue, her daughter in her arms, into view. Surprise filtered across her face at the sight of them, but she quickly mastered it. She took up a firm stance outside the parlor door, rocking her child soothingly.

"You will not speak to me thus in my own home," Mr. Collins said. "I should cast you and that child out of this house."

Beatrice shrank against her mother in reaction to Mr. Collins' angry voice.

"That would suit me perfectly," Mrs. Fortescue snapped.

"Cousin Elizabeth," Mr. Collins called, still out of sight in the foyer. "Where is she?" his nasally voice demanded.

"Does it matter?" Mrs. Collins ventured.

"This is my house. In the absence of Mr. Bennet, she is my responsibility," Mr. Collins declared. "I will see her take the carriage Lady Catherine promised to send. She will be conducted back to Hertfordshire."

Mrs. Fortescue turned slightly. She made a shooing gesture at Darcy and Elizabeth. Darcy stared at her, unsure what she wanted of them. Lifting Beatrice high enough to block view of her face from the foyer, she turned to them and mouthed, 'go out the window.'

Elizabeth clasped Darcy's hand. She yanked. Darcy let her lead him across the room, frowning. He was running from Collins?

Mrs. Fortescue lowered Beatrice. "She's almost certainly in her room."

"I'll go look," Mrs. Collins quiet, worried voice offered.

They reached the window. With her free hand, Elizabeth yanked open the curtains.

"No, I will look," Mr. Collins said. "I'll check all the rooms. She might be using this opportunity to rummage through my things. In her malice, she might destroy my latest sermon." He yelled the name of his manservant and cook, telling the cook to keep Miss Bennet from leaving through the kitchen. The manservant was given similar instructions for the front door.

Darcy could hear a heavy tread on the staircase. In moments, Mr. Collins' legs came into view over Mrs. Fortescue's shoulder. He tugged his hand from Elizabeth's.

"I will not run from Mr. Collins," Darcy stated, not bothering to whisper.

Mrs. Fortescue bustled into the room, cradling Beatrice. "Quickly."

Behind her, Mrs. Collins appeared. Her eyes flew wide at the sight of them. "You're going out the window?" she asked.

Behind him, Darcy heard Elizabeth push open the window. "This

174

is ridiculous," he stated.

Mrs. Collins hurried forward. "Please? Mr. Collins is so angry. I've never seen him like this before. Couldn't you simply go?"

"He wouldn't even permit me to speak with Colonel Fitzwilliam, when he came across the lawn," Mrs. Fortescue added. "My brother flew into a rage. I really think he might have struck the colonel if Mrs. Collins and I hadn't pulled him away."

Darcy looked between the three women.

"Please?" Elizabeth said quietly. "It will be easier for everyone."

Darcy shrugged. He didn't like the idea, but confronting Collins would gain little, especially when Darcy wasn't really in the right. Elizabeth wasn't of age and he hadn't her father's consent. Repugnant as it might be, Mr. Collins truly was her guardian in the present circumstance.

"Fine," Darcy said. "But this time, I will go first, and help you out."

A smile tipped up Elizabeth's lips. Amusement chased some of the worry from her eyes. She nodded. "Certainly."

She turned to Mrs. Fortescue and gave her a quick hug. Above, they could hear Mr. Collins stomping about. Elizabeth then hugged her sister, and kissed Beatrice.

"I'll miss you all," she said.

Mrs. Collins looked as if she might cry but offered only a nod.

Mrs. Fortescue smiled, though the expression seemed forced. "Please tell Colonel Fitzwilliam…" She faltered. "Tell him, I look forward to someday learning what he might have said to me."

Elizabeth nodded. "I will."

"We'll keep Mr. Collins occupied until you're away," Mrs. Collins said, firming her expression.

Darcy bowed, then turned and climbed out the window. As the small parlor stood only slightly higher than ground level, he didn't have far to go. He turned back and held up his arms for Elizabeth.

She sat on the sill and turned, swinging her feet free. He took her by the waist and lifted her down, pleased by the lithe, warm feel of her. A blush sprang to life in her cheeks and he realized he was the first, the only, man to ever clasp her that way. He set her down. The curtains yanking closed behind her. Darcy slid a hand to the small of her back as they headed around the parsonage.

They lingered at the corner, waiting for his carriages to arrive. Darcy sought about for something to say. Anything to ease the tension he read in Elizabeth, or at least get her to look at him. After what seemed an eternity of silence, during which he had more than enough time to worry this would be the state of his wedded life, his carriages arrived.

"I'll instruct them to take your luggage," Darcy said. He strode forward, waving his footman down. "Those are Miss Bennet's trunks. Load them up, please, and someone will need to ride my horse."

The footman nodded. "Yes, sir." He gestured to the footman on the back of the smaller carriage, where Hawkins and Richard's valet must now have been joined by Anne's maid, if Anne had decided to allow one of Lady Catherine's spies to accompany her.

Darcy didn't wait to monitor their progress. He opened the door on the larger carriage. Anne and Richard shared the backward riding seat, for which Darcy was obliquely grateful. He turned back and waved Elizabeth forward. She hurried to his side, expression neutral, and he handed her in. Darcy then climbed up, to be met by Anne's warm smile.

"So, you accepted?" she asked, angling her pleased expression at Elizabeth. "Congratulations, both of you."

Elizabeth flushed. "Thank you."

Richard leaned forward. "Did you see Mrs. Fortescue?"

"We did," Darcy said.

"She asked us to tell you that she looks forward to learning what you planned to say to her," Elizabeth added.

"You couldn't take her aside?" Darcy asked.

Richard scowled. "Collins was in a fit. I believe I would have had to strike him to speak with her." He shook his head. "I couldn't do that. Not in front of his wife."

Darcy nodded, aware that's what the women had sought to avoid at the parsonage as well. "I can't say I blame you."

"We climbed out the parlor window to avoid him," Elizabeth added.

A quick glance found her expression finally relaxed into a smile. Some of Darcy's tension eased.

"A window?" Anne laughed.

"You two are making a habit of that, it seems," Richard added, appearing equally amused.

"Let's hope not too much of a habit," Darcy said dryly. "I prefer doors."

They fell silent as the carriage started moving. Richard yanked open the curtain, turning in his seat to watch the parsonage fade from view.

Anne shrugged. She lifted a small book from the seat beside her and began to read.

"Where are we going?" Elizabeth asked, turning to Darcy.

"I had planned on London, but I will take you directly home if you wish."

She shook her head. "We'd never reach Longbourn before dark. I can stay with Jane and Mr. Bingley."

Darcy nodded. "When we stop to rest the horses, I will send a man ahead to apprise them of your impending arrival."

"Thank you," Elizabeth replied. "And, if they aren't at home, I can stay with the Gardiners." She watched him intently as she offered that alternative. "Jane's written that you've met them on a number of occasions."

It took him only a moment to guess the source of her scrutiny. She wished to know how he felt about her relatives. Mrs. Bingley would have written that he got on well with the Gardiners, which he did, but Elizabeth wouldn't know whether to believe her sister. Mrs. Bingley was apt to say that everyone got on well.

"Yes, we have dined together frequently and socialized at several events." Darcy endeavored for a casual tone. "I have invited them to visit Pemberley. It seems your uncle is quite fond of fishing."

Elizabeth raised her eyebrows. "You invited them to your country seat, even though he's in trade?" she asked, apparently without compunction for her directness.

Darcy realized that she wished to understand him more fully, as they were now committed to wed. Still, he bristled at her accusation he was so shallow... especially since, before he'd met the Gardiners, her supposition of his attitude would have been correct. "Yes, even though they are in trade," he replied, tone touched with ire.

Elizabeth studied him for a long moment, then nodded and looked away.

Silence descended again, almost smothering in its intensity. Normally, Darcy would welcome the quiet. In fact, he expected it from Anne, even from Elizabeth, under the circumstances. But for the generally loquacious Richard to be mute was disturbing. Darcy could only assume the colonel's silence sprang from deference to him and Elizabeth, for being forced into a union. Far from comforting, the consideration gave the inside of the carriage an almost funerary feel.

Darcy cleared his throat. "You are not very talkative, Richard."

Richard turned from the window, letting the curtain fall into place. "You should talk."

"That statement is open to misinterpretation," Elizabeth said lightly.

"I understood the tone," Darcy assured her. "He is not criticizing my current silence but my usual behavior." Which wasn't like Richard.

Anne lowered her book, expression concerned. "Is all well with you, Richard?" Her eyes narrowed. "Is it Mrs. Fortescue?"

Richard gave his cravat a nervous tug. "Well, if you must know, yes, it is."

"What would you have said to her," Anne asked. "If you had been willing to strike Mr. Collins?"

"I would have liked to arrange to meet her."

"So, arrange it," Anne said.

Richard shook his head. "While she's staying with Mr. Collins, it would be wrong to have a clandestine meeting. He is her host, and since he's her brother, he is responsible for her."

"She won't stay with him forever," Elizabeth said. "She has a house somewhere."

"Where?" Richard countered in a frustrated tone. "All I know is that her home is in Essex and not near the sea. That leaves a lot of territory."

"What will you do if you do meet her?" Anne asked, expression suffused with curiosity.

"Get to know her better," Richard said. "I've been thinking of marrying her, but I don't believe marriage should be based on so short an acquaintance."

Beside Darcy, Elizabeth grimaced, evoking an echo of the sentiment in him, which he suppressed. Fortunately, Richard faced Anne.

"Does she have any money?" Anne asked. "You've always said you need a wife with a substantial dowry."

A sudden, somewhat silly grin appeared on Richard's face. "I don't care. If I were a few years younger, I would have yelled my proposal across the lawn. Now, I'm more cautious. Is it love or infatuation? If she gets to know me better, will she like me? I can support a wife, but not in great style. Can she be content with that?"

Anne shrugged. "She seems pleasant enough."

Richard's look molded into resignation.

"I'll be writing her," Elizabeth offered. "I hope Mr. Collins will not refuse the letters but considering how much he doesn't want to upset

Lady Catherine, he might not even let my letters to my sister into the house. I plan to fill my first letter with thanks for their hospitality and praise for Mr. Collins. I'll even apologize that I didn't take advantage of the carriage Lady Catherine was going to provide. Hopefully, that will allow future letters to reach my sister, and perhaps Mrs. Fortescue." She turned to look at Darcy, expression troubled. "Will you read or censor my letters when we are married?"

Richard gave a snort of laughter. "Can you imagine any woman in the Fitzwilliam family putting up with that?"

"No, I cannot." Darcy didn't have to go through the list of women who were Fitzwilliams by birth or marriage to know that none of them would tolerate a husband doing that. What kind of man would deny his wife that little independence? "No. I will only read letters you show me, although I would appreciate it if you do not leave out letters you do not want seen."

She offered a tentative smile. "Thank you."

He frowned. "I am surprised you had to ask." He wanted to understand why she thought so little of him. True, it was within the rights of a husband to read or censor his wife's letters, but Darcy would never consider such an archaic infringement.

Elizabeth shrugged. "I don't know you all that well," she said apologetically. "Which makes me think that Colonel Fitzwilliam is correct in wanting to get to know Mrs. Fortescue better."

"And so he shall," Anne said, her cheery tone sounding only slightly forced. "And I shall write to her as well, and to your sister if you like, Miss Bennet. Mr. Collins will hardly refuse my letters."

Darcy wasn't certain of that, but Elizabeth offered Anne a grateful smile.

Silence descended again. This time, Darcy didn't make any effort to alleviate the quiet, preferring to brood over Elizabeth's apparently low opinion of him. Hadn't he behaved with all honor and cordiality? Why would she doubt him?

He thought about the lie he let Hawkins tell and let others believe, that he'd slept in the servants' quarters on a bet. The lie was exposed. Elizabeth hadn't been in the room, but she would hear. Would her opinion of him sink lower still?

His opinion of himself had. Darcy prided himself on his truthfulness, but allowing a lie, even if told by a servant, should be unacceptable. Yet, it was done almost daily as part of polite society. If people who called on other people were told, 'He's at home, but doesn't want to see you,' a great deal of rancor would develop. Was the difference that they all excepted that lie as necessary for the civility of society?

Men lied to their wives all the time. Men who would challenge him to a duel if he called them a liar, would tell their wives they were with friends when they were with their mistresses. Perhaps Elizabeth's low opinion wasn't of him. Maybe, it was of his entire sex. If that was the case, could Darcy really blame her?

Chapter Twenty-Two

Elizabeth smoothed her skirts, then stilled her hands, aware she fidgeted. They'd left Miss de Bourgh with a friend and Colonel Fitzwilliam at Darcy House, the dwelling a bit austere from the street, where a footman had informed Mr. Darcy that they were expected at the Bingleys'. Now, they were nearly there.

Arrival at her sister's home wasn't the source of Elizabeth's disquiet. She was alone in a carriage with Mr. Darcy. Elizabeth had never been alone in a carriage with any man, let alone one she didn't know well and yet was slated to marry.

A quick glance revealed he watched her. He always watched her. She'd noted as much when he arrived at Rosings. Why his gaze was so often on her, she'd no idea. She'd nearly asked Miss de Bourgh but hadn't wished to start any rumors.

Well, they were to be married now. She must come to know him, sooner or later. "You're watching me," she said, meeting his gaze.

He blinked. "I apologize."

The inclination to smile made her lips twitch. "I don't believe looking at someone is a forbidden act."

"Yet, you brought it up, your tone one of question."

Elizabeth nodded. She could hardly refute that. "Because you often watch me. Why?"

He studied her, his gaze sweeping down her frame, then back up again to meet hers. "You interest me."

She didn't resist the slight smile that turned up her lips now. "Well, that's a better basis for a marriage than not interesting you." When he didn't speak, she cocked an eyebrow. "Why do I interest you?"

"Because you do not wish to marry me," he said. A startled expression crossed his face, as if it surprised him that he'd said the words aloud.

"I always assumed I would choose my husband, perhaps even wed for love," she said, selecting her words with care. "I do not like the idea

181

of him being chosen for me." Foisted on her, rather, but that seemed unnecessarily cruel to say.

"So, it is not me, personally, to whom you object, but rather to the circumstances of my proposal?"

Could that be a gleam of pleasure in his eyes? A touch of hope in his stoic tone? She shouldn't crush those emotions, yet she wouldn't begin their union on a lie. "I also object to you, specifically."

His expression hardened. He looked away, out the window. When he turned back, she could read the hurt in his expression.

"Why?" he finally asked. "I believe I have behaved with all honor and chivalry since that evening in the library."

"Yes, you have," she agreed. "When pressed, when your honor is at stake, you behave wonderfully."

"Well, then?" he demanded.

"It's your behavior when you feel your honor is not at risk that dismays me."

A frown pulled down the corners of his mouth. "How do you mean?"

Elizabeth smoothed her skirt. They should have saved such a conversation for a lengthier carriage ride. They would arrive at the Bingleys' mid-tiff. "When I first set eyes on you, I thought you quite handsome and fine. We all did."

Far from appearing reassured by the compliment, his frown deepened.

"Then, at that first assembly, you proceeded to dance with no one but the women you arrived with," Elizabeth continued. "Nor did you make any effort to be sociable. It was apparent to all that you considered yourself far above our company." She drew in a quick breath. "On top of that, you said I wasn't even handsome enough to dance with."

He blinked, appearing startled. After a long moment, he opened his mouth to speak. "But I was far above the company there."

Elizabeth cocked her head to the side. Could she make him see how unappealing his arrogance made him? "The way Lady Catherine is above the company she keeps?"

"I am not like my aunt," Mr. Darcy snapped. "She is a complete snob who thinks—"

He broke off. He turned to the window again and yanked at already-open curtains. Even in profile, Elizabeth could see his glower.

Elizabeth pressed onward, for the conversation, now begun, ought to be carried to completion, so as to be placed properly behind them. "If the first words you'd ever heard from me had been, 'Mr. Darcy is not handsome enough to dance with,' would you be pleased to wed me?"

He turned to look at her, still frowning. "I believe, the first words you said to me were an acclamation of your own cleverness." His expression turned slightly smug. "Not the most appealing introduction."

Elizabeth blinked, taken aback. She wracked her mind but could scarcely recall her first sally with Mr. Darcy. "An acclamation of my own wit? What, pray tell, were these words of mine?"

"I believe you inquired to know if I felt you had expressed yourself uncommonly well, when you badgered Colonel Forster about giving a ball." Mr. Darcy's expression turned sardonic. "Praise of yourself and a taunt lobbed my way, I believe, to reprimand me for overhearing your conversation. Not the sort of exchange to invite a man to wish for your hand."

Elizabeth felt her cheeks heat. She recalled the conversation now, at Sir Lucas's. Mr. Darcy had, at the time, taken to lurking about, listening in on her conversations with others, and she'd sought to call him out on the behavior. "That was my attempt to delve into your seeming preoccupation with my conversations." She shook her head. "Why were you so interested in my conversations?"

"As I said," he snapped. "You interest me."

"But in what way?" Elizabeth demanded, exasperated. "In the manner of an insect in amber? Or an unidentified smudge on the walk? A strange, mythological beast?"

"In the manor that any beautiful, intelligent woman might interest a man," he snapped back, glaring at her.

Elizabeth's jaw hinged open. She hinged it back closed, then licked her lips. Heat suffused her face and neck. "Are you saying... that is, do you mean to imply..." She shook her head, dumbstruck.

"I am saying," he offered, tone harsh with anger, "that despite some of your family members being rather atrocious, and the fact that your connections in no way augment mine, and your lack of an even remotely suitable dowry, I was already interested in you before the incident in the library, and remain interested, to this very moment."

She shook her head. Incredulous, she said, "That is the most offensive way of telling a woman you fancy her that I have ever heard."

"You express yourself uncommonly well," he muttered. "Put it another way if your pride so requires."

Elizabeth stared at him. He… was interested in her. Had been, for some time. From another man, that would have meant little. From Mr. Darcy, she suspected it meant rather a lot. For him to admit as much, after she'd essentially told him she didn't care for him or wish to wed him, only must do so, spoke even more of the depth of his feelings.

Subdued, she settled back in her seat and turned away from his glower. Mr. Darcy had feelings for her. Could she truly wed him, then? It seemed the height of cruelty to force a man to endure marriage to a woman he esteemed, who did not reciprocate his care.

She stole a quick glance and found his face averted, his profile perfection. He was undeniably handsome. Wealthy, as well, though she placed small enough value on that.

Honorable. Even though she suspected some of his obsession with chivalry stemmed from pride, chivalrous he was. She doubted there existed another man in England who, with Mr. Darcy's wealth, wouldn't simply have offered to buy his way out of wedding her, interested or not. After all, she did have some abominable relations and no dowry. Even her laudable connections offered him little, they being either in trade or connections he already possessed.

As she studied that perfect profile, her thoughts went to the blankets. He'd slept in the servants' quarters, seen the conditions there, and provided a blanket for each member of another household's staff. So, Mr. Darcy was kind, and not too proud, after all, to share sleeping quarters with the staff. How many men would simply have their valet stand guard, ignoring their servant's need for sleep?

And his cousins cared for him, as did Mr. Bingley. All people whom Elizabeth had come to like, whose company she enjoyed, and all of whom had known Mr. Darcy far longer than she. All of them were fond of and respected Mr. Darcy.

In truth, only Elizabeth, her younger sisters, and her mother seemed to judge him lacking. Putting aside her own council, would she really take her mother's and younger sisters' opinions as correct and Mr. Bingley's, Colonel Fitzwilliam's and Miss de Bourgh's opinions as false? That seemed the heart of folly.

"Now you are doing it," he said without turning to face her, tone forcedly light.

"Doing what?" she murmured, her mind spinning. It had been only one evening, that first, when he'd behaved horribly. One, only, but she'd permitted it to seal her judgement.

He turned, his gaze unerringly finding hers. "Watching me."

"Perhaps I find you interesting," Elizabeth offered.

Light sparked deep in his eyes. "Is that so?"

Elizabeth didn't know how to reply to that, or to the intensity in his gaze. Suddenly, there seemed a lack of space inside the carriage. They were quite near. His long legs, stretched out before him, nearly touched the hem of her skirt.

She realized she studied him too intently and wanted to look away, only to have her gaze settle on his lips. Heat rose up her neck. She didn't dare meet his eyes now. He leaned across the empty space between them.

The carriage rumbled to a halt. Elizabeth gasped, somehow surprised they'd stopped. Though too low to hear properly, she thought perhaps Mr. Darcy cursed. The door swung open to reveal fading daylight and one of Mr. Darcy's footmen.

Elizabeth all but leapt out, pleased to find the air cool. She smoothed her skirts. She didn't look at Mr. Darcy as he came to stand beside her, but she did place a slightly trembling hand on his arm and walk with him up a flight of front steps. As a door opened before them, Elizabeth had the impression of a neat, somewhat smaller than Mr. Darcy's, townhouse, into which they stepped.

"Elizabeth, you're here," Jane said, rushing past a well-dressed butler to embrace Elizabeth. "Oh, Mr. Darcy, thank you for bringing her." Jane released Elizabeth and turned to the butler. "Please see my sister's luggage is taken up to her room." She turned back, smiling. "Forgive me," she said, and dipped a curtsy.

"Jane," Elizabeth said, collecting herself. She returned her sister's smile. "There is nothing to forgive."

"Oh, but I'm behaving like Lydia, or Kitty," Jane said. "I'm so pleased to have you visit, though, Lizzy. I should have had you sooner, but Mother forbid it." Jane flushed. "Well, actually, she said you could only visit if we invited her as well."

Elizabeth raised her eyebrows. "I'd no idea Mother had given such an ultimatum," she said as she stripped off her gloves.

"Yes, well, we truly were about to invite you, regardless, but then Mary did…" Jane's voice trailed off, guilt clouding her lovely features.

The butler, who'd remained to collect their outerwear, presumably before seeing Jane's request carried out, accepted Elizabeth's cloak and then turned to Mr. Darcy.

Elizabeth smiled her reassurance to Jane. "I completely understand.

You moved to London to have space from her. You'd hardly achieve that by bringing her here." She lowered her voice to a menacing whisper and added, "And who knows, once she got here, how long she would remain."

"That thought had occurred to me," Jane admitted, still looking a touch guilty.

Elizabeth chuckled. "Jane, dearest, there is nothing to forgive. No one expects you to let Mother encroach, especially so early in your marriage. I'm proud of you for not giving in and inviting her, even to see me. I would have done the very same."

"Would you?" Mr. Darcy asked, expression keen.

So, he didn't wish her mother to visit them? Despite what Elizabeth had only just told Jane, the thought annoyed her. She would not have a husband who couldn't be civil to her relations.

"But do come in," Jane said, calmer already. "I don't mean to keep you standing in the foyer. Aunt and Uncle Gardiner are here. We've been waiting on you. Do you wish to see everyone first or change for dinner?"

"We should see everyone," Mr. Darcy said.

For once, Elizabeth agreed with him. Things needed to be told and she wanted to get it over with.

Jane smiled and turned to lead them into a good-sized parlor. As promised, Mr. Bingley and the Gardiners were within. A flurry of greetings commenced.

Elizabeth studied Mr. Darcy as he exchanged pleasantries with her favorite aunt and uncle. He seemed easy around the Gardiners, and Jane and Mr. Bingley. Relaxed. More... human. For the first time, it occurred to her that some of his stiffness, and his excess thereof at his first assembly in Hertfordshire, might stem from a deep seated shyness.

"So," Uncle Gardiner said once they were all seated. He looked from Elizabeth to Darcy. "How is it you've brought Elizabeth to us here in London, Mr. Darcy? Last we knew, she was in Kent, visiting Mary."

Elizabeth caught Mr. Darcy's grimace. She would have saved him the telling, but he launched into the tale before she could halt him. Nor did he contain his monologue to recent events, going back instead to that fateful evening in the library, though he glossed over her parting warning about Miss Bingley, leaving out what more had happened that evening.

Elizabeth didn't press him on the point, for Mr. Bingley's sake and because she could tell Mr. Darcy was unhappy to recite the whole humiliating story to Mr. and Mrs. Gardiner. What Jane had reported Miss Bingley to have done after Elizabeth and Mr. Darcy had parted ways didn't actually concern Elizabeth or the Gardiners.

At one point, in the middle, Elizabeth took over to mention her conversation with her father, and to speak of Mr. Collins and how he'd gone through her letters. She then turned back to Mr. Darcy. He nodded and recommenced his telling. It warmed Elizabeth to hear how he'd defended her after she quit Lady Catherine's parlor.

When he finished, he turned to Mr. Bingley. "I'm sorry to reveal Miss Bingley's part in all of this but, in view of what she attempted to do to Elizabeth, and Lady Catherine's very public use of her name, I do not think Miss Bingley's reputation can be spared. Lady Catherine's parlor was quite full of people."

Mr. Bingley, face folded into lines of worry, nodded.

Aunt Gardiner and Jane wore looks of equal surprise and sympathy.

Mr. Gardiner cleared his throat. "Yes, well, under the circumstances, I don't think there will be any problem getting consent from Mr. Bennet."

Mr. Darcy dipped his head in acknowledgement. "I believe that as soon as we secure that consent, we should marry in London. I would like to take Miss Bennet to Pemberley once we are wed, to show her new home to her, but the technicalities required to proceed will take several weeks. Even if I apply for a special license, I still must speak with my attorney about settling money on her, and I believe she will need additional clothes, which are more easily obtained in London than in Derbyshire."

Elizabeth turned to him, surprised. "New clothes? I shouldn't know where to begin."

"Oh, we will help you, won't we, Jane?" Aunt Gardiner said with considerable enthusiasm.

"Yes, of course," Jane replied, and added a smile.

Elizabeth attempted to return that smile, but the recounting of what had brought her to the Bingleys' townhouse had left her a bit dazed. How had her life become so twisted into a tight knot? One which she had no way to unravel. She was barely conscious of the agreement they reached to dine at Darcy House the next evening.

That trapped, whirling feeling didn't leave Elizabeth over the oncoming days. She stayed with Jane and Mr. Bingley in their lovely townhouse. She shopped with her sister, her aunt and Miss de Bourgh, spending Mr. Darcy's money. Her father wrote a brief letter, saying she and Mr. Darcy could wed, allowing them to start the reading of the banns. It bothered her that he added nothing more, no personal comment for her, in the letter.

They did all dine at Darcy House the evening after their arrival, though with a notable absence. Miss Darcy, it turned out, had committed to several outings, one each evening, for days. Elizabeth, not having met Mr. Darcy's sister, couldn't be sure, but she guessed from Jane's and Aunt Gardiner's reactions that Miss Darcy venturing out was odd.

Elizabeth enjoyed dining at Darcy House, though she found it incomprehensible that she might reside there someday. The staff was friendly and seemed pleased to be in Mr. Darcy's employ. His cook was excellent. Conversation about the table, with Mr. Darcy, Colonel Fitzwilliam, Miss de Bourgh, the Bingleys and the Gardiners, touched on a wide range of topics, almost all of interest. Even the decor, though a bit stiff, proved pleasant enough.

Still, she felt Miss Darcy's absence more and more keenly as the days wore on. Jane, too, seemed to think the young woman's behavior odd. Not that Jane admitted as much, but Elizabeth knew her sister well enough to tell. Likewise, Mr. Darcy grew increasingly short with any mention of his sister's absence.

After the initial flurry of shopping, Elizabeth's tenth morning in London found her and Jane sewing in the Bingley's parlor. Elizabeth mended one of her old gowns, and wore another, for none of her new ones were ready yet. She also pretended to be unaware that Jane stitched a garment for a babe. Elizabeth knew her gentle sister must have only hopes as of yet, or she would make the announcement, and chose to abide by Jane's wish not to speak on the topic.

From the extra-besotted way Mr. Bingley gazed at Jane when he entered the room to inform her that he was going out, Elizabeth felt certain Jane had shared her hope of being with child with him. Elizabeth had to work to stave off unbecoming sorrow. Once, she was Jane's confidant. Now, Mr. Bingley held that role.

Elizabeth's thoughts went to Mary. Though not even two weeks had passed, it seemed like ages since she last saw her younger sister. Was this vague sorrow, this feeling of being outside looking in, what Mary had lived with all these years? Elizabeth and Jane had one another. Kitty and Lydia also had each other.

And now that she understood better how Mary felt and wished to make amends, Elizabeth couldn't be her sister's confidant. Mr. Collins would read every letter Mary wrote to her, and Elizabeth's replies. They couldn't share intimacies knowing that. So far, all Elizabeth had dared send was a letter full of apology and compliments. Mary had yet to reply. Elizabeth suppressed another sigh and returned to her stitching.

Footfalls sounded in the hall, notably not Mr. Bingley's cheerful tread. Both sisters looked up as the Bingley's butler appeared in the doorway. He bowed slightly.

"Mr. Darcy, Miss de Bourgh and Miss Darcy are asking if you're at home, Mrs. Bingley, Miss Bennet."

Elizabeth shot Jane a quick look.

Jane shrugged. "Show them in, please," she said and began stowing her work.

Elizabeth set aside her sewing as well, though not with the same urgency. She looked down at her drab gown. Would Mr. Darcy be annoyed to see her clad thusly to finally meet his sister? Surely, he would realize her new gowns weren't ready yet.

The Bingley's butler returned to gesture the Darcys and Miss de Bourgh into the room. Elizabeth and Jane both rose. Mr. Darcy bowed, his gaze never leaving Elizabeth's face to note her gown. Miss de Bourgh curtsied with a warm smile. Miss Darcy, who turned out to be even taller than Jane had said, with light brown curls and a somewhat broad frame, emphasized by the jerkiness of her movements, dipped what hardly qualified as a curtsy.

"Please, send for tea," Jane said to the butler, who nodded and disappeared. She turned back to their guests. "Mr. Darcy, Miss de Bourgh, Miss Darcy, what a lovely surprise."

Miss Darcy lifted her gaze to Jane, flushed, and looked back down.

"Please, do come sit," Jane invited, ignoring the young woman's odd behavior.

This simple invitation proceeded awkwardly, as Miss de Bourgh took Miss Darcy by the arm and all but dragged her toward the sofa on which Elizabeth sat, then took the chair to Miss Darcy's right. After watching this as one might supervise a workforce, Mr. Darcy moved to sit in the chair nearest Jane, across from Elizabeth and his sister. Miss Darcy scooted to the edge of the sofa and Elizabeth couldn't help but think it was more to get away from her than nearer the comfort of Miss de Bourgh.

After a moment of strained silence, Jane sat forward in her seat.

"We've been having good luck with our evenings this spring, have we not?" she said. "Perfect weather for outings."

"Yes, quite fortunately," Miss de Bourgh said when it became clear neither Mr. Darcy nor his sister would speak.

"Miss Darcy." Elizabeth angled to face the young woman seated on the sofa with her. "I'm very pleased to meet you at last."

Miss Darcy nodded, not looking up.

Elizabeth looked past her to Miss de Bourgh, who offered an encouraging nod. "You must be enjoying London greatly," Elizabeth ventured.

Miss Darcy shrugged, face angled toward tightly clasped hands.

Silence stretched out to fill the room. Elizabeth strained for any sound of the tea tray, though it was too soon. She shrugged and looked past Miss Darcy. "And how are you finding London, Miss de Bourgh?"

"Since my time has been divided between catching up with old friends and spending time with you and your lovely sister and aunt, I am enjoying London very much." Miss de Bourgh smiled. "Also, please call me Anne. I feel we've grown quite close, and now you are to be my cousin. I shouldn't like to burden you with 'Miss de Bourgh' forever."

Elizabeth answered with a smile of her own. "I should be honored to and you, of course, should call me Elizabeth."

Mr. Darcy nodded, as if approving of their interaction. For some reason, that annoyed Elizabeth, but she strove to keep any indication of such from her face. Jane beamed cheerfully.

Miss de Bourgh reached out and touched Miss Darcy's sleeve. "Georgiana."

Miss Darcy darted a glance at Elizabeth, her expression mulish. "Please call me Georgiana, Miss Bennet." She dropped her gaze again, giving Elizabeth an excellent view of the top of her head.

Elizabeth raised her eyebrows slightly. "And you must call me Elizabeth, of course."

"Good," Mr. Darcy said, just as the first tray of tea things arrived.

Jane turned the conversation back to the weather then, followed by a discussion of the opera from Miss de Bourgh, she and Colonel Fitzwilliam having attended the evening before, with Miss Darcy. Miss Darcy remained silent throughout both topics, and all others raised over the short, somewhat strained tea they took.

When the Darcys and Miss de Bourgh finally left, Elizabeth turned to Jane. "Does Miss Darcy have reason to dislike me specifically? I thought you wrote that you, she and Aunt Gardiner were getting on well, and I know she's close with Miss de Bourgh."

Jane shook her head, retaking her seat. Maids appeared and began gathering up the tea service. Jane took out her sewing once more.

"Miss Darcy is very shy," Jane finally offered. "Maybe more so with you because you will soon live with them?"

"Is she jealous of her brother's time?" Elizabeth mused.

"I can't see how. He never gave her much of it, as far as I can tell. She spends a lot of time on her lessons."

Elizabeth shook her head, bemused, and returned to her mending. She had the fleeting thought that Lady Catherine would approve of that activity. She hadn't made much more progress with her mending when the butler returned. Elizabeth's hands stilled, her first thought that Mr. Darcy had come back to apologize for his sister.

"Mr. Bennet is here, Mrs. Bingley," the butler said.

Jane let out a happy exclamation and leapt to her feet, Elizabeth a moment behind her. She followed Jane as her sister rushed from the room and down the hall in the direction of the foyer. This was so much better than any good wishes in a letter. Mr. Bennet had come in person.

The three of them exchanged a flurry of greetings in the foyer, while the Bingleys' butler made every effort to gather Mr. Bennet's outerwear.

"Oh, Papa," Jane cried. "I'm so happy you've come. You will stay, won't you? With us? How long will you be here? Let me show you our home."

Mr. Bennet offered Jane a bemused smile. He was obviously unaccustomed to his eldest daughter being verbose, a trait Elizabeth was coming to understand that Mr. Bingley's easy, cheerful manner fostered in Jane.

"I would be pleased to stay with you," Mr. Bennet replied. "I'm not sure yet for how long. And yes, I should like to see your home. First, may I speak with Elizabeth alone?"

Jane's eyes grew wide, some of her shed solemnity returning. "Of course, Papa. Let me show you to Mr. Bingley's office. He's out."

Mr. Bennet nodded. Jane led the way back down the corridor and past the parlor. She opened the door to Mr. Bingley's office for them and stood back. "I'll be in the parlor. Elizabeth knows the way."

Mr. Bingley's office was small, though not quite cramped. It had an unused feel, emphasized by the lack of a fire laid in the grate and the few, never-lit candles. Elizabeth crossed and pulled open the curtains to let in more light, then returned to sit on the single sofa with her father.

"Is everything well, Papa?" she asked. Happy to see him as she was, his appearance also invoked a fit of nerves. She wondered if anything was wrong.

Mr. Bennet took her hand and gave it a gentle squeeze before letting go. "I only came to tell you, to assure you, that you do not have to marry Mr. Darcy, if you don't want to, Lizzy. I gave permission, but daily wondered if I should have done so."

Elizabeth let out a relieved breath. "I think it is for the best."

"Are you sure? It's not too late to withdraw." her father pressed. "Well and truly certain? You cannot undo this, Elizabeth."

"I'm sure he's a good man, even a kind one," she said, words coming out slowly, as she selected them. "He's honorable. He's giving." She dropped her gaze. "I don't… I don't love him. Not yet. I come nearer to liking him every day." She shrugged. "I think, in time, what I feel will grow closer to love." At least, she hoped so.

The moment in the carriage, the day they'd arrived from Kent, returned to her mind. In that moment, she had the odd hope Mr. Darcy would kiss her, and she'd craved that kiss. Heat rose in her cheeks.

Mr. Bennet settled back on the sofa. "I have to admit, I'm relieved. I was not looking forward to the scandal of a broken engagement, but I would have withdrawn my consent if you wanted me to."

"I want to marry him, Papa." A thought hit her. "Even though not to would give Mama a real scandal about me."

"I don't think you should make an effort to please your mother in that way," he said dryly. "You should know, Mr. Darcy is trying to please you. He had several documents sent. He's being very generous with his settlement."

Elizabeth looked up, surprised. "I hadn't thought to ask."

Her father smiled. "Well, he is."

Elizabeth shrugged. "I suppose that's good to know."

They chatted on for some time after that, with Elizabeth detailing everything that had happened since she'd left for Kent, most of which she hadn't dared put in a letter to him for fear her mother would read it. They then went to find Jane, and a returned Mr. Bingley. While Jane and her husband happily showed Mr. Bennet about their London home, Elizabeth worked, once again, to stave off a feeling of being trapped. Retelling her tale, no matter how much she'd briefly longed for Mr. Darcy's kiss, still left her feeling desperate.

Fortunately, almost daily socializing with Mr. Darcy over the weeks it took for the banns to be read somewhat minimized that feeling. Enough so that, at least, Elizabeth was able to rejoice that she could wed while her father remained in London. So as not to keep him away from Longbourn any longer than necessary during that busy season, and at Mr. Darcy's request, she and Mr. Darcy were to marry as soon as the last of the banns were read.

Elizabeth couldn't deny that, of all her family members, if she'd been forced to choose, she would have selected to have her father, Jane and the Gardiners at her wedding. For his part, Mr. Darcy would have Mr. Bingley, Colonel Fitzwilliam, Miss de Bourgh and his ever-silent sister, with her companion, Mrs. Annesley, beside her. In addition, the Hyatts, a very pleasant couple who were friends of the Bingleys attended. Elizabeth couldn't be sure, but she felt she knew Mr. Darcy well enough to guess that all the people he cared for most would be with them. All in all, she felt the wedding would be a happy one.

An additional happiness was that, instead of a wedding breakfast, they were to make a brief stop in Longbourn. The idea, in fact, was Mr. Darcy's. When Elizabeth had thanked him for allowing her a celebration with her mother, two youngest sisters, friends and neighbors, he'd simply said, "It would be churlish not to stop, considering it will not take us very much out of our way." This sort of modesty, she was beginning to realize, was as much a cornerstone of his character as his pride.

When her wedding day came, the ceremony was over quicker than Elizabeth could have imagined. It was as if, once the matter began, time contrived to speed her into the union and to her wedding night, which she viewed with mingled interest and dread. It seemed like only moments after the ceremony began that it was over, and the time was upon her to make her farewells to those who would remain in London. Everyone stood in a line, down which she made her way, her loved ones all smiling.

Finally, near the end of the line, Elizabeth turned from Mr. Bingley to Jane. A lump lodged in her throat. She reached out to clasp Jane's hands. "Promise me you'll visit soon? Please?" Elizabeth couldn't believe she was about to leave the warmth of Jane's and Mr. Bingley's home to go off with her grim new husband and his sullen little sister.

"We will," Jane assured her, pulling her into an embrace. "I promise," she added, in Elizabeth's ear. "As soon as I may."

"Thank you," Elizabeth whispered back. "Be well, sweet Jane."

Jane released Elizabeth with an encouraging smile.

Elizabeth would have said more, but she couldn't get words past the hard lump blocking her throat. She was certain she saw tears shimmering in Jane's eyes. Her sister reached to clasp Mr. Bingley's hand.

Then Mr. Darcy offered his arm. Elizabeth placed her hand on it and let him lead her away. It was all she could do not to look back as Mr. Darcy ushered her outside.

Chapter Twenty-Three

Immediately after the wedding, Elizabeth, Mr. Darcy, Miss Darcy and Mr. Bennet rode in a carriage together to Longbourn, a second going on ahead with Mrs. Annesley, Mr. Darcy's valet, Miss Darcy's maid and more luggage. During the ride, Elizabeth was pleased to see her husband and father get along well, but her new sister barely said a word. They weren't to stay the night, but Mrs. Bennet had prepared a large meal for them, inviting all their relatives, friends and neighbors. Although they did not attend the wedding, they did participate in the celebration.

To Elizabeth's relief, Mr. Darcy tolerated her mother's silliness and behaved cordially. Surprisingly, he appeared to get along well with Mr. Phillips. As far as Elizabeth was able to ascertain, they discussed roads.

Marriage to Colonel Forster had improved Lydia's manners. Kitty behaved better than usual, likely because Lydia did. Miss Darcy said virtually nothing and did not act shy but disdainful. She clearly didn't like her new relatives. Elizabeth called to mind what Mr. Wickham had said of Miss Darcy. She certainly seemed more as he'd described than how Jane and Aunt Gardiner did.

Not that Elizabeth cared. Her family was behaving rather well. Even were they not, Elizabeth would not apologize for them to anyone, especially not Miss Darcy. Elizabeth had not sought this marriage. If Miss Darcy wished to blame anyone for new relatives she obviously found beneath her, she should turn her ire on her Aunt Catherine.

After the meal, Elizabeth had a scant half an hour to collect and pack the items she'd left behind before they were scheduled to depart once more. Not that there was much to take. She would leave most of her clothes for Kitty to make over, since she had a completely new wardrobe. In truth, she spent several long minutes simply standing in the center of her empty-seeming former bedroom, feeling bereft.

This room, which seemed rather small now and a bit bedraggled, held the sum of so much of her life. Happiness, sorrow, laughter and tears. Whispered confessions, hopes and dreams. Giggles and even, on rare occasion, grudging silence. She and Jane had grown up together in this room, the closest of friends.

Elizabeth tried to focus her thoughts on Pemberley. It was reputed to be a beautiful place. She would take her possessions and put them in her room there. At first, it would be odd, much stranger than simply visiting a place she didn't mean to stay at for long. After a time, though, surely Pemberley would feel like home? Yes, her new husband, who did have feelings for her, was withdrawn and taciturn and her new sister seemed disdainful, but Elizabeth would make a home at Pemberley. Even if she did not yet love Mr. Darcy.

And even if she felt as if everything she did love was being left behind and like she may have, in going through with the ceremony, made a terrible mistake.

Elizabeth swallowed hard. She blinked back tears and took a last, slow look about her childhood room. All that remained for Elizabeth in that room were memories. In truth, she'd already left, though she hadn't realized it when she did. With a deep breath, she picked up the satchel she'd packed and turned toward the door, and the stairwell beyond.

As the three of them headed for the carriage, Elizabeth turned to find Mr. Darcy watching her, Miss Darcy beside him. Mr. Darcy stepped forward and offered his arm. Elizabeth settled a hand on his sleeve. She drew in another deep breath and mustered a smile. Mr. Darcy turned, once more leading her away.

The mood inside Mr. Darcy's carriage offered no respite from Elizabeth's growing worry that she and Mr. Darcy had made a mistake by marrying. Mr. Darcy sat beside her but seemed almost to ignore her, with Miss Darcy across from them. Miss Darcy's glowering, petulant presence was a solid dampener to any joy Elizabeth may have felt on her wedding day.

If she and Mr. Darcy weren't to be alone, Elizabeth wished Miss de Bourgh would have come. Anne seemed able to break Miss Darcy from her reserve. Furthermore, Elizabeth enjoyed Anne's company, unlike Mr. Darcy's or Miss Darcy's. Anne had, however, elected to return to Rosings to, in her words, speak firmly with her mother.

As the carriage set out, the weight of silence pressed on Elizabeth. Especially Mr. Darcy's. Not that he was ever verbose, but they'd wed that morning. Surely, he'd some words for her.

She glanced down, taking in his gloved hand where it rested on the seat between them. Elizabeth placed hers near it. He didn't seem to notice. She drew in a breath and slid her hand over until their gloves touched.

Mr. Darcy looked down, expression startled. He offered an unreadable look. Elizabeth's heart seemed to shrink. Then, he slid his hand over hers, engulfing it. She could feel the warmth and strength of his fingers as they clasped hers.

A somewhat strangled sound emanated from the other side of the carriage. Elizabeth glanced up to see Miss Darcy staring at their clasped hands, her expression shocked. Mr. Darcy yanked his hand away. Miss Darcy's mien turned smug and she dropped her face, hair coming forward to hide the look.

Elizabeth narrowed her eyes. So, Miss Darcy was more than shy around her. She truly did actively dislike Elizabeth. But, why? Elizabeth had been nothing but kind. She'd made overtures of friendship.

The interior of the carriage took on an eerie silence. Elizabeth dedicated her time to staring out the window. The driver settled into a pattern of walking and resting. Horses were changed with unusual swiftness.

Finally, they arrived at an inn. They found Mrs. Annesley and Mr. Darcy's valet, Hawkins, already there. They were shown upstairs. Elizabeth noted, with trepidation, that she and Mr. Darcy had adjoining rooms.

After a strained dinner, which they took in a private dining room, Elizabeth headed to her chamber to ready for bed. She'd little idea what to expect from her husband after their day of hardly speaking. Her hands trembled as she brushed out and braided her hair, then went to the bed to slip beneath heavy blankets.

To her surprise and relief, Mr. Darcy did not come to her room, or request she visit his. She lay awake for a long time, though, in what many would assume was her marital bed, events running through her mind. Miss de Bourgh's words returned to her, of how Mr. Darcy wanted a loving wife and children. Had he, for the sake of Elizabeth's reputation and future, given up on that dream?

She shook her head against the fluffy pillow. No, he couldn't have. He simply gave her space, and time. That must be all. In fact, she hoped that was all, for, though relieved, she also felt a stab of disappointment. She, too, wanted a home with love and children.

More than that, Elizabeth realized as she drifted nearer to sleep, she wanted fulfillment of the promise of that moment in the carriage. She wished to experience Mr. Darcy's kiss. She would try harder. Be more amiable. Neither of them should give up on the dream of happiness.

Elizabeth hoped, desperately, that they would find it. It didn't help that, since their almost-moment in the carriage, just before they'd reached Jane's new London home, Elizabeth hadn't been alone with Mr. Darcy. They hadn't had another moment of any consequence.

He was polite, of course, and did spend what she felt was an extensive amount of time watching her, but that often seemed to be more in consideration of censure than amorous. At least, if his expression was any indication, and indeed that was the only indication she had, since he didn't speak to her of his feelings as they related to her. All in all, she rather worried he regretted taking the honorable course and wished he hadn't wed her. That worry gnawed at her as she finally found sleep.

The following day, Mrs. Annesley joined them on the second leg of the journey, but her presence did nothing to loosen Miss Darcy's tongue. With nothing across from her but Mrs. Annesley's deliberately blank expression and Miss Darcy's disapproving one, Elizabeth turned to gaze out the window once more, watching the scenery pass.

At the first stop, she learned they hadn't yet reached Derbyshire, the county where Mr. Darcy's home was. She returned to the carriage after stretching her legs to the feeling that they'd been locked in together for days, instead of hours. She settled back into her seat certain, as they started moving once more, that it would feel like rather a long carriage ride. After a time, a light rain started, and Elizabeth let the curtain fall back into place.

With her new sister across from her, Elizabeth couldn't help but dwell on Miss Darcy's dislike. Despite Jane's dismissal of the idea, Elizabeth still suspected that Miss Darcy must be jealous of her brother's time. After all, Mr. Darcy was all she had. No mother. No father. Only her brother.

Or she was a snob, as Mr. Wickham had confided. She'd gotten on well with Jane and their Aunt Gardiner, but there was a great difference between being sociable with people and becoming their relation. The elder of Mr. Bingley's two sister had made that very clear back in Hertfordshire, by changing her behavior toward Jane once Mr. Bingley's interest became apparent. Elizabeth had patience for a young woman jealous of her brother, but none for snobbery.

After what seemed hours, the carriage rolled to a halt. Elizabeth pulled back the curtain to find the rain had stopped, though the world without stood wet and gray. They'd halted in an innyard, staff hurrying forward. With relief, she let a footman hand her down when the door opened.

Elizabeth stepped aside as Miss Darcy was handed out. Miss Darcy took one look Elizabeth's way and set out toward the inn with long strides. As Mrs. Annesley was yet to leave the carriage, Elizabeth hurried after the tall young woman. No matter how much Miss Darcy disliked her and wished to be away from her, Elizabeth couldn't let her enter an inn alone.

Reaching the porch steps, Miss Darcy all but ran up them. At the top, one a foot flew out from under her, sliding on the mud-caked step. With a screech, she grabbed onto the porch rail to keep from toppling, one leg jutting out from under her skirt at an uncomfortable angle.

Elizabeth rushed to her side. "Miss Darcy, are you hurt?"

Miss Darcy cast her a hate-filled look. She pushed away hands Elizabeth hadn't realized she'd placed on her. Mrs. Annesley appeared, scooped up Miss Darcy's reticle, and went to her other side. Miss Darcy squared her shoulders and yanked her gaze from Elizabeth to snatch her reticle from Mrs. Annesley. She shook off Mrs. Annesley's hands as well and marched into the inn, appearing unharmed by her near fall. Mrs. Annesley hurried after.

Elizabeth let out a relieved sigh. Snobbish or jealous as Miss Darcy might be, Elizabeth wouldn't want to see the girl hurt.

"I thought my sister asked you to call her Georgiana," Mr. Darcy's voice said.

Elizabeth turned to find him at the base of the porch steps, putting his head on level with hers. "She did, but in the heat of the moment, I forgot."

"Honor her request." His voice was devoid of inflection.

Elizabeth clamped down annoyance. "Certainly," she said and turned away before he could offer his arm. She strode into the inn, reflecting that Mr. Darcy's request would be easier to carry out if Miss Darcy acted as if they were on a first name basis. In fact, Miss Darcy never used Elizabeth's name, either first or last.

They didn't remain in the inn for long, the mood around the table where they took a brief meal almost hostile. Not that returning to the carriage offered any relief. They journeyed in oppressive silence. Eventually, Elizabeth, seated as far from Mr. Darcy as their bench permitted, yanked back the curtain once more.

A short time later, askance, Elizabeth noted shoulders relaxed and expressions cleared slightly. Her three companions seemed to breathe easier. She could only assume they neared the end of their arduous journey.

A turn brought a body of water into view, the new spring foliage seemingly designed to frame the lawn on the other side, and the manor beyond that. Lightness filled Elizabeth as she gazed on what must surely be the most perfect meld of architecture and nature that England had to offer.

Bright green in the sunlight, the lawn, dotted here and there with decorative shrubs, a fountain, and flowerbeds, raced away from them. At the top of a gentle swell of earth, the manor surely commanded as lovely a view as it made. Smooth stone rose with careful symmetry into a structure with lovely clean lines and tall windows, stately and touched by the memory of a castle of old.

Her breath caught to behold this, her new home, for surely the manor was none other than Pemberley. If Darcy House had seemed an inconceivable luxury, Pemberley was born of children's tales. She turned to Mr. Darcy, a request for confirmation on her lips.

He watched her, as always, yet with more intensity than usual. A glow smoldered deep in his gaze, but his expressionless mien gave no indication of the impetus. Elizabeth swallowed back her question, worried anger birthed that spark. Did he detest the idea of her as mistress of his magnificent home?

She returned to the view, but trees now cloaked the building. She sat back as they rumbled up the drive. She wished Jane had accompanied her. Or Miss de Bourgh. Even Colonel Fitzwilliam. Anyone of a more sympathetic disposition than the Darcys.

She was a Darcy now, she realized. Mrs. Fitzwilliam Darcy. For better or for ill, and, increasingly, she found it difficult to believe not for ill, Miss Elizabeth Bennet was no more.

Pemberley proved as lovely and magnificent inside as without. To Elizabeth's relief, the staff seemed competent and kind. Mrs. Reynolds, the housekeeper, seemed particularly like someone Elizabeth could go to for advice, and count on.

She wondered if Mr. Darcy had selected the staff himself or had a man for that. She couldn't imagine him choosing such warmhearted employees. She wondered how they found him as a master but suspected they wouldn't tell her the truth of that.

Mr. Darcy's gift of the blankets surfaced in her memory. Perhaps he was a kind master. Likewise, she deliberately recalled how much Miss de Bourgh and Colonel Fitzwilliam cared for Mr. Darcy, as did Mr. Bingley. Miss Darcy as well, even if she didn't care for Elizabeth. People liked Mr. Darcy and he, apparently, liked them. People who weren't Elizabeth.

She was given a room that adjoined to Mr. Darcy's, a sitting room between them. To her added relief, she was also given a key. Of course, Mr. Darcy might have another copy, and Mrs. Reynolds certainly did, but it pleased Elizabeth to have one.

Dinner was served very soon after they arrived and proved, as she'd suspected, nearly silent and very strained. At the earliest possible moment without being completely rude, Miss Darcy claimed a sore head and retired. Almost immediately, Mrs. Annesley left to check on the young woman. Mr. Darcy excused himself as well, to attend to his correspondences. Elizabeth was left alone to return to her room and await the possibility of a delayed wedding night with growing apprehension.

Elizabeth opened her wardrobe and studied the scandalous, lacy concoctions Jane and Aunt Gardiner had pressed her to buy. It irked her that those she had, while some of her gowns still weren't ready and would need to be sent on, bits finalized by the seamstresses in Derbyshire, or by Elizabeth. Normally, she might count on her new sister to help with such a task but, somehow, she couldn't imagine Miss Darcy stitching her hems.

Elizabeth pushed the French lace away. She changed into her oldest, most austere nightgown and belted an eminently practical robe overtop. She then took down her hair and sat to brush it out. As her dark locks fell nearly to her waist, the task absorbed her for some time. While she plied the brush, she wondered which Mr. Darcy would come to her room that night, the one who'd ordered her about that afternoon, or the one thoughtful enough to buy blankets for servants?

A knock sounded on the door that linked her room to Mr. Darcy's. Elizabeth nearly dropped the brush. With care, she set it on the dressing table and stood. She pushed in the chair. A tremble returned to her hands and speedily filled her frame.

"Enter," she said, her voice coming out so soft, she wondered if she may have to try a second invitation.

The knob turned. The door swung inward to reveal Mr. Darcy.

Elizabeth clasped her hands tightly before her.

Still dressed for dinner, which made her feel all the more improperly attired to be in his presence, he studied her from the doorway. A faint glow filled the room behind him, indicating the fire was lit but not candles. It was nothing compared to the heat in his gaze.

Elizabeth was alive with nerves. Her body shook. Her mind felt numb. She hardly knew Mr. Darcy, and was somewhat sure she didn't care for him, or he for her.

Yet, the way he studied her… His gaze scorched where it passed over her frame. Down to her toes. Up again. To her loose tresses. Her eyes. Her lips.

Sudden warmth flashed through Elizabeth, not born of amorousness. How dare he look at her that way, when he'd said nary a kind word to her, ever? She may be his wife now, his property, but she would never be servile, and she'd nothing to be ashamed of about wearing a nightgown and robe before him.

She threw back her shoulders and lifted her chin. "Were you coming in, sir, or remaining in the doorway?"

Mr. Darcy blinked. He seemed to collect himself. The passion in his gaze dimmed. "It occurs to me we do not know one another well." He turned and gestured toward the room behind him. "Would you care to join me in the sitting room?"

Elizabeth couldn't help a stab of relief, and thankfulness. "Yes, thank you. I think that would be wise." She started across the room. "I had hoped for some time alone in the carriage at least. I hadn't expected your sister and Mrs. Annesley to join us."

"You wish Georgiana had not accompanied us?" he asked, tone sharp, as Elizabeth drew abreast him in the doorway.

She halted to look up at him, her temper ignited. "I did not say that."

"Yet, you implied it."

"And what if I did?" Elizabeth's hands found their way to her hips. "We've just wed and, as you only now pointed out, we've hardly had time to come to know each other." As she said that, she realized it wasn't true. In Kent, they'd had time, but she'd avoided him. In London, they'd been together often, but always with a seeming crowd of others. Still, she'd made no effort to seek Mr. Darcy out.

"You feel my sister was rude to accompany us."

The accusation in his tone only stoked Elizabeth anger. "Yes, if it was her choice. Who inflicts their presence on a newly wedded couple?"

"Now Georgiana is an affliction?" His full mouth pulled into a frown. "Why do you dislike my sister?"

"I do not dislike your sister nearly so much as she dislikes me, which she chose to do out of hand, so far as I am able to tell."

"Do not be absurd," he snapped. "Georgiana does not take it upon herself to dislike people."

"Well, she dislikes me, and has since the moment we met."

"Perhaps you have not been kind to her."

Elizabeth glared up at him, astonished by his obtuseness. "She wouldn't even have met me, if she could have avoided it. She worked hard not to, until you and Miss de Bourgh dragged her into Jane's parlor."

"You are being overly sensitive and imaginative. She merely has difficulty meeting new people. She is shy, something you would not understand."

"Which is it?" Elizabeth countered. "Am I overly sensitive or insensitive?" She didn't give him time to reply. "Perhaps, as I'm so good at making things up, I've discovered a means to be both at once."

His gaze narrowed. "Perhaps you have."

Elizabeth threw up her hands. "Is this how we're to carry on? Do you not see how we needed time alone, without either of our families?"

"Your animosity is not Georgiana's fault."

Elizabeth tossed manners aside and pointed a finger at him. "You answered an entirely different question than I asked." She sniffed. "That's a sure sign of not having a leg on which to stand."

Mr. Darcy's answering scowl should have been intimidating. Elizabeth found it infuriating. "I've changed my mind, sir. I do not wish to speak with you in the sitting room. If you'll kindly vacate my doorway, I am going to bed." She reached for the edge of the door.

His scowl deepened. He didn't appear as if he meant to leave the doorway. Eyes narrowed with anger, Elizabeth slammed the door in Mr. Darcy's face.

Chapter Twenty-Four

Elizabeth woke the next morning feeling remorse for losing her temper. She and Mr. Darcy had to learn to get along, or, she sorrowfully reflected, at least how to ignore each other better. Furthermore, as Georgiana was quite young and may not wed for years still, Elizabeth must learn to exist with her new sister as well.

She assumed that coming to some understanding of cordial behavior wouldn't be too difficult, residing as they all were at Pemberley, but it soon became apparent that, in so large a home, the Darcys found it easy to avoid her. Mr. Darcy spent every waking hour in his office or riding… and Elizabeth was quite certain he knew she didn't ride. Miss Darcy devoted herself to her studies.

Elizabeth made a foray into the management of Pemberley as a neutral topic, but if she asked Georgiana a question about running the household, she usually replied that she didn't know. If she asked Mr. Darcy, he told her to ask Mrs. Reynolds, which proved the best possible solution to learning to run the household, if not to bridging the gap with her new relations. Sometimes, Mrs. Annesley would step in to answer.

Although Elizabeth spent at least an hour a day learning about the running of Pemberley with Mrs. Reynolds, that was hardly enough to fill her time. Her nearly complete gowns arrived from London, giving her something productive to do. Letters began to catch up with her, including a very stiff one from Mary. Elizabeth wrote all her sisters, her parents, a few friends, the Gardiners, Miss de Bourgh, the Phillips, and Mrs. Fortescue. In her first letter to Jane, she included a fresh plea for the Bingleys to visit, deeming them the guests most likely to garner Mr. Darcy's approval.

With more than enough time on her hands, Elizabeth copied Miss de Bourgh and first wrote a draft for every letter. She also optimistically set up a small file cabinet to house her correspondence. The cabinet had locks, and two sets of keys were helpfully in a drawer. She decided to keep it locked. Her correspondence contained nothing that was private, but Mr. Collins' taking Mr. Darcy's letter still troubled her. The locked cabinet gave her a feeling of security.

She missed conversation. Mrs. Reynolds would provide information about Pemberley and generally answer direct questions but was too deferential to be a confidant. Miss Darcy ignored Elizabeth to the point of rudeness unless Mr. Darcy was present, and then answered only in monosyllables. At dinner, Elizabeth often talked only to Mrs. Annesley, while her new husband and new sister said almost nothing.

Nor did Mr. Darcy make another foray to her room. The first few days, this relieved her. As the week wore on, Elizabeth began to worry. How could she learn to get along with her husband if she only saw him at the dinner table, with the staff, his sister and Mrs. Annesley present?

The rapidity of Jane's reply pleased Elizabeth, but her happiness was dimmed immediately upon opening her sister's letter. Jane could not visit. In fact, she and Mr. Bingley were to take a very slow, very careful carriage ride back to Netherfield Park.

Jane's pregnancy, it seemed, was more than a hope, but the fulfilment of that dream was shaping rapidly into a nightmare. She experienced horrible morning sickness, and other, more dire seeming complications. Their physician and the midwife had both recommended Jane be carefully removed to the country immediately. They felt the commotion and, indeed, very air and water of London to be detrimental to Jane's and the babe's health.

In view of her troubles, Jane still didn't wish her condition made public, a desire Elizabeth sympathized with. Jane also confessed, her hand shaking enough to show in her usually rounded strokes, that she regretted permitting herself to begin baby clothes. She could only pray, she confided to Elizabeth, that her exuberance did not come to haunt her.

Elizabeth folded Jane's letter, read alone in one of Pemberley's many parlors, and wiped tears from her cheeks. Her poor sister. Should she go to Jane? Elizabeth hadn't been requested, but if there was any way she could help…

She shook her head. What excuse could she give to leave now, so quickly and her union unconsummated? Not that she wouldn't trust Mr. Darcy with Jane's and Mr. Bingley's troubles, but her presence hadn't been requested, even hinted at. Jane and Mr. Bingley were so close, closer than even Elizabeth had ever been with her sister. They had each other. If they wanted Elizabeth, she would go to them with all haste, but she wouldn't insert herself. She must be content to tender the offer in a letter.

"Are you crying?"

Elizabeth looked up to see Miss Darcy looming in the doorway.

"What do you have to cry about?" Miss Darcy's tone dripped derision.

"Jane wrote that she cannot visit," Elizabeth temporized and pulled a handkerchief from her sleeve.

"I figured that would happen." Miss Darcy tossed her head and marched away.

Elizabeth stared after her, perplexed by the statement. She'd been there when the mail arrived, with little else to occupy her. No other letters from the Bingleys had arrived, for Mr. or Miss Darcy. Elizabeth felt certain her sister hadn't confided in Miss Darcy and if Mr. Bingley had confided in Mr. Darcy, despite his many flaws, he wouldn't have shared the news with his sister.

Elizabeth shrugged. Likely, Miss Darcy simply intended to vex. Elizabeth had more pressing worries than Miss Darcy's contrary nature.

That evening, Elizabeth didn't go to dinner, begging off due to a headache. It took her a great deal of time to fall asleep, worried as she was for Jane. Then, deep in the night, Elizabeth woke, half sure she'd heard footsteps in the sitting room, and that they'd paused outside her bedroom door. Ears straining, she eventually faded back to sleep when the sound never came again.

In the days that followed, she received letters she could discuss, and so resolved to renew her attempts at conversation over the dinner table. When both her sister Mary and Mrs. Fortescue wrote, Elizabeth couldn't help but share their news. Miss Darcy hadn't met Mr. Collins, but Mr. Darcy had. Surely, they could agree that Mr. Collins had behaved badly and that his behavior warranted change. Especially as his bad behavior had played a large hand in their present predicament.

Elizabeth waited until the first course was served and ventured, "Mary and Mrs. Fortescue both wrote to say that Lady Catherine told Mr. Collins that he should permit them to write whom they please, and that he should allow them to send and receive letters without him reading them."

Mr. Darcy met her gaze, eyebrows elevated. "I am glad to hear that, but a bit surprised. Not that Lady Catherine would believe that, but that Mr. Collins sought her advice on the subject."

"He seeks her advice on everything," Elizabeth pointed out.

Mr. Darcy's slight smile, mostly a lessening of the severity of his expression, sparked a flicker of joy in Elizabeth. "Actually, I noticed that he does not," he said. "He's more astute than I would have first credited. When he does not wish to be advised, he avoids a subject."

"I hadn't realized he is that shrewd," Elizabeth admitted. "Mrs. Fortescue must have, however, for it was she who brought the topic up, in Lady Catherine's presence."

"Was he very displeased?" Mr. Darcy asked with something akin to interest.

"Mary says surprisingly not. She claims he is happy to please Lady Catherine on this."

Elizabeth decided to conceal that Mary also wrote that Mr. Collins' reading of his female relatives' letters had already helped achieve results that Lady Catherine was unhappy with, Miss de Bourgh traveling to London and, worse, Elizabeth and Darcy wedding. Mr. Collins, Mary said, was more than happy to be relieved of the responsibility of deciding which future letters would be a boon to Lady Catherine and which would bring more aggravation.

"It was clever of Mrs. Fortescue to speak out in Aunt Catherine's presence," Mr. Darcy said after a slightly too long silence.

"She's intelligent," Elizabeth agreed. Wishing to keep the conversation going, she ventured, "Do you think she will be clever enough to find a way to meet Colonel Fitzwilliam, if she still wishes to?"

Miss Darcy, who'd been pushing food about her plate with a sullen expression, cast Elizabeth a sharp look.

Mr. Darcy frowned, making Elizabeth worry that he didn't wish for the match. "Was not there something about a lease on a house she owns? Richard hoped that once she moved out of Mr. Collins' home, they could recommence their acquaintance."

Elizabeth smiled, relieved his dower expression was aimed at conjuring reluctant memories, not at her mention of his cousin. "Yes, but there is a complication. The couple who are renting the house are expecting a baby about the time the lease expires. Also, they have an ailing elderly relative with them. It isn't reasonable to force them to leave."

"I suppose she and Richard will have to wait," Mr. Darcy said.

Miss Darcy issued a relieved sigh. She popped a forkful of peas into her mouth.

Annoyance sparked in Elizabeth. Miss Darcy didn't even know Mrs. Fortescue. Did she judge the woman unworthy of Colonel Fitzwilliam simply because Elizabeth was an acquaintance? "Yes, but wait how long? Months? A year? The relative could be ill for a long time." She stole a quick glance, taking in Miss Darcy's smug look. "Is Colonel Fitzwilliam welcome at Rosings?"

Mr. Darcy shook his head. "No. He wrote that Aunt Catherine informed him that he could visit her next spring. She implied he was not welcome earlier."

That resulted in another forkful of peas and a return of Miss Darcy's smug look, which had begun to slip at Elizabeth's suggestion of Rosings.

"Maybe Lady Catherine realizes she needs that time to restore her calm," Elizabeth said, pleased they were having a reasonable conversation over dinner, even if Miss Darcy didn't join in and kept pulling faces. "Or perhaps Miss de Bourgh reasoned with her and next spring is a concession."

"She told you to call her Anne," Miss Darcy said. She stabbed a piece of meat.

Mr. Darcy cast his sister a frown. "She asked Elizabeth to address her as Anne, not refer to her as such." He turned back to Elizabeth. "You should learn the whereabouts of Mrs. Fortescue's home in Essex."

"I will enquire in my reply." It took all of Elizabeth's will not to follow her words by sticking out her tongue at Miss Darcy.

"Very good," Mr. Darcy said and reapplied his attention back to his plate.

"We could invite them both here," Elizabeth suggested, unwilling to let the conversation die. Besides which, if she couldn't talk to Mr. Darcy and Miss Darcy, she could talk to Colonel Fitzwilliam and Mrs. Fortescue.

Miss Darcy frowned. "How will you get her here?" she demanded. "It wouldn't be proper for her to travel alone and I doubt this cousin of yours, this Mr. Collins, will have the time or means to come this far. It would be very expensive for him."

"True," Mr. Darcy said.

He directed his words at Elizabeth, but she watched Miss Darcy. Sure enough, triumph flickered across Miss Darcy's face. Elizabeth kept her own expression neutral.

Later, as she lay in her oversized bed completely alone, Elizabeth couldn't help but ponder Miss Darcy's behavior. Jane was correct. Mr.

Darcy didn't give his sister any more of his time than he awarded Elizabeth. So, Miss Darcy couldn't dislike Elizabeth out of jealousy, could she? That brought the argument back to snobbery. As Elizabeth hardly had occasion to see Miss Darcy interact with anyone but herself, Mrs. Annesley, Mr. Darcy and the staff, she still couldn't decide if the younger woman was aloof or shy.

Elizabeth indulged in a long sigh, momentarily lending sound to her silent chamber. She'd been married for almost three weeks. She'd yet to share a bed with her husband, or even a private conversation that didn't end in argument. She'd made no headway in befriending her new sister. Elizabeth felt she was being isolated, just as Miss de Bourgh had been.

The following day, Elizabeth went to Mr. Darcy's office and requested funds for charitable work. After a lengthy lecture about dispensing charity, delivered in a way which implied Elizabeth lacked all competence, Mr. Darcy directed her to his steward. Elizabeth ignored Mr. Darcy's likely inadvertent insult, thanked him, and went on her way.

Advised by Mr. Darcy's steward, she spent the next week visiting tenants. This gave her more to do but provided no better conversation. The people beholden to Mr. Darcy were too much in awe of Elizabeth to treat her normally. She supposed that might fade over time, but that proved little consolation.

The following week, she received a letter from Lydia, the last of her sisters, other relations or friends to take the time to write her back. Lydia opened with several pages of babble about how happy and wonderful she and her husband were. This was followed by a discourse on how terrible Mr. Darcy was and how awful it was that Elizabeth had been made to marry him, a tirade Elizabeth had also received from her mother and Kitty, and already replied to. Lydia then described, in detail, the numerous social events she and Colonel Forster attended, her recounting full of gossip. Lydia included some tidbit or another about nearly everyone in Hertfordshire, much of what she said absurdly false but at least amusing.

Of particular interest to Elizabeth was mention of their mutual acquaintance, Mr. Wickham. Her mention of Mr. Collins and Lady Catherine, both of whom Mr. Darcy knew, had sparked the only reasonable conversation they'd managed since Elizabeth's arrival at Pemberley. Perhaps talk of Mr. Wickham could do the same. After all, if Mr. Wickham was to be believed, both Mr. Darcy and Miss Darcy knew him well.

The information Lydia passed along was hardly the sort to bring up at dinner, however. It seemed Mr. Wickham had soured of late. First, he'd stopped patronizing the local merchants, which Elizabeth suspected had something to do with the rumor about his using Mr. Darcy's credit. Then, he'd given up speaking well of Mr. Darcy. Instead, he'd begun spreading a tale that Mr. Darcy had denied him a living that should have been his.

Elizabeth had spent only some little time with Mr. Wickham and didn't feel she knew him at all well, but she had trouble believing the claim. As the news came from Lydia, Elizabeth couldn't even be certain Mr. Wickham perpetuated the tale. Still, if Lydia had heard the news, others had as well. It could be that Mr. Darcy might care enough about how people around Elizabeth's home viewed him to wish to set the matter straight. Elizabeth decided that, even though the topic lent itself to easy conversation less than her news about Lady Catherine, she'd be doing Mr. Darcy a service by bringing the rumor to his attention.

That evening, she again waited until the first course was served and most of the servants had left the room, then ventured, "I received a letter from my sister Lydia today. She mentioned someone who says you were once acquainted. A lieutenant in the militia. Mr. Wickham."

Miss Darcy's fork clattered to her plate. A look revealed her features slack with shock. Her chair flew backward as she stood. Without a word, she ran from the room.

Elizabeth turned to Mr. Darcy, a question on her lips.

"Never speak of that man," Mr. Darcy snapped.

"If that is your wish," Elizabeth grated out, swallowing her question. "I believe I've once again developed a headache." She stood with more decorum than Miss Darcy, and more anger. "If you'll excuse me."

Head high, Elizabeth strode from the room with deliberate calm. In her wake, she heard Mrs. Annesley excuse herself to go check on Georgiana. Elizabeth went to her room and remained there for the rest of the evening. It didn't trouble her at all that Mr. Darcy didn't come to her room that night.

Chapter Twenty-Five

The following morning, Elizabeth left Pemberley carrying a basket full of food and clothing for a tenant who'd recently given birth to her first child. When she reached the modest dwelling, she was greeted with warm enthusiasm. Dutifully, she admired the baby, kept all indication of her worry for Jane from her mien, and chatted amiably about nothing.

She then made her slow way back, thoroughly despondent. Mindless chatting with people who were too daunted by her role as Mrs. Darcy to see her as a person would not fulfil her need for companionship. She reached Pemberley, hardly able to appreciate the beauty of the structure, and slipped inside. She wandered through the manor, heading toward the foyer to check on the mail, feeling horribly isolated.

The mail had not yet come, she found when she reached the foyer, depriving her of the respite from loneliness that communication brought. She had Lydia's letter to reply to, but otherwise was caught up on her correspondence. Replying to Lydia seemed… daunting. All Elizabeth had managed was a draft of her rebuttal to Mr. Wickham's accusation about the living, but the draft didn't satisfy her. As Elizabeth had failed to bring the issue up to Mr. Darcy, by his order, she was experiencing difficulty conveying her certainty that Mr. Darcy hadn't done what Mr. Wickham said, though certain she was.

With a small shrug, Elizabeth departed the lovely, sun-filled foyer. Another walk didn't appeal to her, as the sky threatened rain. She had her choice of another lesson with Mrs. Reynolds, finishing the hem on one of her new gowns or replying to Lydia.

Or, she supposed, she could seek the library. She knew from her tours with Mrs. Reynolds precisely where the first floor, two story room stood. Undoubtedly, Pemberley's library was lovely. Elizabeth would, she assumed, enter it someday. For the moment, she preferred to avoid that particular room. The appeal of libraries, especially those in fancy manors, had recently soured.

As she made her meandering way through the halls, strands of music reached her. A slight, wistful smile touched her lips. Miss Darcy practiced on the pianoforte. She played wonderfully, one of the reasons Elizabeth had yet to touch the instrument. The other, of course, was how upset she imagined her use of Miss Darcy's pianoforte would make her new sister.

Elizabeth pivoted and hurried to her room to collect her sewing. Brash anger welling in her, she took her work to the music room and settled on one of the sofas there, opposite Mrs. Annesley. Pretending as if she didn't know Miss Darcy existed, Elizabeth plastered on a serene expression and set to stitching.

When Miss Darcy finished the piece she played, she started on scales. Grimly amused, Elizabeth continued her work. She would not be driven away by the scales. After some time, Miss Darcy fell silent. Elizabeth didn't look up. A moment later, discordant, angry sounds welled from the pianoforte. Mrs. Annesley winced and covered her ears. Elizabeth didn't permit her expression or the rhythm of her stitch to change.

The fallboard slammed closed over the keys. The bench screeched as it slid over the floor. Miss Darcy marched across the room to loom over Elizabeth.

"What are you doing here?" Miss Darcy demanded.

Elizabeth looked up, affecting a look of surprise. "Why, hello Georgiana."

"What are you doing here?" Miss Darcy repeated.

Elizabeth carefully set aside her sewing. She folded her hands in her lap and looked up at Miss Darcy. "Are you so uncomfortable with my presence that you played badly to drive me away?"

"Yes." Miss Darcy stamped her foot. "I am uncomfortable with your presence, and I was hoping to drive you away. I wish I could drive you away from Pemberley, and from my brother's life."

"Georgiana," Mrs. Annesley murmured, her tone one of mild reprimand.

Elizabeth tipped her head to the side. With deliberate calm, she asked, "Why?"

Miss Darcy's face turned red. "Because you trapped Fitz into marrying you."

Elizabeth considered denial, but what good would that do? "I do not believe I did. Did your brother not explain to you what happened?" Was ignorance the trouble? Elizabeth would be angry with someone who

214

trapped one of her siblings, and she wouldn't put it past Mr. Darcy not to deign to explain, even to his sister. "If he didn't explain how we came to marry, I am happy to."

Miss Darcy's face pulled into a sneer. "Oh, he explained." Her voice dripped sarcasm. "But I know the truth. His explanation is the story he wants put out, to protect you. He doesn't want his wife shunned. He put the blame on someone else, someone who can't defend herself, to make you appear what you aren't... innocent."

"How did you come to that conclusion?" Elizabeth asked. She wondered if Miss Darcy meant Miss Bingley. She could hardly refer to another. Had Miss Darcy heard some garbled tale of what transpired at Rosings?

"I received a letter telling me the truth." Miss Darcy looked down at Elizabeth as if she'd sighted a garden slug on the sofa.

"Oh?" Elizabeth prompted, hiding the anger that stabbed through her. A letter, indeed. Elizabeth had a good idea from whom. "And what, exactly, did this letter say?"

"It said that when you were at Netherfield Park, you stole a key and locked Fitz in the library with you, but he climbed out a window to get away," Miss Darcy said, her versions of events familiar to Elizabeth from Lady Catherine's accusations. "But you didn't stop there." Miss Darcy's featured portrayed disgust. "After your first scheme failed, you wantonly climbed into bed with my brother, since you had no proof that you were with him in the library. He still wouldn't marry you, and I don't blame him, and all that would be bad enough," Miss Darcy spat out, "but then I received a second letter disclosing how you made certain a version of the story came out in front of a whole party of people at Aunt Catherine's, Fitz realized he would have to marry you, so he lied to protect your reputation. He knew that you would be shunned if the truth became known."

Elizabeth contemplated the fuming young woman before her. Miss Darcy seemed very righteous in her indignation and anger, as Elizabeth would be if she believed such a tale. "And you believe Miss Bingley, rather than your brother?"

"So you know it was Miss Bingley who wrote to me," Miss Darcy exclaimed, expression triumphant.

"I assume it was," Elizabeth corrected. "She told a similar story to your aunt."

"Then it's true," Miss Darcy accused.

"That Miss Bingley told a similar story to Lady Catherine?" Elizabeth asked in deliberate misunderstanding. "Yes, that is true. Her version of events, on the other hand, is not. I imagine that what your brother told you is the actual truth."

"You mean his lie to save your reputation?"

Elizabeth offered a real frown, honestly perplexed. "You would really believe Miss Bingley over your brother?" she reiterated, unable to fathom such a decision.

Miss Darcy shrugged. "Yes. Why not? I know him well enough to know he would lie to avoid societies censure." She pointed a finger at Elizabeth. "And I know you're hiding something. You keep your letters in a locked cabinet."

Elizabeth's eyebrows swept upward, but she forbore from asking how Miss Darcy knew the cabinet in which she kept her letters was locked. She contemplated the triumphant look on Miss Darcy's face for a long moment. Apparently, there was only one way to satisfy her new sister that Elizabeth was neither secretive nor the sort to trap an unwilling gentleman.

Elizabeth stood, forcing Miss Darcy to take a step back, and gestured in the direction of the music room door. "Come with me."

Miss Darcy's face folded into lines of suspicion. "What? Why?"

"So we may put this matter behind us," Elizabeth said. She nodded to Mrs. Annesley. "You may join us, Mrs. Annesley."

Elizabeth turned and strode from the room. For a moment, only silence followed, but soon enough, she heard two sets of footsteps. They did not join her, but instead trailed her the entire way to her room.

Elizabeth led the way inside and to her cabinet of letters. She held the keys out to Miss Darcy. "Read them. You will know all my secrets. Please lock the cabinet when you are done and leave the keys. I shall go for a walk."

Miss Darcy stared at her, mute. Elizabeth turned to Mrs. Annesley, who accepted the keys with a nod.

Elizabeth headed for the foyer, where she informed the butler she was taking a walk. She strode out into a drizzle, reflecting that she wouldn't get any colder outside than under Miss Darcy's hateful glare. The wind stinging her eyes, Elizabeth strode away.

***

Seated in her favorite armchair, ensconced in her chamber, Anne reread Hawkins' letter, frowning. Hawkins remained well, charming, discreet and faithful, as Anne knew he would. That part of her plan proceeded amiably.

Darcy and Elizabeth, however, were not getting on. Hawkins, loyal as well as the consummate gentleman, gave few details and didn't place blame anywhere, yet Anne could glean their difficulties were serious and had something to do with Georgiana. With a frown, she folded Hawkins' letter and went to her desk.

Georgiana hadn't written lately, which was in itself odd. Anne could admit, she hadn't given that much thought. After all, they'd been in London together. True, Anne had been preoccupied, sneaking off with Hawkins to work on their plans, and so hadn't paid her young cousin much attention. Looking back, it seemed to Anne that Georgiana had been somewhat absent, which was not odd, but also sullen, which was a touch aberrant. Perusal of her last letter from Georgiana, received some months ago, revealed nothing out of the ordinary.

Anne folded Georgiana's last letter and returned it to its place. It would be difficult, she realized, to have her desk moved. The piece was terribly large and heavy, and packed with letters. As well, there were the large locked trunks of older letters in the attic. Perhaps she should have them burned?

Anne shook her head and locked her desk. She stowed the key in her bodice. If Hawkins wished her to know Darcy and Elizabeth weren't getting along, he was worried. More than that, he felt Anne might help. That meant the situation was not lost, only desperate. To help, she would need to go to wherever they were.

First, she must deal with her mother.

Anne had been home for some time, if she still wished to call Rosings her home. While in London, she and Hawkins had purchased a small townhome in a respectable location, near the Bingleys. Anne was grateful that her father had insisted she have control over her money, perhaps not realizing how much her capital would grow. Since returning to Rosings, Anne had been unobtrusively organizing and packing her belongings and had already shipped off quite a lot.

She glanced about her now somewhat barren room, then turned and headed for the hall. Normally, what she'd already accomplished would have necessitated a confrontation with Lady Catherine. Fortunately for Anne, her mother's current mental state could only be described as frothing mad, a condition induced by the news Anne had returned home with. Darcy and Elizabeth had married.

Anne smiled slightly as she padded noiselessly down the hall on slipper-clad feet. Always before, she'd attempted to avoid the worst of her mother's temper. She'd staved off confrontation. She'd never realized Lady Catherine could be driven to such a state that reason and observation were beyond her.

Her slippers producing the faintest patter as she hurried down the main staircase, Anne's smile fell. Likely, she shouldn't have permitted her mother's madness to go on so long. She'd been so much easier to work around this way, though. Anne couldn't seem to help but take advantage.

She turned down the corridor to her mother's favorite sitting room. As she neared, Mrs. Jenkinson, expression harried, ran out. She sighted Anne and hastened to her.

"Mrs. Jenkinson," Anne exclaimed. "Are you well?"

"It's your mother." Mrs. Jenkinson wrung a handkerchief in her hands. "She's begun throwing things."

Anne sighed. Yes, the time had come. She must reason with her mother. Until Lady Catherine was made to see that she'd caused her own misery, she would rage about, blaming everyone and everything else that she could. Somewhere behind Mrs. Jenkinson, a crash sounded. Anne's one-time companion winced.

"I'll speak to her," Anne said with a reassuring smile. She stepped around Mrs. Jenkinson and strode into the parlor.

Lady Catherine stood in the center of the room. She had not, as far as Anne could tell, actually thrown anything. Rather, she held her amethyst-topped cane out like a sword, employing the heavy wood to swipe decorative items from various tables, sending them smashing to the floor or bouncing onto the thick rug. As Anne watched, her mother reversed her hold on the cane, took aim at a porcelain figurine that had landed safely on the thick carpet, and slammed the amethyst down on the poor unsuspecting depiction of a dancer.

"Mother," Anne snapped. "Need I remind you that Rosings and everything within these walls belongs to me?"

Lady Catherine whirled to face her. "And should have belonged to Darcy, if that hoyden hadn't seduced him with her vile, wild ways."

"Seduced, Mother?" Anne walked up to her mother and snatched the cane from her hand. "Don't be ridiculous. You know the truth of the story. Elizabeth had no wish to marry Darcy."

"Impossible." Lady Catherine made to grab her cane.

Anne held it away. "Factual. As Darcy pointed out, Miss Bingley's tale is terribly flawed. He would never climb out a window rather than behave with honor."

"But no woman would endanger herself to avoid marrying Darcy," Lady Catherine all but yelled, as if volume made her viewpoint more correct.

"I would," Anne said quietly. "And so would Elizabeth."

"Don't call her that. I won't hear that name in this house."

"Fine," Anne said sweetly. "Mrs. Darcy."

Lady Catherine let out a screech and made another grab for her cane.

Anne stepped back out of reach, relatively certain her mother wouldn't deign to chase after. "Admit it, Mother. Elizabeth did not wish to wed Darcy. You forced her to by attempting to spread Miss Bingley's lies." Anne worked to keep a touch of unbecoming glee from her voice. "You were duped, easily so, because you wished to be. You let Miss Bingley tell you what you desired to hear and then ran off to repeat the tale. Now, you must live with what you caused to happen. Darcy asked Elizabeth to marry him, and you forced her to accept where she otherwise would have declined."

Lady Catherine let out another screech. Anne took another step back, so she could cover her ears and keep the cane well out of reach. Her mother's voice rose in volume and pitch. Anne clamped her hands harder over her ears, the cane pressing painfully against the side of her head. Askance, she saw Mrs. Jenkinson and several servants pile into the doorway, but none dared enter.

With a final wail, Lady Catherine collapsed into her favorite chair. She covered her face with her hands. A small sobbing sound leaked between her fingers.

Anne slowly lowered her hands. She turned and set the cane on the sofa behind her. Tentative, least her mother's tears be a ruse, she crept forward, then lay a hand on Lady Catherine's shoulder. "Mother?"

"I've ruined your life," Lady Catherine sobbed into her hands. "You were to have Darcy, and I've taken him from you. Me, and that horrible, lying, faithless Miss Bingley."

Pity welled in Anne, but she tamped it down. Lady Catherine would admit fault only once. Her role must be cemented now, before she had time to warp and twist past action in her mind and leave herself inculpable. "You admit, Mother, that you were an easy target for Miss

Bingley's rather obvious lies because you were so very eager to see evil in Elizabeth?"

Lady Catherine let out another sob and nodded.

"And you can see how your attempts to manage the lives of others only lead to sorrow, resentment and strife?"

Her mother's head snapped up. Her eyes narrowed. "What are you saying, Anne?"

"I never intended to wed Darcy, Mother, nor he me. He had other plans for his life and I have other plans for mine."

"Other plans?" Lady Catherine repeated, eyes instantly dry.

"Yes, and you shall abide by them because, if you do not, you will reap what you sow, just as you have with Darcy."

"What other plans?" An edge of command crept back into Lady Catherine's voice.

"You'll learn of them soon enough," Anne said, unwilling to chance her mother's interference. "First, I will finish sending on those of my possessions I wish moved to my new townhome in London. Then—" and, in a flash, Anne realized what the trouble with Georgiana must be. Just as Miss Bingley had lashed out by writing Lady Catherine, so too must she have written another acquaintance... Georgiana. "Then, I shall go visit the Darcys." And answer Hawkins unspoken request to set Georgiana right. Furthermore, Anne realized, Hawkins had reached out to her because he wouldn't wish to leave Darcy's employ until he saw his longtime master and friend happy in his union. Yes, Anne would visit Darcy and wouldn't leave until he and Elizabeth were happy, and Hawkins free to wed her.

"Finish sending possessions to London?" Lady Catherine echoed. "New townhome?" She looked about the room, as if to see if ought was missing.

Anne refocused on her mother. "Yes. While you've been ranting and railing against a union you perpetuated, I've been packing."

"You are... leaving?"

"I am."

"You plan to move to London? To live alone?"

"No, Mother. I plan to move to London and wed."

Lady Catherine shook her head, expression stunned. "Who?"

"I will tell you when the time comes."

"But—" Indignation turned Lady Catherine's words into an angry sputter.

Anne firmed her visage. "If you've learned anything from Darcy's union, if, indeed, you are capable of learning such things, understand this, Mother. Should you attempt to stop me or impede me in any way, you will never see me again."

Lady Catherine stared at Anne through round red-rimmed eyes.

"Have I made myself clear, Mother?"

Lady Catherine offered a mute nod.

"Thank you. I'm pleased I have your blessing," Anne said. She turned and left the room.

Chapter Twenty-Six

Darcy readied for dinner with a feeling of trepidation, which was the way he always felt about attending dinner of late. That evening, however, was worse than usual. He hardly noticed Hawkins' concerned look, nor mustered the will to attempt reassurance.

Earlier, from the window of his office, Darcy had seen Elizabeth stomp through the garden even though it was raining, expression furious. She'd looked angrier than when they'd argued on their first night at Pemberley. Angrier, even, than when he'd lost his temper and ordered her never to speak of George Wickham.

Darcy sighed, then wished he hadn't, for Hawkins actually frowned. How could Darcy expect Elizabeth to know not to mention Wickham? Darcy had assumed the two met in Hertfordshire, aware Wickham was stationed there and knew Elizabeth's aunt and uncle. She would have seen only Wickham's charming side, and Darcy was well aware of how charming the man could be.

After all, he'd charmed Darcy's father into leaving him an inheritance. He'd gotten Darcy to pay his debts on several occasions, though that had less to do with charm than Darcy's pride in his family name. Worst of all, Wickham had charmed Georgiana into nearly eloping with him the previous summer in Ramsgate. With no knowledge of that, how could Elizabeth know not to bring up the man's name, ever, let alone at dinner?

Another sigh threatened. Darcy transformed his frustration into a scowl instead. He would speak with Elizabeth. He wouldn't reveal Georgiana's secret. He hadn't the right. He would, however, explain that his sister must be handled more delicately. Elizabeth must learn not to upset Georgiana.

"Will that be all, sir?" Hawkins said.

Darcy blinked. He turned to the mirror to find he was perfectly clad for dinner. He hadn't even noticed Hawkins tie his cravat, let alone place shoes on his feet, for which Darcy must have lifted first one foot, then the other.

"If I may suggest, sir, perhaps a woman's touch?"

"I beg your pardon?" Darcy asked. His mind felt sluggish, as if trapped down a deep, dark well that brimmed with Elizabeth's anger and Georgiana's misery.

"I would not presume to have any notion what is troubling you, sir, but perhaps a woman's touch is called for. May I suggest Miss de Bourgh, as cousin and friend to both ladies?"

A bit of Darcy's tension stole away, replaced by amusement at Hawkins' phrasing. "You have no notion what is on my mind, yet you have a good idea of how to rectify the issue?"

"Precisely, sir."

Darcy's frown eased. "You may have something there, Hawkins," he admitted. After all, Darcy had no notion how to manage the two. "I will take your suggestion under advisement."

"Thank you, sir." Hawkins hesitated, an act more felt than seen. "I'm afraid I've taken the liberty of alerting Miss de Bourgh to the possibility that you may require her."

Darcy's eyebrows shot up. "You have?" Hawkins must believe the situation dire indeed. Then, was it not? Darcy had been married for weeks and had yet to consummate his union. That could hardly be considered normal.

"I have."

"Well." Darcy had no notion what to say. It wasn't like Hawkins to take such initiative. Yet, he hadn't actually done anything. He was a good man, loyal to a fault, and Darcy had no desire to reprimand him, especially when he wasn't sure a reprimand was required. Possibly he should thank Hawkins.

With a shrug, Darcy turned from Hawkins to take another look in the mirror. He squared his shoulders. Hawkins, as always, had him in perfect order. Not that anyone was likely to notice Darcy's appearance. He wished Elizabeth would.

"Right, then," he said. "Dinner." He turned to march from his room.

He certainly noticed Elizabeth's appearance, he mused as he headed for the dining room. Her lithe form. He gleaming tresses. The new dresses that displayed her beauty as was fitting for his wife. The way her eyes flashed when she was, apparently inevitably, angry.

So far, he found marriage exceedingly frustrating and decidedly unfulfilling. He liked Elizabeth, form, mind and spirit. He'd thought, perhaps, she was coming to regard him more favorably. That was, until they reached Pemberley.

No, he realized as he neared the dining room. The trouble had begun the moment they all got into his carriage. Or had it begun even before that? His frown returned as he recalled how busy his usually less-than-social sister had been when the time came for her to meet Elizabeth. He'd had to, by surprise, drag her away from her lessons simply to take her for tea at the Bingleys' townhome.

Darcy stepped into the dining room and pulled out his watch. Twenty minutes until dinnertime. He looked down the long table, four places set. Twenty minutes was a long time to sit alone with such dire thoughts. Maybe Elizabeth was correct. He should at least invite Richard to visit. Perhaps the Gardiners as well. And Anne, as Hawkins suggested. Darcy and Elizabeth spent no time alone as it was. At least, with a house full of people, they might all be happier.

The rapid patter of feet alerted him and he turned, stuffing his watch back into his pocket. Georgiana rushed down the hall, alone. Darcy opened his mouth to ask after her companion. Not that she required Mrs. Annesley's presence at all times, especially in Pemberley but, ever since Ramsgate, he felt a jolt of worry anytime he found Georgiana on her own.

"Fitz, there you are," she cried before he could speak.

"Georgiana."

She slid to a halt before him, her rapid pace and silk slippers combining to propel her forward. She reached out and grabbed his arm, much to his surprise. "Come with me." She tugged.

Darcy took in her red-rimmed eyes. "You have been crying."

"I have. Come with me."

"Did Elizab—"

"She did nothing." Georgiana's brow furrowed, as though she might recommence weeping. "Absolutely nothing. That's why you must come with me."

"But Elizabeth is likely on her way here." What would she think if she found the dining room empty?

"She's still in her room now, which is where we're going." Georgiana yanked harder, strong enough to sway him. "I must speak with her. We both must, and I should like to do so in her room, alone."

Darcy glanced about. To his chagrin, he realized the dining room was not, of course, empty. Servants stood where they always did, immobile but attentive, ready for dinner to commence. He issued a sharp nod and gave in to Georgiana's attempt to drag him from the room.

"Why did you not go to Elizabeth's room on your own, or with Mrs. Annesley?" he asked as they ascended the stair. "Elizabeth is your sister, after all." Darcy didn't like to think Georgiana somehow feared to speak with Elizabeth.

"I need your support." A look, askance, showed Georgiana's flush. "I misjudged her. I think. Well, I know. I may have to give her a very humble apology."

That wasn't particularly helpful information, but as it was hopeful for their relationship, Darcy made no further protest as they headed for Elizabeth's door.

Georgiana's knock was almost instantly met by the door opening. Elizabeth, lovely in her evening gown, looked between Darcy and his sister in surprise. Her gaze settled on Darcy.

"Am I late for dinner?" she asked.

"No," Darcy said.

"I would, that is, may I speak with you?" Georgiana stammered. "With Fitz."

Elizabeth frowned slightly. "In the sitting room?" she suggested, nodding toward the room which adjoined hers to Darcy's.

Georgiana nodded. "Yes."

Elizabeth stepped into the hall and headed to the next door, which opened into their joint sitting room. She opened the door and led the way inside, then moved to the cluster of sofas before the fireplace. Darcy and his sister followed. A cheery blaze danced in the grate, lit each evening by his ever-hopeful staff.

"Shall we sit?" Elizabeth asked after they all stood for a long moment in deafening silence.

"Yes," Georgiana said and dropped onto a sofa.

Elizabeth took the one opposite her, leaving Darcy to sit with either his wife or sister, or on the sofa in the middle, directly opposite the fireplace. He elected the middle. Georgiana didn't seem to notice, but Elizabeth cast a slightly sardonic look his way. Once more, silence enveloped the room.

"You wish to speak with me?" Elizabeth ventured.

Georgiana turned to Darcy. "Please tell me again how you happened to be locked in the library at Netherfield Park, but this time, please don't leave anything out."

Darcy grimaced. All he'd told his sister the first time was that someone he did not wish to name had, vindictively, locked him and Elizabeth in together, but that they had kept the incident from becoming public knowledge and Elizabeth had not insisted he marry her. He'd left out any other details both as a kindness to Bingley and to protect his pride.

"I think she must hear the whole of the incident," Elizabeth said quietly. "From you."

Darcy drew in a deep breath, then related the details of the evening. He forced himself not to gloss over the amount of work Elizabeth put into her plan for escape, aware of her mild amusement as he spoke. He didn't even leave out the bit about her refusing his coat. When he reiterated her warning that Miss Bingley might climb into his bed, Georgiana gasped.

Darcy turned to Elizabeth. "The story becomes even less appropriate for my sister after that."

Elizabeth, eyes alight with interest, tipped her head to the side. "You never did tell me any more of what happened, though Jane summarized the events and I've pieced together that you spent the night in the servants' quarters." Elizabeth's bowlike lips twitched up at the corners. "Though I never really believed that you slept in there on a bet." She seemed about to add to that but closed her mouth over the words.

"But there is more?" Georgiana asked tentatively.

He may as well have it out, Darcy decided. "There is." He went on to tell how he'd decided to take Elizabeth's advice, how he'd permitted Hawkins to lie for him, and sleep in his bed. He then recounted what happened during the night, and even both meetings the following morning, first with Bingley and then with the whole family. He ended with Bingley's plan to remove Miss Bingley from society.

When he finished, silence fell. Elizabeth appeared contemplative. Georgiana, shocked.

"When I issued that warning, I did so in jest," Elizabeth murmured.

"Well, I am very pleased I took your words to heart," Darcy replied.

"Hawkins is the grandson of a gentleman?" Elizabeth asked. "Miss Bingley should have wed him. From what I've seen, he's kind, loyal and intelligent, which is more than she deserves."

"I'm pleased she didn't," Darcy admitted. "Selfish of me, because he could have had her fortune, but he's one of my closest confidants.

He's invaluable to me and deserves better than Miss Bingley."

"None of that is what Miss Bingley wrote to me," Georgiana blurted.

Darcy turned to his sister in surprise. "She wrote to you? What did she say?"

Georgiana swallowed. "I don't remember everything. She told me to burn the letters once I read them, so I did." Georgiana's face crinkled. She blinked back tears. "In the first, she said Elizabeth stole a key and locked the two of you in the library together and that you climbed out the window immediately." Georgiana's face turned red. "Then, Elizabeth went to your room and climbed into your bed, in the middle of the night, because she realized she'd be sent back to Longbourn in the morning and that was her one last chance."

"I did return to Longbourn in the morning," Elizabeth cut in. "Everyone would know that." She glanced at Darcy. "In your carriage. It's not a far cry for people to believe I was sent away, as my own mother did, instead of that you leant me and Jane your conveyance."

Darcy nodded, a grim, simmering anger forming in his gut. "What else?" he asked his sister.

Georgiana shook her head. "She said that you still refused to marry Elizabeth. You said you had no legal obligation to do so and you wouldn't be tricked into marriage." She turned to Elizabeth. "Miss Bingley said you then forged a love letter from Fitz, promising marriage, and left it out, so Lady Catherine could see it." Georgiana closed her eyes for a moment. When she opened them, they were hollow with despair. "I should have realized she was lying. She said Elizabeth forged your handwriting so well that you realized you were trapped and married her, even though you hate her. Then Miss Bingley said Elizabeth would never be accepted by polite society and that she felt sorry for me." Georgiana dropped her face to her hands.

Darcy stared at her. How dare Miss Bingley craft such lies? How far had she spread them?

"That's even worse than her lies to Lady Catherine," Elizabeth murmured. "She's grown more desperate, or vindictive."

"How could I believe her?" Georgiana's voice came out muffled by her hands. "How would Elizabeth even know what your handwriting looked like? I'm such a fool."

Elizabeth stood and crossed before Darcy to sit beside his sister. She placed a hand on Georgiana's bowed shoulder. "She is very cunning.

She played similar games with your aunt. You couldn't have known she lied. I understand you've known her for years."

"All the more reason," Georgiana sobbed. "I've never cared for her, yet I willingly took her words over Fitz's, and yours."

Elizabeth murmured soothingly, gently rubbing Georgiana's back as she cried. Elizabeth's expression held no rancor, only concern. Darcy wondered if he would be so forgiving, had he been the subject of the unfounded, persistent ire of one of Elizabeth's relatives. Elizabeth had such a loving spirit. She almost seemed too good for him and his circle.

Suddenly, he found he more than liked Elizabeth. His interest in her went deeper than that of injured pride. He'd never stopped thinking of her from the moment they first met at that assembly in Hertfordshire. Yes, his thoughts had often been uncharitable, but to Elizabeth they always, inevitably turned, and to Elizabeth, he now realized, they always would. Did he, then, love her? He still didn't know if he could fully give his heart to someone who held no regard for him.

Georgiana raised a tear streaked visage. She looked past Elizabeth. "I'm so sorry I didn't believe you, Fitz."

"Why didn't you?" Elizabeth asked, head tipped to the side in that endearing way of hers. "From what I know of your brother, he's very honest."

"Because, once, he lied for me." Georgiana's cheeks reddened at the admission. "He takes his responsibilities very seriously. If he lied for his sister, he might lie for his wife."

There was a long pause. Darcy tugged at his cravat, which Hawkins had obviously tied too tight. He remembered the lie. On top of that, he mentally added the additional one he'd only just admitted to, the lie that he'd slept in the servants' quarters on a bet. True, he hadn't spoken the words, but he'd permitted them to stand. He wondered if, moments after uttering her praise, Elizabeth wished she could revoke her kind words.

"Well, one person none of us need lie for or protect, I think, is Miss Bingley," Elizabeth said, a hard edge in her voice. "I wouldn't have passed her name about before, out of a kindness to Jane and Mr. Bingley, but she's made our silence incriminating. If we must mention her, she's brought it upon herself."

Darcy nodded. "Lady Catherine already revealed Miss Bingley's name, that day at Rosings. Much of the story is already out." He grimaced. "A multitude of variations likely circulate through London, and already did even before we wed."

Elizabeth shook her head. "I suppose there's really no way to ever keep something like that a secret."

"You are right," Georgiana said, sitting up straight.

Darcy turned to his sister, surprised, an emotion mirrored on Elizabeth's face.

Georgiana reached for Elizabeth's hands, but looked past her to Darcy. "Elizabeth is right. There's no way to keep such secrets." She turned back to Elizabeth, expression resolute. "About a year ago, when I was fifteen—"

"Georgiana," Darcy said sharply.

Georgiana met his gaze again. "Elizabeth is my sister and I trust her. She should know what happened."

Darcy glared at his sister. He hated this tale. His sister's near ruin. His obvious lack as her protector. George Wickham's ultimate betrayal of any shred of trust that lingered between them. If Darcy had his way, no one, not even Elizabeth, would hear what Georgiana meant to tell.

Chapter Twenty-Seven

To Darcy's surprise, Georgiana matched his glare. Darcy shook his head. Georgiana's expression took on a familiar, mulish cast. His sister at her least yielding. Finally, Darcy folded his arms across his chest and shrugged. Georgiana turned back to Elizabeth.

"I was in Ramsgate," his sister continued. "George... that is, Mr. Wickham, encountered me as if by chance. You've met him, I believe?"

Elizabeth nodded.

"You must realize, at least somewhat, how charming he can be?"

Another nod of those dark tresses. Darcy wished he could see Elizabeth's face, read her expression. The way she sat, her hands clasped in Georgiana's, her nods and silence were all he had by which to guess her thoughts.

Instead, Darcy watched his sister's face carefully for any sign she didn't wish to continue her disclosure. He wouldn't force her to confide in Elizabeth, though it pleased him that, if she must confide the story to someone, she wished it to be to Elizabeth. Georgiana had gone far enough, as well, that he would finish the tale for Elizabeth, in private, if she faltered. Elizabeth must guess much already.

"Mr. Wickham persuaded me to elope with him," Georgiana said in a rush.

Darcy wished anew he could see Elizabeth's face. Her shoulders didn't tense, although his did. She didn't yank her hands from his sister's.

"My governess, Mrs. Younge, supported the idea." Georgiana bit her lip, gaze darting to Darcy and away again. "I was going to do it, run off with George, but Fitz came, and I realized how hurt he would be. I knew he didn't like George, but I didn't know why. I thought it had something to do with our father." Again, she looked past Elizabeth to meet Darcy's gaze.

He gave a shake of his head, refuting her guess.

Georgiana turned back to Elizabeth. "Thinking of how unhappy Fitz would be, I wanted to break off my plans with George, but I didn't know how, so I confessed to my brother." Georgiana winced. "If I thought he didn't care for George before, he definitely didn't after I told him what George planned. I've never seen Fitz so angry."

"And the lie?" Elizabeth asked. "That Mr. Darcy told for you?"

Darcy frowned. It seemed odd for Elizabeth to call him Mr. Darcy. Georgiana called him Fitz, as she had since she'd learned to speak. Richard, Anne and even Bingley called him Darcy. Casting back through his mind, he couldn't recall Elizabeth addressing him as anything, ever, other than Mr. Darcy.

Except when they'd wed. She'd repeated back for the priest that she would take Fitzwilliam George Darcy as her husband. He recalled the thrill that shot through him at those words.

"We were visiting Rosings," Georgiana was saying, her words penetrating Darcy's musings. "Lady Catherine asked why Fitz had let Mrs. Younge go and hired Mrs. Annesley. Aunt Catherine had recommended Mrs. Younge, you see. Fitz said she proved unsatisfactory. Lady Catherine pressed for more detail and he said she had poor judgment when hiring servants."

Darcy grimaced. At the time, he'd wished he could come up with a way to tell the truth without hinting at Georgiana's transgression. He wasn't quick in that way, though. Only later did it occur to him that he might have said Mrs. Younge had permitted Georgiana to associate with a fortune hunter.

"I should have said that Mrs. Younge permitted Georgiana to mingle with an unsatisfactory person," Darcy felt obligated to admit. "Rather than lie."

Elizabeth twisted to regard him over her shoulder, expression thoughtful. "I'm not certain that would have worked. Lady Catherine would have demanded to know who. If you had been evasive, she might have pressed for more information. At a certain point, all you could do was refuse to answer. Knowing what little I do about your aunt, she would have sought the truth and might have revealed it."

"She would have," Georgiana said with an impish grin. "She's a bulldog and never lets go."

Tension eased in Darcy's chest. This was the Georgiana he hadn't seen since before the incident in Ramsgate, the one with a sense of humor. The joyous child within her that was squelched by George Wickham.

Amusement fled Georgiana's features. She released Elizabeth's hands and clasped hers tightly in her lap, then let out a sigh. "Now we are a family full of scandals and secrets." She looked down at her hands, her curls coming forward to obscure her face. "But I have more to confess than believing Miss Bingley. I also thought you were hated by your family."

"Why ever would you think that?" Elizabeth asked, tone surprised. She swiveled to look at Darcy again.

He could only shrug.

"No one came to your wedding," Georgiana said. "Only your father, who looked so sad, and Mrs. Bingley and the Gardiners. I know they're all too nice not to attend. Even the celebration in Hertfordshire seemed more like your mother having a party than celebrating the wedding. Your mother said something to me about how she was glad your behavior hadn't prevented the wedding."

"She knows something happened at Netherfield Park," Elizabeth said, "but doesn't know the details."

"Then, I heard you begging Mrs. Bingley to come visit, and found you crying when she wrote that she would not."

"Crying?" Darcy asked sharply. He didn't like to think of Elizabeth crying. Not for any reason.

"Then there are the letters," Georgiana continued, both women ignoring him. "You keep them in a locked cabinet. I thought you were hiding something." She glanced up at Elizabeth, revealing cheeks suffused with red. "Now that I've read them, I realize you don't have any secrets to hide."

"You read Elizabeth's letters?" Darcy demanded, sitting forward. "Georgiana, that is unacceptable."

His sister cast him a startled look. "She gave me the keys and told me to read them."

Darcy shook his head. He'd no idea how much his sister disliked Elizabeth. No notion of her misconceptions. He hadn't noticed Elizabeth's apparent sorrow that her sister couldn't visit, or known that Georgiana had read Elizabeth's letters. He was beginning to feel as if he had no grasp of what transpired in his own home.

Georgiana's flush deepened. "And I did read them," she said to Elizabeth. "All of them. You're not the person I thought. I hope Mrs. Bingley and her baby will be well. I'm sorry, very sorry, I believed bad things about you."

Darcy pushed a hand through his hair. Mrs. Bingley was with child?

And unwell? All his last letter from Bingley had mentioned was a return to Hertfordshire to take the country air. Darcy had the sudden suspicion that no one actually confided in him. Was he not a good friend?

Elizabeth reached for his sister, drawing her into an embrace. "I forgive you, Georgiana. Miss Bingley misled you." Elizabeth shook her head. "No. Let me be blunt. She lied to you." Elizabeth squeezed his sister tight for a moment. Releasing Georgiana, she turned fully to Darcy. "It seems, on top of the scene that took place in Rosings' parlor, that Miss Bingley has been spreading tales somewhat freely. There can be no hope all of society hasn't heard one version of the incident or another." She met his gaze squarely. "The best we can do now is tell the truth and hope it will be believed."

The full scope of what Miss Bingley had done settled on Darcy. Until that moment, he'd been too focused on Elizabeth, on navigating his new union, to contemplate the reception he would receive when next he set foot in London. "Whether it be the truth or Miss Bingley's lie, I will be the laughingstock of society," he realized. "Either I was trapped by a scheming hoyden or I wed a woman who climbed out of a window to avoid marrying me."

Elizabeth rose from the sofa on which Georgiana sat and came to alight beside him. She placed a tentative hand on his coat sleeve. "But it will pass," Elizabeth said. "I don't know much about the circles you move in, but won't there be another scandal that supersedes it?"

Darcy shook his head. "Certainly, but our scandal will still be there. Those who believe the truth and are kind will not mock me, but they will pity me, and that will be the best for which I can hope."

Elizabeth pressed her lips together. He could see her mind working, seeking words of reassurance. Her fine-boned hand still lingered on his arm. He could feel her warmth through coat and shirt. He wished he dared cover her fingers with his, but he feared she would pull away.

"Not if you are happy," Georgiana said.

Elizabeth's hand fell from his arm as she turned to look at his sister.

Georgiana stood and hurried to the hall door to peek out, then returned to the fireplace to crack open the servants' door, discreetly hidden by the molding. She turned back, took in Darcy's questioning look, and shrugged. "I thought it best to check if anyone is listening."

Darcy nodded.

Instead of retaking her seat, Georgiana came to stand before them. "If you act like you are madly in love with Elizabeth, people won't feel sorry for you," she said, directing her words at Darcy.

He frowned, uncertain his sister's idea held merit. He turned a to Elizabeth.

"It may work," she said slowly. A wistful smile crossed her lips. "Especially if I act like I return that affection."

Darcy didn't know how to answer that, so he resorted to silence.

Georgiana paced away. When she turned back, her face shone red once more. "You don't seek Elizabeth's company during the day," she blurted, voice low. "And... and every servant knows you don't spend the night with her."

"Georgiana," Darcy reprimanded in shocked tones.

His sister's face glowed more brightly than the blaze in the grate behind her. "Your bed is slept in every night. It's the talk of the household."

Darcy made a sputtering sound, too indignant to find words. A quick glance showed Elizabeth's cheeks nearly as red as Georgiana's.

His sister drew in a quick breath. "The servants know everything that goes on. You have to spend time together." She made a vague gesture, encompassing the two of them. "Act as if you like each other."

Elizabeth turned to him, cheeks pink but lovely eyes ripe with question. "I can manage that."

"I will still be laughed at," Darcy said.

Elizabeth flushed more deeply and dropped her gaze.

Darcy silently cursed himself. Here was his beautiful wife, hopeful he might even pretend to care for her, and he still yammered on about his reputation?

"But it will eventually go away," Georgiana said into the strained silence.

Darcy tugged at his cravat again. "Not completely." He scowled.

Georgiana let out a sigh and plopped down on her vacated sofa. She wrung her hands, eyes abstract. Beside Darcy, Elizabeth shifted. She looked from him to Georgiana and back.

"Who will sponsor me?" Georgiana said.

"Sponsor you?" Darcy shook his head, confused by the change of topic.

Georgiana turned to him. "When I have a season. I certainly don't wish Lady Catherine to, and Anne said she will never marry. If you can't bring yourself to at least give the appearance of loving Elizabeth, to put this scandal behind you, who will sponsor me? She won't be accepted into society, so how can I be?"

"I did not say I will not pretend to care for my wife," he protested. Not, really, that he would need to pretend. Not if Elizabeth warmed to him even a little.

"You didn't say you would," Georgiana challenged. "And we both know you do not care to lie. Pretense is an ongoing lie."

"We already established that you believe I will lie for my wife." Darcy felt his patience with the entire conversation waning. Besides which, none of them had gotten dinner yet. He realized he was rather hungry.

"I have family in trade," Elizabeth said, voice quiet and apologetic. "I may never be acceptable."

"The Bingleys have family in trade," he hastened to remind her, not carrying for the forlorn note in her voice. "They are accepted by many. You will be accepted as my wife."

Elizabeth raised luminous eyes to meet his gaze. "Not if people think you hate me."

"Are you willing to pretend you are in love with me?" Darcy asked, wishing he dared ask for more.

"Yes."

Darcy waited, but she didn't elaborate. He realized he very much wanted her to love him. Or at least like him. After a long moment, he nodded. "Then we should try Georgiana's way. But for now, I think, we should head to dinner. The staff must be wondering what became of us." If they didn't already know, as his sister seemed to feel they knew everything.

"There is one other…issue I want to bring up." Georgiana said, halting Darcy when he would have stood. "Elizabeth received a letter from one of her younger sisters, a Mrs. Forster."

Darcy frowned. He didn't care for the idea that Georgiana had read Elizabeth's letters. Her doing so crossed a firm line of propriety and put him in mind overmuch of their aunt. And he especially didn't care for the notion of his sister being exposed to Lydia Forster's rare form of idiocy.

"About Mr. Wickham," Elizabeth said.

Darcy's frown dipped into a scowl.

"Yes," Georgiana agreed. "Mrs. Forster wrote that Mr. Wickham is spreading it all around Hertfordshire that you denied him the living our father left him, Fitz." She met Darcy's gaze squarely. "Is the living why you and George weren't getting along?"

Darcy glowered at Georgiana. He didn't care to speak of George Wickham, friend turned betrayer. His sister's gaze remained surprisingly unwavering, however.

Finally, Darcy shrugged. "No. We both knew he would not make a good clergyman. Only father held an idealized enough view of him to believe he might. I was happy to pay him for the living. Three thousand pounds, to be exact."

"Three thousand pounds?" Elizabeth exclaimed.

"Then why did you stop being friends?" Georgiana pressed.

"He kept racking up debts and expecting me to pay them," Darcy said. "He became increasingly erratic, selfish and unreliable. I had not completely given up on him, though. Not until…" Even though both women knew what he would say, he didn't care to speak of Ramsgate.

"Oh," Georgiana said.

Darcy didn't find her response illuminating. Nor did he care for any more talk. He was sure he hadn't spoken so much in years, and never so intently. He stood. "We are very late for dinner."

Elizabeth obediently rose. "May I write to my sister and correct Mr. Wickham's lie?"

Darcy shrugged. "If you wish." He cared little for the opinion of anyone who would believe Wickham's tales. He frowned slightly. Was that because they were being spread outside of London? He cared a great deal about Miss Bingley's lies, spread among London society.

Georgiana rose as well. "I have one more question," she said. "Why did you have to switch beds with Hawkins? Why not put a chair next to the door with something on it that would fall and wake you if she came in? Or put your key inside the lock? Her key wouldn't have worked then. There must have been something easier than what you did."

Darcy looked down at his sister in surprise. "Those things did not occur to me."

Beside him, Elizabeth chuckled. Darcy turned to take in her smile. Warmth unfurled in him.

"Look at it this way," Elizabeth said. "If your brother hadn't switched beds with Hawkins, the servants of Netherfield Park might never have gotten new blankets."

Chapter Twenty-Eight

Darcy stood in the sitting room he shared with Elizabeth, outside her chamber door, as he had every night since they'd reached Pemberley, though he'd only mustered the courage to knock the very first night. That hadn't worked out as he'd planned, or at all well, and their relationship had seemed worse every day since, until that evening.

After heading to the dining room, to find a somewhat worried Mrs. Annesley waiting, they'd had a convivial dinner. Georgiana had been more her old self. Elizabeth, as well, behaved nearer to how Darcy recalled from Netherfield Park. The evening had been much more in line with Darcy's imaginings of how life with Elizabeth would be.

Now, he stood outside her bedroom door. Again. Only, this time he was clad in his night clothes and a dressing gown. Was that too presumptuous of him? Perhaps he should return to his room and dress. What if…

He drew in a deep breath. They were married. Eventually, she must see him in nightclothes. Hopefully, out of them as well. Darcy fixed their pleasant evening firmly in his mind and raised a hand to knock.

The door swung inward before he could.

"Oh." Elizabeth exclaimed. Mien surprised and likewise clad for her respite, she stood just inside the door. A smile turned up her lips. "I was…"

In the flickering light cast by the fire behind him, Darcy saw a blush steal up her cheeks. His arm dropped back to his side.

"I was about to come find you," she continued, smile unwavering.

Darcy took a step backward, making a sweeping gesture to encompass the siting room. "Would you care to join me in the sitting room?"

Elizabeth tipped her head slightly, then shook it. "I think not. That was the plan the last time you came to my door, and it didn't work well." She reached out, grasped the front of his robe, and tugged.

Elizabeth, rather slight, wouldn't generally have much hope of moving him, but Darcy was so taken by surprise, he let her drag him into her bedroom. She pushed the door shut behind him, then turned back to face him. A fire burned in her grate as well, lending an extra luminous glow to her crimson cheeks.

"I thought we could speak in here," she said, voice a touch breathless.

"Certainly." His hands twitched, as if they would reach for her, but he kept them firmly at his sides. "On what did you wish to speak?"

Her gaze roamed the room. He saw it settle for an instant on the two chairs before the fireplace, then move on, to the large, empty bed. She stared at that momentous piece of furniture for a long moment.

"The idea is to make it appear…" She drew in a slow breath, chest rising and falling, gaze still caught on the bed. "That is, we ought to make it seem as if my bed… that we…" She turned to look him full in the eyes. "Let us lay in bed, side by side, and talk."

"Very well." Darcy knew those calm words were his, yet he made no move. In bed with Elizabeth, his wife, it would be pure torture to restrain himself to talk until she wished for more.

Elizabeth walked to the end of the bed. One delicate, long-fingered hand trailed across the coverlet. "Do you prefer one side to the other?"

Darcy shook his head. What care had he for sides so long as that slender form lay next to him?

She cast him a surprised look. "No? Jane and Mary both tell me married people do. Select a side of the bed, that is."

He wondered what else Elizabeth had been told about wedded life. "Do you prefer one side over the other?" he asked, throwing her question back at her.

Her smile returned, brighter than the flames flickering in the grate. "I've been sleeping in the middle."

"Then get in the middle, and I'll lay down beside you."

Elizabeth chuckled, as if he jested. He did not. Elizabeth in the middle of the bed would be much closer to him.

Her expression resolute, she walked around the bed. "I shall sleep on the side nearer the fire." She halted there and glanced back. "Under the sheets?"

Darcy forced a bland expression, heart thudding in his chest. "If we're to make the bed appear slept in, I feel we must."

She nodded. "I best remove my robe, then. I'll become tangled."

He waited.

She stared at him.

He raised an eyebrow in question.

"Would you mind, terribly, turning away?" she asked.

He did mind, but he turned his back. Every swish of fabric shouted for him to turn around. He heard her robe come off. The bedclothes shift. The slightest creak of the mattress.

"You may turn back, now," she called.

Darcy strode to his side of the bed. He had no qualms about removing his robe. Elizabeth, it seemed, had none about watching him do so. He tossed the garment toward a chair and slid under the sheets.

A gulf of space lay between them. He couldn't even feel the heat of her slender form. Why did Pemberley have to boast such large beds?

"I enjoyed dinner," Elizabeth said.

"As did I."

There came the sound of fabric against fabric as she slid her hand halfway across the empty space. Darcy matched the overture immediately. He covered her palm with his.

"I have a question, but if I'm out of line in asking, please tell me," Elizabeth said. "I wish us to get on and I'm willing to avoid some topics, for now, that we may learn to know each other better."

"What is your question?"

"Why are you so concerned about what people might think or believe about our union?" she asked. "In Hertfordshire, you very noticeably didn't care a wit what anyone thought."

Especially her, he realized, when they first met. He was all too aware he'd insulted her that evening. He wondered if, in large part, his boorishness was the root of her climbing out Netherfield's library window. "I should never have said you weren't worth dancing with. You were the loveliest woman in the room."

"That's very sweet of you, but Jane was there, so I doubt that. I don't mean myself, however. You didn't care what anyone in Hertfordshire thought of you, except perhaps Mr. Bingley. Yet, you seem very concerned about how marrying me will affect your reputation."

"Not how marrying you will," he countered immediately. "At least, not in the way I believe you mean. How people will regard me, either thinking I was fool enough to be trapped, finally, or that I wed a woman who vehemently wished to avoid marriage to me."

"Yes, but why do you care?" She turned on her side to face him, hand leaving his.

He considered his answer carefully. Finally, he sighed, finding no way to soften the truth. "I felt myself so far above the people of Hertfordshire that I simply did not care how they felt about me."

"Ah," she said. "And you are not above the company in London?"

Darcy winced, though her tone lacked condemnation. "I thought I was. I always had confidence that I was better than most people. Richer. More well-read. More athletic. Even more charitable and more intelligent. Now, all of that has slipped away." He studied the way the firelight flickered across the ceiling. "I'm as fallible as the people I looked down on."

"You mean," she said, tone amused, "that you are as human."

He turned his head to look at her. Her hands were clasped under her cheek. Her perfect lips smiled. Intelligent, bright eyes danced with firelight and silent laughter. In this, if nothing else, he should thank Miss Bingley. Unwittingly, she'd ensured Darcy wed the best woman in all of England.

His mood soured slightly, thinking of Miss Bingley. "It will be bad for you if people believe Miss Bingley's story. Your reputation will suffer."

Elizabeth shrugged, her smile unwavering. "I think, interestingly, that I care far less for London opinions than you do. The people who matter to me know the truth."

That was fine for her to say, and brave, but Elizabeth didn't know how cruel the Ton could be. She was under his protection. Her reputation was his concern. He could not ignore his duty toward her. They must reinsert themselves into society before rumor inflicted too much harm.

The Bingleys would be the easiest place to start. They both knew the truth. They were both kind and well-regarded. "We should visit your sister, once she's well enough."

"I would like that," Elizabeth said, her smile growing. "And, maybe, I could persuade Jane to invite Colonel Fitzwilliam and Mrs. Fortescue, although I still think perhaps, in a while, we should have them here."

"Pemberley is rather far from Kent for a woman and child to travel to alone," he said. "My sister was correct in that."

He immediately regretted the words, but Elizabeth's expression, barely visible by the light of the fire, merely turned thoughtful, not angry. Relief eased tension from his frame at this additional confirmation that he'd been fortunate enough to marry a woman who did not collect and cherish slights, saving them for when they could be turned against others.

"There must be some respectable way to get Mrs. Fortescue to Pemberley," she said after a moment. "Still, we must all hope Jane will soon be well, for many reasons, and if she is, Hertfordshire is not so far from Kent."

He read the worry in Elizabeth's expression and voice, and knew it wasn't for Richard and Mrs. Fortescue. He turned fully on his side and reached out to trail gentle fingers down her cheek. "Your sister is strong."

Elizabeth smiled, but her eyes remained shadowed. "She is." A grimace flittered across her face. "I hope Mama isn't helping her too awfully much," she said, the word 'helping' dark with emphasis. "It's a shame Jane hadn't somewhere in the country to go that was near London, but not Longbourn."

"I shouldn't worry." Darcy stroked her cheek again, enamored by the softness. "Bingley may be affable to a fault, but when it comes to your sister, I have every confidence he'll assert himself."

"You know him better than I," Elizabeth replied.

Darcy sought for a change of topic, a way to lighten her mood. "You said, after a time," he recalled.

"I beg your pardon?"

"You said we should find a way to have Richard and Mrs. Fortescue here, after a time," he elaborated, fingers sliding along the curve of her neck. "Why not now?" She had, after all, recently suggested inviting them immediately.

His question had the desired effect, and more. Elizabeth's lips curled, the mischief in her smile matched by a spark in her eyes. "Because, Mr. Darcy, we only recently wed. We require time alone to come to know each other."

Darcy, lying in bed beside his beautiful wife, one hand caressing the smooth skin of her shoulder, had no desire to argue with that.

***

Anne weighed the two letters in her hand. The one from Hawkins, much lighter, likely contained a summary of Georgiana's weighty missive. Eager to hear from her betrothed, Anne opened Hawkins' first.

Dear Miss de Bourgh,

Matters to which I may have alluded have come to a happy conclusion, no intervention required. Therefore, it is my great pleasure to assure you that my

resignation is now yours to tender.
With the utmost respect and care,
~ H

Anne couldn't contain a smile. Respect and care. Yes, that summarized Hawkins to perfection. That was what she loved most about him.

Not love like the Bingleys had, or the Hyatts. Certainly not what her cousin Richard felt for Mrs. Fortescue, of whom his letters constantly asked and continuously referenced. Anne's love for Hawkins was deep and still, like the bottomless, ice-clad lakes she'd read of in Scandinavia. Calm. Fathomless.

She folded Hawkins' letter with care and stowed the page away in a secret compartment under the drawer in which she kept letters from people with last names beginning with Q. Smile lingering, she cracked open Georgiana's plump envelope. The first page unfolded to reveal a letter stained here and there with actual tears.

Anne's smile left her as she perused her young cousins rambling confession of all the evils she'd believed of Elizabeth, of who had perpetuated them, and the steps Georgiana had taken to break up her brother and his bride. Anne could see why Hawkins had become worried enough to write her but, in typical fashion, Elizabeth had prevailed. Anne assayed a new smile when she read of how Elizabeth kept her letters.

Georgiana's letter, when finished, got folded and placed in the flat to-be-answered compartment. Anne would craft a suitably bolstering reply for her cousin later. Georgiana's confidence had been tattered by the incident in Ramsgate the previous year, which Anne knew about from Georgiana, and hadn't even hinted to Darcy that she knew. Keeping the fact that Georgiana had shared her secret almost negated the value Georgiana received from being able to share it. Anne was glad Elizabeth had been openly told about the incident.

Anne's gaze flicked to the drawer with Georgiana's letters. No mention of Ramsgate could be found there. In an act very untypical of her, Anne had burned her cousin's letter confessing her near transgression with Mr. Wickham. She did have every other letter from Georgiana, though. She would keep this one, because her reference to Ramsgate was so oblique as to give no information. Anne also had hundreds of other letters, from many locations in England and scattered even farther afield.

She wouldn't need letters from abroad to address the true concern she'd found in Georgiana's recent missive. A passing note for her cousin, but of importance to Anne. Mrs. Bingley was with child, and not faring well.

Anne had spent little time with Mrs. Bingley but knew, as much from Elizabeth as from those brief encounters, that Mrs. Bingley was a bright, light spirit. Someone who added goodness and joy to the world. Now, she faced the awful dread of being with child, a precariousness all too near Anne's heart. There wasn't much Anne could do, but there was something.

Her hands dipped in and out of drawers, plucking free letters. These, she arranged before her on the desk, in an ever-reaching web of friends, gossip and acquaintances. She organized, placed and moved the pieces until she arranged the array of knowledge she required and reached the line of communication she sought.

Though Anne hadn't met Mrs. Bennet, she knew enough people who had, or knew someone who had, to have a fair depiction of the woman. From her network of information, she'd ascertained that Mrs. Bennet possessed a trying personality and constituted the main reason the Bingleys had taken a home in London.

Anne also knew, though she'd yet to meet either young woman, that Lydia Forster and Kitty Bennet were headed to Brighton soon, with Colonel Forster and his unit, and that Miss Kitty was the sole Bennet daughter now unspoken for. It would take only a few hints, a suggestion here and there that it would please Anne, for a long-lost connection of Mrs. Bennet's to invite her to Brighton as well, to oversee Miss Kitty's attempts to win a husband. Anne simply needed to pull the correct threads—

She plucked a letter from her web with a smile, and another, and a third. Yes, they would do. A return favor might be required. The offer of some weeks in London, if, once Anne's plans became known, she was still deemed acceptable company. By then, though, Mrs. Bennet would be in Brighton for the summer and well away from Mrs. Bingley.

Anne nodded in satisfaction. She returned most of the letters to their drawers, drawers she would soon carefully empty into trunks, for the time had nearly come for her to leave Rosings. Her precious correspondence properly stowed, she assembled her paper, pen and ink and set to writing.

Chapter Twenty-Nine

"The Hyatts are kind people?" Elizabeth asked as their carriage drew near Netherfield Park. "I met them only briefly in London."

She asked about Jane's other house guests not out of real concern, but to draw her husband or Georgiana into speaking, to fill the silence. Elizabeth felt increasingly nervous as they neared Netherfield. Jane had written of being fully recovered when she invited them, along with Colonel Fitzwilliam, Mary and Mrs. Fortescue, but Elizabeth didn't trust her sister's letter. She wouldn't be happy until she assessed Jane's state for herself.

"They are very nice," Georgiana said. "She talks a lot, which is nice, so I don't have to."

Elizabeth smiled, not saying that Georgiana had become much more talkative of late.

"Lord Walter is a quiet man," Darcy offered. "Lady Clara is very curious. She is a bit like Lady Catherine in that, but kind."

Elizabeth raised an eyebrow at that. Not long ago, Darcy would never had admitted fault in his aunt. Not to her, at least.

Across from her, Georgiana grimaced. "No one is as prying as Aunt Catherine. Lady Clara asks a lot of questions, and she knows everything about everyone, but she's nice. She's never mean when she's gossiping." The dour look on Georgiana's face deepened. "Not like Mrs. Hurst."

Elizabeth could appreciate her new sister's expression. Now that Jane's pregnancy appeared to be going well, she'd revealed her state to the world at large, the news prompting Mrs. Hurst to forgive Mr. Bingley for exiling Miss Bingley from their social circle. Sadly, as far as Elizabeth was concerned, this meant the Hursts, too, were invited to Netherfield Park.

At least, as the party was not to be that intimate, Jane had no qualms with inviting Colonel Fitzwilliam and Mrs. Fortescue. Mary, who had also recently revealed herself to be with child, coming along to support Mrs. Fortescue and share the struggles of her state with Jane was a brilliant idea on Mr. Darcy's part. One for which Elizabeth had repeatedly thanked him.

As an added boon, Mrs. Bennet had left Hertfordshire shortly after the Bingleys arrived. Out of nowhere, one of Mrs. Bennet's acquaintances had written and invited her to Brighton. A friend of her youth, now widowed, the woman had heard that Lydia and Kitty were to be there, and Kitty in want of a husband, and selflessly extended the offer. Mrs. Bennet was beside herself with joy both at the trip and that she would be able to singlehandedly oversee Kitty's entrance into Brighton's society.

They rolled up the drive. Once the carriage came to a halt, Elizabeth disembarked as quickly as propriety permitted. She rushed up the steps to the door, which opened for her.

Whatever problems Jane had earlier in her pregnancy, now she looked even more gorgeous than ever. Always serene, she had a kind of a satisfaction in her expression that became her. That looked brightened to joy as she rushed toward Elizabeth to greet her.

Mr. Darcy and Georgiana followed Elizabeth in, no less happy but more decorous. Their arrival met with an organized flurry of activity. Soon, the butler was showing Mr. Darcy to the back parlor, where Mr. Bingley, Lord Walter and Mr. Hurst apparently waited, while Elizabeth and Georgiana followed Jane up to their rooms.

After Jane showed Georgiana to hers, a lovely yellow and pea green affair, she yanked Elizabeth into a sitting room and to a sofa. They both sat, and Jane turned to Elizabeth. "I have my housekeeper delaying your and Mr. Darcy's cases. She's to chat with his man, Hawkins, until I can speak with her."

Elizabeth's brow wrinkled in concern. "Whatever for?"

Jane turned a bit pink, but her smile was full of mischief. "Well, that is, I never thought I would need so many of the bedrooms in Netherfield Park all at once, so I suppose I didn't plan all that well. I even went ahead and turned that smaller one near Charles' and mine into a nursery, which won't go unused because Mrs. Fortescue's daughter, Beatrice, can sleep there. Of course, that means Mrs. Fortescue has the large room on the other side. Oh, and you should know, I had the library moved. It's on the ground floor now, so no need to make ropes of the curtains. I'm turning the old library into a playroom."

Elizabeth took a moment to sort through Jane's words. Fleetingly, she wondered if she hadn't half preferred when Jane had been a bit more reticent, before Mr. Bingley's encouragement saw her speaking more like Kitty and Lydia. That, however, was an unworthy thought, so Elizabeth dismissed it to focus on the matter at hand. "Are you attempting to tell me there's no room for Mr. Darcy and me? Do we need to go stay with Father?" Elizabeth realized she wouldn't mind that at all.

Jane shook her head. "Oh, but before I forget, I also have an unexpected guest. Miss Anne de Bourgh arrived with Mary and Mrs. Fortescue. Of course, it is lovely to have her."

Elizabeth blinked, surprised. "Anne is here? Did you invite her?"

"I did not, but I welcome her, certainly." Jane's blush deepened. "You see, though, I had to give her one of the more elegant rooms, since the granddaughter of an earl can hardly be given a small room."

"You have only one room left, you mean?" Elizabeth clarified.

Jane shook her head again. "I have several left, but none with connecting doors or next to each other. I saved the best large bedroom for the two of you, but if you don't wish to share with Mr. Darcy, you'll be a distance apart. Which would you prefer?"

"So, you're asking if Mr. Darcy and I will share a room?" Elizabeth smiled to see her sister's blush grow all the brighter.

"I am. I don't mean to pry. I simply don't know what else to do. Or, truly, you will need to go stay with Papa."

Elizabeth chuckled, amused to see her married-for-longer, already with child, older sister so embarrassed on her behalf. "Then, be assured, Mr. Darcy and I are happy to share a room." For all her amusement, Elizabeth felt her cheeks heat as well.

"Oh, but that's wonderful news," Jane cried, and hugged Elizabeth. "I'd hoped, from your and Georgiana's more recent letters, but I knew things were strained before, so I still worried."

"Let me assure you, you may set your worries aside."

"I'm very happy to hear that." Jane released Elizabeth. "So, you do love him, then?"

It was Elizabeth's turn to blush. "I'm not sure," she murmured. In truth, she grew surer every day. Now that she and Darcy spent time together daily and conversed with civility and spent nights in the same bed, she'd grown very fond of her husband. So fond, she rather thought she would call it love, but not to Jane. Not when she hadn't dared say as much to Darcy.

A stab of pain cut through Elizabeth. Maybe, if she told him that she loved him, his proclaimed interest in her would grow into something more. Maybe the only reason he hadn't professed love for her was worry she didn't yet return the emotion.

Or maybe, he only pretended love, as they'd agreed to do.

Jane stood, pulling Elizabeth back to the moment. "I'm sure you will soon come to love him," Jane said, supremely confident. "Let me show you to your room. You'll want to ready for dinner."

Elizabeth came to her feet. "Mr. Darcy will, as well. So, your question about our sleeping accommodations is why you ushered him off to the parlor instead of letting him accompany us upstairs?"

"Yes, of course," Jane said as she led the way from the room.

"Why, Jane, how very cunning you've become."

Jane cast her another quick smile and led the way to a large, blue and silver themed sitting room, door open to the bedroom beyond.

"This is lovely, Jane. Thank you," Elizabeth said.

"I'll go have your luggage sent up."

"Did Miss de Bourgh say why she came?" Elizabeth asked, before Jane could leave.

Jane shook her head. "I didn't ask, of course. I assume because we're all here." Jane frowned. "In truth, I should have thought to invite her. Do you know," Jane lowered her voice, "she, Mary, Mrs. Fortescue and Beatrice arrived in one of Lady Catherine's carriages?"

"Did they? I wonder how they managed that." Elizabeth would rather have thought they'd be forced to hire a carriage.

Jane shrugged. "Maybe you can ask her," she said, and slipped from the room.

But Elizabeth didn't see Miss de Bourgh, Mr. Bingley, Mrs. Fortescue and Beatrice, the Hursts or the Hyatts until they all met in the parlor before dinner. She did see Mary, who appeared at her door moments after Jane departed, for a hug and to reiterate, in person, the joyous news that she was with child. Mary, Elizabeth was pleased to see, glowed nearly as much as Jane and seemed equally happy.

Not too much later, when they all convened in the parlor, they were joined almost immediately by a newly arrived Colonel Fitzwilliam. He greeted his hosts first, then headed straight for Mrs. Fortescue and Beatrice. Once he'd said hello to them, Beatrice in his arms and Mrs. Fortescue at his side, he made his way around the room for the remainder of his greetings, already acquainted with everyone there to some degree.

After the Hursts, Hyatts and Mary, Colonel Fitzwilliam greeted

Elizabeth, Darcy and Georgiana. He turned last to Miss de Bourgh, who stood near them. "I say, Anne, it's lovely to see you here, but however did you escape the ogre, as it were?"

"Ogre," Beatrice repeated, and giggled.

"My mother is very subdued," Miss de Bourgh said. "She realizes her actions had consequences. Consequences she didn't want. She also feels she was made a fool of by Miss Bingley."

"I can empathize with that feeling," Darcy said, tone dry.

Lady Clara, small of statue, appeared at Mrs. Fortescue's elbow. "Tell us about what happened," she asked, eyes alight with interest. "I've heard all sorts of rumors, mostly contradicting each other."

"It is not appropriate for us to talk about," Mrs. Hurst snapped from where she stood on the other side of the room.

"I think it is," Georgiana said. "Scandals that are secret are worse than those that are public. I should know."

A sudden silence descended on the room.

Lady Clara turned wide eyes on Georgiana. "Why do you say that, dear?"

"A little over a year ago, I was visiting Ramsgate with my governess, Mrs. Younge," Georgiana began, much to Elizabeth's surprise.

"Georgiana," Darcy exclaimed, tone hard with censure.

Elizabeth placed a soothing hand on his arm, only to feel his muscles rigid with some emotion, be it anger, consternation or surprise.

Georgiana turned to Darcy, her expression firm. "I think it's better to talk about it. What does it say in the *Book of John*? The truth shall set you free. I've been so worried about it getting out, and I'm tired of worrying."

Darcy glared at his sister.

Elizabeth squeezed his arm, but he didn't appear to notice. She stood on tiptoe and whispered into his ear, "Given the other person involved, it's bound to come out eventually. She'll be the better for being brave, both in her own mind and societies, and this way she may set the story."

Darcy still didn't look at Elizabeth. He clamped his lips tightly closed, expression stony.

Georgiana regarded him a long moment. She shrugged and turned back to Lady Clara. "Last summer, when I was in Ramsgate, I agreed to elope with the son of my father's steward, Mr. Wickham. He was my father's godson and raised like my brother. Fitzwilliam came on a

251

surprise visit. I felt guilty and told him. He stopped the elopement, of course. I was told to keep it secret, but I can't keep doing that. When I have a season, I don't want to be constantly worrying about what will happen if one of my suitors finds out. Nothing happened. I mean, there were a few kisses, but nothing more."

About the room, everyone from Mary to Lord Walter looked around, clearly uncomfortable with the exchange.

"That doesn't sound like much of a scandal," Mrs. Hurst said into the silence, with a sniff.

Elizabeth cast her a quick look. She took in the almost smug disdain on Mrs. Hurst's face and realized, in the realm of scandals, Mrs. Hurst was proud of hers. What Miss Bingley had done, and the trouble she'd since caused, was monumental when compared to Georgiana's broken almost-elopement and a few kisses given a childhood companion.

"But it is," Georgiana protested. "Or will be, for a bit, when it gets out. I'm not going to have a season for more than a year. If I let everyone know now, it will be old news when I come out."

"That's a sensible approach," Lady Clara said, nodding. "You said you were in Ramsgate, for a holiday, I presume?"

"Yes."

Lady Clara made a tsking sound. "I'm surprised your chaperone let you get close enough to Mr. Wickham to agree to an elopement."

Georgiana flushed. "She encouraged him. I think he was planning to pay her from my dowry."

"Oh, dear," Jane said.

"That is shocking," Lady Clara declared. "If you didn't like his attentions, there was no one you could go to, being away from home." She turned a look of mild rebuke on Darcy. "How could such a woman have been left in sole charge of you, Miss Darcy?"

Elizabeth's hand tensed on Darcy's arm. She didn't know Lady Clara well, had been assured the woman was kind, but she wouldn't stand for anyone reproaching Darcy. Elizabeth could see Darcy's jaws grind together.

"Actually," Miss de Bourgh said, tone mild, "I believe my mother, Lady Catherine, selected Mrs. Young to chaperone Georgiana."

"And I'm not going to pretend I was forced into it," Georgiana said, recapturing Lady Clara's attention. "I thought it was exciting."

Elizabeth could feel the wave of mingled anger and disgrace that roiled off Darcy. "But you stopped it," Elizabeth said, hoping to do the same with the conversation. "Presumably, your governess would have kept quiet about what was going on. If you also didn't tell anyone, it would have been relatively simple for the elopement to take place once your brother left. Therefore," she firmed her tone, "you did what was correct in the end, no real harm was done, and now everyone can know and, soon enough, forget." This last she aimed at Lady Clara.

"Yes. Yes indeed," Lady Clara said. She turned back to Georgiana. "Don't you worry, dear. We'll stand by you, and everyone will forget soon enough."

"Have you noted, there's a chess board in the corner, Clara," Lord Walter said into the ensuing stillness, tone mild.

"Is there?" Lady Clara laughed, the sound like yuletide bells. "Do you know," she said to the room at large, "Walter and I nearly didn't become engaged, all over chess."

"Truly?" Elizabeth encouraged, happy to find Lord Walter and Lady Clara allies in changing topics.

"Oh yes. Shortly after we met, we engaged in a game of chess." She glanced over her shoulder at Lord Walter, smile warm. "I beat him badly."

Lord Walter chuckled. "I expected to win. My pride was so hurt, the next time I met her, I pretended I thought she was a servant."

"That did not go over well, with me or my parents," Lady Clara said, shaking her head. "Walter had to work terribly hard to make that up to my father."

"Yes, dear, but tell them what you did."

Lady Clara laughed again, but the articulation was companied by a bashful look. "I put a bur under his saddle. His horse threw him." Her expression became a bit stricken as she turned apologetic eyes on her husband. "I could have killed him, and all because he'd injured my pride, making me think he didn't recall me at all and that he thought I was the staff."

"Then she had to make that up to my mother." Lord Walter's tone was kind. "And Darcy was forced to intervene to sort things out."

"What did he do?" Georgiana asked.

Lord Walter cast Darcy a look of invitation, but Darcy still glowered at his sister. Lord Walter shrugged. "For starters, he tossed out the chess set."

The room at large offered an obligatory laugh, ranging from honest amusement to a variety of strained sounds. That was, except for Darcy, who continued to frown. For her part, Elizabeth's amusement was touched with relief. She caught Lady Clara's eye and smiled, aware the Hyatts were trying to tell Georgiana that everyone made mistakes. Elizabeth wondered if Darcy had received the message. Judging by his scowl, he had not.

Chapter Thirty

The following morning, Elizabeth gazed eagerly out the carriage window, taking in every familiar tree, shrub and hillock as she, Darcy, Georgiana and Mary made their way toward Longbourn. She hadn't seen her father since her wedding. She also had in her possession a note, written by Mr. Bingley, inviting Mr. Bennet to join any and all the festivities planned for the upcoming weeks.

"Your father must be eager to see you both," Georgiana said, looking between Elizabeth and Mary.

"More eager to see Elizabeth," Mary said without rancor.

Elizabeth shook her head. "Nonsense. Anything else aside, I'm not bringing him a grandchild." She felt a touch of heat in her cheeks. "Yet."

"Why would your father prefer to see Elizabeth?" Georgiana asked.

"Georgiana." Darcy's tone held mild reprimand.

"Mrs. Collins brought it up," Georgiana replied, and turned to look at Mary, expression questioning.

Mary shrugged. "He's always preferred Elizabeth and Jane. They're smarter, and prettier, and everyone likes Elizabeth's playing better than mine, although I used to practice much more." She gave her head a little shake. "I don't mean to evoke sympathy. I'm accustomed to his preference."

The carriage rumbled down the lane. Elizabeth felt a pang of sorrow for her middle sister.

"You are prettier than I am," Georgiana said. There was no way Elizabeth or Darcy could agree or disagree with that, which made Elizabeth glad Georgiana continued. "But I try to make the best use of the looks I have, which you don't. For one thing, your hairstyle is too severe. You should be less neat. Let a few strands fall next to your face."

"Mr. Collins probably wouldn't approve if I curled them," Mary said doubtfully.

"Then don't. Trim them so they aren't too long." Georgiana pulled one of her ringlets straight and showed Mary. "See? You should have your hair like this." She then swept both sides up, showing how much it changed her face. "Not like this."

"I'll try it," Mary said, "but I want to cut them long enough so I can put them up if Mr. Collins doesn't like them."

"If he's anything like my brother, he won't notice," Georgiana said.

"Papa never noticed what any of us wore," Elizabeth said.

"And Mama always noticed," Mary replied. "As does Lady Catherine. She told me not to wear my yellow dress when visiting, because it clashes with those horrible mustard colored chairs of hers."

Elizabeth winced inwardly at Mary's lack of tact.

"That sounds like Lady Catherine," Georgiana said, not appearing to mind. "She will tell me what the weather will be like tomorrow and never remember if she is wrong."

For the remainder of the ride, Georgiana and Mary compared their memories of Lady Catherine. Most of them were unflattering.

Watching her oft-neglected sister and her new sister converse with growing ease and interest, Elizabeth smiled. She cast a glance at her husband, pleased his expression was bemused, not censorious. She studied his strong profile, aware much of his stuffiness stemmed from a great sense of responsibility. He felt, very keenly, the weight of raising his sister without the benefit of mother or father, and Elizabeth cared for him all the more for that.

A slight smile came to her lips. She slid her hand across the seat, toward him, gaze searching his face. She saw the moment his eyes caught the movement. They flicked in her direction. An answering smile rewarded her as his hand reached out to clasp hers. Across the carriage, grinning, Georgiana leaned over and whispered something in Mary's ear. Both young women giggled.

They reached Longbourn to be greeted at the door by Mr. Bennet, a pleasant surprise. He embraced both Elizabeth and Mary, shook Darcy's hand and bowed to Georgiana. He then led the way into the parlor and, in a second surprise, called for tea.

"We missed you last night, Papa," Elizabeth said as they all settled in the parlor. She held out Mr. Bingley's invitation. "I've a note here for you from Mr. Bingley, requesting you join us from now on."

Mr. Bennet accepted the envelope. "I was invited yesterday," he said. "I thought I'd let all you young people settle in."

To Elizabeth's eye, her father seemed… lighter. Younger in some way. He was almost, nearly, cheerful. Not in the somewhat sardonic way he used to be, but with genuine happiness. "You look well, Papa."

"Do I?" Mr. Bennet nodded. "I am well, Lizzy. You've no idea the change seeing you all settled has wrought in Mrs. Bennet. Do you know, I'd forgotten that she used to read? Once, long ago, we spent our evenings discussing books. Then, Jane arrived, and Mrs. Bennet had less time for books, but we still played chess. Then, you arrived, and chess went away as well."

Elizabeth stared at her father. She'd often wondered, but never dared ask, what he'd seen in her mother. There must have been something. Some spark when they met. "Do you mean, Mama was different before she bore five daughters?"

Mr. Bennet nodded. "Once Kitty is wed, I plan to bring the chess set back into the parlor."

"I think that's a wonderful idea, Papa," Elizabeth replied.

"As do I," Mary added. "I'd no idea Mother knew how to play chess."

The tea service arrived. Elizabeth took it upon herself to play hostess, after a quick look to Mary for permission. Talk between Elizabeth, Darcy and her father turned from chess to a foray into the doings of parliament. Across from Elizabeth and Darcy, Georgiana and Mary chatted about music.

It occurred to Elizabeth that, being younger than she was, Mary was closer in age to Georgiana. Elizabeth recalled being about fifteen or so, and thinking that women of the incredible age of one and twenty were really quite old. She wondered if Georgiana saw her that way, an idea that somewhat amused her.

"Elizabeth, Mary." Mr. Bennet's voice called Elizabeth back to the discussion at hand. "Have either of you received a letter from your sisters, or Mrs. Bennet?"

Elizabeth shook her head and looked to Mary, who did likewise.

"Like as not, the post hasn't caught up to our visit to Netherfield," Darcy suggested.

"True enough," Mr. Bennet agreed. He pulled a folded note from his pocket and set it on the table. "I hope I'm not out of line in bringing the gentleman up, but both Lydia and Mrs. Bennet have written something quite interesting about that Mr. Wickham, whom I believe you were both once closely acquainted with, Mr. Darcy, Miss Darcy."

Georgiana's eyes went wide. Beside her, Elizabeth felt Darcy stiffen. She resisted the urge to glance at him, silently hoping for civility, not the sort of anger that met her first mention of Mr. Wickham to her husband.

"We were, once, well acquainted with the man, yes," Darcy said, expressionless.

"You should know, then, that he spread a lie about Meryton, and now down in Brighton, that you wrongfully denied him a living, Mr. Darcy," Mr. Bennet said.

"I had heard as much." Darcy's voice lacked inflection but wasn't cold.

"How do you know it's a lie?" Georgiana asked.

Mr. Bennet offered an amused look. "For one, I've met your brother and know him to be an eminently honorable man." He inclined his head to Darcy, who nodded back. "For another, I've Lydia's and Mrs. Bennet's letters."

Elizabeth darted a look at Darcy to check his temperament. Finding him calm, she asked, "What did they say, Papa?"

"It seems Lydia had written to you of Mr. Wickham's lies," Mr. Bennet said. "And that you wrote back, correcting them."

Elizabeth nodded.

Mr. Bennet's expression took on a touch of the sardonic look Elizabeth was more familiar with from him. "Instead of quietly telling Colonel Forster, Lydia blurted out the entirety of her knowledge on the subject before a crowd of people, which included her husband."

Across from Elizabeth, Georgiana gasped. Mary turned to her, mien concerned.

"Under Colonel Forster's insistent questioning, Mr. Wickham admitted he'd lied." Mr. Bennet's gaze lit with inner glee. "He was forced to resign his commission. He was also found to be deeply in debt."

Darcy nodded. "I would expect him to be. He has never been one to control his spending."

Mr. Bennet tapped the letter where it lay on the table beside his saucer and cup. "Lydia also writes that Mr. Wickham sold everything he had and was last seen boarding a ship bound for Canada."

Elizabeth turned to her new sister, to gauge her reaction.

Georgiana sat straight backed on the sofa beside Mary. Her face a touch pale, she held her head high. She looked square at her brother. "Well then. I don't suspect we'll ever see Mr. Wickham again."

"No," Darcy agreed. "I do not suspect so."

Elizabeth hurriedly moved the conversation on to other topics, but she knew her father must note Georgiana's particular interest in the subject of Mr. Wickham. Nor would her father remain uneducated as to why. Even without Mrs. Bennet or his youngest two daughters in the house, word of Georgiana's scandal would spread so quickly, even Mr. Bennet would hear. Elizabeth could only hope interest in the news would pass as swiftly.

They spent nearly half an hour more in Longbourn. Mary and Georgiana disappeared upstairs for a time. When they returned to the parlor, Mary's hair had been cut with strands framing her face. Elizabeth, quite sincerely, told her the new hairstyle suited her.

When it came time to depart, Elizabeth lingered for a moment in the parlor while the others headed to the foyer. She turned in a slow circle, taking in the room. She noted more books than usual, and newspapers, and fewer figurines cluttering the space. A small table, which used to be in her father's office, stood in one corner. Elizabeth realized it awaited the chess set.

Unlike when last she'd departed Longbourn, Elizabeth wasn't full of worry and regret, and unlike the room she and Jane had shared, the parlor didn't look forlorn. It looked loved, tended and refreshed. Footsteps sounded behind her. Mary appeared at her side.

"It's time to go, Lizzy."

"I know." Elizabeth smiled, though she knew tears shimmered in her eyes.

"Whatever is the matter?" Mary asked in a low voice, barely heard over the commotion in the foyer. "I… that is, Jane and I both, we thought you and Mr. Darcy were happy?"

"We are," Elizabeth assured her. "I was only thinking of Mama and Papa, and this room, and how life changes."

Mary looked about. "I can keep it this way, if you like, so it will be the same here when you visit." She frowned. "Of course, Mother and Father will be here for years more, so they might change things, and Mr. Collins must have a say, and Jane will have Netherfield Park, where I'm sure Mr. Darcy would rather stay, but I'll do my best."

Elizabeth turned to face Mary, smile growing. "That's right, you're to have Longbourn." She frowned slightly. "That was Lady Catherine's idea, was it not?"

"That Mr. Collins marry one of us, so we could keep Longbourn?" Elizabeth nodded.

"It was."

Elizabeth threw her arms about Mary and squeezed her tight. "That may be the very best, and so far as I know the only, good idea Lady Catherine ever had. I'm so happy for you, Mary, and Mr. Darcy and I should be delighted to stay here with you someday." Elizabeth blinked rapidly, hot tears behind her lids. She let her sister go to dab at her eyes, hoping Mary didn't notice.

Mary wiped her own eyes, but she smiled. "Thank you, Lizzy. That means a great deal to me."

"Well," Elizabeth said staunchly. "You mean a great deal to me, and I really do love your new hairstyle."

Elizabeth threaded her arm through Mary's. She took one last look about the room, which seemed even brighter now, knowing that someday the house would be under Mary's stewardship. With a gentle tug, she turned them toward the door.

"Of course, you needn't keep the parlor the same," she said as she and Mary left the room. "For one thing, I know you've always disliked Mother's obsession with porcelain pigs."

Mary cast Elizabeth a surprised look. "I didn't think anyone knew that."

"We all did, except Mama. Lydia even recommended once that we smash them for you, since you were always in here practicing and Mama has them all lined up in the shelves, facing the pianoforte."

Mary let out an exaggerated sigh. "The one time Lydia didn't act on her more silly impulses, and the one time I would have wanted her to."

Elizabeth chuckled. Her sister joined in her laughter as they strode from the parlor, to where their father, Georgiana and Darcy waited. Mr. Bennet came forward to tender his farewells.

When he hugged Mary he said, "Pregnancy must agree with you. I've never seen you look lovelier."

Mary blushed. "Thank you, Papa," she offered with a slight stammer.

Mr. Bennet bid Elizabeth goodbye as well, then stepped aside to let them depart. They strode out into the bright morning and clambered back into the carriage.

As soon as they were moving, Georgiana turned to Mary. "Your father just noticed how nice you look," Georgiana said smugly.

Mary mustered another blush, obviously unaccustomed to so much attention. "Yes, he did."

Georgiana whirled to face Darcy and Elizabeth. "You didn't warn him, did you, that we'd spoken of changing Mrs. Collins' hair?"

Elizabeth raised her eyebrows. "Can you truly see your brother speaking with our father about women's fashion?"

That evoked a smile from Mary, but Georgiana narrowed her gaze at Elizabeth. "Did you warn him, while we were above stairs?"

Elizabeth shook her head. "I did not. On my honor."

Georgiana gave a satisfied nod, expression regaining its smugness. Elizabeth smiled. Georgiana had earned the right to be smug, and Mary was well-deserving of their father's attention.

The rest of the return ride had Georgiana and Mary talking about music. As they approached Netherfield Park, Mary said, "I think I will offer to play for Lady Catherine. We don't have an instrument in the parsonage, but it would please me to play for her, rather than listen to her, and Mr. Collins will be happy if I make Lady Catherine happy. I'm sure she will let me practice on the pianoforte in Mrs. Jenkinson's room."

Elizabeth, and the others, could only agree to that.

Chapter Thirty-One

Darcy enjoyed dinner that evening more than he would have thought. He didn't normally care for large gatherings but aside from Mrs. Hurst, who was in a sour mood, and Mrs. Collins and Mrs. Fortescue, neither of whom he'd yet come to know well, he realized the party consisted of his closest friends, and Mr. Bennet. To Darcy's surprise, Mr. Bennet added a great deal to the conversation, often serving to elevate it in a way Bingley and Richard never proved capable of and Mr. Hurst and Lord Walter generally declined to.

Drinks after dinner, taken with Richard, Bingley, Lord Walter, Mr. Hurst and Mr. Bennet in Netherfield's new library, turned out to be quite pleasant as well. Mr. Bennet and Lord Walter, in particular, were very knowledgeable and engaged with Darcy in a lively discussion of history and government. Bingley seemed content to banter with Richard off to one side. Mr. Hurst sat between the two groups, perhaps listening to both or perhaps simply enjoying a respite from his wife's dourness.

The library, too, was a pleasant surprise. Situated on the ground floor in a long, narrow room which Darcy believed was the selfsame one he and Elizabeth had entered when they snuck back into Netherfield after climbing out the old library's window, the space had been set with armchairs and tables and fitted out with shelves.

Engaging as the conversation was, Darcy began to miss Elizabeth about halfway through his port. They'd been spending nearly all their time together, ever since agreeing to put on the appearance of being in love. Now, when they were apart for too long, thoughts of Elizabeth crowded Darcy's mind. Silly as he knew it to be, as she stood but a few rooms away, he felt her absence keenly. He wondered with whom she spoke. Did she laugh, and he wasn't nearby to hear?

"I say," Richard said, voice raised to catch the attention of the room at large. "Wonderful chaps, all of you, but ought we not get back to the ladies?"

"I wouldn't mind," Bingley said cheerfully, knocking back the remainder of his drink. "Jane looks particularly lovely this evening."

"Smitten, the both of you," Lord Walter said with a chuckle, though he too drained his glass.

Mr. Bennet turned to regard Darcy with assessing eyes. "Mr. Darcy?"

"If the consensus is to return, I agree," Darcy said.

"Hm," was all the response he got from his father-in-law. Mr. Bennet, rather than finish his drink, set his half full glass on a tray.

Darcy followed Mr. Bennet's example.

Mr. Hurst drank down his port, stood, went to the sideboard and poured another. "I'll be along."

Bingley shrugged and led the way from the room.

Even from afar, Darcy could hear the chatter of the women, though the words were still indistinct. He picked out Lady Clara's bell-like tones, and Georgiana's slightly deeper voice. He didn't hear Elizabeth speak, but did hear her chuckle, the sound bringing a smile to his face. A voice he thought was Mrs. Collins spoke, and Mrs. Fortescue replied. He half expected to hear Beatrice, then recalled the child had been sent to bed already. As far as Darcy could discern, neither Anne nor Mrs. Hurst spoke.

As they drew nearer, the familiar figure of Hawkins rounded the corner down the hall. He halted, as if surprised, then resumed his course. Darcy had the oddest impression his valet hadn't expected the hall to be occupied and, indeed, wished it were not.

"If you'll excuse me," Darcy said to the other gentlemen.

Bingley offered a nod as they continued into the parlor occupied by the ladies. Cheerful chatter rose within. Darcy strode past the doorway to meet Hawkins.

"Sir," Hawkins greeted with a bow.

"Is something amiss?" Darcy couldn't imagine what would have brought his valet there.

"No, sir."

After a long moment, Darcy frowned. "You are looking for me?"

"No, sir."

"I do not mean to pry, Hawkins, but what are you doing?" Darcy asked with mild exasperation. Behind him, cheerful babble spilled from the parlor.

"I came to ascertain at what time I might be required."

Darcy's frown deepened. Did Hawkins normally pop by while they all chatted, to estimate when Darcy would need him in the evening? Was that how he always seemed to appear the moment Darcy called?

Or... was Hawkins feeling neglected? Darcy considered his valet something quite near a friend. There were times, since Darcy's father died, that Hawkins had, indeed, been Darcy's only true confidant.

Now, with him spending all his time with Elizabeth, Darcy had seen little of his valet. When he did interact with Hawkins, of late, Darcy had been rather perfunctory. Remorse touched him.

Darcy reached out and clasped Hawkins on the shoulder. "You know I appreciate you, Hawkins? You have been a pillar in my life, especially since my father left us."

"Thank you, sir."

"I simply need to spend time with Elizabeth now," Darcy continued, pressing aside his embarrassment at their conversation. Hawkins deserved reassurance. "That is, with Mrs. Darcy. You understand?"

"Certainly, sir."

"Good man." Darcy gave Hawkins' shoulder a final squeeze and dropped his arm. "Well, then, I will be in the parlor, and you can stand down, you know. Take the evening off. Enjoy yours-"

"I see all the other gentlemen, but where is Mr. Hurst, and where is Mr. Darcy, Mrs. Darcy?" Lady Clara's cheerful, ringing tones cut into Darcy's awareness, robbing him of what he planned to say. "You two simply must tell us what happened. I've heard so many rumors. Did you truly climb out a window?"

Darcy whirled toward the parlor. Fond as he was of Lady Clara, he didn't need that story told yet again, to even more people. The truth had been aired at Rosings. Would he be expected to trot out the tale at every gathering from now on?

A rich chuckle met Lady Clara's query. "You must call me Elizabeth, and if I did climb out a window, it would have been a terrible error. Mr. Darcy is the most wonderful of husbands."

"Oh, I'm very sure of that," Lady Clara continued. "I've seen the way he looks at you. Really, though, do tell us. I've heard so very many rumors."

"I should go," Darcy said over his shoulder to Hawkins.

"Certainly, sir."

Darcy strode back toward the parlor door.

"Who's still interested in that?" Mrs. Hurst's voice was brittle.

"What I wish to know, honored as we are by your presence, is why you're here, Miss de Bourgh? Don't you have many friends in London? Whatever brings you to Charles' little country manor?"

Darcy strode into the parlor to find all eyes on Anne.

"I do have a number of friends in London," Anne said. "As well as a new London home I must see to arranging."

"You purchased a house?" Richard asked, surprised.

"You can't live there alone. Do you have someone in mind to hire as a chaperone?" Lady Clara queried, obviously distracted from pursuing the scandal surrounding Darcy and Elizabeth.

Darcy moved to take the seat beside his wife. She offered him a smile, and her hand, which he clasped. He cast a quick look Mrs. Hurst's way, taking in the strain on her features. As much as she enjoyed being near the heart of the season's greatest scandal, she obviously didn't want the full truth revealed.

"No, I am not going to hire a chaperone," Anne said. She turned to Darcy, an odd smile on her face.

Darcy frowned, confused. Had Anne lost her senses? Forgotten he'd wed?

Lady Clara, ever observant, followed Anne's gaze. She looked to Darcy, then back at Anne. "I don't understand."

"No," Anne agreed. "I doubt any of you do." She turned to the door. "Hawkins," she called, voice raised slightly.

That set the room a murmur. Darcy glanced to Elizabeth, but she shook her head, expression as baffled as he felt. He looked to the doorway to see Hawkins, as impeccably clad as always, step into the room.

"Is this the famous valet?" Lady Clara said, voice eager.

Hawkins raised his eyebrows. "I couldn't say, my lady."

Anne held out a hand. "Hawkins, if you would please come here."

Hawkins nodded and crossed the room. Darcy felt as if his eyes might pop from his head when Anne clasped Hawkins' hand. Not a few of the people in the room gasped. Anne drew Hawkins to her side, to face the room with her.

"I have a problem," Anne said, voice raised to be heard. "I do not wish to have children. Ever. Yet, an unmarried woman is at a severe disadvantage in society. I like people. I do not want to be shunned."

She looked up at Hawkins. He smiled down at her. Darcy stared, unable to help himself.

266

"My solution is to marry the kind, intelligent, caring man you see beside me. Hawkins."

Silence filled the parlor.

"But, couldn't you simply marry someone who can't have children?" Mrs. Hurst gasped out.

Far from appearing offended, Anne turned an amused look on Mrs. Hurst. "How can I be certain a man can't have children? A man could have buried three childless wives and it was their fault, not his. No. I need to marry someone who I can count on to not ever do what needs to be done to have a child. I also need a husband who will not walk off with my money. Someone who can be relied on, when in company, to behave impeccably."

"But, Mr. Darcy's valet?" Mrs. Hurst squawked.

"Yes, Darcy's valet," Anne said firmly. "I've known Hawkins for years. He is the most dependable, respectable man I know."

"But, my dear, he's a servant." Lady Clara's tone was gentle. "You'll never be accepted in society."

Georgiana stood, expression resolute. She strode across the room to stand beside Anne. "My cousin is right, Hawkins will always behave impeccably," Georgiana said. "And I agree with your faith in him, Anne. He will keep to any agreement you've come to. Both my father and brother have great respect for him and trust him implicitly."

This brought attention back to Darcy. He freed his hand from Elizabeth's to tug at his cravat. A cravat Hawkins had tied.

Anne raised an eyebrow, gaze meeting his. "Darcy, will you shun me if I marry Hawkins?"

"No," Elizabeth said firmly.

Anne offered her a quick smile, then refocused on Darcy. "Cousin?"

"No," Darcy said, voice quiet but firm. "How could I? Hawkins is one of my oldest, dearest friends."

Anne nodded. She then, hand clasped firmly with Hawkins', turned to each person in the room and repeated the question. For the first time, Darcy noticed Richard and Mrs. Fortescue were suddenly conspicuously absent. Everyone there agreed that they, too, would accept Anne. When she reached Mr. Bennet, he, in particular, appeared exceedingly entertained, as did Lady Clara and Lord Walter. Only Mary Collins appeared unsure of her yes, her mind almost certainly on her husband and how he would react, which would depend entirely on Lady Catherine.

Finally, Anne turned to Mrs. Hurst. "And you, Mrs. Hurst?"

Mrs. Hurst looked about the room. Her gaze snagged on the doorway. Darcy turned to see Mr. Hurst had finally arrived.

He turned to Anne and Hawkins and offered a slight bow. "We will accept you both."

Mrs. Hurst's lips pulled down in a scowl. "She can marry a servant, but Caroline must be snubbed for a harmless flirtation?"

"Harmless flirtation?" Georgiana gasped. "She locked my brother and Elizabeth in a library. She climbed into Fitz's bed. She wrote to my Aunt Catherine and to me, and who knows how many others, and spread lies about Elizabeth. Very hurtful lies. Her behavior has not been harmless."

Darcy winced.

Across the room, Lady Clara's eyes sparkled with interest. "Did all of that really happen?"

"Yes," Elizabeth said quietly.

"No," Mrs. Hurst snapped. "It wasn't like that. Caroline did none of those things."

"Louisa," Mr. Hurst said, "you heard your sister confess. I've no knowledge about what she may have written, or to whom, but we both heard her confess not only to locking them in, but to climbing into Darcy's bed later that night. There is no point in trying to defend her."

Mrs. Hurst looked about the room, expression beseeching. "You're right, I know," she said, tone cajoling. "I realize Caroline is in the wrong, but, please, if we could keep this quiet a little longer. She's going to be married in a matter of days."

Everyone looked about the room at one another. Darcy shrugged. He'd be pleased to keep the matter as quiet as could be expected for all time, let alone a few days.

"Oh, but this is wonderful," Jane Bingley exclaimed. "I'd no idea she'd found love. I'm very happy for her."

"Love?" Mr. Hurst snorted. "She's found a wealthy man, rather, who doesn't yet know what sort of woman he's hitching himself to."

"Mr. Hurst," Mrs. Hurst gasped.

"No, she must be in love." To her credit, Jane Bingley appeared honestly happy for her sister by marriage. "I wrote her and told her that Charles informed me Mr. Kenley recently lost all his holdings. She wrote me back thanking me for the information, so I know she received my letter. If she's still going to wed him, it must be love."

"Yes, Caroline told me about your false friendship." Mrs. Hurst sniffed. "Fortunately, she saw right through your lie. Really, a letter telling her the man is poor, to put her off him? You must be more creative if you wish to fool Caroline."

"Louisa," Bingley snapped. "Jane does not lie."

Mrs. Hurst turned a disdainful, skeptical look on her brother.

He shook his head. "She doesn't. She wished to help Caroline. Kenley squandered most of his inheritance, then he took the last bit and put it all into a trading venture, which sank off the coast of India. The moment the last ship went down, he turned fortune hunter. I thought you knew."

Mrs. Hurst's face went white. Someone, Darcy didn't look quickly enough to see who, chuckled. Both Mr. Bennet and Lord Walter grinned, making them prime suspects.

Mrs. Hurst whirled to face the parlor door. "I must send an express. Send for your best horseman, Charles."

Bingley's expression turned stubborn. "Jane told her. If Caroline thinks my wife acted out of malice, that Jane would stoop to her level, I don't have any sympathy."

"But she believes Mr. Kenley is wealthy," Mrs. Hurst moaned. "I must warn her. Your servants will tell me who your best rider is. Oh, Caroline," she cried and rushed across the room. Mr. Hurst, still in the doorway, stepped out of her way as she left.

Darcy, along with the others, turned to watch her go. He looked to Elizabeth, who wore the near-to-bursting expression of someone who was greatly amused yet strove to keep the feeling hidden. As Miss Bingley's behavior only brought more attention to their scandal, Darcy couldn't find her predicament entertaining, but he did see a sort of grim justice.

"Let me get this straight," Lord Walter drawled from where he stood near the fireplace, with Mr. Bennet. "Miss Bingley connived, lied, tried to ruin the happiness of others, and now seeks to marry someone she believes to be rich, yet didn't believe Mrs. Bingley, obviously the most gracious of people, and will soon be wedded to a fortune hunter?"

"But how do you know about Mr. Kenley's squandering and ill fortune and your sister does not?" Lady Clara asked.

"It's simple," Bingley said. "I decided my rejection of my roots in trade was wrong. I enjoy the society of everyone here, but I also have family that I am not going to ignore. Jane and I have been corresponding with them all regularly. Once you all depart, many of them are coming here to visit. We expect to thoroughly enjoy ourselves." This last he said with mild defiance.

Anne laughed. "I'm the last person to object to that."

There was a rustle near the far side of the room. Everyone turned to see Richard and Mrs. Fortescue slip in through one of the tall windows along the outer wall. They went still when they saw all the faces turned their way.

Richard grinned. "Yes, well, none of you noticed us leave, so we didn't think you'd notice us come back in." He turned and closed the window.

"Oh, this is a wonderful party, Mr. Bingley," Lady Clara declared, clapping her hands in glee.

"You climbed out a window together," Elizabeth said with a wide smile. "I can only assume that now you will be married?"

Mrs. Fortescue's expression was radiant. "We have reached such an agreement, yes."

"And we could hear you all from out there," Richard added. He bowed in the direction of Anne and Hawkins. "And yes, of course we accept you both, gladly."

Mr. Bennet stepped forward from his place near the mantle. "I may be a touch out of line, as this is not my home, but I say this calls for a toast. Let us drink to love, lies and letters, and to accepting our friends."

Chapter Thirty-Two

They talked cheerfully for a long time after that, Hawkins seamlessly joining the party. As Darcy watched his former valet, who didn't leave Anne's side, he reflected that any newcomer to the room would be hard pressed, if informed that one member of the party was only recently elevated from the role of servant, to select the correct gentleman.

The only downside to the remainder of the evening was Lady Clara's insistence on hearing the full of Darcy's and Elizabeth's scandal. When Darcy proved unwilling, Elizabeth related the tale. Only Lord Walter and his wife listened. Darcy realized, taking in the room, that everyone else was already quite familiar with the story. He supposed two more people knowing the whole truth couldn't do any harm, but it still grated on him to listen to the recounting.

When Lord Walter and Lady Clara moved away to speak with Richard and Mrs. Fortescue, Mr. Hurst came up and quietly told Darcy that he would confirm the truth at their club. A short time later, Darcy overheard Georgiana asking Lady Clara to publicize her scandal. He grimaced, wishing his sister might take a different tack.

Finally, people began heading off to bed. Mr. Bennet kissed all three of his daughters good night, told each of them that they were more lovely than ever, and departed for the evening. In short order, Darcy stood alone in the parlor with Elizabeth.

He didn't want to be with anyone. Not even his lovely wife. "You go ahead. I saw a book in Bingley's collection I wish to peruse."

Elizabeth regarded him with assessing eyes. "You'll come to bed soon?"

"Certainly."

She nodded, popped up on her toes to brush a kiss across his lips, and slipped from the parlor.

Netherfield Park was a large, rambling house and the sounds of the others heading off to sleep soon faded. Darcy took a candle and headed down the hall. Slow steps took him back to the library. Darcy stood for a long moment, gaze traveling the shadow-draped room.

He would be a laughingstock. There were so many scandals surrounding him that the gossips would chatter on for months. This stay at Bingley's house would be the center of conversations for years to come. Everywhere he went, his peers would look at him with knowing eyes, whisper behind raised hands.

Possessed of deep desire to be alone, Darcy went to the door and felt about the top frame. Sure enough, he found the key. He closed the library door and turned the key in the lock.

He selected a chair, lit several candles and sat to brood. His life was in shambles, socially speaking. Didn't they all see what hardships, what trouble, they'd invited?

Would he bring Georgiana to London for her season and have Elizabeth preside over parties which no one attended? Would the invitations not come in and people never be at home when they called? It was his duty to protect those he loved. Not simply from the obvious dangers of their world, but the subtle ones as well. Ones that would see his wife ostracized and his sister unable to wed. He couldn't protect them from the repercussions of so much scandal. He had failed.

Someone tried the door. A soft knock sounded. Darcy ignored it. He'd no wish for further socializing. Whoever it was gave up. He returned to his brooding. As always, no matter his intention, his thoughts soon turned to Elizabeth.

He loved her. Fully and completely. He knew that now. He should have known it from the start.

Pretend to be in love, his sister had said. For all his worry over keeping a part of his heart until his wife loved him, Darcy had quickly realized he couldn't. When it came to loving Elizabeth, he had no need to pretend.

Reach to caress Elizabeth's cheek. Hold her in his arms while he slept. Sit down to dinner and share the events of his day. What need was there for pretense in any of that? Each action he took was only what he truly wished to do.

But Elizabeth didn't love him. As much as he'd cared for her all these months, she didn't care for him. What would their lives be like with one-sided affection? Could he persuade her to continue to pretend?

On the other side of the library, something creaked. Darcy squinted into the darkness. Did he see movement? He stood and swiped the candle from the table. Would people forever be lurking in libraries, tormenting him?

A window opened as he started across the room. He halted in surprise. A burglar?

A familiar, slender form climbed through the window. Darcy hurried forward, but Elizabeth's feet were on the floor, her hands smoothing her skirt, before he could reach her to offer assistance.

She raised an amused look to meet his gaze. "Someone should really fix the latch on that window."

"What are you doing here?" Darcy asked, the words coming out harsher than he intended. "Why did you climb through the window?"

"I did try knocking first." She tipped her head to the side, expression curious. "Why did you lock yourself in?" She left off staring at him to look about the room.

"You could have called out," he said, ignoring the question. "At the door. I'd no idea it was you."

"I could have." She bit her lip.

"Why didn't you?" he asked, thoroughly perplexed.

"Because you locked the door."

Darcy shook his head, unable to follow her logic.

Elizabeth's face colored, the red deep enough to be seen by candlelight. She drew in a breath. "You seemed to wish for no one to disturb you."

He still had no notion what road her mind traversed. "That's true."

Elizabeth nodded. "Yet, I could see you were in need of consoling. So, when I found the door locked…not that you're that sort of man, but still…" she trailed off with a shrug.

"You thought I was seeking consolation in the arms of another woman?" he asked, shocked.

"The thought may have passed through my mind."

Darcy was too stunned to be offended, too baffled to be angry. How could Elizabeth think there could ever be anyone for him other than her? "How could you possibly believe that?"

She gave another small, forlorn shrug. "I didn't say I believe it, only feared it," she said in a near-whisper. "After all, it isn't as if you really love me. I mean, it's all been pretend."

Darcy set the candle on a nearby table. "Has it?"

Wide eyes that danced with candlelight gazed up at him. "Hasn't it?"

"There's no one here to pretend for," he murmured. He slid a hand up the back of her neck, fingers tangling in her hair, and tipped her head up toward his. "No one to see if I do this."

He touched his lips to hers. He meant for a fleeting gesture, to prove a point before further taking her to task for ever imagining he might be in the library with another woman, but Elizabeth's arms wrapped about his neck, urged him closer. Both arms about her now, he pressed her to him, deepening their kiss.

After a long, yet all too brief moment, he lifted his head. "I do not believe I was ever pretending, and I promise you, I am not pretending anymore."

A smile curled the corners of Elizabeth's perfect lips. "Neither am I."

Darcy swept her up in his arms and carried her to an overwide chair. He sat, Elizabeth firmly in his lap, and reapplied himself to kissing her. Once he felt she could not possibly imagine him in the library with another woman, he raised his head to take in her features, lips bright pink from his kisses, eyes closed. A contented sigh whispered from her lips.

Her eyes fluttered open. "I didn't truly mean to accuse you of..." She blushed again, obviously unwilling to say the words.

"And I did not mean to cause you concern. I was merely thinking."

"What about?" she asked, snuggling against him in a rather distracting fashion.

"Nothing."

She raised an eyebrow. "You must have been thinking about something." A soft hand came up to caress his cheek, rough with stubble so late in the evening.

"Society. My place in it. Our place. Georgiana's come out. Scandals. Everything."

"That's a lot more than nothing," she said, expression grave.

He brushed loose locks of hair back from her face. "Most of all, I was thinking about how much I love you, and wondering if you love me back."

Elizabeth's smile was so radiant, he would wager he could blow out the candle and still see it.

"Scandals come and go," she said. "These, like all others, will pass. Even if they somehow don't, we have the friends who were here with us tonight. Do we really need more?"

"No, I do not suppose so, but—"

"And even if we do need more, we also have all of Mr. Bingley's relatives, and the Gardiners. We have more family, above those currently in Netherfield. We won't lack friends or connections. In truth, I imagine we have more of both than you even care for, given your general dismay at socializing."

She made a good point. "Yes, but—"

Elizabeth pressed a finger to his lips. "And I do love you, Fitzwilliam Darcy. I love you now, and I'll love you always."

With those words, the ones he'd waited so long to hear, he realized Elizabeth was right. He had everything he needed, right there. All thoughts of other people fled. Darcy once more drew Elizabeth into his embrace.

Epilogue

~ Five Years Later ~

Darcy stood on the mezzanine in Darcy House, Elizabeth at his side and a sea of guests below. He shook his head, ruefully, taking in the sheer volume of people. He wouldn't have thought Darcy House could fit so many. He was sure the London home had never held such numbers before.

"Everything is so lovely," Elizabeth said. "And everyone is having such a marvelous time. Georgiana's wedding will be the talk of the season."

"I should hope so," Darcy replied. "I spent a small fortune on it."

Elizabeth cast him an amused glance. "That is your fault. You reap what you sow."

He shook his head, rueful. "I know. I know."

To his relief, Elizabeth forwent pointing out that she'd warned him. When Georgiana began planning for her wedding, he'd stipulated she could only invite family and close friends, to keep the guest list small. Elizabeth had pushed for him to set a number, a limit for Georgiana to adhere to, but he'd scoffed at the idea that his parameter would see Darcy House even half full.

Yet, day after day, Georgiana approached him with more names for the guest list. Each one, he'd been forced to admit, was either a close friend or a relative. Usually both. Before long, she'd invited so many guests that he realized the house would be quite full.

Giggles filled the ballroom. Adults adroitly moved aside as a train of children ran through. Little Bingleys, Darcys, Fitzwilliams, Gardiners, Collins, Forsters, Kitty Bennet's, now Kitty Parker's as she'd married a lieutenant, twin boys, and even a lone Hurst ran, skipped and trundled across the room, the youngest dragging a blanket and followed by a harried-looking nanny.

"I suppose it was too much to hope that they could be contained,"

Elizabeth said with a laugh.

Darcy nodded. Fleetingly, he noted the lack of any Kenley children. By all reports, the former Miss Bingley, who hadn't been invited regardless, had a very strained marriage. Trouble had begun immediately following the ceremony, when Mrs. Hurst's messenger had burst in, demanding on a stop to the union on the grounds that Mr. Kenley had lied. Rumor, not that Darcy gave much credence to hearsay, reported that Miss Bingley had fainted on hearing she'd wed a pauper.

Not that the room required more children, Darcy noted as more nannies joined the chase. Mrs. Collins, in particular, had managed a miraculous four offspring already. Wonderingly, the moment Mr. Collins set eyes on his first born son, he'd undergone a change, shifting from Lady Catherine's toady to doting husband and father in an instant.

Lady Catherine, who had been invited but declined to accept, likely felt Collins' defection deeply, but Darcy could only guess at that. His aunt had cut all ties with anyone who accepted Anne and Hawkins. So far as Darcy knew, that left Lady Catherine isolated and alone, though Anne had made it clear, for her part, that she wouldn't hold socializing with her mother against anyone.

His gaze sought his cousin. He gestured to where she and Hawkins danced, both with sublimely happy expressions, neither giving any indication they'd even heard the children. "Anne chose well."

"Of course, she did," Elizabeth said. "You, of all people, could never have doubted her selection."

"True." He hadn't, only the wisdom of making it.

Elizabeth let out a sigh. "Look how grown my cousins are." She pointed to where the Gardiners stood with their brood, most no longer relegated to the playroom.

"Georgiana tells me the Gardiners' eldest has benefited greatly from the instructors she recommended."

Elizabeth nodded. "She's sure to make a wonderful match."

Darcy glanced at his beautiful, elegant wife. Elizabeth carried their third child, but they hadn't made the announcement yet, not wishing to distract from Georgiana's day. The eldest Gardiner daughter, he'd noted, bore some resemblance to Elizabeth. Yes, she would make a good match, and he'd no worry, not any longer, of past scandal getting in her way.

Years ago, there were a few acquaintances who had not accepted Elizabeth. Darcy dropped them. Many more would not accept Anne.

Darcy made a point of telling them that they might meet her in his house. Georgiana ran into problems with a few society matrons who didn't want her to corrupt their daughters. She also met a few men who thought she had loose morals. With Darcy, Elizabeth and the rest of their relations decisively on her side, Georgiana had no trouble putting such men firmly in their place.

They also had a problem with people who would not accept the Gardiners, or Bingley's relatives, who were added to their ever-expanding number of friends. Elizabeth, in her usual adroit way, had shown him how to find that sort of snobbery amusing. Now, looking out over his crowded ballroom, Darcy couldn't deny he had a considerable number of friends and an exceedingly large family. They weren't all the best people by the Ton's definition, but they were by Darcy's.

"You're thinking," Elizabeth said. She reached to clasp his hand.

Darcy brought her fingers to his lips. "I am."

"About our friends and family?" she asked. "About this great, happy gathering that's filled our home to the seams?"

"Yes."

"And what, Mr. Darcy, are your thoughts on them?" Her eyes danced with amusement, and a touch of challenge.

He kissed her hand again. "That I wouldn't want my life to be any other way."

~ The End ~

About the Authors

Renata McMann

Renata McMann is the pen name of Teresa McCullough, someone who likes to rewrite public domain works. She is fond of thinking "What if?" To learn more about Renata's work and collaborations, visit **www.renatamcmann.com**.

Summer Hanford

Starting in 2014, Summer was offered the privilege of partnering with fan fiction author Renata McMann on her well-loved *Pride and Prejudice* variations. More information on these works is available at **www.renatamcmann.com**. Additionally, in 2016, Summer was lucky enough to be asked to join Austen Authors, a great place for fans to get more Jane Austen. To explore Austen Authors, visit **www.austenauthors.net**.

Summer is currently writing solo Regency Romance works, partnering with McMann, providing content for, creating and managing websites, and is a fantasy and science fiction faculty member at AllWriters' Workplace and Workshop, LLC., an international creative writing studio. She lives in Michigan with her husband and compulsory, deliberately spoiled, cats. For more about Summer, visit **www.summerhanford.com**.

36298856R00173

Made in the USA
San Bernardino, CA
19 May 2019